Born and raised just outside Toronto, Ontario, **Amy Ruttan** fled the big city to settle down with the country boy of her dreams. After the birth of her second child Amy was lucky enough to realise her lifelong dream of becoming a romance author. When she's not furiously typing away at her computer she's mum to three wonderful children, who use her as a personal taxi and chef.

Julie Danvers grew up in a rural community surrounded by farmland. Although her town was small, it offered plenty of scope for imagination, as well as an excellent library. Books allowed Julie to have many adventures from her own home, and her love affair with reading has never ended. She loves to write about heroes and heroines who are adventurous, passionate about a cause, and looking for the best in themselves and others. Julie's website is juliedanvers.wordpress.com.

D1144263

THE DOCTOR
SHE SHOULD RESIST

AMY RUTTAN

THE MIDWIFE
FROM HIS PAST

JULIE DANVERS

MILLS & BOON

First Published in Great Britain 2022
by Mills & Boon, an imprint of HarperCollins*Publishers* Ltd,
1 London Bridge Street, London, SE1 9GF

www.harpercollins.co.uk

HarperCollins*Publishers*
1st Floor, Watermarque Building,
Ringsend Road, Dublin 4, Ireland

The Doctor She Should Resist © 2022 Amy Ruttan

The Midwife from His Past © 2022 Alexis Silas

ISBN: 978-0-263-30127-4

05/22

MIX
Paper from
responsible sources
FSC™ C007454

This book is produced from independently certified FSC™ paper
to ensure responsible forest management.
For more information visit www.harpercollins.co.uk/green.

Printed and Bound in Spain using 100% Renewable Electricity
at CPI Black Print, Barcelona

THE DOCTOR
SHE SHOULD RESIST

AMY RUTTAN

MILLS & BOON

To my amazing friends,
who encouraged me these last couple of months.
Your support means so much to me.

PROLOGUE

HAZEL REES WAS FURIOUS, but she was trying to keep it under control. This was not St. Raymond's fault, rather it was the doing of a greedy board of directors.

She knew how they all worked.

When she and her best friend, Bria, had applied to open their birthing center across from St. Raymond's hospital, the chief of staff, Dr. Victor Anderson, had been so supportive.

Then the city planning commission had slapped them with a whole bunch of red tape, which had delayed them.

And the reason?

St. Raymond's board of directors had *concerns* about the Multnomah Falls Women's Health Center even existing. Not the staff of the hospital, just the board, and Hazel knew that the new chairman of the board, Timothy Russell, had friends at city hall.

Politicians were corrupt, as far as she was concerned, but she and Bria had come too far now to let anyone stand in their way. This whole thing was ridiculous.

It was a complete waste of time, and now they were here at this tribunal to see if the city would even approve of them opening at all. Their reason was some idea about being in direct competition with the hospital, because it was apparent that the hospital's bottom line was more important to the board of directors than providing great health care to Portland's pregnant women.

As far as Hazel was concerned, why else would they be here?

All the work on their birthing center had just stopped, and they were forced to plead their case in front of the city commissioner.

Bria reached out and squeezed her hand, as if sensing she was angry.

Bria was far calmer than she was.

Which made sense.

Hazel's father had always said she had rather a fiery temperament. She had never believed him, until now, sitting here, waiting for the hospital representative to come in and give their report.

On what, exactly, she didn't know.

All she knew was that the hospital representative was late.

Which ticked her off all the more.

The door opened.

"Sorry I'm late," a male voice said.

Hazel turned and was taken aback by the gorgeous, albeit frazzled-looking man who'd walked into the tribunal room.

He was probably the most handsome man Hazel had ever laid eyes on.

He had a mop of well-tamed dark brown curls, with a sexy bit of silver at the temples. The well-tailored and expensive suit he was wearing showed off an impressive set of broad shoulders. There was an air of dignity around him and she wasn't quite sure what it was, but he made her heart go pitter-patter.

It had been some time since she was so instantly attracted to a man.

Not since Mark, in fact.

She thought she'd learned from that terrible mistake. She tried not to look at the man, but she couldn't help herself.

What was wrong with her? She needed to focus.

Get ahold of yourself. You're in a crucial meeting!

"I take it you're the representative from the hospital?" the meditator inquired.

"Yes. I'm Dr. Caleb Norris, the head of obstetrics at St. Raymond's."

Bria glanced at Hazel and leaned over. "I thought Dr. Anderson was the head of obstetrics?" she whispered.

"No. He's the chief of staff. The head of obstetrics wouldn't speak to us before because he was too busy."

So this was the man who had no time to speak to them, according to his secretary and his residents.

Seems he had found time to speak *against* them, though!

"And you are here on the hospital's behalf, Dr. Norris?" the mediator asked again, for the record.

He nodded. "Yes. The board of directors said you required facts, and I have the data necessary for your inquiry relating to births in this area and in the state."

"By all means, Dr. Norris," the mediator said.

"Thank you." Dr. Norris pulled out a chair and took a seat at the table, right across from Hazel.

Their gazes met; his blue-gray eyes pierced her to her very soul. It caused her stomach to do a flip, but she folded her hands carefully and straightened her spine, meeting his cool look with a lift of her eyebrow.

His eyes widened, as if surprised to see her. And there was suddenly a spark, a twinkle warming his gaze that made her cheeks heat and a zing of electricity flow through her. Like she had been struck by something.

Focus. Keep calm.

He looked away, clearing his throat as he shuffled papers.

"Dr. Norris?" the mediator asked.

"Yes. Sorry." Caleb put down the papers. "I lost my train of thought there for a moment."

Hazel smiled in satisfaction that he seemed to be a bit discombobulated by her.

Good.

It would bode well in their favor if he struggled to get his point across.

"My board of directors asked me to tell you the percentages of births, etcetera, that come through St. Raymond's and why our hospital is vital to the area and can more than handle the needs of the community."

"Our midwife clinic is also vital," Hazel interrupted hotly.

Bria grabbed her wrist as if to silence her.

Dr. Norris's eyes narrowed as he glared at her.

"Yes, I am already aware of your projected figures," the mediator stated. "I am interested in Dr. Norris's facts, his proven figures, if you please, Ms. Rees. Yours are not fact yet."

Hazel subsided and nodded. "Of course. My apologies."

"Dr. Norris, please continue," the mediator said.

"Thank you." Caleb stacked his papers. "Last year we had eight maternal deaths, two hundred and eleven infant deaths, and there were one hundred and thirty-eight neonatal births and one hundred and fifty fetal deaths. That is, of course, in the whole county, not just St. Raymond's. Out of forty thousand births in the state, the county had nine hundred live births, and four thousand patients came through our doors. Multnomah is a large county. We do see the majority of the state's births, but there are other hospitals and other midwives in this county."

"Thank you, Dr. Norris," the mediator said. "There's a lot to consider and to take to city planning. We'll adjourn and meet again in two weeks."

Hazel was fuming, but she got up and left the tribunal room. Everything was going to be delayed again.

It was so frustrating.

She followed Bria outside.

"Why didn't they bring in a midwife with an established clinic too?" Bria asked. "The mediator said our numbers weren't fact yet, but an established midwife would have those proven numbers."

"Why didn't they ask a pregnant woman about her comfort of care either?" Hazel groused. "You and I both know there's a huge demand in this area of the city. A lot of women don't want a hospital birth."

"Some women don't have a choice," a stern voice said behind her.

Bria took a step back to answer a phone call that came through, so Hazel was alone to fight this battle against Dr. Norris and she crossed her arms. "I'm well aware of that. Still, it would have been good to have had a pregnant woman's perspective. As head of obstetrics, I would think you, of all people, would agree."

"I do agree, as it happens, but the board of directors simply asked me to present the figures and I have done so."

"Births are more than just data," Hazel said, bristling.

His blue-gray eyes narrowed. "Look, I'm not your enemy."

"No, but you represent people who wish to deny women access to having a choice in their health care. Not all women want a clinical birth. Some prefer a more holistic approach."

"Hardly denying access."

"Our center opening is being delayed, thus you're denying access."

"And as I've already explained to you, that isn't my fault. I will not stand here and continue this discussion, Ms. Rees. I have patients to see. Good day."

He turned to walk away.

Hazel scowled.

Why did the good-looking ones always have to be so stubborn and so prideful? So prickly.

She only hoped that when this all blew over, when their birthing center finally opened, she could work with Dr. Norris if she had to.

Right now, she wasn't so sure she could.

That fiery temper her father always teased her about suddenly kicked in as she glared at his retreating figure. It took a lot for her to keep her cool, especially when she was so passionate about something and the center was her and Bria's whole world.

She couldn't let him walk away.

Hazel might regret it, but as they were opening their center across from St. Raymond's, she planned on working with him in the future. Therefore, this discussion was far from over.

She marched after Dr. Norris and darted in front of him.

His eyes widened in shock again, as if no one had ever confronted him before.

"Madam, please…"

"No, I don't think we're quite done talking about this."

"I beg to differ."

Hazel cocked her eyebrow. "Do you now? Well, I beg to differ too."

A small, brief smile quirked his lips and his eyes narrowed. "Is that so?"

"We're going to have to work together."

"Are we?" he asked. "I thought you were opening a birthing center not starting a job at St. Raymond's."

"You're being a bit pedantic." She was so infuriated with him, and she had to keep reminding herself that it was all for the benefit of the center, finally realizing Bria's and her dream. She could deal with the likes of Dr. Caleb Norris for that.

Can you?

"*I* am being pedantic? I thought our discussion was over. As I said, I have patients to see. I'm a very busy man."

"Yes, you made that very evident when Bria and I came to speak with you. Your secretary made it quite clear when you wouldn't even deign to grace us with your presence."

"As I have stated, I have a lot to do..." He tried to side-step her, but she was having none of that.

"You're not the only one who has better things to do, Dr. Norris. Do you have any concept of what you've done here today?"

He looked confused. "I presented the facts and figures that my hospital's board of directors asked me to. What's wrong with that?"

"They're the ones who are trying to stop us from opening," Hazel said, hoping she wouldn't burst out crying, which was what she always did when she got as angry as she currently was.

"I don't think that's what happened here. Your center will open."

"It's being continually delayed. Your report today, your lack of willingness to confer with us so we could explain things to you has done irreparable damage. Do you even care about women's health at all?"

There was a flash of pain across his face and Hazel flinched, cursing her temper under her breath. She didn't mean to attack him like that, and she instantly regretted it.

"That was unfair," she said. "I know that you do care..."

"Yes," he said absently. He wasn't looking at her, but she could see the hurt still etched in his face and the air of vulnerability that suddenly cloaked him, and she couldn't help but wonder why he was so pained.

That's not your business.

"Our birthing center will give women more choice, which can only be a good thing," she said calmly.

"I understand." His eyes were cold now, and he could barely look at her. "You do understand my information was not a personal attack on your center, don't you? I was merely doing my job."

"I get that," she said with a sigh.

"You would do well to do the same, Ms. Rees. As you say, we'll most likely have to work together in the future. Perhaps, for now, we should go our separate ways before we say anything else we might regret."

"Agreed, but Bria and I could really use your support. It would be nice to know that you respect a woman's right to choose her own health care."

His lips pressed together in a firm line. "I always do respect that decision, but what I wonder is, will you accept that same choice?"

"What do you mean?"

"If a woman chooses to have a, as you put it, clinical birth, will you stand by her decision? Will you stand in the way of the hospital doing its job?"

Hazel crossed her arms. "I'm kind of insulted you are insinuating that, Dr. Norris."

"Tit for tat, Ms. Rees. You assumed the same of me."

Damn. He had a good point.

"No, I wouldn't stand in the way. I meant what I said. I want us to be able to work together in the future."

He smiled, slightly, but she could tell that his feathers were a bit ruffled still. "That remains to be seen. Good day, Ms. Rees. Again."

This time she didn't try to stop him. She stepped to the side and watched him walk away. She had overstepped her bounds a bit and she regretted it, but there was a lot at stake here.

She and Bria had worked so hard.

What she had to do now was swallow her own hurt pride, her temper, and just focus on the next steps to get their center approved and opened. She had to believe that the board of directors at St. Raymond's wouldn't keep trying to put a stop to it, even though there was a part of her that was worried they would.

But one could live in hope, right?

CHAPTER ONE

Six months later

DON'T TURN AROUND. *He's staring at you again.*

Hazel Rees could feel that she was being watched. Ever since she and Bria had decided to open the Multnomah Falls Women's Health Center, Hazel felt like she was under complete scrutiny from the board of directors from the hospital across the road. Especially at that tribunal where they'd sent their head of obstetrics to delay their building permits.

Although, Dr. Caleb Norris hadn't known what the actual agenda of the board of directors was. He'd just been doing his job presenting figures as requested. The members of the board of directors weren't medical people, and they only cared about money. The chairman of the board was particularly devious. Hazel could tell, just by his actions. Whatever Caleb claimed, Timothy Russell definitely wanted to ruin their center.

It's because you're a threat to their bottom line.

And that fleeting thought made Hazel smile to herself. She liked being a threat. Especially after the hospital board had delayed them so many times by going to the city.

St. Raymond's birthing hospital had had the monopoly on births in this area for far too long. There was a huge need for a birthing center here, and that's what she and Bria had provided. Both of them were certified midwives, and

Hazel was also a nurse practitioner. She wanted to offer not just an amazing, safe birth experience, but also provide postpartum support for years afterward. Hazel had seen the difficulties her sister had experienced after her C-sections, how her sister's adhesions after surgery had left her with pelvic floor problems and pain. Hazel had grand plans to help women with their whole health.

This had been her and Bria's dream since they'd met during midwifery training. Hazel usually kept people at a distance, but somehow Bria had weaseled her way through her defenses and they'd become fast friends with the same goals.

It had been a fight to get here, but they were here now and Hazel couldn't be more proud if she tried. Delays hadn't stopped them from what they had managed to achieve so far.

Even if the head of obstetrics, the surly, brooding Dr. Caleb Norris, grumped at her all the time. Hazel hated that she was so attracted to a man who had apparently taken it upon himself to become her sworn enemy.

Enemy was probably too strong a word, but ever since they'd met at the tribunal every single time she saw that man they got into an argument over the most foolish things.

He was intelligent.

Incredibly professional.

He seemed so put together too. Caleb made her weak in the knees, but then he would open his mouth and it would go downhill from there.

Always sniping at one another.

He grated on her nerves.

They were on the same side in the grand scheme of things, yet when she was around him her temper got riled up. He was just so infuriating!

There was a part of her that wanted him to just take her in his arms and kiss her. Then she recalled the hurt look on his face during the tribunal and the feeling she'd got that she'd wounded him in a particularly vulnerable place. Maybe he was broken and needed love? But that instinctive need to heal had got her into trouble before, and she'd ended up in a very bad relationship because of it.

Mark had been a man she thought she could heal with love. He was a surgeon she'd met at hospital after completing her nurse practitioner training. He'd been jilted practically at the altar, and he'd told her that's why he'd pushed her away when they first met, but that in the end, he couldn't resist her.

It was like something out of a romance novel.

He'd driven her crazy too, at first. Then came the passion. She'd thought his heart had finally been mended, by her. That she had helped him over the pain and hurt of being so cruelly jilted. But after she'd let her guard down, and once he was firmly planted in her heart, then he'd betrayed her trust by cheating on her.

It was then she'd learned his ex-fiancée had left Mark because he had cheated on her too.

Hazel had also discovered that everyone they'd worked with had known the truth all along.

They had been watching the drama, gossiping, predicting when Mark would do the same to her. And they were right. She'd been made to look like a complete fool.

It had broken her.

Completely.

What she needed to do now was listen to the logical part of her brain. The one that was telling her that Dr. Caleb Norris would probably be just like Mark, and she needed to keep him squarely where she put him, which was on her "do not resuscitate" list. She wasn't going to put her heart on the line again for a vulnerable-looking man.

Or any man, really.

She laughed to herself thinking about how foolish she

was to be so attracted to another brooding, wounded doctor. She certainly had a type, didn't she? She didn't know what had caused the look on Caleb's face that day at the tribunal, and although she still felt bad about it, it certainly wasn't her business.

She tucked back a loose strand of hair that had escaped her braid and glanced over her shoulder at the hospital across the street. The large, looming, multimillion-dollar birthing hospital that seemed to have a revolving door policy when it came to babies and women's health.

When she and Bria had researched a location, they'd picked a spot across from St. Raymond's because it was a stellar hospital with a good reputation.

The chief of staff was welcoming.

It was a good fit.

It was beneficial to the community.

Then politics from the board of directors had reared its ugly head and delayed them.

It was certainly a facility like St. Raymond's that had dealt with her sister so quickly. The Arizona hospital had shuffled Hazel's older sister and niece out of the door so fast just because her sister didn't have the best insurance.

Then her sister had hemorrhaged, and she'd almost died.

It was at that moment Hazel decided to pursue midwifery once her nursing training was complete, and her dream had been to open a birthing center. One that wouldn't push women through a revolving door. A center that would see a woman through the entire journey, right into postpartum care and beyond, and to help those women who couldn't always afford to pay.

Health care needed to be equal access for all. Not just for a select few.

Lack of funds, lack of insurance that decided who received the best health care put lives in jeopardy. Like what had almost happened to her sister. The thought of losing her had utterly terrified Hazel.

It had been one of the worst moments of her life.

That and Mark's betrayal.

An ache filled her chest, and she shook those painful memories away. That was all in the past. Her sister was healthy. Her niece was seven and thriving. She'd moved on from Mark. Everything was good.

She was here now to help those who needed her, and it didn't matter to her that the big bad wolf's house was just across the road. Or that the wolf in question was standing outside hospital's main entrance, his hands in his pockets, scowling at her as usual.

Hazel raised her hand and waved politely.

"Hello, Dr. Norris. Beautiful day, isn't it?" she called out breezily.

Caleb looked away and she couldn't help but smile. She didn't know what it was about her that irked him so much. She'd apologized for upsetting him, but it didn't seem to matter to Caleb. Nor, so she'd told herself, did she care. The problem was, she really did. Still, no matter how many brooding glares he sent in her direction, he wasn't going to alter her course. They were here to stay.

Hazel pulled out her keys and saw out of the corner of her eye that Caleb was headed her way.

Damn.

What did he want now?

She turned to face him, trying to plaster the fake smile on her face that she had recently mastered whenever she had to deal with him. Her jaw was beginning to ache at how much she had to clench it around him. Bria always warned her to play nice, and she'd do it to keep her friend happy.

"Dr. Norris, to what do I owe the pleasure of your company?" she asked through gritted teeth.

"You called me over," he said tersely. "I abhor shouting."

"I didn't call you over," she responded dryly. "I greeted you, instead of ignoring you."

"Yes, you greeted me by shouting across the street like…"

"A fishwife?" she asked when he seemed temporarily lost for words.

"A what?"

"Something my grandfather always said. He was from Cornwall."

Caleb's lips pressed together in a firm line at her rambling. "I deduced that you wanted to speak with me, since you took the time to shout across the street."

"No. I really didn't need to speak with you. I'm sorry for exchanging pleasantries. I'll remember that for next time and just ignore you." She turned to try and end the conversation, but he stepped in her path. Just like she had done to him six months ago. She braced herself for an argument, but instead he looked like he was struggling to say something.

Like he didn't want to say whatever it was he was thinking and her stomach twisted in a knot, expecting the worst.

This was so not how she wanted to start her day.

"Actually, I do need your assistance," he finally said in a lowered voice, as though imparting a scandalous piece of gossip.

Hazel took a step back and cocked an eyebrow. "You what?"

Caleb's own jaw tightened. "I said I need your help."

Hazel couldn't quite believe what she was hearing. Since their little run-in, Caleb had largely kept his distance and mostly dealt with Bria, whom he didn't fight with. Bria was definitely more of a balm when it came to dealing with the staff at St. Raymond's, so Hazel let her be the voice of reason over there.

There was just no talking to the man. Hazel had tried, but he reminded her of every pompous jackass she had dealt with when she had been studying to be a nurse. And he was just as emotionally closed off as Mark had been. He was everything that Hazel didn't want. She wasn't getting involved with a man who was clearly lugging a lot of baggage.

He drove her completely bonkers and yet she was highly attracted to him.

She had a problem.

A serious problem.

And now, here he was, two months after their triumphant opening, and he was asking for her help.

"Do my ears deceive me or are you asking *me* for help?"

"Don't make this harder than it already is," he said tightly. "Will you do it or not?"

"It depends on what it is. If it's to help you figure out a way to shut down our health center, then I'm going to have to decline."

Caleb rolled his eyes. "Hardly. I've told you repeatedly that I was merely presenting the facts that the board of directors asked me to."

She knew that, but did he have to be so grumpy about it? Or maybe it was just her who brought it out in him?

"Fine. Still, you usually go to Bria. You don't usually talk to me."

"She's more logical," he remarked.

Hazel cocked her head to the side. "Is she? Then speak with her."

"She's not available."

"I'm busy too."

Caleb sighed and pinched the bridge of his nose. "Please, Ms. Rees, can we just have a normal conversation?"

She sighed. "Of course."

"Thank you." He looked at her with his gorgeous blue-gray eyes. The color reminded her of the sea when a storm came in. Cool, yet mysterious and dangerous with hidden depths.

She felt she could get lost in them, if they weren't attached to someone as annoying as him. As she stared up at the man, his eyes narrowed and went a bit flinty, and she couldn't help but wonder what it would be like if he smiled.

He was such a handsome man. His dark brown hair, cut short on the sides, but with a curl on top, was streaked with a little silver to match that on his temples, but it so suited him. His white lab coat, his tailored pants and polished shoes made his athletic six-foot-one build look pristine.

Everything about him gave off an air of a put together, well-to-do man, and she had no doubt that if this were Regency times he would be polishing his hessian boots with champagne.

He exuded power and control.

Whereas she was a bit of a mess, but she liked being that way. More down to earth, comfortable and approachable for her patients. She was pretty sure she was all the things that annoyed Caleb greatly.

Which was a shame.

She couldn't help but wonder what it would take to get Caleb to loosen up a bit. To see him smile. To kiss him.

You've trodden down this path before. Don't make the same mistake again.

Mark had been broody, untouchable.

Intelligent and charming.

She'd been like putty in his hands and he knew it. He'd woven a web of lies so easily about being heartbroken. She'd felt like she'd connected so deeply with Mark. Like they were soul mates.

She'd been such a fool.

Men like Mark didn't have a shred of empathy. She didn't know Caleb well, but she'd bet her money on him being exactly like her ex. It was apparent he was hiding a deep hurt of some sort, but she had no desire to find out what it was.

She had her heart to protect.

Caleb was off-limits.

Hazel blew that thought away, hoping that the heat she felt from her fleeting, ridiculous musings wasn't creeping up her neck for the whole world to see.

"Look," he said, breaking through her introspection. "I'm not here to bandy words with you. I need your help. I have a patient I'd like to bring to you. One that wants a midwife's opinion on a vaginal birth after caesarean."

"Of course. When?"

"In about an hour or so if that's all right?" he asked.

"Sure."

Caleb nodded. "I'll see you then."

He didn't thank her, but just left as abruptly as he'd arrived, marching back across the street to the hospital with his white lab coat fluttering behind him. Hazel shook her head, still slightly stunned over the exchange that had just taken place between them. Why hadn't he simply called and booked the appointment with their receptionist, Joan?

There was no point in trying to figure him out. Hazel didn't have time to waste on the intricacies of Caleb's mind, though there was a part of her that really wanted to. He was just the kind of man she always fell for.

And therein lay the rub.

She just didn't trust her own judgment around men like him. And she certainly couldn't trust again; her heart couldn't handle another betrayal like that. When she'd walked away from Mark, she'd sworn never to get seriously involved with anyone ever again.

She had plans.

Romance and love were not in those plans.

The universe had made it perfectly clear she should steer clear of love and focus on her career.

She headed into their clinic and Bria was already there, going through files at the main desk.

"Hey," Bria said brightly. "I didn't think that you were coming in so early."

"I couldn't keep myself away. And apparently I now have a patient to see."

Bria cocked an eyebrow. "Oh, really? Who?"

"Dr. Norris is bringing her over in an hour. A consult about a vaginal birth after a caesarean."

Bria leaned forward. "Oh, that sounds kind of intriguing."

"Why?"

"The broody obstetrician that you constantly butt heads with is bringing you a patient. You, the proverbial thorn in his side."

Hazel chuckled softly. "I suppose it is kind of like the opening of a book club type of novel."

"They could so make a movie!" Bria teased.

"Noted." Hazel picked up a blank patient file and poured herself a cup of coffee. "If he comes barging in, just point him to my office."

Bria nodded. "Will do."

Hazel headed to her office, set her bag and the file down, and took a sip of her coffee. She was expecting a busy day, but she'd hoped her morning would be quiet so she could go over inventory and prep for later.

Instead, she was catering to Caleb.

Except that she wasn't. She had to put it out of her mind that this was about him. She was helping someone in need. And if it was a woman in need, she didn't care if the woman was the devil's wife.

There was a knock.

"Come in," Hazel said, trying not to sigh as she set down her coffee, knowing full well that it would be cold by the time she got back to it.

Joan stuck her head around the door. "Good morning! A walk-in patient has come in. Can you see her?"

"Sure. If Dr. Norris comes with his patient, just ask him to wait."

Joan eyes widened. "Dr. Norris?"

"Yeah."

"Coming to see you?"

Hazel laughed softly. "Yes. I know. It caught me off guard too."

Joan smiled. "Sure. No problem."

Hazel got up and walked out into the waiting room. There was a nervous young woman sitting there. She had long blond hair and was twisting the hem of her T-shirt. A backpack was at her feet, and she was tapping her leg.

Joan handed her the intake form.

"Lizzie?" Hazel asked.

The young woman looked up. "Yes."

"I'm Hazel. It's nice to meet you."

They shook hands. Lizzie was trembling.

"Nice to meet you, Hazel," she said. "Thank you for seeing me so quickly."

"Not a problem. How about we go into my office?"

Lizzie nodded and Hazel led her into her office. The young woman took a seat, and Hazel shut the door so they had privacy. Lizzie was wringing the hem of her shirt again.

"How can I help you?"

Lizzie swallowed hard. "I had… I'm late. I'm usually pretty on time with my cycle, but my period's about two weeks late."

"I see. Have you taken a pregnancy test?"

"No." Lizzie blushed.

"Are you underage?" Hazel asked, although if Lizzie were, she could be lying about her birthdate. Not that it mattered. She wouldn't deny this young woman care. Still, if she was underage, she would have to get Lizzie's parents involved.

"No. I'm eighteen," Lizzie said. She worried her bottom lip. "I just didn't want to go to my regular doctor. He's friends with my dad and…"

"It's okay. We can do a test here."

Lizzie looked visibly relieved. "Thanks."

"I'm curious. Why not go to the hospital across the road?"

"My father works there."

"Ah, I see." Hazel got up and opened the door to the bathroom. "There are sterile bottles. I'll need a sample, and then I can do a test."

Lizzie nodded. "Okay."

She disappeared into the bathroom and Hazel sighed.

Eighteen.

So young.

Her own mother had been eighteen when her brother was born, and she knew how tough it had been for her parents to make ends meet. She knew how much her mother had to give up to take care of them all.

Lizzie came out of the bathroom, and Hazel took the sample into the center's testing room. She placed a strip into the bottle and waited.

The strip confirmed it.

Lizzie was pregnant.

Hazel headed back into her office. Lizzie was tapping her leg again, her blue-gray eyes wide as she looked up at her.

"You're pregnant. When was the first day of your last period?" Hazel asked, sitting back down across from her.

"The twenty-first. As I said, I'm two weeks late and pretty much regular."

"So you're about five weeks, then."

"Yeah." Lizzie sighed.

"What're your plans?" Hazel asked gently.

"I would like to keep the baby. The father, my boy-friend—we're planning to get married after college."

"Okay. You might have to put college on hold at some point and tell your parents."

"I'm eighteen and an adult. I don't have to tell my dad yet."

"I know, but they may notice a bump when you go home at Christmas," Hazel said.

Lizzie smiled. "I'm from Portland, but you're right. I live with my dad. He'll notice for sure."

"If your dad won't be supportive, can you stay with your mother?" Hazel asked, assuming that her parents were divorced because Lizzie kept talking about her father only.

"No," Lizzie said quietly. "My mother died when I was born."

Hazel's cheeks heated. "Oh. I'm so sorry."

"It's okay. I'll tell my dad…when I'm ready. You won't tell him, will you?"

"No. Patient confidentiality. I won't be making that call," Hazel assured her.

Lizzie smiled, relieved. "Good."

"Shall we determine a due date? It's too early to do an ultrasound, but we can talk about when that will happen as well. That's if you would like to stay under my care and if you want me to be there for the birth of your child."

"Yes. I would much rather have my baby here. My dad would like me to go to medical school, but I've always been fascinated by midwifery and would much rather deliver here than a hospital."

Hazel nodded. "And you're in college you say?"

"Bachelor of Health Science, to appease my father, then midwifery after I get my bachelor."

Hazel didn't want to remind her that her career plans might change slightly with having a baby, it wasn't her place. Lizzie seemed smart enough to know what she was taking on.

She was of legal age. She didn't need to keep drilling it into her that her life would become so much more complicated with a newborn baby and college to deal with.

Hazel was not her mother.

She took down Lizzie's health information and figured out the baby's due date. The baby was due to arrive early next year. In January.

After Hazel had set up the next appointment, she got up to walk Lizzie out. As they left her office, a loud male voice boomed across the waiting room.

"Lizzie?"

The young woman groaned. "Hi, Dad."

Hazel spun around and saw Caleb, frowning and confused. Then it hit her.

Lizzie was Caleb's daughter?

He had an eighteen-year-old child? And Lizzie had said her mother had died when she was born...so he was a widower.

Hazel couldn't help but wonder what had happened to his wife. It explained why he was so closed off. The pain of losing the woman you loved must be unbearable. She felt bad for him. It also solidified her resolve to not get any closer to him.

It was way too complicated.

Caleb came over. "What're you doing here, Lizzie?"

"She's interested in midwifery, so we were talking about that," Hazel said quickly.

He frowned, crossing his arms and looking at Lizzie. "Is this true?"

"Y-yes," Lizzie stammered. "Th-that's it. Hazel was so kind to let me know what training was needed and how long it takes to become a certified midwife. Jeez, why else would I be here, Dad?"

Caleb didn't look convinced. "You're sure you're not pregnant? That boy you're dating... I swear..."

"Derek's not a boy, Dad! He's the same age as me. He's in college too. Could you keep it down? You're embarrassing me," Lizzie hissed.

"Fine. We'll talk about this later."

Lizzie rolled her eyes and turned back. "Thanks again, Hazel, for being so reasonable, unlike some people I know."

Hazel bit back a chuckle as Caleb watched his daughter leave, looking flabbergasted.

"You're early," Hazel remarked. "And here without a patient I see."

"She's on her way. I thought we could talk about her case before she arrives."

"Of course." Hazel stepped aside so he could enter her office.

She hated keeping such a secret from Caleb, because he had the right to know he was going to be a grandfather, but that also wasn't her place as Lizzie's midwife. Lizzie had to be the one to tell her father.

She was still a bit shocked he had an eighteen-year-old daughter. All right, he had a touch of gray, but he certainly wasn't over forty. He couldn't be, but all of what Lizzie said about not wanting her father to find out made complete sense to her now.

If her dad was an obstetrician like Caleb, he would definitely be spouting off his disapproval. Hazel had seen it enough in other parents of teenage children. And she was certain raising a child on his own and becoming a surgeon hadn't been easy, so he wouldn't want that for Lizzie as well.

However, what she needed to do was take care of Lizzie and not get involved in anything beyond personal care for her patient. It was most definitely not her business what happened between Caleb and his daughter, unless it affected Lizzie's or her baby's health.

* * *

Caleb sat down in Hazel's office still a bit distracted by the fact that he'd just seen Lizzie here.

She said she's not pregnant.

And he believed her. Lizzie had never lied to him before.

For the last eighteen years, he had been trying to hold it all together, and not always very successfully in his opinion. Most days, he felt like a complete failure when it came to Lizzie. One time they had been extremely close, but then she'd hit the teenage years and something had changed.

He knew, biologically, what had shifted in his relationship with his daughter. She was a grown woman now. She was self-reliant and really didn't need him anymore. He was no longer the center of her world.

Her boyfriend, Derek, was.

He'd seen it happen to other parents; he just didn't know how to deal with it himself. He was frozen, and it felt like his world was spinning out of control.

Lizzie was very like his late wife, Jane, in so many ways.

Same temperament.

Same drive.

Same expressions.

Jane had got pregnant when she was young and he was still in medical school. At the time, he'd been thrilled. He and Jane had felt like they could do anything. She'd left school so that she could stay home to raise Lizzie.

Everything would be okay.

Then Jane had died, and he'd had both medical school and a newborn to cope with. With so much to juggle, he'd just done the best he could to get through each day.

Seeing Lizzie here had scared him.

She'd only just started college.

He didn't want Lizzie to give up her schooling like Jane had done—that had been Jane's choice, but Lizzie wanted other things. And he painfully remembered his days of interning while parenting a young child. It was brutally hard.

She says she's not pregnant.

Still, he couldn't calm his nerves. There had been a lot on his mind lately, and this just added to the unrest. Most of his thoughts during the last six months had centered around a certain midwife at the new birthing center across the road and how he could best avoid her.

Except now here he was. In her office.

Hazel was one of the most fiery, intelligent, attractive, stubborn women he'd ever met. That day he'd walked into the tribunal had changed his life.

He could not stop thinking about her.

He'd gone to present facts about birth rates in the county. He'd genuinely had no idea the board of directors was trying to prevent the birthing center from opening. He'd been so taken aback when he'd discovered that, and he knew that he had probably ruined any chance he might have had with Hazel.

It had been a long time since he'd been so attracted to another woman.

Then Hazel had opened her mouth and infuriated him by jumping to conclusions about him.

It was like he'd been hit with a bolt of lightning.

He'd been mesmerized by her.

If he wasn't a single dad trying to keep his life together, if he wasn't so afraid of getting his heart obliterated again, he suspected he'd already be pursuing Hazel Rees.

But it was clear she didn't particularly like him, and he'd been out of the dating game for far too long to even think about starting up a relationship with a woman like her.

What would a young, vivacious woman want with a middle-aged father of a young adult anyway?

He cocked his head, staring at her as she talked. He could never find the right words to say.

She was one of the most beautiful women that he'd seen in a long time. Hazel had this rich auburn hair, with a slight curl. Her hair was untamed, just like her spirit. The dark brown eyes were keen and her heart-shaped lips were quick to deliver a barb.

She was an intellectual challenge, just as much as she was beautiful.

And Caleb wanted to get to know her further.

It unnerved him how much he wanted to get to know her. How much he liked her.

He had to remind himself that she was off-limits. He didn't have the space for her in his life. It was better for his heart to be alone.

He had his work and his daughter. That's all he needed.

Is it, though?

"So you wanted to talk about your patient?" Hazel asked, shutting the door.

"Yes." Caleb cleared his throat. "She's pregnant with her second. She's a new patient. Her first baby was delivered in California via caesarean section. They, my patient and her husband, just moved here from Oxnard. She would like to try for a vaginal birth after caesarean and would like a midwife to consult."

"And what's so strange about that?" Hazel asked, sitting across from him.

"I didn't say it was strange," he snapped. "Why are you constantly putting words in my mouth?"

"Usually obstetricians that I've dealt with in the past are wary of a vaginal birth after caesarean. So I assumed…"

"You assumed incorrectly. Again."

She lowered her eyes. "I'm sorry. Please continue."

He was taken aback. She'd never apologized before. What had changed?

She eyed him curiously. "Why are you looking at me like I have antlers or something?"

"I've just never heard you apologize before."

She laughed softly. "Bria said I have to be nicer to you."

"Well, I appreciate the apology. Thank you."

"You're welcome."

He narrowed his eyes. "Lizzie told you about my late wife, didn't she?"

"She did."

"I don't need your pity if that's why you're apologizing."

"I'm not pitying you," she said quickly.

"Oh, no?"

"No," she replied gently. Her dark eyes held a soft gleam, and he found he quite liked this side of her.

"I appreciate that. Often I get pitying comments. My late wife died eighteen years ago. I think I'm doing okay by now. I've had enough of the sympathy, and I feel like it's insincere sometimes."

"Of course. You raised a smart young woman, by the way," Hazel stated.

"Thank you. It was difficult, I won't lie. I was in medical school when she was born and interning during the toddler years, trying to become an OB/GYN. Day care cost a fortune. Raising a baby alone is incredibly hard for anyone."

"You didn't have help?" Hazel asked.

"No. My parents were both gone as were my late wife's. It was just me and Lizzie."

Although, as Lizzie grew older, she didn't need him anymore. Not as much. Lizzie was the one encouraging him to move on and find someone, but he just didn't have the time or the inclination.

He always had Lizzie as an excuse not to date or get serious with anyone.

There was nothing stopping him now, except himself and his fear of losing someone else he loved. Whoever coined that phrase about it being better to have loved and lost than never having loved at all was so wrong.

The pain of loss felt like it had swallowed all the love fully.

"So why don't we talk about your patient and how I can help," Hazel suggested.

He smiled in relief. "I'd like that."

He was glad to return the talk to business.

Business was safe.

Emotions never were.

CHAPTER TWO

ALL HAZEL WANTED to do was focus on work with Caleb, but it was hard to concentrate on just that when he was so close and she could drink in the spicy, clean scent of him. Then her brain started wandering, wondering what kind of cologne he used or was that just him.

Hospitals were usually scent free.

Seriously. You need to focus, she chastised herself yet again.

She took a discreet step back as he gave her the particulars of the patient. She made her brain concentrate on the facts and the figures that he was presenting, rather than how good he looked or how great he smelled.

The last time she'd had such an intense physical reaction like this to a man was with Mark, and her heart didn't have to remind her what had happened in that situation. How he had completely obliterated her trust and humiliated her.

The memory began to unfurl in her head, and she couldn't stop it.

She'd been bursting with good news because she had got into the midwifery course of her choice, and she was so excited to be starting that journey.

Mark was a surgeon, and he had been the one to tell her to pursue her dreams of becoming a midwife. She had been saving up for the course and paying off her nursing course debt since they met.

She'd wanted to share with him how she had got a scholarship, but when she'd gone to the ward where she'd known he would be working, he was nowhere to be found.

It had been kind of odd.

Mark had lived for work, and the ward was really busy.

So she'd asked the charge nurse if she'd seen him.

"No. I haven't seen him lately. The last I saw him he was heading with his surgical fellow to the intensive care unit to check on a patient. I'm sorry I can't be of more help, Hazel."

Hazel smiled. "No worries. I'll just go and see if I can catch him on the way back from the ICU."

She headed down the hall that was used for staff only.

A group of interns sniggered by a closet door.

"What's going on?" Hazel asked.

The interns tried to regain their composure. "A couple is having sex in the supply closet. We tried to go in to get suture trays to restock, but the door is jammed."

Hazel frowned. "They shouldn't be in there."

"At least let them finish," an intern joked.

"It's unsanitary," Hazel groused. She knocked several times, but no-one answered. Finally, she grabbed a pen from one of the interns and applied the old trick her father had taught her to jimmy open a door. With an easy pop, the door swung open and her whole world toppled over when she saw Mark, with his pants down, and behind his body, pressed against the wall, his surgical fellow, Melody.

"Hazel?"

She heard shocked gasps and a snigger of laughter behind her. Tears stung her eyes, tears of rage and humiliation, as she slammed the door and ran off...

Hazel shook the painful scenario from her mind.

She hated it when those old memories came back to haunt her. She had thought, in the last six years since it happened, that she'd firmly locked them away. That she had put them in their place, but apparently not.

"What do you think?" Caleb asked, intruding on her morose thoughts.

"Sorry, what?"

He looked slightly annoyed, pursing his lips. "I asked you if you think she's a good candidate?"

Hazel stared down at the facts and figures. It was all just numbers. Their patient was a good candidate. Her last caesarean section was a low transverse incision. She didn't have any other previous complications, and her latest ultrasound showed that the placenta was in a good position with the baby down.

"I don't see why not. I haven't met her or examined her, but I would like to do that and I could go from there."

"What do mean, go from there?" Caleb asked dubiously.

"Using my instincts. Facts and figures are great, Dr. Norris, but sometimes there are things you can't predict."

He looked utterly crestfallen for one moment. "Yes. I'm very well aware of that."

And she knew then that she had intruded into the memories of what must have happened to his late wife. Not that Hazel knew exactly what had happened, only that she had died when Lizzie was born.

"I don't see why she can't attempt a vaginal birth this time. What I'm saying is that I would feel more comfortable if she did it in a birthing suite in the hospital."

Caleb cocked an eyebrow. "Really? You're suggesting she gives birth in the hospital?"

"Why do you sound so surprised?"

"I just figured that since you want to get to know the patient and go with your instincts, that you would want her to give birth here in this homey environment and not at a sterile hospital. Not that this place isn't sterile like a hospital, it's just…it's not so bleak. The decor makes it more comfortable."

She frowned. "Hospitals have their place. I am a nurse practitioner as well, you know. I worked in a hospital for a couple of years. And since this is a vaginal birth after caesarean section with a patient that neither one of us is familiar with, my instinct tells me that it would be better if she delivered in a birthing suite with access to an obstetrical team that can give her a repeat C-section if needed."

"That makes sense."

"Now you really sound surprised," Hazel teased.

"Well, the few times I actually try to strike up a rational, logical conversation with you we seem to always end up at cross-purposes."

"That's not my fault," she responded swiftly.

He chuckled. "Oh, it so is."

"What?" she asked, feeling kind of affronted.

"You have a temper."

"I don't!"

Only she knew she did. Her father said it came from his grandmother who was Irish and Scottish. Hazel didn't really believe that; her father was military and she knew that it came from him.

Completely.

He was just too stubborn to admit it.

Just like she was doing now.

Hazel threw up her hands. "I don't want to argue, but if the patient wants a midwife there for her, I'll be at the hospital and willing to help her in any way that I can."

"I agree. I don't want to argue, and I appreciate that you are willing to work with me. I think it would be safer for our patient if she gave birth to her child at St. Raymond's, under both our care."

"Good. I'm so glad we're in agreement."

He was laughing softly to himself.

"What?" she asked.

"In the last six months, with all our interactions since that day at the tribunal, this is the first time that we've really agreed on something."

Hazel cocked her head to the side. "I suppose it is. Don't let it go to your head. When did you say your patient is coming?"

"I thought she'd be here by now. Hold on a moment," he said as he fished his phone out of his pocket and checked it. "Ah, they've had to rearrange some things, so they're not coming right away." Caleb just shook his head. "So, I'll arrange an appointment for later, if you're free?"

"I think I am. Just check with Joan. She's the one who books in all the appointments. Of course, that appointment could be interrupted if a patient needs me."

"Of course, the same goes for me."

Hazel nodded. "I look forward to working with you, Dr. Norris."

"And I you."

He left her office, and she sat down in her chair weakly.

After that tribunal, if Hazel had been told she was going to make a deal with the devil and work with Caleb, she would've laughed in everyone's faces.

Who was laughing now?

After Caleb made the arrangement for his patient to come to his office and meet Hazel, he got called down to the operating room to do an emergency caesarean section on one of his patients. He liked being in the operating room; it cleared his mind, because he was solely focused on the work that he was doing.

And he really needed to clear his mind.

He couldn't believe that he'd asked Hazel Rees to consult on a patient with him, but this new patient had been insistent that she have a midwife attend. To add to that, the chairman of the board of directors, Timothy Russell, who Caleb detested, had insisted that Caleb do whatever he could to make this particular patient comfortable.

Apparently, her husband was wealthy and she also came from money.

Caleb knew that Timothy's agenda wasn't about the health or care of the newborn and mother, but whether he could hit them up for donations. He knew how people like Timothy thought.

It drove him crazy, but he kept his head down and focused on his work.

His work was security, and the only thing to keep him sane since his wife died. It's what had provided a living for him and Lizzie, but there was a part of him that wished he could branch out on his own, open his own practice someday.

Provide the same level of care that Hazel gave to her patients.

Sometimes, it felt a bit like a revolving door at the hospital, and he missed the human connection and interaction.

The problem with walking away from St. Raymond's and opening his own practice was the financial risk, and he wasn't sure that he wanted to risk so much on something that might fail.

Playing it safe was always better. The one time he'd played fast and loose, Jane had conceived Lizzie. Not that he ever regretted having Lizzie, but he'd lost Jane in the process.

No, it was better to stay put. To not take the risk.

Even though he had taken a huge risk to talk to Hazel over Bria. He wasn't attracted to Bria, therefore she was safe. Hazel, on the other hand, was a gorgeous ball of uncertainty.

Caleb shook those thoughts away as he scrubbed out after completing the caesarean section. What he couldn't quite believe right now was that he was going to be working with Hazel. Why was he taking the chance? Temporary insanity must be the reason.

Loneliness? Boredom? a little voice suggested.

He silenced it.

Hazel was like this tempting thing he wanted so much, but he couldn't deny he was worried about getting bitten. When they'd had their little disagreement at her office, there was a moment when he'd started to regret asking her to consult on the case, but then she completely surprised him agreeing with him.

It was the first time they had really agreed on something.

Maybe this would be a new leaf? Or an olive branch maybe?

He could only hope.

He left the scrub room and headed out onto the operating room floor. He needed to change out of his scrubs and get ready for his meeting with his new patient, Tara Jameson, and her husband, Wilfred. He had to make sure he had all his information ready for when he and Hazel consulted with them in an hour.

"Ah, Dr. Norris. I wanted to have a word with you before your meeting with the Jamesons."

Caleb froze in his tracks and groaned inwardly as he turned around to see Timothy standing there in his expensive suit.

"This is the operating room floor. You shouldn't be wearing street clothes here. It's a sterile environment."

Timothy looked nonplussed. "I'm not in the operating room."

"No, but patients pass through here. Women. Children."

"Well, I did go to your office and you weren't there."

"I was in surgery." Caleb continued to walk and Timothy followed. He needed to lead this dunderhead away from the operating room floor and into a conference room or something so they could speak. There was an empty gallery room that was used to train residents, where they could view surgeries, but since there was no surgery in there and no residents, it was a quiet place to listen to what Timothy had to say now.

Caleb shut the door. "I'm meeting with the Jamesons soon. Is there a problem?"

"Hazel Rees. In particular her and the birthing center she opened with Bria Thomas."

"What of it?"

"The Jamesons are under the belief that she'll be attending the consult too."

"That's correct."

Timothy's eyes narrowed. "Why?"

"Because that is what the Jamesons requested, and since Hazel and Bria are the closest midwives in proximity to the hospital, they were the most logical choice."

"The Jamesons will want to have their baby at their birthing center, and that will take away revenue from us. Suppose they want to give donations to the birthing center instead of St. Raymond's?"

Caleb frowned. "So let me get this straight. You're not concerned about the medical wishes of our patients…"

"Of course I am," Timothy snarled. "Never assume that about me."

"What else am I supposed to think when you immediately talk about money?"

"Money is what pays your salary," Timothy said stonily. "Please don't forget that."

"What exactly do you mean?" Caleb asked.

Timothy turned around slowly. "What I mean is that the more money siphoned from the hospital, the less we have to pay staff. Think about that when you're inviting that Rees woman in here."

Timothy left the gallery and Caleb fumed inside.

He wouldn't forget that, but he was never going to put his patient's health at risk for money.

Never.

Hazel was pleased with how the meeting with the Jamesons and their little girl, Vanessa, had gone. She was fairly confident that Tara would be able to deliver her next baby vaginally without too much worry. The placenta was in a good place—they'd checked again at the appointment— and she was healthy, young and her scar didn't seem to be giving her too much pelvic floor trouble. And the Jamesons were very happy to have both her and Caleb working together on this.

Honestly, Hazel was glad to be working with him on this case too.

Her hands were tied when it came to surgical cases.

It was nice to have a good working relationship with him now.

At least, the start of a good professional relationship, if they could only stop arguing for long enough!

Although, she could tell that something was off about him during the consultation.

Something had clearly been bothering him. When she came over for the consult, he was even more closed off than usual and there was an air of anger in the room. Hazel was pretty sensitive to mood changes as well, and it was definitely a tense atmosphere.

"They're a lovely couple," Hazel said, trying to make conversation after the Jamesons left while Caleb was cleaning up the exam table in his office.

"Yes." His back was to her and it was stiff. His spine ramrod straight.

"Dr. Norris, are you regretting your decision to ask me here to consult?" she asked point-blank.

"No." He turned around and scrubbed a hand over his

face. "I'm sorry. I had to deal with the chairman of the board just before this meeting and it's still affecting me, I suppose."

"Ah, that's Timothy, isn't it?"

"Yes."

"He's definitely not a fan of our clinic being across the road."

"No, he's not," Caleb responded. "The staff has no problem with you and Bria. I hope you know that. It's just him and his precious bottom line."

"I get that. I've worked in a hospital. I understand it."

He smiled, relieved. "Good. I'm glad, because Tara Jameson clearly wants you on this case and I do too. You can see she's close to delivering. There isn't much time to form a game plan."

"No. There isn't. Maybe we could meet tomorrow?"

"Or we could meet tonight?"

The invitation caught her completely off guard. "What?"

"You could come over for dinner. Lizzie is cooking, and I know that she loves to have company. Especially company for me so that she can sneak off and be with her friends. She always worries about me being alone."

Hazel chuckled.

She didn't know Lizzie well, but she could already tell that she was a caring girl who would be worried about her father, but Hazel wondered if Caleb knew exactly who Lizzie was sneaking off to see.

She seriously doubted that Lizzie had told her father yet that she was pregnant.

Maybe that's what Lizzie was planning on doing tonight, hence why she was cooking for him.

"I don't know…" Hazel said doubtfully.

"Is it because we really didn't get off to the best start?" he asked.

"No, it's just… I don't want to burden Lizzie. She has so much schoolwork."

"I know, but think of it as a way for us to pay you back for letting her talk to you about midwifery. As well as talking to me about Mrs. Jameson and her VBAC. It's a working slash thank-you dinner."

"Okay." She couldn't believe the words were coming out of her mouth until they did.

Did she really just agree to a dinner with Caleb? At his house?

"Great. I will email you the address, and I'll see you around seven?"

"Sure," she said. She grabbed her purse and left his office.

She walked out of the hospital a bit stunned and back to the Women's Health Center, still going over the chain of events that had just happened.

Bria walked into her as Hazel was entering the building. "Whoa, there you are. I was wondering where you got to. You look like you've seen a ghost!"

"Dr. Norris just invited me over to his place for dinner. Tonight."

Bria's mouth fell open. "You accepted? You accepted dinner at the terrible ogre's house?"

"What?"

Bria's eyes twinkled. "Don't you remember? After your first run-in with him, you were calling him the devil and an ogre."

Hazel chuckled. "He's not a terrible ogre. I was wrong. There's nothing ogreish about him."

"So you said you've accepted. Are you regretting it already?"

"No," Hazel said softly. "No, because he said it was a working dinner. And we're going to be consulting on a case, so really it's the smart thing to do. We need a good relationship with St. Raymond's in order for our center to survive."

"I was thinking of having some kind of fundraising event. It would be great to have the hospital on board," Bria said.

Hazel wrinkled her nose. "I will help, as long as I don't have to plan it. I hate those kinds of things."

Bria chuckled. "Deal. So what're you going to wear when you go over there tonight?"

Hazel felt the blood drain from her face. "What do you mean? This isn't a date, Bria."

Her friend just smiled knowingly in that annoying way she sometimes did. "Sure, sure."

"What I'm wearing is fine."

"Sure." Bria nodded.

Hazel rolled her eyes. "Get back to work."

Bria smiled again and continued on her way.

Hazel just shook her head. She could focus on the rest of her work, even though she had a bunch waiting for her. All she could think about was Caleb, and her pulse quickened. He was so prideful, so stubborn and moody, but now she understood why. He was a widower. Still hurt and grieving.

Why was she always attracted to men like that? The wounded ones.

The broken ones.

The wrong ones.

CHAPTER THREE

CALEB'S HOUSE WAS in a posh area of Portland, and Hazel had to admit that she felt a little bit intimidated heading into this part of town. She grew up in a firmly middle to lower income family. They didn't have much, but they had enough.

Still, she was a bit overwhelmed by his wealth.

Why are you letting these thoughts bother you now?

The only thing that she could think of was that she was nervous.

That wasn't a lie.

It was nice that Caleb invited her for dinner, and she had to keep reminding herself that it was just a working dinner.

Still, his invitation had surprised her.

She should've said no, but maybe it was curiosity that propelled her to accept.

Curiosity killed the cat.

As she chuckled to herself, all the tension she was feeling melted away.

This was good.

Lizzie wasn't her only patient, but she wanted to be a midwife too, plus she and Caleb were working together on Mrs. Jameson's case. There were a lot of pros to accepting his invitation to dinner, and that's what she was going to remember.

They were colleagues now.

This dinner was a great way to get to know one another

and maybe end the sniping that they had been engaged in the last six months.

Hazel took a deep, calming breath and rang the doorbell.

The door opened and Lizzie greeted her.

"Hazel! I'm so glad you made it."

"You sound surprised," Hazel joked.

"There was a part of me that wondered if Dad was pulling my leg saying you were coming to dinner and you were just saying yes to him to be nice. I was half expecting you to call him and cancel," Lizzie said excitedly as Hazel stepped inside the house and Lizzie closed the door.

In truth, Hazel had thought about that option, but didn't take it.

It was the coward's way out and she didn't want to disappoint Lizzie, who had opened up to her. She wanted to earn the young woman's trust so that she could help her.

Lizzie would need her help and support until she told her father the truth about why she had been at Hazel's clinic.

"Hazel would never do that. She's too kind. Annoying, but kind." She looked up and saw Caleb standing at the top of the stairs, leaning casually over the banister.

He was smiling as he said it, so it was meant as a gentle tease.

"I'm not the only annoying one," Hazel quipped.

"True."

Caleb came down the spiral staircase in the foyer. Her heart skipped a beat. He was wearing a V-neck sweater in a deep navy that brought out the color of his eyes, and she was surprised to see him in jeans.

She'd never pictured him as a denim kind of person.

Of course, in all her interactions with him he'd been dressed in a suit and a white lab coat.

She hadn't even seen him in his scrubs. Hazel's cheeks heated as their gazes met. He was smiling, just slightly as he came down the stairs.

"Dad, she's hardly annoying," Lizzie interjected. "Although, you certainly can be."

Hazel chuckled as Caleb cocked an eyebrow at his daughter's muttering.

"Oh, really?" he asked his daughter.

"Where do you think I get it from?" Lizzie asked, crossing her arms.

Caleb shook his head. "Would you let our guest in?"

"Right." Lizzie ushered Hazel in. "I hope you like lasagna, Hazel."

"I love it," she said, tearing her gaze from Caleb and holding out the plastic container she'd been gripping so tightly. "I brought pie."

"Yum. Thanks. I'll take it to the kitchen." Lizzie turned to her father. "Dad, can you be nice to our guest for one minute?"

Caleb rolled his eyes, but was still smiling. "I'm certain I can."

Lizzie nodded and left them.

Hazel was still standing in the foyer, her coat on, her boots on. The only thing missing was the pie that she had bought at a local bakery. Caleb closed the gap between them.

"I am really appreciative that you came," he said. "I didn't expect you would."

"I'm not mean. Well, I guess I am annoying, but I like your daughter. She's delightful. Unlike you," Hazel teased.

"You just don't know me yet. I'm an absolute delight."

"That remains to be seen."

"I can show you some figures," he teased.

They both laughed, and the tension instantly melted away.

Caleb smiled. "Can I take your coat?"

Hazel nodded and undid the buttons. He stepped behind her, and she was suddenly aware of how close he was. Her pulse was thundering in her ears, and she was suddenly so nervous being near him and in his home.

This man who'd got under her skin for the last little while was making her weak in the knees. She never thought she'd be here, laughing with him.

And now she was in his home and he smelled so good.

You need to get control of yourself. Remember Mark? You're not a good judge of character.

The Women's Health Center was the only thing that mattered. Their relationship had to be strictly professional.

Hazel slipped off her coat and gave it to him, then sat down to slip off her boots. As soon as the boots came off, she realized she'd forgotten to change her socks and she was wearing her rainbow-striped toe socks. The rainbow toe socks that reached up to her midcalf didn't exactly go with the casual dinner skirt and shirt she'd picked out.

She'd been planning on wearing tights.

Caleb instantly saw them and there was a twinkle in his eyes. "Those are quite the socks."

"Right. I knew I forgot something," she mumbled, embarrassed.

"There's a pocket for each toe. Doesn't that drive you slightly crazy?"

Hazel glanced down at her feet and wiggled her toes. "Nope. They're quite comfortable, which is probably why I forgot to change them."

"Well, I think they look great. Unusual, but great." He was smirking as he took her jacket to the closet and hung it up. "Would you like a drink?"

"I would love one, but maybe I should go help Lizzie?"

"No. She won't want that. This is her project, and I learned over the years not to get involved with her projects. She gets testy and says I'm interfering."

Hazel chuckled softly. "So the apple doesn't fall far from the tree, then, does it?"

Caleb laughed again. "No, I suppose it doesn't."

Hazel followed him into a formal sitting room. It was decked out with antique furniture, all dark wood, and bookcases full of leatherbound books, floor to ceiling. There was also a fireplace with a fire flickering in its hearth. It was actually kind of cozy, and she could easily spend many a rainy, cold evening curled up with a good book in here.

It looked like a den of a wealthy lawyer or doctor.

And then it struck her, Caleb was just that. Although, the books looked more for show than reading. The bookcase in her loft apartment had paperbacks with creased spines from all the times she had read her favorites over and over again.

Though lately, those had been few and far between.

She didn't have much time for reading right now. Her life was all about work.

She walked over to the big bay window and there was a large maple tree outside, with leaves softly fluttering in the rather brisk wind that had got up.

"Scotch?" Caleb asked.

"Is it though?" she asked.

He cocked an eyebrow. "Pardon?"

"I mean, is it really scotch. Scotch is only scotch if it's from Scotland. If it's from here, it's whiskey."

He glanced at the bottle. "It's from Scotland."

"Ah, then it is indeed scotch." She was rambling again. She always seemed to do that when she got nervous.

"You didn't answer my question," Caleb said.

"And what's that?"

"Would you like some?" he asked.

"No, thanks. Not keen on the stuff."

"Would you prefer a gin and tonic? The wine is being saved for dinner I'm afraid."

"A gin and tonic would be wonderful." She wandered over to one of the bookcases and stared up at all the classics.

She'd taken some English literature classes in university, and she recognized some of the tomes she'd had to read.

And she remembered some of them putting her to sleep.

"Have you read many of these?" she asked.

"All of them," Caleb responded.

"Seriously?" she asked.

He nodded and handed her a highball glass with her gin and tonic in it. "I loved English literature when I was in school. So I've read all the greats. I'm a bit of a collector when it comes to first editions."

Her eyes widened. "So you're telling me this is a first edition of Mary Shelley's *Frankenstein*?"

Caleb nodded. "It is. A classic feminist piece."

A smile quirked on her lips. "And you're a feminist?"

"I am an OB/GYN."

She shrugged. "It doesn't mean you're a feminist though."

"I am. I believe in the rights of women and them having autonomy over their own choices."

She was impressed. "That's very admirable. So why are you so against the Women's Health Center then?"

He sighed. "I told you I'm not. The board asked me to present the facts, and I felt my hands were tied. I only did my job."

There was an exhaustion in his voice. She remembered how boards of hospitals could be. She knew they could be money hungry. Money was really the source of all evil. She felt bad for him.

He had so much on his plate and was now having to deal with this pressure from the board. And he also didn't know yet that his college-aged daughter was pregnant. She couldn't help but wonder how he was going to handle that.

It was a lot for any one person to deal with.

All she wanted to do was reach out and comfort him.

Only she couldn't.

She had to keep her distance.

"Well, we're there now and I hope that we can work together," she said. Although, she wasn't going to hold out too much hope. She wanted to believe that everything was going to work out all right, but she'd been disappointed before.

She'd been hurt before.

Caleb's lips pressed together in a firm line, and he was staring at his shelves of books in consternation. "I would like that."

"I would like to be able to send my clients, the ones I can't help, to you. We could have a beautiful partnership." Hazel was putting a lot on the line, but it was the truth. It was, after all, another reason why she and Bria had chosen a site across from the hospital. They wanted to be able to send their surgical cases to St. Raymond's.

It wasn't to stick it to the hospital, far from it. It was so that there was another option available for their patients. It was a safety net. That was Hazel's hope always, that their midwife clinic and St. Raymond's would work in a sort of symbiotic relationship together.

Only, that wasn't the case at the moment. The board of directors had made it clear that they didn't want to work with them. At least Caleb seemed to want to, and Dr. Anderson, the chief of staff, had also been so helpful and friendly.

"You're right," Caleb said. "I hope you know that you have my full support. My board of directors won't like that, but this is about the patients. I would gladly consult on any case, and I'll send on any patient that would prefer your midwifery services over mine. Which is why I asked you to consult on my vaginal birth after caesarean case. Mrs. Jameson's case. I sincerely respect midwifery. I hope you know that."

She was a bit taken aback and didn't know quite what to

say to that. This didn't seem to be the man she's assumed he was. Only she didn't know him well enough yet to be sure. She wanted to believe he was who he appeared to be, but her trust had been broken and it was hard to take Caleb's integrity at face value.

She really wanted to believe him, but she couldn't let herself.

"Thank you, Dr. Norris," she said quietly.

He smiled, his eyes twinkling in the dim light. "Caleb."

A blush crept up into her cheeks and she couldn't stop it, even if she wanted to. "Caleb then."

"You're welcome, Hazel," he said softly.

Her heart was racing and her knees began to tremble.

"Dinner is ready!" Lizzie announced, popping her head into the room and breaking the tension that had fallen between them.

"Perfect," Caleb said, turning around. "I'm starving."

Hazel took a deep breath and followed him out of the formal sitting room. Relieved to put some distance between them and this strange whirl of emotions that he was causing.

Caleb didn't quite know what overcame him. One moment they were discussing the feminist implications of Mary Shelley's *Frankenstein*, and then the next thing he knew he was forming some kind of partnership with Hazel and fighting back the urge to pull her in his arms and kiss her.

She looked absolutely adorable in her rainbow-colored toe socks.

And then he watched as she admired his books.

There was a part of him that wanted to discuss English literature with her. Curl up in front of the fireplace and talk. That's what he and his late wife had done. They had met in English literature class in college.

Jane had loved the classics just as much as he did.

When he'd first started collecting these books, she had been the one to start giving him first editions. And she was the one who had found and tracked down the first edition of *Frankenstein* for him.

"What is it?" he asked, shaking the package.

Jane made a face. "Don't do that!"

"Is it breakable? Will it explode?" he teased.

"Just open it. Or I'll open it for you," Jane threatened.

He laughed. She always was impatient, especially when giving gifts. It was one of the most endearing things about her, and he loved teasing her.

"Maybe I'll open it later."

She jumped at the package, and he'd held it over his head as she crawled across his chest in a futile attempt to get it.

"Just open it, Caleb. Stop teasing me so much."

He grinned. "Fine. I'll open it."

He torn into the paper and been stunned at the old book wrapped in parchment paper. "Is this what I think it is?"

"Well, your essay and thesis on this book was the best in our class. It's why I fell in love with you." She leaned over and kissed him.

"Is it?"

"Your sympathy for the devil. Or, in this case, the monster, was truly inspirational. The monster is definitely misunderstood."

"You fell in love with me because I sympathized with a monster?" he asked, teasing.

Jane smiled and kissed him again. "Happy anniversary."

Caleb tucked the memory away. It was a good memory, but it was just that. He had lived in the past for far too long. When Jane died, he'd had to focus on Lizzie and his career. There was no time to grieve properly. No time to move on.

It had been easier that way.

Was it easier now?

He looked across the table to see Lizzie and Hazel laughing over something as they enjoyed their dinner. He couldn't really recall the last time Lizzie had laughed like this. Actually, when was the last time there was this kind of mirth in his home? Probably not since Lizzie was a little girl. They loved one another dearly, but as she'd grown older she'd naturally preferred hanging out with her own friends.

It was nice to hear her giggling again. Both of them had got so busy lately, they'd barely had time to sit down and have a meal together.

He was alarmed to realize he was struggling to remember the last time they'd connected like this.

He couldn't help but smile at her joy, but there was a part of him that was worried. Any spare time he had should really be spent with Lizzie. There could be nothing between Hazel and him.

They were colleagues, and he didn't want to mix business with pleasure anyway. Even if in Hazel's case he wanted to break that rule.

It's not like she'd want you.

He was a widower with an adult daughter, and Hazel was young, vibrant, beautiful.

Hazel can be your friend.

The only problem was, he didn't just want to be Hazel's friend. The moment he'd laid eyes on her he was drawn to her, attracted to her, and the more he got to know her, the more he wanted to know. He was putting his heart in a dangerous situation.

He was going to have to try and put some distance between them. Which would be hard given they were going to be working together at times. But it was the only way he could get over this infatuation with her.

He'd been attracted to other women before and got over

it easily. He'd even had a couple of flings, but no real relationship. All he had to do was get some distance. That was the key.

Not that inviting her to dinner was helping any.

Hopefully, they wouldn't have to confer on too many cases together.

"Do you want me to get out the pie?" Caleb asked, trying to escape this happy scene so he didn't get too caught up in it. It was one that he wanted to have continue, but knew that it couldn't.

"No, Dad. This is my dinner. I'll go get it." Lizzie got up and took everyone's plates.

She disappeared into the kitchen.

And an awkward silence fell between him and Hazel. This was not part of the plan. Logically, he didn't want to be alone with her, but another part of him did.

"Would you like some more wine?" he asked, clearing his throat.

"Please." Hazel held out her glass, but wasn't exactly looking him in the eye. He hoped that he didn't make her too uncomfortable.

"So, are you from Portland?" he asked, trying to lighten the tension and make conversation.

"No. I'm not. I was born in New York. We moved around a lot. My father was in the armed forces so I've lived all over. One of the longest places we stayed was in Portland though, so I've always thought of it as home. And I did my midwifery training here, which is where I met Bria. It seemed like the perfect spot. I'm glad to be back. And you? Are you from Portland?"

"No, I'm from California. I am a West Coast native at heart, but I much prefer the mountains and forests to the city."

"Portland is quite a large city," she reminded him.

"Not as large as Los Angeles, which is where I'm from."

"I would've pegged you as a WASP from the East Coast. Somewhere like Connecticut. Old money."

Caleb frowned. "What makes you think that?"

"You're a bit...well, you're a bit stiff sometimes. I guess that's a polite way of saying it."

Caleb chuckled under his breath. "So you're saying that your first impression of me, you felt like I had a stick up my backside?"

Hazel laughed. "I guess so. You were so rigid. Aren't Californians usually more relaxed?"

"Aren't military brats rigid too?" he asked.

"We're efficient," she countered.

"So am I, but I assure you I am not a WASP. My parents were actually a bit hippyish. We had money, because my father was a movie director and my mother was an actress. Quite a big name in her heyday. She was even in a Bond movie at one point."

Hazel's eyes widened. "Are you serious?"

He nodded. "Yes. So there was a lot of Hollywood parties, and A-listers at our home. I was sent to boarding school on the East Coast. So I guess that's where I probably picked up that WASP vibe that you're feeling."

Hazel leaned in. "I'm fascinated by old Hollywood. Who came to your house? Did you go to anyone's house? Oh, my goodness, did you go to any grotto parties?"

"Hardly. I was a child, but I did attend a party once at the Black Dahlia murder house."

"What is that?"

"You don't know about the haunted Black Dahlia murder house?" he asked incredulously.

She shook her head. "No, but I do read a lot of true crime."

"You said you were fascinated by old Hollywood and you read true crime. You should know about those murders. I'm not going to tell you anymore until you've read about it yourself. Then you can ask me questions, but needless to say, that was really old Hollywood and it firmly entrenched my belief in ghosts."

Lizzie opened the door and brought in the pie. Holding it proudly like she had baked it herself, but he could tell it was from Fleishem's bakery, which was a popular new bakery in the more artsy section of Portland.

"What kind is it?" he asked.

"It's pumpkin," Hazel said. "I know it's spring, but it's been so chilly and drizzly lately, I felt pumpkin pie was appropriate. This weather today certainly called for a good, old-fashioned pumpkin pie with whipped cream on top. Something to warm your belly."

"I agree," Caleb said appreciatively.

Lizzie grinned. "I love pumpkin pie."

Hazel beamed, her eyes twinkling. "It's my favorite too."

It warmed his heart to see his daughter so happy, and there was a part of him that this felt was right. The problem was, it couldn't last. He had no time to even think of romance right now. He had a teenage daughter, a job, and didn't have the emotional capacity to give more. Not to mention that whenever he'd mentioned Lizzie in the past, women weren't interested.

Which was fine by him. He didn't have time for them either.

Except now it didn't feel that fine.

There was also a part of him that was scared of letting someone in again.

He remembered the visceral pain of Jane's loss still.

He was terrified of that deep, gut-wrenching agony he'd felt the night he'd held his newborn daughter in his arms and learned that his wife was gone.

That pain he kept buried deep inside, to remind him that he was never going to go through that again. He couldn't.

His heart wouldn't survive it.

"Lizzie, are you okay?" Hazel asked.

He glanced up to see that Lizzie looked a bit green around the gills.

"Lizzie?" He got up and touched her head. "You're feverish."

"I just feel a bit sick. I think I'll lie down for a bit."

"Can I get you anything?" Caleb asked.

"Maybe Hazel could help me?" Lizzie asked.

"Sure," Hazel said. She helped her up and they left the room.

He was confused.

Usually he was the one who took care of his daughter when she was sick. Why was she asking for Hazel?

Of course, the older Lizzie got the less she wanted him to help.

Hazel came back. "She's fine. Just a bit queasy."

"Queasy?" he asked.

Hazel's eyes widened. "Yes, well, stress, classes and you know how it is at this age."

"I do."

Although, he felt like she was holding something back. *Are you sure about that?*

"Let's finish our dessert, shall we?"

"That would be great," Hazel said promptly.

They ate their pumpkin pie and talked about nothing in particular. After the pie was finished, Caleb walked Hazel to the door.

She pulled on her sensible boots over the rainbow toe socks.

"Thank you for having me over for dinner. Lizzie is a wonderful cook."

Caleb smiled. "Thank you for coming. You made her night. Sorry she got sick."

"She's a lovely young woman. Seriously, any time she

needs anything, just tell me. I know we haven't exactly gotten along before…"

He winced. "That is my fault. I do apologize. I could've explained myself better at the tribunal."

"You're not the only one at fault. I was exceptionally mad that day."

He smiled gently. "You certainly were."

That blush tinged her cheeks again. "Well, I'm sorry too."

"I appreciate that. I'm glad we cleared the air."

Hazel nodded. There was a small dimple in her right cheek. One that he wanted to kiss. The impulse caught him off guard, so he took a step back to disconnect. He couldn't let this go too far. Even if his instincts were telling him that he should kiss her, pull her into an embrace. He couldn't do that.

She was a professional colleague.

That's all they could be. That's what he wanted.

Isn't it?

"Well, good night," he said abruptly, not sure what to do.

"Good night, Caleb." She opened the door and headed out into the drizzly spring night. He watched her from the door as she made her way to her car. His head was a jumbled mess as she drove away.

There was a part of him that so wanted more.

Only she wasn't his for the taking.

CHAPTER FOUR

A FEW DAYS had passed since Hazel had been over to his place for dinner, and Caleb couldn't stop thinking about her. And it wasn't just the dinner; it was her collaboration on Mrs. Jameson's vaginal birth after caesarean case.

As head of obstetrics, his work was fairly solitary, other than teaching his residents or conferring with anesthesiology, nurses and the chief of staff.

It was rare to have such a collaboration with a professional colleague.

It was nice.

He stared out at the birthing center across the road.

There was a knock at the door.

"Come."

Victor Anderson stuck his head in. "Hey, how are you doing today?"

Caleb glanced over his shoulder and then turned to face him. "Good. And you?"

"Very good, surprisingly, considering I just had a meeting with the board of directors." Victor winced and Caleb chuckled as his colleague came into the office and sat down.

"So what did the new chairman have to say this time?" Caleb asked.

"Timothy is still so convinced that the Women's Health Center across the road will be detrimental to St. Raymond's finances."

"Why is he so concerned about St. Raymond's bottom line? According to the last fiscal statement the board passed around to staff heads, we're not hurting for money. We both know the Women's Health Center will be mutually beneficial. Why can't he see that too?" Caleb asked.

Victor shrugged. "Who knows? It's quite frustrating. If I had my way, there would be no more endless meetings about it. I wish Timothy Russell would just accept that the Women's Health Center is going to stay, and there's nothing to be done about it. It's time to move on to the more pressing needs of the hospital. Those midwives aren't villains, they're just doing their jobs. Like we need to be doing ours."

Caleb sighed. "It seems to me that our time or rather the board of directors' time could be used in a much better way."

Victor tapped his nose. "But you didn't hear it from me."

"Maybe I should go to speak with them."

Victor raised his eyebrows. "You want to talk to the board? To Timothy? You two don't exactly see eye to eye."

"Sure. There's a huge benefit to working with the midwives. They can send over surgical patients to us. It's a win-win."

"You know that and I know that," Victor said, agreeing.

"I'm currently utilizing Hazel Rees's knowledge on Mrs. Jameson, who Timothy is very eager for us to help. Well, for me to help."

"That's great! Just don't mention it to Timothy that Hazel is involved."

"What do you mean?" Caleb asked, confused. "Timothy already knows Hazel is involved."

Victor groaned. "Oh, no. He'll definitely try to do something about that."

"Are you serious, Victor? You mean he would try to stop the collaboration even though he knows it's what the patient wishes?"

Victor sighed. "Yes."

"That's ridiculous."

Victor nodded. "Agreed. I'm still going to try to get the board to agree that working with the birthing center is the best thing for everyone involved, but with Timothy Russell at the helm, it'll be hard."

"Should I present them with some more facts?" Caleb asked hotly. "Since they got me to present so many at that tribunal."

Victor grinned. "If you'd like to, you can tell them the senior staff will put up a united front to support the birthing center."

"That could work."

Victor stood up. "It sounds like a plan."

"Is that all you wanted to discuss?" Caleb asked.

"Yes." Victor winked. "Just making my rounds and I peeked in and saw you staring out your window in quiet contemplation. Usually you're hard at work, head down at charting."

Caleb grinned. "Well, maybe it's time to stop and smell the roses."

He had been so distracted lately. All he could think about was Hazel. Her smile, her laughter, that dimple in her cheek. It was more than a bit consuming. It had been a while since he'd felt this way about someone, not since Jane. No other women had held him in this kind of thrall in a very long time.

It had also been forever since he'd let someone take up this much space in his brain.

Victor left his office with a wave as he shut the door. Caleb was left feeling incredibly frustrated that Timothy Russell didn't see the value of the birthing center.

What was happening to St. Raymond's? It used to be such a great place to work. He'd always loved coming here every day, but lately it was all becoming too much like a big corporation.

It was more about the money than the medicine.

The old board of directors would have been all for a collaboration. The new chairman would ruin this hospital's reputation if he wasn't careful.

"Hey, Dad!"

Caleb turned to see Lizzie come in. She still looked a little pale, and he was worried about her.

"How are you feeling?" he asked.

"Fine. It was just a bit of a stomach bug. Stress about midterms." Lizzie set her bag down.

He wasn't sure that was completely it. There was something else going on, but she was being tight-lipped.

Maybe she broke up with Derek?

He knew he had to tread lightly with her private life, or he'd get pushback.

Lizzie could be as stubborn as he was.

"What're you doing here?" Caleb asked.

"Can't I come see my dad?" she retorted.

He chuckled. "Of course."

"Good." She worried on her bottom lip. "There's something I need to talk to you about."

"About midwifery? It's okay if you want to study that. I'd prefer it if you went to medical school so you could follow in my footsteps," he teased.

Although, he didn't care what she did for a career, as long as she was happy and could take care of herself.

Lizzie's eyes were wide. "Right."

"Was that it?" he asked.

"Yes. That was it."

"If you're going to learn midwifery then Hazel is one of the best."

"She's great," Lizzie agreed.

He had a feeling that there was more she wanted to talk about, but then his pager went off.

"One of your patients?" Lizzie asked.

"Yes. She's been brought in and I have to check on her."

"Go." Lizzie got up and kissed him on the cheek. "I'll see you later."

Caleb left and headed down to the labor and delivery floor. He was so distracted today. He had to get his head on straight.

He had to concentrate.

Caleb hated this loss of control over his own thoughts. Being in control was how he'd managed his life for the last eighteen years.

It's how he'd raised his daughter, made his way through medical school and it would be how he got over his infatuation with Hazel.

"What in the world are you reading?"

Hazel startled with a slight jump and looked up to see Bria hovering in the doorway of her office. She didn't even hear her come in. Hazel had been so engrossed in reading about the Black Dahlia murders, she had tuned out the world.

It had been a few days since her dinner with Caleb and Lizzie.

And all she could think about was how much she missed them. How nice it was to have dinner with a family again. Her family was scattered all over, and it had been some time since she'd got together with her parents and siblings.

It was lovely to have that feeling of belonging.

She had Bria, but both of them had been so busy trying to get the center up and running that when they'd each got to their respective homes, they'd simply crashed. Hazel's whole life had been this center, and her dinner at

Caleb's home with Lizzie suddenly had her longing for something more.

Something she wanted so much, but she'd been burned before.

Her heart was still on lockdown because Mark had crushed her so completely. It was just better to be alone and focus on her career.

And to get her mind off Caleb, she had purchased a book about the old Hollywood murders. She hadn't heard the door open, and now her heart was racing a mile a minute! She set the book down, trying to regain her composure.

Bria cocked her head and looked at the cover. "What in the world is this about? Black Dahlia?"

"An old Hollywood murder that Caleb was talking about. I thought I would read up on it."

Bria smiled knowingly and cocked an eyebrow. "Caleb?"

Hazel's cheeks heated. "Dr. Norris... I mean."

Bria chuckled. "No, I don't think that you do. I think you meant Caleb. You went to his place for dinner, didn't you? How did that go?"

Wonderful.

Marvellous.

It felt like home.

"It was good," Hazel said quickly. "He grew up with the Hollywood elite. His mother was a film star and his father a director."

Bria's eyes widened. "Are you serious?"

"Apparently his mother was in a Bond movie."

"That's wild! He doesn't seem like the type."

"Oh?" Hazel asked, but then she had thought the same thing too.

"Aren't all native Californians supposed to be laid-back?"

Hazel chuckled. "That's a stereotype. Being a military child, or brat, I would also like to sweep away text-book stereotypes."

"And he recommended you read about these Hollywood murders?" Bria asked, glancing at the cover of the book again.

"He did."

"Maybe he's a serial killer?"

It was a joke, but Hazel just shook her head and puffed out a breath. "What is it that you need?"

Bria nodded and held out a file. "New patient. She's coming in. I'm swamped, and Joan said you weren't answering your texts."

Hazel glanced at her phone and cursed under her breath. "It's on silent."

Bria handed her the file. "The patient will be here in ten minutes. Look sharp. Read on your own time and all that nonsense."

Hazel laughed. "Right. Thanks."

Bria nodded and left.

Hazel texted Joan to let her know when the patient came in. She glanced down at the book and sighed. It had been a long time since she had escaped into a book or done anything beyond work, eat, or sleep.

She was feeling slightly burned out lately. Getting their center off the ground had left her with very little time to relax, but that was the casualty of running your own business. She took another deep breath and opened the patient's file from their general practitioner. It was all standard stuff letting her know that the patient was pregnant.

This was her first pregnancy.

And it looked very textbook.

Hazel set down the file and then began to tidy up her desk.

Joan called her.

"Hi," Hazel answered.

"Your next patient, Sandra Patterson, is here," Joan said.

"Send her in." Hazel hung up and waited to greet the patient.

She walked into the room with her husband, and the first thing that Hazel noticed was that the woman was considerably larger than she should be for fourteen weeks. She shouldn't even be showing that much, especially for a first pregnancy.

Instantly she saw a red flag.

"Sandra, it's a pleasure to meet you. I'm Hazel."

Sandra smiled. "The pleasure is all mine. This is my husband, Dan."

Hazel shook Dan's hand.

Dan looked a bit frazzled, a bit stunned, which wasn't uncommon for a first pregnancy, but he was also smiling, so he seemed to be happy to be here.

"Have a seat," Hazel said, motioning to the chairs.

Her mind was already going a mile a minute as she looked at Sandra, and her instinct was telling her there were multiple fetuses. She'd seen it once before, a case of quadruplets when she was in her nursing training, before she decided to completely focus on midwifery.

High-order pregnancies were always difficult.

Sandra and Dan sat down, and Hazel shut the door to her office.

"Congratulations on your pregnancy," Hazel said brightly.

"Thank you!" Sandra was beaming, but poor Dan still looked a little shocked.

"I was told that I didn't really have to see a midwife straightaway," Sandra said.

"No, not right away," Hazel agreed.

"My cycle is so unpredictable," Sandra said.

"I've had a glance at your file. You're about fourteen weeks along?"

Sandra nodded. "I was prepping to do in vitro fertilization. We had been trying for some time, but again I'm not totally sure. My cycle was so sporadic."

"Well, we can do a dating ultrasound to confirm. Were you taking any medication for egg production?" Hazel asked, another red flag rising to attention that this was multiple gestation.

"Yes, we were getting ready to harvest, but then I noticed my temperature was right and we just got pregnant." Sandra smiled at Dan and he returned that loving smile, squeezing her hand.

"Have you had an ultrasound?" Hazel asked.

Sandra shook her head. "No. When my doctor confirmed my pregnancy, I weighed my options. I really wanted to see a midwife first. Which is why I'm here. It takes me some time to think."

Hazel smiled as she inputted the information into Sandra's chart.

"That's not a problem, but given that you were taking medication to start an egg harvest, there is a good chance that you could be carrying multiples."

Dan's face went paler. "Multiples?"

"We'll do an ultrasound and see, shall we?" Hazel suggested. "That way we can give you a good date estimate."

Sandra nodded. "Okay."

"Climb up on the exam table, and I'll pull out my handy-dandy portable ultrasound."

Sandra nodded again. "If I have more than one, will I still be able to deliver here? I really don't want to go to the hospital. It's not in my birth plan."

"I'll lay it out straight. We can for sure safely deliver twins here. We've done that before. Anything above two, though, I'm going to bring in an obstetrician to consult. You can absolutely continue to have your care here as long as you and the babies stay healthy, but there are risks for anything over two. Ninety percent of births over two are delivered via caesarean section, but there are some small percentages that can still deliver vaginally. It's not hopeless."

"Okay." Sandra eased onto the exam table and lay down.

Dan stood next to her. "I just want Sandra to be healthy."

"Of course," Hazel said, smiling.

Hazel got everything ready to do the ultrasound. She hadn't meant to terrify the new parents, her new patients, but the fact was they had to be made aware of the possibilities. If they were in the process of upping Sandra's egg production and it wasn't a controlled procedure, there was a huge likelihood of twins or even triplets.

Sandra lifted her shirt and Hazel did measurements of her belly. Her patient was definitely measuring large for fourteen weeks, which was confirming her suspicions.

"Okay, this jelly is a bit cold." She squirted the jelly on Sandra's lower abdomen and flicked on her ultrasound.

It didn't take long for Hazel to find the uterus and her hunch was correct, but as she counted the egg sacks, the little flickering of heartbeats, her hope for a safe delivery of twins was quickly dashed. She counted five.

Five viable heartbeats.

Five little lives.

"Well…" And Hazel was at a loss for words. "How long have you two been trying?"

"A long time," Dan said. "We always hoped for a large family, but as the years went on that kind of became a pipe dream."

"You're going to get your wish." Hazel moved the monitor. "There are your babies. Five of them in fact."

"Five!" Sandra gasped, tears welling in her eyes. "Five! Like as in quints?"

"Quints occurring naturally are extremely rare," Hazel remarked. "And though you were taking medication to increase your harvest, this is still pretty momentous news. It also means I would definitely like to have an obstetrician brought in. With a multiple pregnancy like this, we're looking at a preterm birth, possible gestational diabetes…so this is the safest thing for you and your babies."

Dan looked down at Sandra, smiling. "Okay, but we don't know any good obstetricians. We're new to Portland."

"I happen to know an excellent one, who is just across the street." Hazel saved a picture of the babies and wiped off the jelly. She handed Sandra the printed picture. "If you two wouldn't mind waiting here, I'll give him a call now and see if he can come over to meet you."

Sandra and Dan nodded. Not saying much as they stared in wonder at the sonogram.

It warmed her heart.

High-order pregnancies were dangerous, but she could see the longing etched in Sandra's and Dan's faces. They were happy. Terrified, but happy with their outcome.

Hazel slipped out of her office and pulled out her phone. She typed in Caleb's office number.

This was too important for a text or even an email.

This warranted a call.

"Dr. Norris speaking," he said stiffly.

"Caleb, it's Hazel."

"Hazel?" he asked, confused. "I haven't input your number, but it came up as a private caller."

"Yeah, I have it set that way. Sorry. Anyways, you remember how you said you'd be willing to consult with me?"

"I do," he said cautiously.

"I have a need for one. Big time."

"What is it? You sound a bit shaken."

"It's quints. Conceived naturally…for the most part. They're here now, and I could really use your help with this one."

There was a slight pause. "I'll be there in twenty minutes."

She could hear the excitement in his voice. She couldn't blame him. This was thrilling. She hadn't seen quints since her days of training, and even then she'd just observed. She wasn't involved in the delivery.

High-order births, especially ones like this, were just so rare. This would be an exciting case. A challenging case.

Hazel hung up and then took another deep breath. She headed over to Joan at the reception desk.

"Hazel?" Joan asked. "You look like you've seen a ghost."

"Not quite. Dr. Norris is coming in. Please show him to my office right away when he gets here."

Joan nodded. "Of course."

Hazel headed back to her office.

When she had asked Caleb to work with her, she thought it would be once in a while, or not very often, but fate had apparently found a way to bring them together yet again.

First Mrs. Jameson's VBAC, Lizzie's pregnancy and now the quints.

It looked like for the next several months she and Caleb would be working very closely together. So much for putting distance between them.

Thanks, karma.

Caleb shook Dan Patterson's hand as he and Sandra left. The Pattersons had made it clear that they wanted to keep coming to the center to have their checkups, and Caleb didn't see a problem with that as long as the babies were small.

He ordered a bunch of tests.

Including monitoring Sandra for gestational diabetes, more often than he would with a singleton pregnancy.

He still couldn't quite believe that it was quints.

Although Sandra had taken medication to aid her with in vitro fertilization, she had still conceived the babies naturally and he found that fascinating. It was rare that he came across that. Usually the high-order births that came through St. Raymond's were because of IVF.

He was really glad that Hazel had asked him to consult on this case.

He knew she was a nurse practitioner and a midwife, but cases like this needed a bit more help. And he was only too glad to be involved.

"Thank you for coming over so quickly and for letting my patients continue their primary care here," Hazel said.

"You mean *our* patients. I'm glad to help, but there are so many complications we have to watch for, and when she gets to a certain point then I'm going to want her on bedrest."

"At the hospital?" Hazel asked.

"No, not necessarily. I mean the board of directors, I'm sure, would love me to assign her to months of hospital bed rest and rack up her medical bills."

"Of course. It's all about the money," Hazel groused.

"Indeed, but if she's well and the babies are fine, then I don't see why she can't stay at home for the time being. Eventually, we'll have to monitor her frequently the further along she gets. It's a huge adjustment and shock."

"Well, it doesn't matter how many babies are in there. I still see a lot of fathers with that deer in the headlights look on their face," Hazel said lightly.

"Agreed. I had a similar expression when my late wife told me the news."

They shared a smile.

"I can only imagine," Hazel said. "You must've been like…what, a young man when your late wife had Lizzie?"

"A lot younger indeed. I'm forty now."

"That's still very young to have a grown daughter!"

He smiled. "Perhaps."

And he thought back to that moment Jane had told him

she was pregnant. He had been so surprised. A child that early hadn't been a part of his and Jane's plans, but the shock had been momentary, because then he'd felt an unending amount of joy when they'd learned they were going to be parents. He'd always wanted to be a father.

He wasn't always the most demonstrative when it came to his feelings, but he still felt those moments very deeply. It was just hard to feel anything when he'd had to keep it all together just to get through medical school and take care of Lizzie.

His little girl had never wanted for love, but that was all he could give for so many years as he'd chipped away at his enormous student debts.

Being wracked with pain and yet having a beautiful piece of yourself and your wife to love and protect. It had been such a fine line to walk for so many years, being a loving supportive father on the outside, maintaining a professional demeanor at school and work, but being a raw, broken mess inside when you were alone.

"I can only imagine," Hazel said, breaking through his thoughts. "Still, I'll need your expertise. At first, Sandra was quite adamant about her birth plan."

"Her birth plan will have to change," Caleb said bluntly.

"That's a bit harsh," Hazel responded.

"I've had run-ins with very controlling patients."

'That's quite the judgment of people you've only just met!"

"I'm just generalizing," Caleb said defensively.

"Well, a mother's birth plans are important."

"They are important, I agree, but they also need to be fluid. You can't predict every detail. Things happen during labor and delivery you can't control." He knew firsthand about those changes. It hadn't ever imagined he'd end up being a single father and a widower.

"I think it's something practical parents can do to ease stress, and what's wrong with that?" Hazel asked hotly.

"Look, I don't want to argue. I get why birth plans are important for a woman. It's their body and it's their right to dictate what they need, but I'm just pointing out that most times those birth plans are just that. A plan. An ideal that is meant to ease anxiety. Nature has its own agenda sometimes. I've rushed countless women into surgery who were adamant right up until the spinal epidural froze that they weren't going to cop out the easy way and have a C-section."

Hazel frowned. "A C-section is not a cop-out, nor is it easy. I see patients all the time who are post C-section and are working with adhesions and scar collapse, prolapse issues…just the same as someone who gave birth vaginally."

Caleb nodded. "Exactly, but misinformation and internet research can be misleading. People make ill-informed choices when they do their own medical research. Dr. Internet Search Engine is the worst kind of quackery."

Hazel relaxed as she chuckled. "Quackery?"

He grinned. "Exactly."

"It must be that undergraduate English literature coming out in you. You talk like a disgruntled hero from a Jane Austen novel."

"Do I?" He smiled at her. Her mention of literature had him remembering their dinner again; he'd been thinking about her a lot since that night. In fact, he couldn't get her out of his head, and that was a bit worrisome.

What was it about her that attracted him so? He never normally had this kind of preoccupation with a woman.

But Lizzie is an adult now. She doesn't need you now as much. You're free to pursue happiness.

And maybe that was it, but honestly he didn't know if it was the whole story. Perhaps it was simply Hazel.

Instead, he'd thrown himself into his work to try and not think about her. It had been working until she called him today, but he was still glad that she did. Quints were something special, and he was more than happy to be a part of the patient's care.

And it also would be interesting to see how working more closely with Hazel would be.

When they'd finally opened the clinic here, he'd done his research on her. He wanted to know who he could be potentially working with. So he'd learned what he could about the midwives, in particular Hazel. He knew where Hazel did her training and what papers she had written. She was impressive, and he was looking forward to working with her closely.

Truth be told, he was growing seriously tired of hospital politics.

And he was becoming more envious of her freedom to open her own practice. There was a part of him that wished he could leave Portland behind, open up his own practice somewhere up north…like in Alaska. Alaska had always been a secret dream of his since reading books set there when he was a child.

It was so different from his lonely life in Los Angeles and growing up as a Hollywood child.

Alaska made him think of peace, quiet and adventure.

Only, he couldn't do that to Lizzie.

His daughter needed security, and security meant him keeping a stable job. Opening up his own practice meant he'd be wholly financially responsible for its continued success. Caleb wasn't sure he could invest in himself and take that risk when Lizzie still needed him.

So he was stuck for now. At least until Lizzie was finished with school and was independent with her own life and that was fine.

Everything was fine.

Is it?

"You do. A bit," Hazel answered, interrupting his train of thought. "Except for the American accent. It's not quite as dignified as Mr. Darcy or anything."

"Thanks," he replied sardonically, deciding a change of subject was in order. "I'm glad your center will be able to handle the tests I need."

"We can't do an amniocentesis here. Not yet."

"We can handle that at St. Raymond's," Caleb answered. "It's a delicate procedure when it's a high-order pregnancy. We want to draw out the fluid, but not hurt a fetus. And then there's trying to figure out whether it was one egg that split and if there's different embryonic sacs."

"I remember seeing one set of quints, but it was from IVF, so they were different sacs. It's not too early to determine gender. If they were all the same gender, then we could probably deduce that they were from the same egg," Hazel said. "Like that case in Canada in the thirties...the quints they put on display because they were the first to live."

"Yes. They were all identical."

"I'll say it again, I am glad that you're willing to help me. I have other patients, and I'm a little out of my depth here. It's a lot of babies, potentially."

"Potentially?" he teased. "I think it's a fact."

"Of course. I don't know why I jumped to the idea that they might not all make it."

"It's a sobering thought, but with the right health care and with us working together, I think her babies have a great shot."

"All five of them," Hazel said brightly.

He smiled. "Indeed."

It was going to be a very high-risk pregnancy, but Caleb had this instinctual, gut feeling that working with Hazel would make things so much easier for them all. That this was the best course of treatment for Sandra Patterson and her babies.

"I think we'll make a good team."

"I do too."

They gazed at each other for a moment. His pulse was thundering between his ears. A pink blush tinged her cheeks, and it took all his willpower not to reach out and let his fingers brush across her skin.

He wanted to feel her softness.

Hazel looked at her phone. "Oh, I have to run! One of my patients is in labor and they're outside the city."

"Can I help?" he asked. "I have the afternoon off, and Lizzie is studying late tonight at her boyfriend's."

"You say that so disparagingly," she teased.

Caleb grunted. "Derek is an okay person. So can I help you?"

"I think I'll be fine, but thank you," she said quickly.

Caleb was slightly disappointed, but he couldn't blame her. This was her work. Would he really want her in the operating room with him while he was doing a surgical procedure?

Yes.

But he pushed that niggly little voice away.

"At least let me walk you to your car and help carry something?"

Hazel was grabbing the prepacked birthing kits. "Okay. If you can grab that other duffel bag, you can help me lug it to my car so I can get out of here. It's a two-hour drive."

Caleb picked it up and followed Hazel out of her office and the building to her car. She opened the trunk, and they heaved everything in.

"Thanks again," she said, quickly shutting her trunk. "I'll call you later and we can talk further about Sandra Patterson."

"Sounds good."

Hazel smiled at him quickly and climbed in the car. He took a step back as she turned the ignition. Nothing happened. There was a small sputter of the engine, but it didn't turn over. She tried again, but had the same result.

She rolled down her window, wincing. "Can I ask another favor?"

"You need a lift to your patient's?" he asked.

She nodded. "If you don't mind."

"Not at all. Stay put. I'll be back in a few minutes with my car."

"Thanks." She leaned her head against her steering wheel and banged it gently a few times in frustration.

He couldn't blame her.

Normally, he'd be swamped, but today he was not on rotation for the delivery room and he had no patients to see. It was a day he usually dedicated to dictation, reports and research. It would be nice to get out of the office for a few hours and take Hazel to attend a birth. With Lizzie at Derek's, there was nothing waiting for him at home.

Except loneliness.

Even if he was used to it, he was glad for the excuse to have some company.

CHAPTER FIVE

HAZEL WAS VERY THANKFUL, but still shocked that she was sitting next to Caleb as they sped their way through curvy mountain roads toward her patient's house. Of all the days for her car to break down, it had to be today.

Her patient was no stranger to home births.

This was her seventh child born at home.

Hazel was more worried that she wasn't going to make it in time.

The roads were a bit slick from drizzle, and it was midafternoon. School buses were making their runs, and the trip became longer and longer. And the more time that went by, the more Hazel was worried that she would be too late and that she would've wasted Caleb's time driving out here.

It's not a waste of time. You're checking on your patient.

They hadn't said much as they raced out of the city to her patient's rural address, but it wasn't an awkward silence. It felt like it was normal. Like they had done this many times before, and Hazel couldn't help but wonder what had shifted in the last week.

For the last few months, he had been such a thorn in her side.

A sexy, broody thorn, but a thorn nonetheless.

Now it was as though they were friends or something.

It was weird, but also kind of nice.

She had Bria, but no one else thanks to her family being spread so far and wide.

And she didn't realize how lonely she had become. Of course, part of that was her own doing. She pushed people away, in particular men. It was safer for her heart. Especially after what Mark did to her.

She'd been destroyed after catching him in the act with Melody. It was so dehumanizing. It had broken her trust, and it was hard to let go of that pain. It was almost impossible to think about opening her heart again.

It was much easier to keep people out. Except for Bria. She still didn't quite know how her friend had managed that, but she was glad for it. The one thing she was certain of was that Bria wouldn't ever hurt her.

The wall she had erected around herself was for her own good, and she had to remember that. Even if there was a part of her that was telling her she was settled in Portland and it was okay to let people in now.

"You know," she said, finally breaking through the silence, "I really do appreciate the lift here. I could've called a cab. I'm sorry for burdening you."

She didn't know what had made her ask him for a ride, but she was glad she did as they followed the Columbia River before turning south to go around Mount Hood National Park.

"You're not burdening me. Not at all. I told you that I was able to help you out. It's a nice distraction, this drive. It's a beautiful rainy spring day. Not a fan of the unseasonable cold though."

"I just hope we get there in time."

"You said this is her seventh child?" Caleb asked.

"Yep."

His eyebrows raised. "I think I'll go a wee bit faster."

She chuckled. "Don't get a ticket, but I'm very glad your

GPS has the ability to provide alternate routes to bypass traffic and accidents."

The usual highway that she would take from Portland down past Warm Springs was backed up with a tractor trailer that had rolled over on the interstate.

Caleb had got the information and altered his course before the rest of the traffic was detoured the same way. Following the Columbia River took a little bit more time, but it was definitely better than sitting in a traffic jam and probably missing the birth.

As an added bonus, this was the more scenic route as far as Hazel was concerned. With Caleb driving it gave her a chance to sit back and prepare for her patient's birth.

"Is your patient fairly healthy? What I mean is, do her deliveries usually go smoothly? Do the infants fare well?" Caleb asked. "Should I call an ambulance on the off chance there's a problem?"

"No, she does fairly well. She's a pro and her babies are strong. We haven't had to call an ambulance yet. If we did, it would have to be an air ambulance as they live a little off the grid and just outside of Warm Springs."

He raised his eyebrows. "I really hope you make it on time. I almost wonder if they really need you."

"I do feel like an ornament sometimes with her," Hazel acknowledged. "But they like to have me there, and I don't blame them. You just never know what could happen."

"That is true," he said quietly, and she couldn't help but wonder if he was thinking of his late wife again. "I wish we knew how she was doing. I'm getting a bit anxious as well."

"I know. I've been getting texts from her husband and she's still laboring. Even if she does give birth before I get there, I can still do an assessment of the baby and make sure mother and baby are both okay."

"Seven kids," Caleb murmured. "I had a hard time raising one."

Hazel chuckled. "At least it's not seven all at once!"

"I've seen that once," he said sadly. "Almost lost the mother, and two of the babies were born with difficulties. One did not survive and…" He didn't continue his thought, but trailed off.

"What?" she asked gently. Although, she knew. It was the worst part of the job, when there was nothing to be done and a life was lost.

"I was only a student, but I remember the hospital bill that family faced. It still haunts me."

"Yet you work for a hospital that does similar things. Charges astronomical amounts."

"I needed to provide for my child," he said stiffly. "It doesn't mean I always like it. I don't set the fees. The board of directors does that."

He didn't need to say more. Hazel was quite familiar with the board of directors and their greedy policies at St. Raymond's.

"Do you do a lot of pro bono work?"

"I try to," he said. "Not as much as I would like."

Her heart softened. When she'd first met Caleb, she had painted a completely different picture of him. This was a different side to the man, one that she could relate to. She also wanted to help others. She'd grown up in a large family, and medical expenses could be tricky.

She'd seen families struggle.

Health care should be more affordable. That had always been her stand.

Not that it was a particularly popular opinion always, but she was glad to see that Caleb was sympathetic.

She tried to help where she could too.

She was glad that her first impression of him was incorrect.

He was a lot better than she thought he was. More honorable, and they had a lot more in common than she thought they did.

Don't get too attached, that persistent little voice reminded her. It warned her of the last time she'd let herself get too involved with a man she'd thought she was on the same wavelength with and how much that betrayal had hurt.

She was never going to risk her heart again.

Friends. Yes.

Lovers. No.

The thought of Caleb as her lover immediately made her blood heat and she shifted in her seat, hoping he didn't notice a blush in her cheeks.

"So I started reading about the Black Dahlia and those murders in old Hollywood," she said, trying to change the subject.

"Did you?" he asked, intrigued.

"In fact, Bria caught me reading it. She was kind of horrified, but she doesn't get my fascination with history and true crime."

"I don't get your fascination with old Hollywood. I told you, I lived the aftermath. It's not all that glamourous. It was kind of a miserable childhood, if I'm honest. My mother on sets, my dad at constant parties trying to make connections."

"You said your mother was in a Bond movie. Which Bond?" she asked.

He chuckled. "It was a small part."

"Oh, come on, which one?"

Caleb cleared his throat and tried a very garbled Scottish accent that was terribly bad. "Guess."

"Really? That's exciting. He was so handsome. Even right up until the end, when he was older."

"Never understood why women were so entranced by him."

"Did you ever meet him?"

"No. Bond was before my time. My mom became pregnant shortly after that movie, and I was born."

"Maybe you're really his love child."

Caleb laughed. "Uh, no, I can assure you I am very much my father's son. Though, whenever I got mad at him I did fantasize that James Bond was indeed my father, and he was going to rescue me to take me on exciting adventures. I'm talking about the fictional version, by the way, the character from Ian Fleming's books. I was very much over Hollywood as a child."

"Still, it's kind of exciting. We were a transient family, being military and all."

"So where was the most exciting place you moved to?" he asked.

"Alaska. Nome, Alaska. Like far up there."

"See, and now I'm jealous of that."

She quirked an eyebrow. "You're jealous of me living in Alaska?"

"Completely. It was sort of a dream for a long time to move up there and open a practice, but my late wife didn't want to leave Portland and then I had Lizzie and those dreams just became that. Dreams."

"I understand that. Although, I have to admit I'm living my dream at the moment."

"Oh?" he asked.

"It was always my dream to open a midwife clinic with Bria. I love being a midwife and taking care of women in all stages of health. There were some places where I've lived and worked where women's health wasn't freely discussed, and I was a bit sad to learn of places where a woman didn't have autonomy over her own body. I guess I wanted to change that. It took a long time. There were things I had to give up to make it happen."

What she didn't tell him was that she'd given up on the idea of finding Mr. Right after Mark. It was hard to believe in love when your heart was broken, though there was a part she kept locked away that still secretly hoped for a family of her own.

One small ember of hope left burning that she would find love.

That she could heal. But the logical part of her just had a hard time trusting again. She had sort of settled on the idea that she would be alone for the rest of her life, but that was okay with her.

Is it?

She ignored that thought again.

"I'm glad that you're living your dream," he said. They shared a brief glance, and she could see the sincerity in his eyes.

It made her stomach do a flip.

Silence fell between them again as they drove through the town of Warm Springs. It was down in the foothills of Mount Hood, which rose in their rearview mirror. They drove for another thirty minutes until the GPS told Caleb to take a sharp right and then a left down a bumpy, gravel track through the woods.

At the end of the long tract, Hazel could see the little log cabin that was nestled into the woods. Her patient Clarissa and her husband, Matt, had chosen to live like old-time homesteaders. The land had been in Matt's family for a long time.

They had modern conveniences, but those conveniences were run off solar power, water power and wind.

Matt was waiting outside as Caleb parked the car. Pacing more like it, holding his phone.

Matt looked worried, which made Hazel's stomach do another flip, this time in anxiety. Matt was never the one to be worried. Especially when this was Clarissa's seventh child. Hazel had delivered the last two, and she'd got to know the couple quite well.

So seeing Matt outside pacing, his face creased with worry, made her stomach knot in apprehension.

Hazel got out of the car and grabbed her first duffel.

Matt ran down the stairs from the front porch, out into the rain. "You're a sight for sore eyes, Hazel. I was getting so worried."

"Sorry. Car troubles and then that accident on the interstate. I had to take a different route. This is Dr. Norris from St. Raymond's. He's accompanying me today. He was my ride."

Matt nodded, barely glancing at Caleb. "This labor is taking too long. None of the others have ever been like this. She's in a lot more pain than usual."

She began to mentally list in her head everything she had been worried about. All the reasons why this labor wasn't progressing.

Hazel nodded. "Let's go."

Caleb carried the other duffel bag full of her equipment as Matt gave her the full rundown about how labor had been going.

Or rather, how it hadn't, in this case.

The house was unusually quiet, but Matt explained that the kids were with his parents in town, so Clarissa could focus. Hazel was glad that the other kids were gone, because she needed the space to think.

When she walked into the bedroom, Clarissa was on all fours, panting and sweating. Hazel could see the pain etched on her face. More pain than was usual for her.

"Clarissa, tell me what's going on," Hazel asked as she opened her duffel bag and started to get the items out of her birthing kit. Clarissa was quite in tune with her body, and Hazel knew she would be able to articulate what wasn't right.

"It's taking too long. Feels. Stuck." Clarissa groaned. "This position felt better than lying down."

"You do what feels good," Hazel said encouragingly.

Hazel sanitized her hands and then pulled on gloves as Clarissa's glassy expression fell on Caleb.

"Who's that?" Clarissa asked.

"He's a doctor. A friend of mine. He's an OB/GYN, and he was working on an earlier case with me. My car broke down," Hazel said as she continued prepping.

Clarissa laughed weakly. "Your car is in bad shape. Told you that before."

Hazel grinned. "I know."

"What do you need me to do?" Caleb asked, setting down the other bag.

"Pull out the equipment and sanitize. I think the baby might have its shoulder stuck."

"Shoulder dystocia?" Caleb nodded. "She's had six natural births before?"

Hazel nodded. "It'll take some maneuvering, but I don't think we'll have to cut her. Just in case, though…"

Caleb nodded. "I'll prepare the instruments for an episiotomy."

"Thank you." Hazel made her way over to the bed. "It feels better this way? On all fours?"

Clarissa nodded, her gaze focusing as another contraction tore through her. Hazel coached her through it.

"Good, Clarissa. Breathe, and I'm going to take a look if that's okay with you?"

Clarissa nodded. "Please."

Hazel knelt down. She could see the baby crowing with the contraction, but as the baby moved forward, it retracted, like a turtle.

Yep. She was pretty positive it was shoulder dystocia.

"Caleb, I'm going to need your help. Matt, I would like you to hold Clarissa's shoulders. I can't have her move." Hazel sat down behind her.

Caleb came over. "I have resuscitation equipment at the ready."

"Good. I don't think I need to do an episiotomy. If I can get her to deliver this way, there's going to be a little shift and we'll deliver the posterior shoulders first. I'll need your help keeping her steady, and I may need you to push on her abdomen."

"Of course." Caleb knelt down.

Hazel watched closely as the next contraction was coming. "Okay, Clarissa, I'm going to need you to push. As hard as you can."

Clarissa cried out. Hazel guided her hand to press on Clarissa's abdomen, while Caleb steadied her hips. The turtling effect stopped and the posterior shoulder appeared. There was a release and the baby began to slip through, no longer stuck.

"Push, Clarissa. Push!" Hazel urged.

Clarissa gave one final push, her body shaking as the baby was born into Hazel's hands. The baby didn't cry, and Clarissa was bleeding. Hazel quickly clamped the cord and Caleb took the small baby girl in his strong, steady hands.

"It's a girl," Hazel announced. "Matt, help me get her to lie down," she added, looking over her shoulders as Caleb took the baby over to the table, to where the portable oxygen tank she'd brought with her was kept.

"Why isn't she crying?" Clarissa whimpered.

"She was stuck, so Dr. Norris is tending to her. I'm going to see to you," Hazel said gently. Her pulse was thundering in her ears and her ears were pricked, listening for that cry of life. That first breath, but the room remained quiet.

Hazel kept her focus on making sure that Clarissa was stable.

Then she heard it.

The thin little wail through the room.

Hazel smiled and sighed internally. Matt and Clarissa cried out in relief.

Caleb was in awe of Hazel. She knew exactly what was wrong at almost first glance. She knew her patient so well and trusted her. For the first time, in a long time, since Lizzie was born really, he had felt absolutely the bystander during a birth.

It was clear that Clarissa was in very capable hands.

If Clarissa had walked into St. Raymond's and been in his care, he would've done the same thing. Although, there might be a surgeon or two who would've gone instantly to a caesarean section, but it was clear to him that it wasn't needed here.

He looked down at the tiny girl who had got stuck.

She was a little blue, but once he cleared her throat and nose with suction and gave her a bit of oxygen, she was improving. Her color was pinking up nicely.

Usually, when he delivered an infant that had a hard time breathing at first, the infant was whisked off by the attending pediatrician. His concern was the delivery. It was rare that he really got to be here and hold the new baby.

Hazel came over. "How is she?"

"Doing well. She just needed some help," Caleb said gently. "She's seven pounds three ounces. I took the liberty of measuring her. Her clavicle is broken, so they should get it checked by their pediatrician, but it's not uncommon for births like this. It'll heal on its own."

"She won't be in pain?" Clarissa asked.

"Should we give her pain meds?" Matt asked anxiously.

"No, she's too young. Just be mindful of the way you hold her," Hazel said.

She smiled as Caleb handed her the baby. Hazel took the little girl over to the happy parents, and he watched them.

A bit jealous, like he always was when he saw first-time parents with their newborns.

He was happy for them, but it always brought him back to that moment.

The moment when he should've been the happiest he'd ever been and yet instead his world had shattered into a million pieces.

"Look at you. You're the most beautiful girl in the world. Your mommy is going to just love you."

He gently rocked his newborn daughter back and forth.

"Little Lizzy. It's what your mommy, Jane, wanted to call you. So you could be Lizzy and Jane, from Pride and Prejudice.*"*

He walked the hallway outside the delivery room. Jane went in for an emergency caesarean. Her spinal hadn't worked, and they'd to put her under. It wasn't uncommon. It happened to patients of his before, so he just waited.

It was when he glanced up at the clock and saw the time that passed that he began to worry. Only he couldn't freak out. He had a little life in his hands.

A little cherubic angel.

His daughter.

Still, watching the clock soon became an obsession for him.

And then a nurse ran by carrying blood.

His heart sank, because the nurse wouldn't look him in the eye.

His stomach knotted and he focused on the operating room doors. Waiting.

Time seemed to stand still.

Then his colleague came out. It was then that Caleb knew what happened. He held Lizzie closer.

"Tell me," Caleb said softly.

Though he already knew.

"I'm sorry, Caleb. We did everything we could. She bled

so heavily, and then there was a pulmonary embolism. Her heart stopped. We brought in a cardiothoracic surgeon, but her heart... I'm so sorry."

Caleb sat down on the bench.

Numb.

Frozen.

Lizzie began to wail.

A wail that filled his heart with an unspoken scream of pain.

Caleb shook that memory away as he stared at the happy family now. That wasn't their story, and he was genuinely happy for them. Hazel was doting on the baby, and he couldn't help but smile at her.

There was just so much to like about her.

He hated that the board of directors was so against the midwife clinic.

The board of directors, in particular Timothy Russell, should work with Hazel and Bria's birthing center. It would be beneficial to all the pregnant women in the area. There was so much potential for a successful collaboration.

If only Timothy, the new and clueless chairman of the board, could see it. Caleb wished he and Hazel could be partners. Full on partners working on every case together.

Only, he worked in a hospital and she had her own business.

They couldn't be partners.

They could be friends, but that was it.

Even if there was a part of him that wanted more. In this moment, he wanted so much more and he was genuinely terrified of that. For so long he had been holding back. He'd had a child to raise, so much on his plate.

He hadn't thought he could love again, had believed that if he did try to open his heart he was somehow betraying Jane. The thing was, it was all just excuses, and he knew it, but he was still scared of what he was feeling. The need to move on and start anew was unknown.

Wanting more out of life was something he hadn't felt in a long, long time.

CHAPTER SIX

CALEB DIDN'T SAY MUCH.

All he could do was help Hazel clean up. The baby was doing well and Matt had made a call to their local doctor, who came out and checked on the baby. Once they were sure that Clarissa was well and everyone was stable, he carried the bags back out to his car while Hazel said her goodbyes.

He knew that Hazel was planning to come back out here to check on Clarissa and the baby. At the hospital, it usually depended on the shift rotation if he'd see his patients once after the birth, then six weeks after and then maybe not again.

Hazel had more of a chance to have a real relationship with her patients. He didn't really get that personal connection at St. Raymond's.

It was getting dark, and they still had a long drive back to Portland.

The rain was coming in harder.

He checked in with Lizzie, who told him she was still studying with Derek and then would be going to her friend's for the weekend. He hoped it was a friend and not Derek's. He knew that Lizzie was an adult, but he didn't want her to end up young, pregnant and still in school. That had been a challenge he hadn't enjoyed. Still, Caleb didn't really relish the idea of going back to an empty house.

It had never bothered him much before, but tonight he didn't want to be alone.

Hazel climbed into the car and they both waved at Matt, who had walked them out. Caleb didn't say much as he turned around in the drive and headed back down the bumpy track to the main road.

He didn't want this night with Hazel to end. He was enjoying his time with her. He liked working with her, and when they spent time together he forgot how lonely he was.

"You okay?" Hazel asked, breaking the awkward silence that had fallen between them.

"I'm fine. It was just…it's always a bit emotional watching new parents. You'd think I'd be used to it by now."

"I get it," she said wistfully.

"I'm sorry. I know I sound completely maudlin." He glanced over at her, sending her a smile. "I'll be okay though. Would you like to stop and get something to eat? It's well past dinnertime."

"Yes. I would love that, but it'll be my treat since you drove me out here and made dinner the last time."

"There's a small diner on the main interstate. It looks like a reasonable place. I've passed it before."

"Let's go there."

After a forty-minute drive from Matt and Clarissa's small homestead and back into the foothills of Mount Hood, they saw the neon lights through the dark and rain. The diner was sort of themed like a mountain lodge and was called Elkoholic, and there was a huge neon, animated sign of an elk looking extraordinarily happy with a stein of beer in its hoof.

It was tacky and kitschy, but it was warm, dry and provided food.

He just hoped it wasn't a dive.

"It's got great reviews, although the restaurant name is slightly dubious," Hazel said, holding up her phone.

"If it's got good reviews, then I'm slightly more relieved," Caleb said.

"Not into game meat?" she asked.

"It's how it's cooked and the cleanliness of the kitchen that's the concern."

"I wouldn't mind an elk steak or caribou. It's been some time since I've had either of those."

"Can't say that I've had caribou," he remarked. "What else have you eaten?"

"Let's see, deer, elk, caribou, moose and seal."

"Seal?" he asked, surprised.

"Nome, Alaska, remember? A friend of mine was Inupiat, and her mother let me try some seal oil and some of the seal."

"What did you think?"

"I wasn't overly keen, but it keeps you warm during a cold Alaska night."

"I'm sure."

He parked the car and they both made a mad dash through the rain to the entrance of the restaurant, just as the downpour was ending and the sun was coming out. Not that the sun would be up for much longer anyways. Inside was all wooden beams, hunting paraphernalia, canoes and other woodsmen and outdoors stuff.

It was like a lodge.

"Table for two?" the girl at the counter asked.

"Yes, please," Hazel said. "A booth would be great if you have one?"

"I do. Follow me," the girl said, smiling. She led them past happy patrons, lots of families to a back corner. There was a hidden booth that was covered in red flannel and dark wood. The table looked like it was a living-edge piece.

It was cozy and quiet, and he was thankful for the break to collect his thoughts.

The waitress placed two menus on the table. "I'll be back with some water and cornbread."

Caleb thanked her and slipped off his damp coat, sliding into the booth next to Hazel as she scooted to the far side of the table.

"This looks great! It sort of reminds me of a lodge my dad went to a lot in Nome. Only, it might've had something to do with moose or caribou."

"I've never seen a moose and you've eaten one," Caleb remarked, trying to change the subject from the recent birth and the feelings that had threatened to drown him afterward. Maybe if they talked about something else he wouldn't think about the day he'd lost Jane or about how much he liked being with Hazel.

Except for the fact he was with Hazel right now.

Alone.

He glanced up and saw a stuffed elk hanging on the wall above her head. Its glassy eyes were staring at him, in what looked like horror.

Well, maybe they weren't totally alone.

"You're frowning. Actually, scowling is more like it."

He shook his head. "I was staring at your company there."

Hazel glanced over her shoulder and chuckled when she saw the elk head. "Oh, you know it's fake, right?"

"It's fake? How can you tell?"

"There's a tag that says it's from China. Also, it's felted. That's not real fur. It's close, but it's definitely not a real elk head."

"It's creepy anyway," he murmured, staring back down at the menu.

"Not a hunter?" she asked.

"Are you?" he retorted, cocking an eyebrow.

"No, but my dad was. Elk is not my favorite."

"What was your favorite then?"

"Are we really having a discussion about what my favorite kind of meat is?" she asked, her dark eyes twinkling.

He chuckled. "I suppose we are. I do have to apologize for that. I'm not one for a lot of sparkling conversation."

"I don't know about that. I thought our conversation a couple of nights ago at your place was quite engaging. You're easy to talk to." A blush tinged her cheeks, and his heart began to beat a bit faster.

"You're easy to talk to as well."

The waitress came back and took their orders and then left again. He couldn't tear his eyes off Hazel's animated face. "You impressed me today."

"I seem to keep doing that, and I think it's quite unfair!"

"Oh?" he asked.

"I haven't had the chance yet to really see you in your element, but I suppose that your hospital board won't like me poking around too much."

"Probably not, but you know I would love to have you come and work with me being my on call consultant."

She cocked an eyebrow. "Are you serious?"

"You're a licensed medical professional. You're a midwife and I'm head of obstetrics. The board may not have the warmest attitude toward your health center, but they can't actually stop you from coming to the hospital. Besides, when Mrs. Patterson comes for a more extensive ultrasound, I would like you there. She is our patient, after all."

Hazel smiled, the little dimple that he found completely delectable showing up again. "I would like that."

"Then you can compliment me," he teased.

"Oh, so that's the game you're playing at then?" she joked.

"Well, you didn't want to discuss my previous topic about the various meats that you've tried and liked. Have you tried bear?"

Hazel started to laugh and she shook her head. "You are persistent, Mr. Hollywood."

Caleb wrinkled his nose. "That's the best you can do?"

She leaned across the table. "I tell you what. I'll tell you if I've had bear and you tell me about the time you stayed at the Black Dahlia murder house!"

"The supposed murder house," he corrected her.

"Is it a deal?"

"Fine." He leaned back at crossed his arms. "What do you want to know?"

"Is it haunted? It's supposed to be haunted."

"If it is, I don't know. The only thing I remember about that house was that it was architecturally beautiful."

"Boring. Seriously."

"What do you want me to say? I was only ten at the time."

"At ten you were already appreciating architecture?" she asked with a smile.

"Not completely, but I remember thinking it looked cool. Is that good enough for you?" he asked.

"'Cool' I can believe. Especially for a ten-year-old."

"Now it's your turn," he said.

"Yes. I've had bear. I don't recommend it either."

"Was that so hard?"

The waitress came back with their drinks and their dinner on a large serving tray that she was balancing on one hand, quite impressively. All talk about consuming weird meat and the murder house that he went to when he was ten and growing up among the Hollywood glitterati dissipated, and instead they discussed the quints.

It was so easy to talk to her about medicine.

Jane hadn't been able to talk shop with him, but she had been a very good listener. It was kind of refreshing to talk about cases with Hazel, and for the first time in a long time he really enjoyed himself.

He completely lost track of time.

Instead of standing still, time sped up and soon the diner was shutting down and Hazel was stifling a yawn. They still had the best part of a two-hour drive to get back to Portland. Hazel paid the bill and he got a coffee to go.

It felt natural as they left the Elkoholic lodge and walked back to his car.

Only this time, when the silence came, it wasn't awkward. It was because Hazel had drifted off to sleep.

He glanced at her a few times, and he couldn't help but smile.

It felt so right with her here beside him, but he was afraid.

Afraid that if he did let her into his heart fully, she wouldn't want to reciprocate. If she rejected him, it would make working with her even more awkward. Why get involved with someone you often worked with? A middle-aged widower with a hefty amount of emotional baggage wasn't exactly appealing, at least that's what he thought.

Hazel certainly didn't appear to have that kind of baggage with her. She was young still, only late twenties, and unencumbered. He wasn't going to burden her with his past because he knew it would only drive her away in the end. His heart just couldn't take that kind of loss again.

Hazel hadn't realized that she'd drifted off until the car slowed down. She opened her eyes to see the lights of Portland in the distance. She touched her face gently, just to make sure that she wasn't drooling. She sometimes had the habit of doing that when she was very tired.

And today had been emotionally draining on so many levels.

She was pretty sure that her walls were still strongly in place. At least she liked to think they were. Except, when it came to Caleb, she could feel him edging around those barriers and it drove her crazy. Every time she saw him or spent time with him she always told herself that she was going to distance herself from him.

Then she didn't.

Caleb was a good man. What would he want with someone like her? A person who was not a particularly great judge of character. Someone who had been easily duped by a false love and made to look a fool. And if that wasn't enough, it was now clear to her why Caleb was still single. Because he'd never found anyone that could take the place of his late wife.

Hazel was not worthy of that kind of love or devotion.

She didn't want to get hurt again.

She was so scared of that.

She needed to build up her defenses better, even though her heart didn't really want to.

Come on, Hazel. You can do this.

Only when it came to Caleb she was so weak.

Apparently her subconscious thought so too, because she usually didn't fall asleep around just anyone.

"I'm so sorry," she said groggily, trying to sit up straighter. "I didn't mean to do that."

"It's okay. I'm used to front seat nappers. Lizzie often drifts off during long car trips. I am glad that you've woken up though, as I don't know exactly where you live."

"Jade Street. I'm just around the corner from the center and the hospital. I live above a coffee shop."

"I know the place."

"That's my little apartment. It's not exactly the most exciting place, but it's mine and it's convenient."

"We should be there in no time. I'll help you carry up your equipment."

"Actually, we should probably stop at the center first so I can take it there. They are my birthing kits, and I'll have to replenish them and sterilize the equipment. If I have to walk to work tomorrow, then I don't want to have to lug two large duffels with me."

"I understand, but tomorrow is Saturday. Your center is open?"

"Not for regular appointments, but babies don't take the weekend off," she said lightly.

"That's true. I'm not on rotation, so it's my day off and Lizzie is staying with friends."

He sounded so sad and though she knew she shouldn't, she offered, "Well, if you want to hold on to the bags, you can bring them by the center tomorrow morning for me and I'll buy you breakfast."

"You bought dinner tonight."

"Yeah, but I still feel like I owe you for driving me."

"I'll gladly drop the bags off to you tomorrow. Maybe if you don't get called out, we can do something together?"

Her heart skipped a beat. Was he asking her out?

She didn't know quite how to answer that.

She knew what she had to say. She should say no, she should resist him. The problem was, she liked being with him. Even though they'd had to attend a birth and diagnose quints together, it wasn't the work that she enjoyed the most.

It was the company.

Bria had her own patients, and they had both been so busy recently.

It would be nice to get out and do something with someone else.

"What were you thinking of?" she asked.

"Have you been to Multnomah Falls? I mean your center is named after them."

Hazel smiled. "No, I haven't actually been there."

"Well, it's only thirty minutes outside of Portland. It's spectacular with all the leaves starting to bud. Every season has its merits."

"I would like that."

Caleb pulled up in front of her apartment. "What time will you be at the center?"

"Around ten?"

He nodded. "I'll bring you back your equipment then."

"Sounds good. Thank you again." She got out of the car quickly.

She waved as Caleb drove away, leaving her standing there.

Still in shock.

What was happening here?

Caleb hefted the two duffel bags out of the trunk of his car and carried them to the center. He didn't know what possessed him to invite Hazel out today. All night he'd tossed and turned about his decision, and part of him was trying to figure out a way to get out of it.

It was only a small part though, because there was a much louder part of him that was lonely and really wanted to spend more time with her.

There was an off chance that their day would be interrupted by her need to attend a birth, but he couldn't rely on that as an excuse not to go.

What else did he have to do today?

There was a bunch of emails from several members of the board of directors, particularly Timothy Russell, who was asking for yet another meeting, and for Caleb to provide more facts and figures. He wanted birth rate stats since the Women's Health Center had opened. Something about wanting to investigate the negative impact the opening of the center had had on the hospital.

It was pointless and a waste of time.

Timothy was grasping at straws.

Caleb was ignoring the mounting emails.

They were getting on his nerves.

It annoyed him that the board was clearly trying to sabotage the birthing center. He was so bothered by it, he was beginning to resent being tied to the hospital. Even though the hospital and its staff were stellar.

Timothy Russell had been a problem ever since he'd become chair last year. Even Victor hated him, and the chief of staff didn't hate anyone.

Caleb had no time for this meeting, nor had he pulled together the required information.

He was not looking forward to Monday, but that was Monday's problem.

Today, he didn't want to think about that, because he was simultaneously dreading and excited for his day out with Hazel.

She was waiting for him at the door.

"Right on time," she said.

"I'm always punctual," he replied as he carried the bags in for her.

"Still, there was a part of me that wondered if this was one of the hospital's ploys to whisk away my equipment and force me to leave."

Caleb frowned. "The board of directors may not like you, but I can assure you that the hospital staff isn't that devious. Though I certainly wouldn't put it past the chairman. However, I am not him and I've brought you back your equipment."

Hazel laughed softly. "We'll take it to the sterilization room and I'll repack it."

"Have they figured out what was up with your car?" he asked.

"Yes, it's the alternator. It was towed away yesterday, and Bria texted me to let me know what was happening. I might have to invest in a new to me vehicle soon. I've had Sally for ten years."

Caleb cocked an eyebrow. "Sally?"

"My car," Hazel explained. She undid one of the bags and began washing and sterilizing the equipment.

"I've never named a car before," Caleb stated with a bemused smile.

"You should. It's fun. I get to cuss at something in traffic. Helps keep down the rage in a traffic jam."

Caleb chuckled. "I don't think I have the heart to name my car. I wouldn't know what to call it anyways."

"How about Rex?" Hazel offered.

"That's ridiculous."

"I think people called Rex would argue with that."

After the equipment had been properly sterilized, they finished repacking the bags. She tucked them away, as she currently didn't have a car and wouldn't get hers back until tomorrow, and she told him that she didn't have any patients that were due to deliver any time soon. She had some downtime.

"So, what were you thinking of doing today? Besides just going to the falls?"

"You need to know everything?" he asked.

"I like to be prepared."

He cocked an eyebrow. "How about we just wing it?"

"Whoa."

"What?" he asked.

"Seems kind of relaxed for a surgeon," she teased.

"Must be a bit of my leftover West Coast California vibe then."

Hazel laughed. "Must be. Have to say I like it. The relaxed bit, not the unknown."

"Well, let's get in…in Rex and drive there," he said grudgingly.

She smiled brightly. "I'm so glad that you're warming up to the name."

"I assure you I'm not," he groaned.

They walked out of the center and Hazel locked up.

It was a crisp, cool and misty spring day. It wasn't the best weather for a walk across the bridge by Multnomah Falls, but they could make it work. It had been one of his late wife's favorite places to go.

It had been a long time since Caleb had driven out there.

Lizzie often liked to go when she was a child because Jane had loved it, so Lizzie wanted to feel connected to the mother she never knew. Whenever he brought Lizzie here, he would bury the hurt and the memories deep, deep down, and he never came out here if he absolutely didn't have to. He wasn't sure what made him think of bringing Hazel out here. For some reason, it didn't seem quite as painful as it had in the past, and he found himself actually looking forward to it for once. It alarmed him how comfortable he was getting with her. She was becoming a part of his life and moving beyond just a colleague. She was becoming something more.

Something he wasn't sure he wanted.

He didn't say much as they drove out of the city and followed the river to Multnomah Falls.

"You've gone all quiet and broody again," Hazel commented.

"Sorry. I was just thinking that it's been some time since I've been out here."

"I've driven by it, but never stopped."

"It was my late wife's favorite place," he said quietly.

"You told me she died in childbirth."

"She did. A pulmonary embolism during her emergency C-section. Her heart stopped, and they couldn't resuscitate her. She lost so much blood and…" He trailed off, because it was a hard thing to talk about. "I'm very mindful of blood clots during emergency caesareans for my clients."

And he was.

When he'd returned to school after his wife died, it had

been hard for him for one second to pick up a scalpel, to focus on what he needed to do to become a doctor, but he had managed to compartmentalize it all. He'd put away his own trauma about how his wife had died on the operating table.

He'd concentrated on his work, the patients and the fact that he wasn't going to allow another woman's partner to feel the same kind of pain that he'd felt when he was told that Jane was gone.

"Childbirth is a scary thing," Hazel said quietly. "We lost a mother during one of my first rotations as a midwife in training. It was crushing. We did everything we could. She gave birth in a hospital, but there was no stopping the bleeding. It almost, for one moment, deterred me."

"Yet you persisted," he said.

"As did you."

They shared a smile.

"Have you ever been married?" he asked suddenly. He was a bit uncomfortable talking about it, but he was surprised that a beautiful, intelligent, vibrant woman like Hazel Rees was unattached.

"I came close. Once. He was a surgeon. We met at the hospital I worked at after I became a nurse practitioner. He pursued the general surgery program, and I was trying to save up to study midwifery. We were both busy and then… I found him with another woman. In a closet. It was absolutely soul crushingly painful. I decided then I would focus on my own dreams. I became a midwife, worked in a hospital in southern Arizona for a couple of years, then focused on opening this center with my best friend."

"He was an idiot," Caleb murmured. "I'm glad you didn't let him deter you from pursuing your dreams."

"My dad would've kicked my butt if I'd given up. He taught me to fight for what I want." There was a hint of sadness to her voice.

And he couldn't help but wonder what it was, what was causing her sadness.

It's not your business.

Except he badly wanted to comfort her. He'd thought she was too young to carry wounds as deep as his own, but maybe he was wrong about that. Inside that professional exterior of hers, she had been living with pain just like he had.

And he hated that she'd had to do that.

She deserved so much better than her ex.

You're better than he is.

He pushed that thought away immediately.

"You father sounds like a smart man." He was trying to change the subject and steer it away from the reminder of lost love.

Hazel smiled. "He is, but don't tell him that! He'll never stop gloating over it."

Caleb chuckled. "My father couldn't care less about my desire to pursue medicine. He wanted me to be in with the Hollywood crowd."

"Why did you go into obstetrics?"

"My wife. I had planned on being a general surgeon, but when she died in childbirth I wanted to devote my life to saving others from what I went through."

"That's admirable."

"I don't regret it." He smiled. "How about you?"

"My sister. She was pushed through the hospital system so fast and had some complications after the birth of my niece. I wanted to provide more personalized care for women like her."

"I think we both have pretty good reasons."

A blush tinged her cheeks. "Some more common ground."

They neared the parking lot of the falls. Caleb found a parking spot. It was busy, but then this site was always busy as it was one of the more popular places to visit in

Oregon. They picked up a map and started the steep climb up to the Benson Bridge.

There was a definite chill to the air, which was unusual for May.

Hazel reached into her pocket and pulled out a woolen beanie and pulled it down over her head. It was multicolored and looked quite monstrous. He couldn't help but chuckle.

"What?" she asked.

"Your beanie. It's quite vibrant, much like your toe socks. Just hairier."

"My grandma made this for me when my father first got stationed to Alaska. It was to keep me warm, and it always has. It's made of alpaca. She had several of them on her ranch in New Mexico."

"Don't tell me you ate those too?" he asked.

"What? Why would you assume that?" she choked out.

"You've eaten a seal."

"Not a whole seal and I told you why!"

He grinned. "Okay, you did. I'm sorry."

"Thank you. The most I did was shear a few alpacas for wool."

"Sheared them?" he asked.

"Yes."

"You never cease to amaze me. You're quite surprising."

"As are you."

"Hardly," he muttered.

"Your mother was in a Bond movie. That trumps everything."

They smiled together. And all the tension and sadness caused by their previous conversation melted away in an instant.

The bridge was cluttered with groups of people wanting to take pictures of the dramatic falls cascading down a high mountain cliff. It was truly spectacular, but they walked away from the crowds trying to get selfies and post things to their social media.

Instead, they found a quiet corner of the bridge to gaze up at the water.

The mist was sprinkling moisture on her face, and she was smiling up at the water.

Not complaining about the cold or the damp.

Much like Jane, but also different.

There was a real zest for life in Hazel.

It had been a long time since he had seen such a spark of vitality in someone. It just softened him, and he found he really wanted to take a chance on her. Baggage be damned. Hazel made him feel alive and not so lonely. He frowned. She was shaking; he could hear her teeth chattering!

"Are you cold?" he asked.

"A bit. I thought the hat would help, but there's quite the chill in the air. It's spring, so logically it should be warmer."

Without thinking he opened his large overcoat and pulled her close against him. She gasped, staring up at him. Her cheeks were rosy, and he could see how long her lashes were. Her body was so warm flushed against him, so soft. He hadn't been thinking when he'd made the gesture, and now his pulse was thundering between his ears. All he wanted to do was kiss her. To taste her lips. The temptation was overwhelming.

Hazel didn't step away, and he could smell her delicious perfume.

Vanilla.

Like something sweet baking.

"Hazel," he said gruffly.

"Yes," she whispered.

"I would very much like to kiss you now."

"I'd like that too."

He didn't need any more encouragement. He bent down and kissed her lightly on her soft, supple lips, drinking in the honeyed taste of her. She didn't push him away. Instead, her arms came around him and he cupped her rosy cheeks, kissing her deeper.

He wanted her closer. His body was thrumming with need, and all he wanted was her.

And then he realized what he was doing, and he reluctantly broke off the kiss and stepped away. This couldn't happen.

They were professional colleagues and nothing more. And now he knew she'd been hurt badly before. He wouldn't be the one to hurt her again. It was far too risky.

He hadn't been thinking straight.

"Hazel, I'm sorry. That shouldn't have happened. My apologies."

She nodded, her cheeks pink. "No need to apologize, but you're right that shouldn't have happened. It can't happen again."

CHAPTER SEVEN

HAZEL DIDN'T KNOW what had come over her. She was staring up at the falls and thinking about her late grandmother and freezing. It wasn't as cold as Alaska, but she had spent the last couple of years with her sister in southern Arizona where it was considerably warmer and drier. She was instantly regretting her choice to dress nicely rather than sensibly. Jeans just didn't cut it when it was cold and damp out, but she'd wanted to dress a little bit more stylishly knowing that she was going to see Caleb.

She had clearly lost her mind, because she would've never done that before.

She'd spent years in Alaska, and she knew exactly how to dress for the weather.

Up there, dressing for the weather meant life or death. And she didn't know why she was trying to impress Caleb so badly.

Nothing could happen between them, even though she wanted it to. She was fighting with disaster, but it seemed she couldn't help herself.

She had been trying to hold back the teeth chattering, and then he'd opened up his coat to embrace her and she'd stepped into his arms without thinking. It just felt like the most natural thing in the world to do.

Wrapped up in his arms she felt warm and safe. Like she was supposed to be there.

Like she belonged.

And then he'd asked to kiss her and she'd melted.

Caleb's kiss had seared her soul. It made her toes curl in her boots and her body combust. The primitive part of her brain wanted much more, but the logical side was screaming at her that this was all wrong. She'd willfully ignored that part.

Thankfully, he'd broken off the kiss.

She was still shaking, and it wasn't because of the cold. It was because of him and that spectacular kiss.

She was trying to get ahold of her emotions, her senses, but right now she felt like a big pile of goo and she couldn't even focus on the falls right in front of her.

"Why don't we head down to the little restaurant and get some coffee?" he suggested.

"Coffee sounds good."

Anything to get her mind off what just happened.

Hazel usually didn't let herself get too carried away around men, even the ones she was attracted to. She was in control of herself, and she was always careful. She wasn't going to let another Mark into her life. She had learned her lesson. Staying in control was a way to protect her heart from pain.

From disappointment.

She operated better this way.

So what was it about Caleb that destroyed the defenses that she had carefully cultivated for so long?

It was seriously annoying.

She was still a little chilly, and as they walked down to the little coffee shop off the parking lot, she wished she could crawl back into his warm arms and be wrapped up. Safe and sound.

Stop that.

It was very dangerous thinking.

The coffee shop wasn't too busy, and they grabbed some

hot coffee and found a little table in the corner, away from the rest of the tourists but where they could still see the waterfalls. She cupped the warm cup in her hands.

It was a way to ground her.

"I'm sorry if I overstepped," Caleb said awkwardly, breaking through the silence.

"No. You weren't the only one who overstepped our boundaries. You weren't the only willing participant. You asked and I said yes."

He half smiled. "Still, we're supposed to be colleagues."

"Exactly." Hazel swallowed the lump in her throat.

She completely agreed with what he was saying, but why did it feel like a slap in the face? She wasn't sure, but some stubborn part of her knew this was for the best.

It really was.

She wanted to have a good working partnership with him.

It would benefit the patients of the Multnomah Falls Women's Health Center in the long run to be on good terms with the head of obstetrics at St. Raymond's.

So even though it felt like a complete gut punch and every part of her body was telling her to kiss him again, it was for the best.

Completely.

If they got together and it didn't work out, it would make things between them awkward.

And he had a daughter.

A grown-up child, to be sure, but he still was a father and that daughter of his was pregnant. She was pretty sure Lizzie still hadn't told her father what was going on. Hazel couldn't tell him. She was the young woman's midwife.

But she didn't like keeping secrets or lying.

Mark had done both with all his affairs and lying about why he was jilted. She abhorred lying, and it ate away at her that she was keeping this huge secret from him. Caleb deserved to know; only professionally her hands were tied.

It was all getting too complicated. She just wanted things to be simple again.

She had to convince Lizzie to tell her father the truth. Caleb would understand. She was sure of it. If Caleb knew, then she wouldn't have to keep this secret from him.

She was going to suggest that they go home when someone came running into the restaurant. It was a highway patrolman.

"There's a massive pileup on the highway. A logging truck lost control. There are several people injured. Is anyone here a doctor?" the panicked man asked. "We can't get emergency services in on the ground yet, and a fog bank is delaying helicopters."

"I am," Caleb said, standing up.

Hazel nodded. "We can help."

"Great," the officer said, relieved. "I'll take you to the accident. If anyone else has any kind of first aid or triage training, we really need your assistance."

A couple more patrons raised their hands.

They followed the highway patrolman out. There were a couple of squad cars. He sent off the first aid volunteers with another patrolman and then turned to them.

"I have the worst victims. The logging truck hit a couple of cars. I need the medical professionals right at the scene. It's pretty bad."

Caleb's lips pressed together in a thin line. "I'm an obstetrician, but I'll help any way I can."

"I'm a midwife, but I'm a nurse practitioner too. As long as you have first aid kits, we can help," Hazel said, hoping that her voice didn't shake. It had been a long time since she did a rotation in the emergency room.

The fast pace of trauma never did suit her, but this wasn't the time or place to quibble. Lives were on the line.

There was a rock in her stomach, but she pushed all of her nerves out the door when the patrol car turned on its sirens and they headed up the highway a short distance. As they rounded the corner, she could see smoke billowing into the sky.

"Oh, my God," Caleb whispered.

Her heart skipped a beat, and her adrenaline kicked in at the sight of scattered twisted metal and cars. The logging truck had spewed its load across the entire width of the highway and the truck itself was lying on its side, flames billowing outward.

The patrolman stopped and they got out of the car.

"The driver is the worst. He's pinned, and we're waiting for the fire crew to get here and use the Jaws of Life on him, but the car he hit, the driver is lying over here and he's in pretty bad shape."

"Take me to him," Caleb said, whipping off his coat and putting it into the patrol car. Hazel followed him as he rolled up the sleeves of his white cotton shirt.

The man was lying on his back, barely conscious, and his pregnant wife was kneeling next to him, weeping.

Hazel went to her.

"Ma'am?" Hazel asked gently. "I'm a midwife. Can I check you?"

"I'm fine," the woman said. "I'm only seven months along. I'm okay, the baby is kicking. I'm fine. It's my husband who's hurt." The woman was rambling, clearly in shock.

"Dr. Norris is going to take care of your husband. What's your name?" Hazel asked, kneeling next to the distraught woman.

"Jennifer," she said, not tearing her gaze from her husband.

Hazel could see a small laceration on her temple that was bandaged, but most likely needed to be stitched.

"Jennifer, how about we let the doctor see to him? I would really like to check you over," Hazel suggested.

The woman finally looked at her. "Okay."

Hazel guided her away and grabbed one of the blankets that a highway patrol man brought her. She wrapped Jennifer in the blanket to keep her warm and had her take the seat in the open door of a squad car.

"I'm going to check your pulse, if that's okay?"

Jennifer nodded, distracted.

Hazel took her pulse and it was thready.

"Can I feel a kick?" Hazel asked.

"Of course."

Hazel placed her hand on Jennifer's belly. It was hard, and Hazel felt the beginning of a contraction. Jennifer's body was pumping so much adrenaline through her that Jennifer couldn't feel it.

Hazel worried her bottom lip.

Jennifer was going into preterm labor.

The baby did kick, but there was nothing more she could do. There was no way to stop her labor.

Then Hazel noticed the blood running down Jennifer's leg. It was either from a cut or it was from the baby. She really hoped it was from a cut and not the womb.

Hazel heard the wail of an ambulance siren. She glanced over her shoulder to see the flashing lights wind their way through the tangle of cars, and she breathed a sigh of relief.

The first paramedic crew headed toward Caleb, and the second crew went to the truck driver as the fire crew was fast on the heels of the ambulances.

Caleb finished up with his instructions to the paramedics, and they loaded up Jennifer's husband in the back of the ambulance. Jennifer began to groan, and Hazel began to time the pain and heavy breathing. The contractions were close together. There was no denying that Jennifer was in labor.

"Where are they taking Teddy?" Jennifer asked.

"To the hospital. He'll be fine. Jennifer, you're in labor," Hazel said gently.

"What?" Then Jennifer winced and clutched her belly. "No, I can't be. I'm only thirty weeks. It's too early."

Jennifer's water broke and Hazel saw blood, so not from a cut then. She winced internally.

Caleb looked up as the ambulance with Teddy took off toward the hospital.

Hazel waved him over.

"What's wrong?" Caleb asked.

"This is Teddy's wife, Jennifer. She's thirty weeks along and is in labor."

Caleb nodded. "Has her water broken?"

"Yes," Hazel said quietly. "There's blood."

"Grab a first aid kit and a blanket from the back of the squad car. I've delivered these extreme preemies before. I don't have what I need here to stop the birth," he said.

"Agreed." Hazel turned to Jennifer. "This is Dr. Norris. He's an obstetrician from St. Raymond's."

"My husband?" Jennifer asked wildly.

"He's stable and on the way to Portland," Caleb answered patiently, reassuring her again as it was clear the poor woman wasn't focusing on details at a time like this. "I need to check on you and your baby."

Jennifer nodded, and they got her settled back into the squad car.

Hazel got the supplies they would need and helped get Jennifer's skirt off. Her water had definitely broken, and there was a bloody show. Hazel draped her for modesty as best she could and then climbed into the back of the patrol car to support Jennifer, who was terrified and in a lot of pain.

"You're ten centimeters," Caleb said.

"Already?" Hazel asked with a raised eyebrow.

Caleb nodded. "Adrenaline, the accident, have speeded it up."

"I can't have this baby without Teddy here," Jennifer cried.

"You're going to have to push your baby out with the next contraction," Caleb stated firmly, but gently.

"It's too soon," Jennifer wailed piteously.

"I know, sweetie, but you have to do this. Your baby isn't going to wait for the emergency services," Hazel said encouragingly.

Jennifer nodded, crying as she pushed with the contraction.

Caleb frowned. "Your baby is breech and I'm going to turn them. Try to stay as still as you can for me."

Jennifer winced, and Hazel leaned over to help Caleb by turning Jennifer's abdomen to help with the breech position. He didn't have to tell her to do it. She knew what to do. Their gazes locked, and she could see the gratitude in his eyes.

"There we go," Caleb said.

Hazel held on to Jennifer's hands as she no longer needed to push on her abdomen.

"Come on, push," Hazel urged.

Jennifer's legs shook, and she gave one large push and Caleb caught the small, wrinkly preemie in his hands.

"It's a boy," he said as he quickly cut the cord.

Hazel made sure that Jennifer was comfortable and went through the other passenger door to go and help Caleb. The baby wasn't breathing.

Another ambulance pulled up, and the emergency services team opened their doors.

"We need an incubator and oxygen," Hazel said. "Thirty-week preemie has just been delivered. Also need a large bore intravenous, fluids and antibiotics for the mother."

"Right away," the paramedic said.

Caleb had wrapped the preemie in a blanket and was gently massaging the little boy's back. Willing the early bird to breath.

The baby was so tiny in his large hands.

It made Hazel's heart skip a beat.

There was a thin cry. So quiet, like a cat, almost, as the little boy gasped for his first breaths. The paramedics brought over the incubator, and Caleb helped them load in the tiny infant. Hazel returned to Jennifer, who was beginning to get uncomfortable as she delivered the placenta.

There was a lot of bleeding and Hazel suspected a tear, which could be from the accident.

Caleb returned and saw what she saw.

"I need to get her into surgery as soon as possible. I'll need to go with them to St. Raymond's," he said.

"I'll take your car back to Portland," Hazel offered. "I don't need to go. Just take care of her."

Caleb nodded, but he didn't look her in the eye. They hadn't really had a chance to talk about what had happened at the falls.

Maybe it was best they didn't. They could just forget about their kiss and go on.

"Thank you for your help. I didn't have to tell you what to do."

"I know. It's kind of my job," she said, grinning.

He smiled at her, his blue-gray eyes twinkling, and then he leaned down and her breath caught in her throat, thinking he was going to kiss her again. Her pulse quickened.

He moved away quickly. "The keys are in my jacket."

Hazel nodded, feeling a bit foolish now thinking he'd been going to kiss her again. "Go. Save a life."

"I will see you later."

She nodded again and watched as he climbed into the back of the ambulance with Jennifer and the little boy. Her pulse was racing as she watched the ambulance race away.

"Ms. Rees?" the patrolman asked.

"Yes," she said. "More injured?"

"Some minor stuff. I could use your help."

"I'm glad to help. Let's go."

And she was. She followed the patrolman into the fray, watching as the flashing lights disappeared down the highway.

Caleb's kiss felt like it was still burning on her lips. His kiss had been like a promise. One she knew that he most likely wouldn't keep. She wasn't going to get her hopes up. It was safer for her heart this way, even though there was a little part of her that wanted to hope.

There was a small part of her that wanted him.

Even though it put her heart at risk.

It terrified her.

Hazel got back from the accident scene and carried Caleb's jacket to his office, but when she left and headed back out of the hospital she found Mrs. Jameson wandering the halls.

Clutching her abdomen.

Oh. No.

"Mrs. Jameson? Tara?" Hazel asked, coming over.

"My water broke. Wilfred is out of town. My mom is with my little girl. I'm alone." Tara winced. "It hurts."

"Come on. Let's get you to labor and delivery."

Hazel found a wheelchair and got Tara settled. She rushed her down to the labor and delivery floor.

"Ms. Rees?" Janet, the head nurse familiar with her, asked.

"Janet, this is Tara Jameson. She's para two, gravida one and thirty-five weeks pregnant. She had a low transverse C-section three years ago. Her contractions are five minutes apart. Dr. Norris needs to be paged."

Janet took over the wheelchair. "He's still in surgery on that uterine rupture."

"Okay."

"I'll have another nurse get you some scrubs," Janet said. "And we'll help Mrs. Jameson."

"I want Hazel," Tara said. "She's my midwife and she knows my birth plan."

"Of course," Janet said. "We'll get her ready to help you, and we'll let Dr. Norris know."

"I'll be with you soon."

Another nurse handed Hazel a set of scrubs, and Hazel made her way down to the staff change room.

She was exhausted, but this was part of the job. She had to put everything from her mind.

Even that kiss.

Hazel changed and then headed back to the labor and delivery suite.

Hovering outside was Timothy Russell, who had clearly gotten wind that Mrs. Jameson had come in. She paused and he turned to look at her, sneering.

"Where is Dr. Norris?" Timothy demanded.

"In surgery." Hazel tried to move past him.

"Where do you think you're going?"

"To deliver my patient's baby. She requested me."

"You don't have privileges here."

"So give me privileges. Either way, I'm her midwife and I'm going to help her. You have a problem, take it up with the patient who is in a lot of pain right now—see where it gets you." Hazel pushed past him.

Janet was trying to calm Tara down, but the labor was progressing quickly.

"Her contractions are coming more frequently," Janet stated.

Hazel pulled on gloves. "I'm going to check you, Tara. Okay?"

Tara was crying and Hazel did an internal. The baby was head down, and she was eight centimeters dilated. It wouldn't be long now, and it was too late for pain relief. What she had to watch for now was the baby's heart rate, and excessive bleeding.

Both signs that the vaginal birth after caesarean section was failing.

Janet got monitors on Tara to watch the heart rate and her contractions, and Hazel helped get Tara hooked up to an IV for liquids, so she didn't get dehydrated.

It wasn't long before Caleb came into the room.

In a fresh change of scrubs, bags under his eyes.

"I came as soon as my surgery was over," he said, pulling on gloves. "How is she?"

"She's eight centimeters dilated. Baby's heart rate is good," Hazel stated.

Caleb nodded. "I'm going to check you, Tara, okay?"

Tara nodded.

Hazel held her while Caleb did his exam. "She's fully dilated now. There's a bit more blood than I'm comfortable with."

Hazel stood next to him and looked. "You don't think she needs to go into surgery?"

Caleb shook his head. "We'll watch, but so far, no."

The baby was coming fast, just like the last delivery. This baby was early too, but closer to the due date than Jennifer's little boy. Their main concern now was Tara.

"With your next contraction, I need you to push, Tara!" Hazel urged.

Tara nodded and pushed, crying out.

The baby began to crown.

There was no sign of the shoulder being stuck, which could often be a sign of a failed vaginal birth after caesarean, and the heart rate was still favorable.

Hazel took point next to Caleb.

Both of them encouraging Tara.

A few more pushes and her little boy came into the world, screaming and shouting.

"It's a boy," Caleb announced.

Tara was crying, and Hazel took the baby as Caleb cut the cord. She placed the boy against his mother's chest, so he could get skin to skin contact and covered his back with a blanket.

Caleb watched for the placenta to be delivered.

If there was a real problem with uterine rupture or the placenta imbedding itself too deeply, they would be able to tell when it was delivered.

A few minutes later, Tara's placenta was delivered whole and everything was going smoothly. It was a successful vaginal birth after caesarean section.

"Thank you both, so much."

"My pleasure," Hazel said.

Caleb smiled and nodded. "I'll come and check on you later."

Hazel was a bit annoyed that he only referred to himself coming and checking on her, but she wasn't going to get into an argument with him in front of the patient.

She helped Janet clean up and then headed out into the hall after Caleb, who'd left a few minutes before.

When she got into the hallway, she saw Caleb talking to Timothy Russell.

And she knew it was about her. She didn't know what they were saying. There was a lot of frowning and nodding going on.

It made her stomach twist in a bunch of knots.

Timothy came over to her. "You need to leave now, Ms. Rees. It's after hours."

Caleb stood there, not saying anything. His face just a professional mask.

"Of course."

There was no point in arguing.

The board of directors had spoken and Caleb hadn't said much, but she figured his hands were tied too.

Or perhaps he just didn't care about her work as much as he said he did.

Once more she was falling into a trap of trusting again, even though she didn't really want to believe it this time.

CHAPTER EIGHT

IT HAD BEEN two weeks since Caleb had seen Hazel and they'd delivered their vaginal birth after caesarean section patient successfully. Mrs. Jameson was doing well as was her little boy.

After he'd completed Jennifer's uterine repair surgery, he'd wanted to talk to Hazel about their kiss, but Tara Jameson went into labor.

They didn't get a chance to talk about it, and then Timothy Russell had been seriously annoyed that Hazel was there.

It was ridiculous and he'd been cross about it, but then Hazel had left St. Raymond's.

It was the last he'd seen of her and though he should be relieved by the space, he'd missed her.

It had been a long time since he'd missed someone like this. It alarmed him because the only other woman who had made him feel like that had been Jane. Since his wife died he'd been attracted to other women, but he'd had no drive to do much about it, other than the odd fling. With Hazel it was so different, and it was apparent to him that she had been just as freaked out by what had happened at the falls.

It was better to get some distance from one another.

Wasn't it?

He groaned and stared at all the reports in front of him. All the facts and figures the board had requested.

Now he was finally forced to hand them over, but he really didn't want to.

Bringing money to the hospital was all that mattered to the board, not necessarily the work that he was doing, that the rest of the hospital staff was doing.

Caleb could only delay the inevitable for so long, and two weeks was all the board had been willing to wait. So as he made his way to Timothy's office he girded his loins for a serious talk.

He didn't know what Timothy wanted now, but Caleb couldn't help but wonder if he was getting some flak from investors. Caleb was so over it all. He would walk away, except he had Lizzie to take care of.

Yes, Lizzie was in college, but he was helping her with tuition so she could focus on studying.

This job was his stability, and he did still love his work here. He just hated the politics of it all.

He straightened his spine and knocked on Timothy's door.

"Come in."

Caleb opened the door and shut it as Timothy stood and smiled.

"Caleb, so good to see you. Please have a seat."

Caleb took the aforementioned seat. "I'm sorry that I had to postpone this meeting. These last two weeks have been incredibly busy."

"I know. You helped out at that traffic accident. It brought us a lot of good press. That couple wouldn't have made it without your help, Dr. Norris. And everyone in the accident survived. Even the little baby. How is the baby?"

"Very well. He's under Dr. Prince's care in the neonatal intensive care unit."

Timothy smiled. "Good. Good. As I said, the press on that was so good for St. Raymond's."

"Medicine and saving lives are good for the hospital. As is working with other health care practitioners."

Timothy's eyes narrowed. "The midwives you mean?"

"Yes. Hazel Rees helped me deliver that baby too. And assisted me in the successful delivery of Mrs. Jameson's child. Your tirade on them is not good press."

"It may not be, but that birthing center threatens our financial future."

Caleb sighed. "I don't know what you expect me to do about it. I'm the head of obstetrics and my focus should be on patients, not worrying about a midwife clinic across the road that's not breaking the law."

"I understand."

Timothy folded his hands on his desk, and Caleb caught a glimpse of his expensive watch. Everything about Timothy was meant to intimidate.

Caleb wasn't so easily pushed around.

"So then I don't see the problem," Caleb stated.

"The problem is Mrs. Patterson."

Caleb frowned. "Why is Mrs. Patterson a problem?"

"The board of directors and myself are concerned that Mrs. Patterson still has Ms. Rees listed as her main practitioner."

Caleb shrugged. "And?"

"She won't be delivering quints over there. She'll deliver them here. Your reports state the obvious outcome."

"What does it matter who the main practitioner is listed as being? As long as the babies and Mrs. Patterson survive."

"It matters to the press."

Caleb saw red and clenched his fists, trying to calm down. "So the board is simply concerned that Mrs. Patterson is Hazel Rees's patient?"

"Yes."

"Well, Hazel did refer Mrs. Patterson to me. So technically it is true. Hazel Rees is the main practitioner on the case."

"The board doesn't want Hazel Rees to have hospital privileges here."

Caleb was shocked, but also not really. "You mean you don't. But you are aware that decision puts lives in danger, Timothy. We have always given privileges to midwives here at St. Raymond's."

Timothy sighed. "The midwives having privileges undercuts the hospital. How better it would be, for all of us, money wise, to have you as Mrs. Patterson's main practitioner, not Hazel. Mrs. Jameson is already telling her friends, wealthy friends I might add, that Hazel delivered her child."

"This conversation is ridiculous."

"I assure you, it's not. Mrs. Patterson is carrying quintuplets, and we would like you, as the head of obstetrics, to be the main practitioner on such a high-profile case."

"Mrs. Patterson is not a PR stunt. She's a patient and I won't jeopardize her health."

"You know with high-order births that the best chance of the mother and the babies surviving is having them in a hospital."

Caleb sighed. "I know, but I won't force Mrs. Patterson or Hazel into that decision. However, both the patient and Hazel Rees are quite aware of the complications, and I will not deny Mrs. Patterson health care just because she lists Hazel Rees as her main practitioner. The babies will likely be born here with my help and Hazel's. Hazel will still officially be the main practitioner."

Timothy nodded slowly. "I see."

"I don't think you do, but as long as I'm head of obstetrics, the midwives will be allowed access and privileges here, understood?"

"I'm glad you have made your position known. I look forward to reading your report," Timothy said calmly, but

Caleb got the distinct impression this wasn't over. He took that as his cue to leave and he was glad to.

As he left Timothy's office, he ran into Victor.

"Hey, I've been looking for you," Victor said.

"Have you?"

"Yes. You haven't checked your email, have you?" Victor asked.

"No. I've been busy."

Distracted was more like it.

Constantly thinking about Hazel. Worried about Lizzie, who seemed to be catching the flu, but insisted she was fine.

There was a lot going on.

"There's a lecture on high-order births that you're supposed to attend in Seattle tomorrow."

Caleb paused. "What?"

"You signed up to go a few months ago. The hospital got you a hotel room and booked your flight, for tonight. The lecture is tomorrow morning.

"I have to attend this lecture?"

Victor nodded. "You do. You requested to go, and the hospital is footing the bill.

"I completely forgot."

"You've been a bit scatterbrained lately. Are you okay?" Victor asked with concern.

"I am. Truly. I would still like to attend."

"Well, the details are all in your email."

"Thanks, Victor."

Victor turned to walk away. "Oh, I saw your daughter waiting for you outside your office."

"Lizzie's there? She's supposed to be in class."

Victor shrugged. "She said she'd wait."

"Thanks, Victor."

Caleb made his way back to his office and sure enough

Lizzie was outside, waiting for him. She looked uncomfortable and a bit pale.

Immediately he was concerned.

"Lizzie?"

"Hey, Dad," she said.

"Are you okay?" he asked, sitting next to her.

"Fine. Just tired. Midterms took a toll on me."

Although, he didn't think it was midterms only. He touched her forehead, but she didn't have a fever. She just felt clammy.

"I'm supposed to fly to Seattle tonight. Why don't I cancel?"

"No, Dad. You have to do your job. I just wanted to stop by and see you, but I didn't realize you were leaving tonight. I have class later." Lizzie leaned against him.

"What class?" he asked, relishing the small moment of affection she'd used to give him more frequently when she was smaller, when she would often want to cuddle with him. It had been some time since she just wanted to see him.

He hated to see her grown up. Even though those days of juggling school and a newborn alone were hard, he sometimes missed them.

"Anatomy," she groused. "Cadaver night. Not looking forward to it."

"You'll do great. And if you want to go to med school still…"

"I don't though. I want to be a midwife."

He smiled. "I know. You've told me. Don't worry. I just want you to be happy."

Lizzie sighed, then stood up. "Thanks, Dad. I better prep for class."

"Be safe."

"I will. When will you be back from Seattle?"

"Sunday. I think."

Lizzie nodded. "Okay."

Caleb watched her walk away. He was worried about her, and he was worried about leaving her.

Maybe Hazel could keep an eye on Lizzie. He called her cell number, but it went straight to voice mail. So he texted instead, but it just sat there.

Unread.

She was ignoring him after their kiss and it hurt a bit, but she was justified in being upset with him after he hadn't discussed it with her afterward. It was best that it was all forgotten.

If he wanted to protect his heart, he would have to stop thinking about Hazel Rees and how much he was falling for her.

Hazel stared out of her hotel room at the Space Needle. She checked her phone, but there was no message. Not that she was expecting anything. She hadn't heard from Caleb in a couple of weeks, and even though the logical side of her brain was telling her that it was good, she'd missed him.

It was like this hole, this ache in her soul.

After the successful VBAC of Mrs. Jameson and the confrontation with Timothy Russell, she was upset that Caleb had stood there and not said anything to defend her.

Of course, she hadn't exactly given him time to say anything.

She'd just left.

She had been so angry, hurt, frustrated, not least of all because she and Caleb also hadn't talked about the kiss they'd shared.

That had been the most stressful thing. She couldn't stop thinking about that kiss. She was angry at herself for letting herself kiss him and be so affected by it.

She closed her eyes and touched her lips. She could still

feel his mouth against hers. Her body tingled just thinking about his strong arms around her.

She was so distracted, which was very unlike her.

She'd almost forgotten about this symposium and the lecture she'd wanted to attend about high-order births, until the notification about her flight had pinged her.

Maybe some time in Seattle would get her mind off Caleb and his kisses.

And how ridiculous the chairman of the board was. Maybe it had been a huge mistake to build across from St. Raymond's.

No. It's not and you know it.

It wasn't Caleb's fault. It was the hospital board's, she told herself, but there was a small nagging part of her that didn't quite trust him completely. She'd seen Timothy and Caleb's discussion, but didn't know what it was about and Caleb's face had been so cool when he'd looked at her afterward. A professional wall had been dropped. Was he truly being honest with her?

You're not being honest with him.

She did know something important about his daughter, but that wasn't her secret to tell. Even though keeping it from Caleb it was eating her alive.

Lizzie had to tell her father soon.

What Hazel needed to do was protect her heart and her business.

No money hungry chairman of the board was going to edge out Bria and her. They had worked too hard to get where they were now.

Hazel sighed and tore her gaze away from the Space Needle and the city of Seattle, which was waking up on this hazy, late spring morning.

There was fog rolling in, which was usual for Seattle, though she'd been hoping for some sun.

So she was glad that she was going to spend all day locked in a lecture.

It wouldn't make her feel so bad for missing out on a beautiful day.

She finished getting ready and left her hotel room. She made sure her door was locked and headed to the elevator, glancing at her phone to make sure that she had time to grab some coffee before heading to the lecture.

The elevator dinged and the doors opened. She walked on and stopped dead in her tracks at the other occupant of the elevator.

"Caleb?" she asked in confusion.

Caleb glanced up from his phone and stood up straight. "Hazel?"

The elevator closed behind her. "What're you doing here?"

"I'm attending a lecture by Dr. Marquez on high-order births today at the insistence of my chief of staff. I had forgotten that I'd asked to go. What're you doing here?"

"Attending the same symposium apparently," she said.

"Well…good."

She stood next to him in awkward silence as the elevator made more stops and more people got on.

He was so close to her. This was not going to help with her resolution to keep herself from him emotionally and maintain her walls. It was easier when she didn't see him. At least that's what she told herself.

Being next to him in such a confined space, she could recall the warmth of his arms around her, the scent of him.

Spicy and masculine.

The strength and security of his embrace was still fresh in her mind.

She had to get control of herself.

"I haven't seen you in a couple of weeks," he said offhandedly.

"I've been busy. I had to check on Clarissa and Jade."

"Jade?"

"Her baby girl."

He nodded. "Nice name."

"I think so too."

"How is the baby's clavicle?"

"Healing really well."

"Good."

Someone else got on and they just stood there. Side by side, saying nothing, but her palms suddenly felt very sweaty.

Finally at the main lobby every one filtered off and they were still standing there, neither of them moving.

"I was on my way to get coffee. Would you like to join me?" she asked.

"Yes. That sounds acceptable," he said stiffly. "I will need something to keep me awake."

They began to walk to the hotel's coffee bar.

"Are you that sure another doctor's lecture will put you to sleep?" she asked.

"I have heard Dr. Kevin Marquez speak before. He's brilliant, but a public speaker he is not."

"Oh, dear. I was going to get decaf. Perhaps I will splurge for the caffeine."

"It's in your best interest." A smile played at the corners of his mouth.

It made her heart beat a bit faster. They were just two colleagues at a lecture.

Out of town.

Even though it was for the best that she resist him, she still missed him. She'd enjoyed their time together, which she'd never thought she would ever think, but there it was. As much as she didn't want miss him.

She did.

And she was glad he was here.

They stood in the seemingly never-ending lineup to the coffee shop.

"I'm sorry that I didn't really speak to you after Mrs. Jameson's delivery. It all took me by surprise. I was so angry with Timothy Russell for asking me to leave."

"Don't worry. I understand…it's ridiculous, really."

"It seems to be that way," she groused.

"Tara Jameson's family is well connected. The board thought delivering her baby at St. Raymond's was good press for them. Just like the accident. They used that to elevate their status in the media too. But that behavior after the VBAC was really immature. I'm sorry Timothy acted that way."

"You say that with such distaste. Not that I blame you."

"It's all well and good that everyone survived. It's fantastic. It's what we strive for as physicians, surgeons, nurses, as health care providers and emergency services, but to use it for PR bothers me deeply. Using it as leverage to get more business or more funding. It just rubs me the wrong way. I was never very good at schmoozing or anything to do with politics in the medical workplace."

"A necessary evil these days, I agree. Funding and grants do help keep beds open, but I know what you mean."

He sighed, and she could tell that he knew exactly what she was talking about. It was so much better being your own boss.

Except their center could use some more funding, and that was a worry that she and Bria had been recently discussing. Bria was a strategist though, and was trying to formulate some kind of fundraiser that Hazel really wanted nothing to do with. Only because Bria was so much better at it. Hazel didn't have the calming demeanor her friend seemed to have.

Hazel would do whatever was needed to help out though.

They placed their respective coffee orders and then headed to the main ballroom of the hotel, which was packed full of other medical professionals.

She was really looking forward to learning all she could about high-order births.

What the complications were, prenatal care of the mother and even learning about postpartum recovery for the mother after the babies were born. A high-order birth was not only precarious for the babies, but also the mother and her body.

She had also seen singleton pregnancies carry complications for the mother postpartum, even years later. Things like adhesions and bladder prolapse. Hazel didn't want to just deliver the babies, she wanted to help the mother afterward too.

It was a service that was seriously lacking.

Especially when it came to postpartum recovery and physiotherapy. She just wanted to be prepared for Mrs. Patterson and she wanted some facts and figures herself, solid information to use against Timothy Russell if he ever tried to deny her access to her patient again.

"Would you like to have dinner tonight?" Caleb asked, as they took seats in the back of the ballroom. It came completely out of the blue, taking her off guard.

"Dinner? Do you think that's wise?"

"Why not?"

Because the last time we were together, we kissed and we can't seem to get past that. There was always heat bubbling under the surface ever since they'd met. Why couldn't she resist him?

"I...I can't think of a reason." She was lying through her teeth. There were so many reasons to say no to him. But right now, staring up into his blue-gray eyes and that strong jaw, those lips that she knew so well, she couldn't think of the million reasons she had gone over in her head for the last couple of weeks.

The reasons why she should resist him, because when it came to Caleb she was so weak.

"Great. I was going to have dinner at the Space Needle alone, but it would be nice to have company and talk about Mrs. Patterson. Go over our game plan and all the scenarios involving the quints."

"A working dinner, at the top of the Space Needle?" she asked.

He nodded. "It's a great view."

"Okay. Around seven then?"

He nodded. "It's a date."

She wanted to say no, it wasn't a date, only she couldn't say anything. She lost her ability in that moment to speak.

Dr. Kevin Marquez walked onto the stage and all further discussion about dinner was done. She had to focus on the guest speaker and the couple of other workshops she planned to attend. Instead, all she could think about was how close Caleb was to her.

How it felt when his leg brushed hers.

And as she secretly glanced at him out of the corner of her eye, her heart beat just a bit faster and every word that came out of the speaker's mouth was like a muffled trombone inside her head.

All she could think of was Caleb saying it was a date.

What had she gotten herself into?

Hazel didn't know what she'd agreed to. She had, thankfully, packed one little black dress on the insistence of Bria, who'd warned her there might be a fancy dinner or a cocktail hour. Hazel had done away with her rainbow-colored socks and all the other clothes that made her feel comfortable.

What am I doing? she asked herself again as she looked in the full-length mirror. She didn't know how to answer that, but at least tonight she wouldn't be sitting in her hotel room alone.

Thinking about Caleb.

* * *

She grabbed her purse and a pashmina and headed down to the lobby. Caleb was there, waiting for her. He was wearing that same overcoat, the one he'd wrapped around her just before they had kissed at the falls.

And just thinking back to that moment made her swoon a bit. Though she had no right to swoon when she was feeling guilty about holding back something so important from him because of patient confidentiality.

She didn't like keeping secrets from anyone.

Especially from him.

He smiled when he saw her and it made her heart skip a beat.

"You look lovely, Hazel."

"Thanks." She was a lot a loss for words when he came closer.

He leaned over her and whispered against her ear. "I miss the rainbow socks though."

Heat unfurled in her belly as he placed a hand on the small of her back and they walked outside to a waiting cab. Her pulse was thundering between her ears, and she didn't know what to say as they sat in the back of the cab, his arm around her shoulders.

It was a short cab ride to the Space Needle, and they took the full elevator to the top and the rotating restaurant.

All she could do was focus on moving forward because her legs were shaking so bad it was hard to stay upright, especially in heels.

The maître d' led them to their table. The city of Seattle was lit up against the darkness. It was all twinkling lights and romantic music, and she couldn't hear anything but her heart beating erratically with her nerves.

Caleb pulled out a chair for her and she sat down. He handed his coat to the maître d' and she took in the sight of him in a well-tailored suit. It made her mouth water, thinking about what might lie underneath that expensive suit.

He took a seat across from her, tucking in his tie as he sat down. His gaze locked with hers across the table. "Are you quite all right?"

"What?" she asked.

"You seem distracted."

Hazel laughed nervously. "It's the lack of rainbow socks. They're the source of my superpowers, you know. So I guess I feel out of sorts without them."

He grinned. "I knew it."

"It's been a while since I've been out...like this. The last person who wined and dined me was my ex-boyfriend and even then it was all a show. I found out later that he'd had so many other girlfriends on the side. Although, I only ever caught him with one. That's what you get for trusting someone," she said a little bitterly.

"You can trust others," he said.

"Can I? I trusted him completely, and he broke my heart. I should've seen the signs."

"He sounds like a fool."

"Maybe I was the fool for being duped?" she said sardonically.

"Doubtful."

"Why doubtful?"

"He was a user. He took advantage of your caring nature. He's the vilest type of person."

A blush crept up her neck and she looked away. "Well, it's lovely to get out anyways."

"Agreed." They shared a brief smile. "It's been some time for me too, and it's apparently nice to do this or so I've been told."

"Who told you that?" Hazel asked.

"Lizzie, actually. 'Dad, people date all the time. Dinners out are nice,'" he teased.

"That's a smart girl you have there. How is she doing?"

He shot her a worried look. "So you've noticed her sickness as well?" he asked.

Her palms began to sweat again. Yes, she'd noticed her "illness." It was pregnancy, and apparently Lizzie still hadn't told her father yet. "Yes, she mentioned how stressed she was, and of course flu is going around at the moment."

She really hated lying to him.

Caleb frowned. He didn't look convinced.

"In any event she'd like to have you over for dinner again soon. She enjoyed your company very much."

"And did you?" she asked, her breath catching in her throat.

"I did as well. I do." He smiled, those blue-gray eyes twinkling in the dim light. "We don't have many people over. There's no one to invite."

"You don't have any extended family?" Hazel asked, trying to make conversation, even though she already knew the answer.

"No. As I said, my parents are both gone and I was an only child. My late wife had no family either. It was just us, and then it was me and Lizzie. It can get lonely sometimes."

"I'm sure. I have a large extended family, but we're spread out all over. It's hard to get together often. I miss them a lot."

"So you understand how isolating it can be," he stated.

"Yes," she agreed. She was lonely, but she put that out of her mind. She didn't like to think about it. Maybe she'd been so blind to Mark's cheating because she'd been lonely when she met him. He'd filled a hole in her heart.

Only she realized he hadn't.

Not really.

"I should have more people over," he groused. "When my wife died, I just focused on raising a baby and working. It was all I could do to get through the day, but I meant what I said… Lizzie wasn't the only one who enjoyed your company that evening. I did too. Immensely."

"Really?"

"It's nice having you around. You keep things…interesting."

She laughed. "Oh, dear, we do have our moments of not seeing eye to eye, don't we?"

"I'm telling you, it's the socks." His eyes twinkled in the dim light of the restaurant. "I enjoy your company, Hazel. I've missed you recently."

She wanted to tell him that she liked being around him too, but the waiter came and took their order. The conversation over dinner shifted to the lecture and discussion of Mrs. Patterson. They both agreed that Sandra, as long as she was stable, could stay at home. As long as she rested.

Sandra wanted a natural birth, if at all possible, but they would determine that next course of action when the babies were further along.

Hazel agreed the quints had to be delivered at St. Raymond's. It was clear to her they both wanted the best care for Sandra and the quints.

After they split the bill, they both decided to walk the short distance back to the hotel.

The night had cleared and the crisp air was lovely.

She shivered slightly.

"Are you cold?" he asked.

"Just a bit." What she didn't tell him was that she wanted him to wrap her up in his arms under that coat again.

What're you thinking?

She didn't know.

This was not keeping her distance from him at all, but also their conversation about loneliness had got to her. She'd forgotten how lonely she really was. He walked her to her room and they stood at her door, for what felt like an eternity.

The thing was, she didn't want him to go.

She didn't want this night to end.

"Thank you for inviting me out tonight," she said nervously.

"Thank you for agreeing to come with me. I was surprised to see you here."

"Same."

"It was a good surprise though," he admitted. "I didn't want to come here."

"Why?" she asked.

"I don't know," he said. "Work has been busy, and it seemed like a hassle."

"It's hard to get to these kinds of conventions."

"I texted you. You didn't respond."

Hazel bit her bottom lip. "I didn't get it. I thought…"

"Is this about the kiss again?" he asked, taking a step closer. "The one we didn't talk about."

"Yes."

"I scared you away?"

"No. It's just…" Only she couldn't think of the why she shouldn't pursue this. Even if just for one night. That logical part of her brain went quiet, and all she wanted to do was kiss him again.

So she did. Her body thrumming with anticipation as she pulled the lapels of his overcoat close and kissed him the way she'd been thinking about for so long. Only she didn't pull away afterward. Instead, she deepened the kiss, opening her mouth, their tongues entwining as she pressed her body against his.

"Hazel," he murmured against her neck as she slipped her arms around him inside his coat. "I want you. I think I've wanted you since the moment I met you."

"I thought you detested me?" she teased. "Especially after I was so mean to you at that tribunal."

"No, just myself for being such an ass to you and yet so attracted to you at the same time."

"I want you too. Even if it's just for tonight. I want you to know I don't need forever."

And she didn't. At least that's what she was telling herself.

There was a part of her that did, but that part of her was deathly afraid and remembered the hurt. It reminded her that forever was not an option for her.

How could she trust another man again?

She'd been blinded before.

She'd given her all to a man who'd callously thrown her love away. She was never going through that again.

Ever.

Even if forever was what she'd always wanted.

She could have tonight though, and maybe after tonight she could forget about how Caleb made her feel. She could get him out of her system and move forward with her career plans.

"Are you sure?" he asked hesitantly, confirming her fear that he might not really want her. That he would hurt her in the end, but she forced those thoughts away. It was all about being here in this moment.

She kissed him again and then opened the door to her hotel room, pulling him in. "I'm sure."

She was sure about him and tonight.

Tonight she wanted to not feel alone.

Caleb couldn't believe what was happening, and he was glad she wanted him as much as he wanted her. When she kissed him, it fired his blood. This was what he'd wanted ever since he met her. His blood was singing with want.

With need.

He wanted to touch her all over and have nothing between them.

Hazel pulled off his overcoat and then his suit jacket, kissing him and touching him. He ran his hands over her and unzipped her dress, marveling at the exquisite view of her in her lace underthings. Her long auburn hair fell down over her shoulders. As he ran his fingers through it, he discovered it was soft and silky, just like her skin. He ran his hand over her body, trailing his fingers over her flesh, leaving a trail of goose bumps in their wake.

She sighed.

It was too much to take in.

He was burning up.

"Hazel, I've dreamed about this for so long." He pressed a kiss against her neck, feeling her pulse fluttering under his lips.

"Same," she murmured, wrapping her arms around him.

Her hands undid his tie and shirt. They made quick work of the rest of their clothes. Except she left on her black stockings and high heels. He liked that.

She pulled him over to the bed beside her.

He reached for her, feeling her quiver under his touch. His hand moved between her legs, gently stroking her.

She moaned and moved her hips against his fingers. All he could think of was burying himself inside her. It was driving him crazy.

"What about protection?" he groaned. He didn't carry it because random sex was never his plan.

There was never time for trysts in hotel rooms.

Until now.

The couple of times he had been with a woman had always been at her place, and she'd been prepared.

"It's okay. I carry some," she whispered. "I them to hand out in case they're needed by patients at the clinic."

She got the condom, opened it and before he could react she rolled it down his shaft. The touch made him burn even more. It was so simple, yet it drove him crazy with need.

He wanted her so bad.

He pressed her down and showed her how much he wanted her. Kissing and licking her between her thighs.

Her hips moving against his mouth as he tasted her.

"Caleb," she murmured. "Please."

"What do you want?" he asked, though he knew because he wanted it too.

"Take me."

Caleb smiled and shifted his weight, teasing the folds of her sex with the tip of his shaft. She moved against him and he gritted his teeth, not wanting this to end. He thrust into her.

Sinking deeply.

Filling her completely.

"You feel so good," he moaned, and she did.

She was so soft, so wet and hot.

He was entirely lost to her.

"Oh, God," she murmured. Hazel met his slow thrusts, urging him to go faster until he complied. Soon, he couldn't hold back and he moved harder, faster, driven by a primal need to possess her completely.

He wanted this to last longer.

And he wanted her to come.

"Come for me, baby," he whispered against her neck.

She clutched his shoulders, her nails digging into his shoulder as she tightened around him, crying out as she came. He knew he was a lost man, and he came swiftly after her.

Melting in her exquisite heat.

When he floated down from heaven, he rolled over on his back and Hazel curled up beside him. He pulled her close, not wanting to let her go.

There was no need for words. He didn't even know what to say.

He was falling in love with her, and that was a terrifying prospect indeed.

CHAPTER NINE

HAZEL WOKE UP and gazed at Caleb sleeping soundly next to her. She smiled because his usually neat hair was curly and mussed.

It was all discombobulated because of what they'd been up to. They'd spent half the night in each other's arms. Hazel didn't know how good it could be with the right person. Being with Mark had been great, but last night with Caleb had been something she had never felt before.

It had consumed her.

And it had terrified her with how earth-shattering it had been.

It scared her how much she wanted more.

She'd been so sure one time with Caleb would be enough. Now she wasn't.

Caleb wasn't looking for forever, which was apparent since he hadn't moved on after his wife died. And neither was she.

Aren't you?

She shook her head, trying to banish that niggly thought from her mind. Of course, it was hard not to let her walls down and think that way when she was with him, especially after last night.

He'd been that broody, stubborn, by the book doctor with an air of vulnerability, who'd always made her groan when she saw him. How could she be falling in love with him?

Why did she always seem to fall for the wrong kind of man?

Is Caleb the wrong kind of man though?

Her brain told her that he was, but her heart was saying that he was everything right. Her heart was convinced that Dr. Caleb Norris was everything she wanted in a man, but she just couldn't wrap her mind around that. Especially since she didn't really know how he felt about relationships, and she was still so wary of being hurt.

She rested her chin on her stacked fists watching him sleep.

A thrum of excitement coursed through her as she thought of his hands on her last night. The way his kisses had burned into her flesh, the pleasure that he'd made her feel. It had been a long time since she'd been intimate with a man, but she couldn't recall ever feeling that kind of heat or intensity with anyone else.

"I can feel you watching me," Caleb murmured without opening his eyes. "Why? Are you plotting my demise? Was this your goal all along?"

She laughed softly. "I'm not plotting anything. I'm discreetly trying to make a dignified exit, and I got caught up in your cuteness."

"Cuteness? I'm hardly young enough to be considered cute," he said, quirking an eyebrow but still not opening his eyes. "Why are you trying to leave? The bed is so warm and comfy."

"My flight back to Portland is in three hours."

He opened his eyes and glanced at the time. "Damn. I meant to text Lizzie last night."

He jumped up, and she admired his bottom as he searched for his trousers in their tangled pile of clothing. He dug out his phone and frowned. "I turned the ringer off for the lecture. Blast."

"What's wrong?" she asked, her stomach sinking.

"No text from Lizzie, but missed calls and pages from Dr. Victor Anderson at St. Raymond's. He's the chief of staff there."

"Yes. I know. I've met Victor," Hazel replied. What she didn't say was that Victor had been the first person she and Bria had met. The one who'd welcomed the idea of their birthing center with open arms. "You better call."

Caleb nodded and called Victor back. She grabbed her phone and saw Lizzie had texted her.

The texts were frantic.

Lizzie was in pain and needed help but was alone. Something about feeling shoulder pain. More like agony.

Hazel's heart stopped for a moment, and a lump formed in her throat as she stared at the texts.

"Hi, Victor. It's Caleb. I forgot to turn my ringer back on."

Caleb's face drained of color as he listened. "When? Right. What's wrong? Okay. I'll be there as soon as I can. What? Okay great. I'm on my way."

He ended the call and ran his hand through his hair, looking frantic.

"Lizzie texted me," Hazel said. "She was in panic. In pain."

"Yes. She collapsed, and her boyfriend took her to St. Raymond's last night. Victor said they've sedated her and did an MRI. They suspect an ectopic pregnancy."

He didn't look at her.

"I couldn't tell you. She had to tell you herself. She's an adult," Hazel stated. She hated that Lizzie's secret had finally come out this way. She'd known that she couldn't tell him, and it broke her a bit that Caleb wasn't looking at her now.

He, of all people, should understand patient confidentiality, but it was obvious he was hurt that she couldn't tell him about Lizzie. Just like it had pained her to keep it from him.

Caleb didn't respond. "I have to get back. The fallopian tube could rupture. I have to be there."

"Oh, Caleb," Hazel said softly. Her heart was sinking for Lizzie, so alone and afraid.

"Dr. Anderson has arranged for a helicopter flight back to Portland. Lizzie wants you there as her midwife. Since you diagnosed her pregnancy."

It was the way he said that last part that caused a shudder to go through her.

Almost like he was blaming her, but she wanted to give him the benefit of the doubt.

He was worried about his daughter, that was all.

"I'll come to Portland."

"Thank you," he said curtly as he pulled on his clothes. "I'll go pack, and I'll meet you downstairs in twenty minutes."

"Yes."

He left her room and her heart was still in her throat.

Other than Lizzie's illness, there had been no other signs of ectopic pregnancy.

Except her extreme feelings of sickness, but that could be present in any pregnancy and her HCG levels had been consistent. Sometimes with an ectopic, they weren't as high.

She felt like the she was at fault. Only, she wasn't. An MRI could pick up the ectopic pregnancy. She couldn't by examination alone. But all she knew now was that she wanted to help Lizzie any way she could.

If it wasn't dealt with right away the tube could rupture, as Caleb had mentioned, and if it did that she'd bleed to death.

It broke her heart that there was no saving the baby because she knew Lizzie had wanted it, even though she was so young, but most likely the baby was gone. They usually were at this point.

Hazel got dressed as fast as she could. A shower could wait until they got to Portland.

After she was dressed and packed, she headed to the lobby and checked out. Caleb was already waiting and pacing by the main door.

"You ready?" he asked abruptly.

"Yes. Let's go."

Caleb hailed a cab.

It was a short ride to the private airfield just outside of Seattle, and it helped that it was a Sunday morning. Traffic was minimal. The helicopter was being primed and ready for them. All Hazel could think about was Lizzie and getting home to her safely.

She could tell that was on Caleb's mind too.

They were given headphones to muffle the sounds of the chopper, and it wasn't long before the aircraft took off, flying away from Seattle down toward Portland.

Hazel reached out and took his hand in hers. Caleb looked down but didn't smile, and instead of accepting the gesture he pulled his hand away. It stung. It wasn't her fault she couldn't tell him about Lizzie. He knew why she hadn't, yet he was still blaming her.

And it broke her heart even more.

Why did she let herself fall for Caleb? She knew better than this.

"Thank you again for coming at Lizzie's request," he said mechanically over the microphone.

"Where else would I be?"

He didn't say anything else, but she could tell he was both mad and worried.

It was like a slap in the face. After their night together, somehow she was taking the brunt of his shock over learning Lizzie was pregnant and the terror that he might lose his child. That he was able to push her aside so easily after their night together really hurt, but she understood all the same.

That's what you wanted, isn't it? For him to keep his distance from you?

Except she wasn't so sure about that now, and she was scared. She'd risked her heart once again, against her own better judgment, and got burned.

She was utterly crushed.

The helicopter ride took a couple of hours, and it landed on the roof of St. Raymond's. They headed down to the surgical unit.

Dr. Anderson was waiting there when they got to Lizzie's room, as was Dr. Gracie, Caleb's OB/GYN fellow.

"How is she?" Caleb asked.

"Stable and we gave her some pain medication. As Victor told you, we did an MRI and the fallopian tube has not ruptured yet. We need to get her into surgery," Dr. Gracie said.

"Fine. I'll go get prepped…" Caleb started.

Victor shook his head. "You're her father. You can't. She did ask for Ms. Rees though."

Caleb was going to argue, but closed his mouth. "Then I want Hazel in there with her, since that's what Lizzie wants."

Dr. Gracie looked confused. "The midwife?"

"Yes, I'm Lizzie's midwife," Hazel replied firmly. "I'm also a nurse practitioner."

Dr. Gracie didn't look that impressed. "Fine. She can be in the operating room."

Lizzie was her patient, and she was going to advocate for her.

"I'd like to see the MRI," Caleb said.

"I figured." Victor brought up the MRI on a tablet. "You can see the mass here in the fallopian tube. It's a nonviable pregnancy."

Caleb's lips pursed in a thin line. "When is the surgery scheduled?" he asked quietly.

"As soon as possible now that you're here," Victor responded. "Right, Dr. Gracie?"

Dr. Gracie nodded. "The operating room is being prepped as we speak."

"Well, I'll sign the forms, since I'm her next of kin and she's sedated, and let's get her into surgery," Caleb stated.

"Timothy won't be happy Ms. Rees is in there," Dr. Gracie said.

Caleb frowned. "I don't care. Hazel is Lizzie's midwife. She diagnosed Lizzie's pregnancy. Lizzie trusts her. If I can't be there, Hazel will be."

Dr. Gracie nodded stiffly. "Very well. Ms. Rees, I'll show you where to get scrubs."

Caleb went into Lizzie's room and sat next to her bed. Hazel's heart hurt seeing him so distraught, but she was going to make sure that Lizzie was taken care of. She may not be welcome in the hospital and Caleb might not be very happy with her right now, but that didn't matter.

She was still Lizzie's midwife.

Maybe even a friend?

She was a trained medical professional, and she belonged here.

Dr. Gracie showed her into the staff locker room and handed her scrubs. "We do respect patient wishes here, Ms. Rees. I'm not against you or your center."

"I get it. Your board of directors is. I'm familiar with the politics of the hospital."

"Are you?" he asked stiffly.

"I worked at a hospital as a midwife and as a nurse practitioner. I know how they work."

"I'm glad you understand," Dr. Gracie said. "I'll meet you at Lizzie's room, and we'll take her down to the operating room."

She had a feeling he wasn't particularly glad though.

Hazel nodded. She put her suitcase in a locker and got changed.

Lizzie looked so small lying sedated in her bed. She was so much like Jane, with her long blond hair fanned out across the pillows. The only difference was that Lizzie had a purple streak in her hair.

Purple streak? When did she get that? Why hadn't he protected her better? Why couldn't he have stopped this?

He would've noticed her pregnancy sooner if he hadn't been so obsessed lately with Hazel.

He was the worst father.

He could've stopped her from seeing that boy, and Caleb was about ready to throttle Derek for getting his daughter pregnant when they were still in college.

Lizzie is an adult now, remember? And it takes two to tango.

Caleb sighed and sat down in the chair by her bedside.

He'd promised Jane that he would take care of Lizzie. They'd had that talk when she was pregnant, that if anything happened to either of them, the other one would always put Lizzie first.

He'd thought he was doing that, but how did he miss this?

Because you've been preoccupied for too long.

He'd basically just concentrated on getting through each day ever since Jane died. He'd thought work would help keep the pain away. Hold back all that grief, but really it had been numbing him to life.

He'd been missing things for years.

Important things like this.

Lizzie was sick and he'd thought it was the flu.

Now, looking back, he could see the pregnancy signs.

He hadn't seen anything at the time, and now this was all his fault.

He was so selfish.

"Caleb, it's time."

Caleb turned to see Hazel in dark blue scrubs, her hair tied back and covered by a scrub cap. He barely recognized her.

Hazel had lied to him.

She'd known for weeks that Lizzie was pregnant and didn't tell him.

He felt betrayed, hurt that Hazel had kept from him what was going on with his daughter. Did she know it was an ectopic pregnancy?

Did she do all the right exams?

He was questioning everything and he wasn't sure what to believe, but none of that mattered right now. All that mattered was Lizzie.

"Take care of her," he said, hoping his voice didn't shake.

"Of course," Hazel said gently as the porters came in to wheel Lizzie's bed away.

Caleb took a step back and watched his daughter go, feeling completely helpless and powerless.

It was an ectopic pregnancy.

That could've been his grandchild. Now it was putting his only child's life at risk.

She could die on the operating table. Just like Jane had.

Don't think like that.

Lizzie was going to be okay.

She had to be okay.

CHAPTER TEN

HAZEL SCRUBBED IN. She stared through the window that separated the scrub area from the operating room, which was in front of her. It wasn't one of the main rooms, but one that was used for day procedures. It had been some time since she'd attended a surgery. When she had been in nursing school, she had done several surgical rotations.

It wasn't her favorite place to be, but Lizzie wanted her here so this is where she'd be.

Lizzie had been transferred to the surgical table and was being prepped for the surgery. Depending on the damage, they might be able to save her fallopian tube.

Dr. Gracie had scrubbed in and was standing next to the bed as the equipment for the surgery was laid out and set up by the scrub nurse.

As she looked at a fully functioning and state-of-the-art operating room, a shudder ran down her spine. Not because of the sterile environment, but because Lizzie was going to be here on the operating table.

Exposed.

At the mercy of the surgeon.

A lump formed in her throat. This was the part of obstetrics she hated.

The loss of life.

Except it would kill Lizzie if her body tried to hold on

to a baby that wasn't viable. And her life, here, was the most important.

She hated seeing Lizzie on the table.

Hazel toweled off and stepped into the operating room. A nurse helped her into a gown and gloves.

Dr. Gracie looked up. "Are you ready, Ms. Rees?"

"Yes. I'm ready." Hazel glanced down at Lizzie and swallowed the lump that had formed in her throat. She cared about Lizzie, just like she cared about Caleb, and there was a part of her that wanted to be part of their little family. But Caleb blamed her for Lizzie's situation, so the chances of that dream ever happening were slim indeed.

She put those thoughts out of her mind and took her place by Lizzie's side. Although the young woman was sedated and unaware, Hazel was here for her.

This was where she needed to be.

"Okay, let's get started," Dr. Gracie announced. "Scalpel."

The instrument was handed over.

"Ovary and mass located," Dr. Gracie said once Lizzie was opened up. "Making an incision."

Hazel watched the monitor with bated breath as Dr. Gracie removed the nonviable pregnancy. The tube was pretty scarred, so he had to remove the damaged portion of the fallopian tube and seal it. She tried not to watch the clock as the procedure went on.

"Ready to close," Dr. Gracie finally said. "She should make a full recovery."

Hazel checked Lizzie and saw that everything looked stable, for now. Dr. Gracie placed a dressing over the incision.

The nurses took Lizzie out of the operating room to wheel her back to her room.

Hazel pulled off her surgical gown and scrubbed out. She hoped the lab results wouldn't take long. She wandered out of the scrub room and made her way back to the staff room to change.

As she walked along the hallway, she ran smack-dab into Dan Patterson.

"Mr. Patterson?" Hazel asked, shocked.

"Hazel, I didn't expect to see you. They said you don't work here."

"I don't…is everything okay with Sandra?" Hazel asked.

"So far. We came in for an ultrasound on Friday, and she was admitted. We wanted you paged, but I'm not sure they did."

"Sandra was admitted? Do you know why?"

Dan shrugged. "Yeah, on Friday. We're here waiting for Dr. Norris to tell us why."

"Dr. Norris?" Hazel asked.

"Yeah. We didn't see him, but the fellow who saw us on Friday said that our care was moving from the Mult-nomah Falls Women's Health Center to St. Raymond's per Dr. Norris's orders. We didn't question it because you referred him to us in the first place."

"Of course. You're right, I did."

"Sorry, Hazel. We would rather be at home or your center, but if it means the babies and my wife are safe, then we have to stay here."

"Absolutely," Hazel said in shock. Dan headed back to his wife's room. Hazel stood there, in hospital scrubs, stunned. She felt like she'd been betrayed. Why had she let down her walls? Why had she trusted Caleb?

And just like Mark, Caleb had obviously lied to her. He hadn't told her that she'd been removed from the case, but he must have known. It was what Timothy Russell and the board of directors had wanted right from the start.

Only, she'd thought Caleb was on her side. Why hadn't he fought to keep her on the case, where she belonged?

Dr. Gracie had said Timothy wouldn't be happy she was

here, and Caleb had promised that he would make sure she was. That she would stay as the main practitioner on Sandra's case. She felt like she had been kicked in the gut. She'd thought she and Caleb were colleagues.

Friends.

No, she'd thought they were something even more.

She'd trusted him.

Once again she'd been betrayed by a man she'd come to care for, and she was angry at herself for trusting him.

For falling for him.

Her walls were there for a good reason. Why had she forgotten that?

Because you fell in love with the wrong person. Again.

Tears stung her eyes and she quickly wiped them away. She was a fool. She was going to rebuild her walls, stronger this time, and she was never going to let them down ever again.

Lizzie was still a bit groggy as she started to wake up.

"Dad?" she asked.

"I'm here," Caleb said, gently stroking her face. "I'm right here."

"Is Hazel here? I texted her…"

"Yes," Caleb said. "She was in Seattle at the same lecture as me."

Lizzie nodded. "I like her."

Caleb smiled a little stiffly. "I like her too. She's a good…midwife."

He was still hurt Hazel had kept him in the dark about his daughter, but that didn't detract from Hazel's talent.

Lizzie wrinkled her nose. "Come on…"

"What?"

Lizzie shook her head and didn't answer. "What's wrong with me?"

He wanted to tell her that the baby was gone, that she'd

lost one of her fallopian tubes, but she was still coming out of anesthetic.

He didn't even know how Lizzie had felt about the baby. He wasn't sure how he was feeling now. All he knew was Lizzie had come through the surgery successfully.

She was alive.

That was all that mattered to him.

Lizzie drifted off to sleep again, and he scrubbed a hand over his face. Not sure of what to think.

Hazel knocked on the door. Instantly he noticed something was off about, her and it sent a shiver of dread down his spine. Had something happened during the surgery he didn't know about?

She seemed tense.

"How is she doing?" Hazel asked, her arms folded across her chest.

"Groggy. I'll tell her what's happened when she's more alert."

Hazel smiled slightly, but he knew something was wrong with her. The smile didn't reach her eyes the way it had done just last night.

It was like a wall had been put up between them again. Like when they had been standing in the elevator in Seattle. She was suddenly shutting him out.

Not that he could blame her.

He was still annoyed that she'd known about Lizzie, but said nothing. Especially with his daughter's life on the line like that.

He'd been thinking so much about Hazel, he hadn't seen Lizzie's pregnancy signs for what they were.

"Hazel?" Lizzie asked groggily.

"I'm here," Hazel said gently, coming closer to the bed.

Lizzie smiled. "I'm glad you're here."

"Of course, where else would I be?" Hazel responded, touching Lizzie's shoulder gently.

Lizzie just nodded and drifted back off again.

Hazel smiled at her fondly and then looked up at him. The smile that was in her eyes for Lizzie fizzled out when their gazes locked. Red bloomed in her cheeks.

"I've got to go," she said quickly.

"Hazel, what aren't you telling me? Did something bad happen during the surgery?"

"The surgery went off without a hitch. Nothing unexpected happened." Hazel walked out of the room, and Caleb followed her into the hall. He closed the door to Lizzie's room.

"Hazel."

"Now you want to talk?" she asked bitterly.

"What's that supposed to mean?"

"You were pretty curt to me on the way back to Portland."

"I was worried about Lizzie."

"So was I." She turned to leave.

"Hazel!"

She turned around, seemingly annoyed with him. "What, Caleb?"

"What's wrong?"

"I ran into Dan Patterson after the surgery."

Caleb was confused. "I don't understand."

"He told me that Sandra was admitted, and they don't know why. And they tried to page me, but that under your orders I've been removed as her practitioner."

"She was having contractions during a routine ultrasound. My fellow called me, and it was only right to admit her until the results of her other tests came through."

Hazel nodded. "Okay, then why was I removed as one of her health care providers?"

"What?" Caleb asked, stunned.

"I have been removed as one of the Pattersons' health care providers. You're their primary doctor now."

"I will correct it," Caleb stated.

"Don't bother. It's what you wanted from the get-go. It was evident when you didn't stand up for me with Timothy Russell after Mrs. Jameson's VBAC."

"What are you talking about?"

"Since the moment we met you've been trying to shut down our center and get me to leave. Why not take my patients too?"

"That wasn't me," he said hotly. "You know that. You're letting your temper get the better of you."

"Why? Why did you take me off the Pattersons' case? I thought you at least respected me professionally. I thought—"

"I do," Caleb snapped. "And you thought what?"

He was hurt that she thought he could be this cruel. He was going to find out why she was removed from the case, but he wanted her to understand that it wasn't his fault. He wanted her to believe him. If she cared about him at all, she would understand what he was trying to say, but she hadn't been up front with him either. She hadn't let him know what was going on with Lizzie.

"No. You don't and it's nothing. It doesn't matter what I think."

Caleb took a step closer. "It does matter. Why aren't you listening to what I'm saying? Why are you throwing up walls again? Why do you keep shutting me out?"

"I'm not shutting you out and you're one to talk. You've been doing it since your wife died. Isolating yourself."

It was like a slap in the face, but it was true. Why couldn't she see that he wasn't like that with her? Why was she being so obtuse about this?

"You're pushing me away. You can trust me," Caleb said.

"Can I?" she asked, glowering at him.

Caleb crossed his arms. "Hazel, I don't fully understand what is happening here."

"I've been betrayed before. You know that. You know I've been used and hurt before. You got so close to me, slept with me and while my back was turned you undermined me."

"I didn't undermine you! And I'm not trying to hurt you. You're the one with the walls firmly up. You're pushing me away now to protect yourself. And don't forget, I'm not the only one withholding information, am I?"

He knew this was going to happen. He'd put his heart on the line, and here he was getting hurt again. He couldn't think straight.

She looked stung. "I couldn't say anything about Lizzie's pregnancy. She's eighteen. I had to abide by patient confidentiality. You're using that as an excuse to have a go at me, and you're being totally unfair. You would've done the same thing if our situations were reversed, and don't deny it. It killed me that I couldn't tell you what was happening. I hate deceit and you know why."

"But I could've lost Lizzie. She's all I have! You have no idea how that feels. You have no one." He regretted what he said the moment he said it, but he was too angry and scared.

Right now, he felt like his world was spinning out of control. He hated this loss of control.

"Caleb…"

"Don't," he said quickly.

"I'll let you have some time to yourself," Hazel said. "It's clear neither of us is ready for anything more."

He could hear the sadness in her voice, and he felt the pain his heart.

Maybe she was right.

So he let her walk away.

And he was left with just his own thoughts.

Today had started so perfectly. He had woken up next to Hazel after an amazing night in her arms. He'd foolishly opened his heart to her, and she'd pushed him away. Now, his daughter had lost her baby, and he hadn't even known what danger signs to look out for because he hadn't known about the pregnancy.

How was he going to tell Lizzie? He didn't know.

He was alone, and right now he needed a friend, except the friend he'd had, the woman he'd loved, didn't want him. There was no point in denying it. He'd fallen in love with Hazel. It had been so long since he had felt this way, he'd almost not recognized it.

He never thought he'd feel love again.

He'd ruined his chance with her. He'd accused her of lying to him in the heat of his despair over Lizzie. But he could see that, really, she'd had no other choice.

She was right. If the situations were reversed, he would've done the same. He couldn't have told her.

But there was no trust between them. How could they move forward without that essential building block of any relationship?

Hazel didn't believe him about not being involved in taking away her case. He was angry at Timothy for that, but he was sad Hazel couldn't trust him.

Wouldn't trust him.

Hazel's heart was breaking, and she had a hard time holding back the tears that were threatening to spill over.

Why?

Why did she have to fall in love with him?

It was clear he didn't want a relationship with her. Now she had to work with him while trying to repress her feelings. It was going to be a nightmare.

She was not going to hide. She had important work to do at the birthing center, and although it would still be hard to see him, she'd have to sometimes. She wiped away the tears on the back of her hand.

Hazel went into Lizzie's room to check on her.

Lizzie woke up when Hazel shut the door to her room. "Hazel?"

"Yes." She walked over to the bed and sat down on the edge.

"What is it?" Lizzie asked.

Hazel sighed, trying to make sure that she could control all the emotions going through her. "Lizzie, your pregnancy was ectopic."

"What?"

"It means your baby grew outside of the uterus. In your fallopian tube. It wasn't viable and your tube was so scarred. We couldn't save it."

Lizzie paled. "My baby is gone?"

"Yes. I'm so sorry," Hazel said, fighting back tears.

Lizzie nodded. "Does my dad know?"

"Yes. They had to tell him. You were sedated. Your life was in danger."

Lizzie frowned. "I didn't want him to worry. It's why I could never tell him. I tried several times, believe me. He always worries, and he'd been so happy lately with you around. So I just kept my pain to myself. I knew he'd be so disappointed in me. I couldn't bear it. I did try and tell him. I swear."

"I was going to talk to you about telling him," Hazel said.

Lizzie nodded, breaking into sobs. "I know. I wanted to, but I just couldn't."

Hazel's heart broke, and she fought to regain her composure. Lizzie had tried to do what was best for her dad, but that hadn't worked out and it hurt her that Lizzie had only wanted her dad to be happy with her.

"He will always worry about you, because he's your father. It's kind of the job," Hazel said, clearing her throat.

"Yes, but he's had no life because of me. He raised me all on his own."

"It's not because of you." Although, Hazel didn't really know why Caleb didn't date or socialize more. He just seemed to work.

As do you. So why don't you date?

Hazel shook that niggly logical thought away. "Lizzie, you need to talk to him. You need to tell him everything. How you felt about the baby. How much you love Derek. I know you didn't want to tell him to protect him and not raise his stress levels, but he deserves to know."

Lizzie nodded. "Okay. I'll talk with him, but what if he doesn't…what if…"

Hazel pulled a trembling Lizzie into her arms. "He loves you. He won't ever disown you. It'll be okay. After all, you're here, aren't you? You survived the surgery. And you can still have babies. One day, when it's the right time for you."

Lizzie nodded and lay back down. "Okay. Can you get my dad?"

"Sure."

Hazel got up and left Lizzie's room.

Caleb was pacing. He was still processing everything.

Lizzie's pregnancy, the fact she'd hid it from him, that she'd felt the need to.

His fight with Hazel.

He'd messed so many things up.

Hazel came out of Lizzie's room. Her face stained with tears. Seeing her so broken up about his daughter melted his heart.

"I told her about the baby. She's an adult, and I'm her health care practitioner. I had to let her know."

"I understand," he said. And he did. It was her duty to tell Lizzie.

"Lizzie needs to speak with you."

Caleb nodded.

Lizzie was sitting up and looking worried. He could see she had been crying too.

Caleb walked into the room and Lizzie looked at him, wringing her hands.

"Dad." Her voice caught in her throat.

"I'm here." He went to her side and stroked her hair.

"Are you mad?"

"No."

"So you're not mad that I…?" Her lips began to tremble.

Caleb choked back his pain. "No. And I wouldn't have been even had I known. Why didn't you tell me?"

Tears slid down her face. "I didn't want to stress you out."

"You kept something so important from me because you were worried about stressing me out?"

Lizzie sighed. "You take such good care of me, Dad. I just didn't want you to worry. You've spent my whole life worrying. I'm an adult now. I want you to be free."

Caleb pulled Lizzie into his arms. "Worrying about you is my job. Whether you're an adult or not."

Lizzie cried on his shoulders. "Dad, I worry about you too."

"That's not your job," he said gently. "Your job is to get healthy."

"It's just the two of us though."

"I know."

"Dad, I really want you to be happy, and you've been so happy recently with Hazel."

His heart skipped a beat. He had been, but he had been trying to hold it back. "I want you to be happy too, Lizzie."

Lizzie nodded. "Derek and I want to get married after college."

"Okay."

Lizzie took a deep breath. "I know you wanted us to take it slow, because you and Mom were so young…"

"We were, but I was in love with her, and I don't regret ever having you or marrying your mom."

"It's going to crush Derek about the baby."

"Of course it will. I'm crushed too." He smoothed back her hair. "It's a part of life, sadly. He'll be happy you're safe and well though. I know I am."

Lizzie broke down crying again, and he held her in his arms. "I love you, Lizzie. So please don't worry and don't hide anything else from me."

"I won't, Dad, but I need you to be happy too. I mean Hazel…"

"She has her own life," Caleb said quickly. "Don't worry about me. Right now we have to focus on getting you better. I can't lose you, Lizzie. I promised your mother I would take care of you."

Lizzie gasped. "I promised her too, Dad. In my dreams. When I was a kid."

Caleb's eyes filled with tears. "You did?"

Lizzie nodded. "She wants you to be happy too and to let her go."

Caleb didn't know what to say. He just held his daughter until there was a knock at the door. Hazel stuck her head in, and his heart skipped a beat seeing her.

"Is everything okay?" Caleb asked, not sure he wanted to let his daughter go.

"No. It's Mrs. Patterson. I'm afraid they need you."

Caleb looked at Lizzie.

"Go, Dad. I've got the television and my phone. I'm fine."

Caleb kissed her on the forehead and followed Hazel out.

"What's happened?" he asked.

"They wouldn't tell me. I'm not on the case, remember," she said quickly.

"Yes, you are."

"What're you talking about?"

"I'm putting you on the case. I'm head of obstetrics, I'll petition the hospital board, and if they try to stop me from doing it, I'll leave. After we take care of Mrs. Patterson of course."

Hazel was stunned. "Thank you."

"It's the least I could do."

Only he could do more. He could apologize and make things right. Repair the trust between them. He could finally stop being such a fool and tell her how he really felt. Only he couldn't find the words in that moment, and there was no time right now.

Right now, he had several lives to save.

CHAPTER ELEVEN

CALEB GOT CHANGED into some scrubs and headed into Mrs. Patterson's room, with Hazel close on his heels. His fellow, Dr. Gracie, who'd admitted Mrs. Patterson when Caleb had been traveling to Seattle, was also there.

Mrs. Patterson was being comforted by her husband, and looked in distress.

"Dr. Gracie?" Caleb asked, taking the chart. Hazel looked over his shoulder to read all the labs and the information that had been collected since Sandra had been admitted.

Including the blatant removal of Hazel by the chairman of the board, which was not Caleb's wish at all. Her eyes widened and she blushed. He knew then that she'd spotted it wasn't him. It was Timothy all along.

"Patient is having signs of labor and upon examination there's a shortening of her cervix," Dr. Gracie remarked.

"Signs of labor?" Hazel asked, crossing her arms. "What kind of signs?"

Dr. Gracie barely glanced at Hazel. "Back pain, contractions. They're intermittent though."

"Thank you, Dr. Gracie," Caleb said. "Hazel Rees is going to assist. Can you check up on the post-op patients for me?"

Dr. Gracie was shocked, but didn't argue and left the room.

"What's wrong?" Sandra asked. Dan was holding her hand, and they both looked frightened.

"You're having some small, very irregular contractions and we're going to find out why," Caleb said. "Hazel, I'm sure you're familiar with cervical cerclage?"

"Yes," Hazel stated.

"Well, as Mrs. Patterson's practitioner, would you be the one to check?"

Hazel's eyes widened. "Of course."

Caleb stepped back and let Hazel sit down as he eyed the monitors.

"This is going to be cold, Sandra. I'm going to use the speculum," Hazel said as she prepared Sandra for the insertion.

Mrs. Patterson nodded and winced. "Okay, I'm ready."

"Just some pressure," Hazel said reassuringly.

Caleb peered over Hazel's shoulder and could see the cervix shortening. He and Hazel exchanged a knowing look. They both knew in that instant that Mrs. Patterson needed to have the cerclage to prevent preterm labor.

"Sandra, we're going to get anesthesiology in here and give you a spinal epidural before we put a tiny stitch in your cervix. That stitch should stop the shortening of your cervix and prevent you from going into labor or miscarrying," Hazel said. "Do you consent to this procedure?"

"Absolutely," Sandra said, her voice shaking. "I thought I could go home today, but do whatever you have to, to save my babies."

"When will it be taken out?" Dan asked.

"Usually by the thirty-seventh week. By then it's safe to deliver the babies. If labor starts and we're past thirty, at the minimum, we'll just remove it. Ideally I would like you to get to thirty-seven weeks," Caleb said. "Which will be a challenge. In your case, anything past thirty weeks is good enough when it comes to quints."

Hazel glanced at Caleb, and he felt bad that he wasn't here when Sandra was admitted by his fellow. He was also furious that he hadn't been here when Timothy had removed Hazel as main practitioner.

Dr. Gracie was young and did what he was told.

He'd been that way once too.

This whole thing was a mess and frankly, Caleb felt, it had made the hospital look bad. It wasn't a horrible hospital by any means, but the way the board was currently running things, it was a disgrace and would have a bad reputation soon enough.

"You're going to have to rest here for a couple more days and then, if you're stable, you can return home," Caleb said. "There is no reason to keep you here if everything looks fine."

Hazel removed the speculum and took off her gloves. "All good."

"I'll put in a call for anesthesiology," Caleb said. "Right now your contractions have ended, but we need to get this procedure done. I'll have an anesthesiologist come to do your spinal, and then we'll take you to the operating room."

"Okay," Sandra said. "Thank you, Hazel, Dr. Norris."

Caleb left. He had to get an operating room prepped.

And then there was Lizzie, who was mourning her own loss.

Caleb knew something about that, and he wanted to be there to help her through it.

Then there was Hazel.

They both had trust bridges to rebuild, and he wanted to do that. He wanted to make things right again. He just wasn't sure how best to go about it.

Caleb scrubbed a hand over his face.

He went to the nurses' station and made the appropriate arrangements for the cervical cerclage. After he made sure that anesthesiology was on their way, Hazel came out of Sandra's room and approached him at the nurses' station where he was trying to focus on the paperwork and not think about everything on his mind. He had to concentrate on his patient.

He just had to get through this surgery, and then he wasn't sure what was going to happen next. He was incredibly frustrated with the board of directors at this hospital. Maybe it was time to open his own practice and not worry anymore about how this hospital was running.

There was a part of him, a long time ago, that had thought he might become a chief of staff at a place like this one day, but with all the political nonsense he'd seen here, he didn't want that now.

He could see the pressure that Victor was under. And how he kept an upbeat attitude about it was commendable.

Now he understood Hazel a bit better, why she'd pursued something that she was so passionate about and why she'd fought so hard for what she believed in.

Hazel was filling in some paperwork herself, so that she could officially have operating room privileges and access to everything she needed. Midwives shouldn't be treated like this. This hospital should be open and accepting of them.

He admired Hazel all the more for doing what she believed in.

He was completely in love with her.

He was going to make everything right. Even if she still didn't want him, he wasn't going to regret their night together. He was going to take a chance.

At least then he would know.

He was so tired of being alone and protecting his heart.

Life meant pain sometimes, and he was willing to risk that again if it meant that he could have Hazel. As long as he hadn't completely blown his chance with her by accusing her of things that weren't her fault and breaking her fragile trust in him.

He was finally willing to embrace the thing that scared him the most, and that was opening his heart back up to the possibility of love.

Hazel was back in the operating room. Sandra Patterson had taken her spinal epidural well and was awake on the surgical table. The scrub nurses were draping her, and Caleb was prepping what would be needed for the cervical cerclage.

Dan was sitting on the opposite side of the drape and comforting his wife. Right up to the last moment, Hazel wasn't sure if she would be allowed in here, because the hospital had been so hell-bent on making sure that she didn't have privileges.

She'd seen from the file it wasn't Caleb who'd taken her off the case, and she had been foolish to jump the gun and blame him. She had been so hurt before by a man that she loved, Hazel had expected Caleb to do the same.

She'd thought Caleb was different, but he had badly hurt her when he'd blamed her for not telling him about Lizzie's pregnancy.

You know he was just scared for his child.

She might not know how he felt in that situation, but she understood it. She cared for Lizzie too.

Being in that operating room, watching Lizzie have surgery, had terrified her.

Caleb hadn't cheated on her or lied to her. She had lashed out at him before she knew the whole truth about why she'd been removed from the case. It was that fiery temper of hers again. She needed to find Caleb and have a calm discussion so they could sort this whole mess out. She had to stop pushing him away.

Not that it took much. She'd known all along that he wasn't ready to open his heart again. He had a lot on his plate. And even more now with Lizzie healing from surgery and loss.

A lump caught in her throat as she finished scrubbing up.

Hazel was absolutely exhausted, but she was going to be there for that young woman. She wished she could be there for her more.

She longed to be a part of Caleb and Lizzie's family.

But if Caleb wasn't ready that was fine.

If Caleb was too hurt because he felt she had let him down by not telling him about Lizzie's baby, then that was fine. They could still be friends. They could still be colleagues. Even if St. Raymond's was still going to give her a hard time about coming to work here, at least she would have an advocate on the other side. Caleb would make sure that she got access if her patients needed it.

She only hoped that the same courtesy would be extended to Bria.

Hazel finished her scrubbing in. She shook off her hands and dried them with a paper towel, slipping on her mask and then stepping into the operating room. A nurse helped her on with a gown and a surgical shield with light.

Sandra looked in her direction as she walked toward the surgical table.

"Hazel, am I going to be okay?" Sandra asked, her voice shaking.

"Yes. This is done all the time," Hazel said gently. "You won't feel a thing and neither will the babies. I promise."

Sandra nodded. "Thank you, Hazel. I'm so glad you're back on my case. I'd go elsewhere to have you."

"I'm glad too." Hazel made her way down to the end of the surgical table. Mrs. Patterson's legs were placed in the stirrups, and Hazel sat down on the rolling chair. Caleb sat next to her.

They didn't have to say anything. Caleb was there to hand her what she needed. Hazel made sure that Mrs. Patterson was numb and went to work. It was a simple procedure, and she had done this on her midwife patients before.

It was nice working with Caleb beside her.

She finished the stitch and everything looked good.

"I'm all done, Sandra!" Hazel finished and removed the speculum. "We're going to move you to post-op, and it can take some time before the effects of the spinal wear off."

Sandra nodded. "Everything is okay?"

"Yes. I don't see any complications. I will check on you later."

"Thank you, Hazel and Dr. Norris," Sandra said.

Hazel nodded and left the operating room and headed back to the scrub room. Caleb followed her and started scrubbing out as well.

"I got a page from Victor while you were doing the cerclage," Caleb said, not looking at her.

"Oh?"

"Besides Timothy being livid, Victor wanted me to tell you that the staff of St. Raymond's are behind you."

"Are they?" she asked in surprise.

"Yes. I am too. The rest of the board now knows the Pattersons will leave if you're not on the case."

"What about you?"

He shrugged. "That doesn't matter. They came to you first. Besides, I have a lot to think about and Lizzie to take care of."

"She'll be okay, Caleb."

He smiled at her. "I know. I can't lose her. I'm tired of losing the people I love."

He left her standing there.

Did he love her?

Is that what he was implying? Then she shook her head, because he obviously meant his late wife.

Not her.

CHAPTER TWELVE

HAZEL FINISHED HER operative report on Sandra Patterson's cervical cerclage as fast as she could. It had been a long time since she'd done a report like this, but it all came back to her quickly.

She made sure that Sandra was settled in the postoperative unit and was comfortable and gave instructions to the residents and nurses who were monitoring her, asking them to page her or Caleb if there was any change.

She grabbed a quick bite to eat, because she hadn't eaten since they came back from Seattle.

Not that she was going to be doing anything else now.

All she had to do was change and go home, but first she was going to see Lizzie and check on her for a final time before she went home.

As she walked through the postoperative wing, she saw that Caleb was in the waiting room. He was back in his street clothes. The white sleeves of his dress shirt were rolled to his elbows, and his hair was still mussed. There were large bags under his eyes, but he was resting.

As if he knew that she was watching, he looked up.

Their gazes locked and her heart skipped a bea,t and her eyes filled with tears.

He nodded encouragingly.

Hazel returned the nod and left to him to his thoughts. She didn't know what his plans were next or if he had forgiven her for not telling him about Lizzie's pregnancy, but he'd made it clear he was on her birthing center's side. That meant so much.

When she went into the room, Lizzie was lying there, looking pale.

"Hazel!" Lizzie said brightly. "I wasn't sure if you were coming again."

"I wanted to say good-night," Hazel said, stroking Lizzie's hair through the scrub cap that they had put on her. "I wanted to check up on you, see if you needed anything."

"Thanks for being here for me." Lizzie took her hand. "I finally talked to my dad."

"I'm so glad."

"He isn't going to murder Derek. He gave his blessing for us to get married when we graduate."

Hazel smiled. "I'm glad."

"I'm nervous how Derek will feel," Lizzie said. "About the baby."

"You don't have to be nervous about anything. If he loves you, you will be all that matters and he'll mourn with you."

Lizzie squeezed her hand. "Dad has been having a great time with you the last couple of weeks."

"He's a good friend."

Lizzie grinned, but it was the kind of grin that was kind of dopey as the painkillers started to kick in. "Couldn't you be more than friends? It would be cool to have you as a…a mom."

Then Lizzie drifted off.

Hazel's stomach twisted in a knot, and she fought back the tears.

I'd like that too, but your dad doesn't trust me anymore.

She straightened her spine and wiped the tears away as she headed to the doctors' lounge. On her way there she bumped into Timothy Russell, and he didn't look pleased.

"I thought you'd be gone by now."

"I'm sure you'd like that, but you know that it's actually hurting your hospital not letting midwives have privileges. It looks petty. Just thought I would make that clear. The Pattersons are leaving."

"Doubtful. St. Raymond's is the best," Timothy said, but she could see the worry in his face.

"Ask the Pattersons. You take away their right to the health care team they've requested, and they'll walk. That's an awful lot of PR and money your board will lose. Think they'll like that?" Hazel asked smugly.

"Are you threatening me?" Timothy asked furiously.

"No. Just telling you because you know and I know there will be a vote of no confidence in you if word gets out how you treat midwives here at St. Raymond's."

Timothy said nothing, but stormed away.

Victor came around the corner, smiling at her. "I heard that."

Hazel chuckled. "Did you?"

"I did." He grinned. "You're smart, Hazel Rees. I like you."

Hazel nodded. "Thank you, Dr. Anderson."

"You're welcome and please, call me Victor." He headed off down the hall.

Hazel swallowed the lump in her throat. All her emotions were overtaking her. She was exhausted.

She needed some space and distance.

You need Caleb.

She pushed that thought away.

Caleb glanced at the clock on the wall.

There were certain things that people did in the waiting room while waiting for loved ones. His thing was apparently this, watching a hand seemingly go backward around a wall clock.

This was what he'd done when Lizzie was having her surgery.

Now he was waiting for Derek to come and he hoped the young man did. Although, there was still a part of him that wanted to throttle him because he'd impregnated his teenage daughter.

Derek came rushing into the waiting room, panicked.

"Dr. Norris, is Lizzie…"

"She's okay. I'll take you to her."

It was up to Lizzie to tell him about the baby.

Caleb let him into the room and Derek hesitated. He could see the pain on the young man's face.

"It'll be fine," Caleb said. "She needs you."

Derek nodded and went to her side. Caleb watched as Lizzie broke the news to Derek, who held her as she cried.

Their shared grief made his heart hurt, but Derek stayed with Lizzie and it was clear they were in love.

He envied them.

Why envy them? Do something about it. You can have love too.

He wanted more.

But right now, he had to think about Lizzie and the next steps on the road to her recovery.

Derek came out. "I'm going to get some water."

"Everything will be okay," Caleb said.

Derek smiled. "I know. I'm just glad she's here. I love her, Dr. Norris."

"I know you do. And please call me Caleb."

Derek nodded. "Thanks. She'd like to see you. She's a bit groggy."

"Thanks."

He went over to Lizzie's bed. She'd fallen asleep again.

Caleb nodded slowly and touched his daughter's pale face. She looked so small and fragile in that big hospital bed. Yet Lizzie was stronger than he thought.

She was stronger than him.

He had been foregoing love because he didn't want to hurt her. He'd been holding back his grief for the same reason. He'd wanted to protect her just like he'd promised Jane he would. Then Lizzie had said she'd dreamed about her late mother telling her to take care of him.

Lizzie was so worried about him being alone.

Which he was.

He was a fool.

"Hazel Rees is quite impressive. I've thought that all day. She should've been a surgeon," Victor remarked quietly, coming into Lizzie's room.

"Why do you say that?" Caleb asked. "Midwives are just as important as surgeons."

"That's not what I mean. Hazel thinks three steps ahead."

"She's an excellent midwife."

Victor nodded. "I wish she was on my staff."

"Does this hospital respect her though?" Caleb asked. "They don't seem to."

"We're working on it. Timothy Russell is in deep trouble with the other members of the board. I don't think he'll be around much longer. The new vice chair is more sympathetic to the vision of St. Raymond's that all the staff share."

"Working on it isn't good enough," Caleb said. "Victor, I have…"

The chief of staff took a step back. "You're leaving, aren't you?"

"Perhaps it's time I formed my own practice."

Victor smiled with approval. "I'd hate to lose you though."

"You're a good chief, but I need to start running my own life. I need to live. I need a new start and a fresh challenge."

Victor nodded. "Let me know when you're ready to talk this through further."

He left and Caleb glanced down at his daughter. He'd meant what he said about needing a fresh start. He'd never really grieved Jane fully. He'd never let her go. All these years, he'd used work to act as a buffer to keep all these feelings away.

He was numb.

Caleb sat down in the chair next to Lizzie's bed, and tears stung his eyes.

It all came out.

The pain, the loss.

It erupted out of him.

He'd been going through the motions for so many years he wasn't exactly sure how to live again. All those dreams he and Jane had shared, all the chances he'd been to afraid to take suddenly seemed possible again, and it was overwhelming.

Looking at Lizzie, who was stronger than he thought, more resilient than he gave her credit for, was begging him to return to the land of the living. When he'd met Hazel, he'd resented the board of directors for making him deal with such a headstrong, fiery woman.

It was that stubborn woman who'd breathed life back into him.

Things were going to change.

Maybe he'd blown it with Hazel, and he'd live with those consequences if that were the case, but he wasn't going to live in fear anymore. He was going to try.

"Dad?" Lizzie murmured, rousing and wincing.

He reached out and took her hand. "I'm here, sweetie."

"Where's Derek?"

"Gone for water. He'll be back." The postanesthesia care unit nurse popped her head around the door and he motioned for her to come over. She checked on Lizzie and gave her some more morphine.

"You'll feel better soon," Caleb said.

Lizzie nodded, but didn't open her eyes all the way.

"Is Hazel still here?" Lizzie asked groggily.

"No."

His daughter frowned. "I wish you'd see sense."

"What're you talking about?"

Lizzie opened her eyes. "Come on, Dad. You love her."

It shocked him. How did she know?

It's the sedatives. People are always loopy out of surgery.

Except he didn't think so.

"Okay then," he chuckled softly.

"Dad, you're blind. She totally loves you too."

"How about you concentrate on healing?"

Lizzie nodded and drifted back to sleep. Now was not the time to get into it, but Lizzie wasn't wrong.

When she was awake and not drugged up on painkillers, then he could talk to her about what to do. Maybe Lizzie would have some ideas on how to rectify the situation he was in.

Maybe she could help him figure out how to get Hazel to forgive him, because he wanted her in his life.

He wanted them all to be a family.

CHAPTER THIRTEEN

Three weeks later

HAZEL STARED OUT the window of her office, watching the rain fall. She pulled her cardigan around herself tighter. At least the cold snap was over now that summer had officially begun, and despite the rain today, they'd had a couple weeks of sunshine.

She was enjoying the summer warmth, especially after several years of living in southern Arizona.

It had been three weeks since she'd last been at St. Raymond's. She wanted to go and check on Lizzie and Caleb, but she also wanted to give them their space. She had pushed Caleb away, so it was her own fault.

When she and Mark had finished, she didn't remember feeling this kind of pain and longing. She'd just picked herself up and carried on, because she had done the right thing and walked away from him.

So why was it so sore and tender?

Why was it so lonely without Caleb here?

Because you love him.

It was like Caleb had disappeared off the map.

There was a knock on her office door and Bria poked her head in. "Feeling any better?"

"What do you mean? I'm feeling fine."

Bria cocked her eyebrow and came into her office, shutting the door behind her. She joined Hazel at the window. "Come on, be straight with me. I know a lovelorn look when I see it. Remember, I've been through heartbreak before."

"So have I."

"Don't get mad, but I don't think that you have," Bria said, defensively putting up her hands.

"What're you talking about? What about Mark?"

"He was scum," Bria said bluntly. "But I don't think that you were in love with him the same way you are with Caleb."

Hazel swallowed the lump in her throat. "Really? I'm in love with him?"

"Why are you denying it to me? I can read you like a book," Bria said.

Hazel smiled, her lips quivering. "You're right. I love him. I'm in love with him, but I think I ruined everything."

Bria put her arm around her, and Hazel leaned her head against her friend's shoulder. "I don't think you've ruined it at all, Hazel. I believe in love."

"Do you?" Hazel asked sardonically.

"Okay, well, maybe not for me, but I believe in love for others."

Hazel chuckled. "You're such a weirdo."

"Thanks. So tell me what happened in Seattle. You didn't say much when you got back."

Hazel sighed, because just thinking about that time in Seattle brought back all the memories she'd tried so hard to forget. The sensation of his strong arms around her, his kisses and the way he'd made her feel the best she ever had, because she was so in love with him.

"Caleb and I made love," she admitted.

Bria's eyes widened. "And you don't think that he cares for you?"

"Some men just want to get laid."

"And you think Caleb is like that?"

"No."

Hazel felt foolish. Caleb was not that type of man at all. She knew that the first moment he took her in his arms. Caleb was so different from Mark. She could see it now. When she was first attracted to Caleb, she'd questioned why she always fell for the wrong man.

Only this time she hadn't, and she'd ruined it anyways. She missed him.

Missed their talks.

She missed how easy it was to fall into a conversation with him.

She missed his smile, his laugh and how safe she felt in his arms.

Tears welled in her eyes and she began to cry. Like a fool.

She'd ruined everything.

They both had with their stubbornness.

Bria pulled her into an embrace and just held her for a few minutes.

"Sorry," Hazel said, sniffling. "We got into a fight. He blamed me for not telling him about his daughter. I blamed him being taken off the Patterson case, when it wasn't him."

"That's nonsense. If Caleb doesn't understand patient confidentiality, then he's an idiot."

"I don't think we can work together anymore. Him and me that is."

"You're both professionals, and if he can't see that, he wasn't the right one for you."

"The thing is, I think he is."

Bria sighed. "You're just as prideful and stubborn as he is."

"I suppose so."

"You need to go tell him how you feel. It's scary, but don't let him slip away. Trust me when I tell you that if you find love, don't let it go so easily."

They hugged again.

"I'll go see him tonight and try to make it right. Or at least I'll know the answer and not keep worrying about it."

"Right. You have a meeting with a new tenant, by the way," Bria said. "For that office space we're renting out to help fund our center."

"I do?"

Joan knocked on the door and stuck her head in. "Sorry for interrupting, but Hazel this package just came in from St. Raymond's."

Bria and Hazel exchanged surprised glances.

"Do you know what it is?" Hazel asked.

"No idea." Bria got an alert and looked at her phone. "Oh, shoot, one of my patients has gone into labor. Fill me in later about what's in the package."

Hazel nodded. "Thanks, Bria."

Her friend blew her a kiss and left.

Hazel took the package from Joan and opened it.

It was a letter from Dr. Victor Anderson with an offer of a closer working relationship between their clinic and the hospital, in particular, for Hazel. The chairman of the board, or rather the new one, had also written her a letter of apology.

Hazel was floored.

It was starting to pay off. This was what she'd devoted all her time to. She was so proud of her and Bria's clinic. It had filled a need for a long time, but there was now a part of her that wanted more than just work in her life.

She wanted good talks about books, laughter and pumpkin pie.

She wanted to be a part of Lizzie's life, more than as just her midwife, and she wanted Caleb.

And maybe a child of her own.

Her alarm went off and she cursed under her breath. She tucked the contract away.

She was glad for the privileges at St. Raymond's.

She collected what she needed and headed downstairs to meet the prospective new doctor who wanted to set up a practice. Joan had booked it, Bria had arranged it and now Hazel was going to meet the doctor.

Hazel unlocked the empty space they planned to rent out and waited.

The door opened behind her and she turned around. Her breath caught in her throat.

"Caleb? What're you doing here?"

He smiled and glanced around. "I had an appointment to see this new rental space."

"Why? You already have an office at the hospital."

"Not for long. I'm forming my own private practice. I have to work out my notice period yet, so my practice will build slowly."

"You are?"

"Yes." He took a step closer to her.

"But… You're head of obstetrics at St. Raymond's."

"Was."

"Was?"

"I quit."

"You quit?"

"I'm following a dream I had that I put on hold because I was too afraid to take a risk while raising a young child. I was numb. You inspired me though."

"I inspired you?"

"You opened the Women's Health Center. You took a chance and followed your dreams."

"Yes. I suppose I did. I'm surprised St. Raymond's offered an apology for Timothy's behavior and a promise to work with Bria and me more closely. I thought that had been your doing, but not if you've handed in your notice."

"No. Not my doing. Victor was impressed with you."

"And were you?"

"Yes. I am." Caleb smiled at her and took another step closer to her.

Her heart skipped a beat, her body trembling. "You are?"

"Yes. I'm sorry for what happened with Timothy taking you off Sandra's case. I had nothing to do with that."

"I know and I'm sorry that I overreacted. I've just… I'm so used to being let down and hurt." A tear slipped down her cheek.

"And I'm sorry for lashing out at you about Lizzie. I was scared for her, that's all. I know you couldn't tell me about the pregnancy."

"I would never, ever harm her intentionally."

"I know that." Caleb reached up and wiped the tear away with the pad of his thumb. "Hazel, I've been numb for so long. You breathed life back into me. I fell in love with you."

"Fell? Like past tense?" she teased, her body melting as she gazed up into his blue-gray twinkling eyes.

"Not past tense. I am in love with you, Hazel, and I want to be with you. Only you. I've been afraid of love for so long, afraid of losing again and having my heart broken, but you give me the strength to want to try again. You brought me back to life." He stroked her cheek and then leaned in to kiss her.

She didn't have to say anything and just melted into his arms.

Melted into his kiss.

Caleb savored the feeling of Hazel's lips against his. It had taken all of his courage to tell her how he had been feeling. He had been planning this moment for three weeks. Once Lizzie was stable, she had actually helped him plan this and got Bria in on it.

He'd wanted to make a grand gesture to let Hazel know how much she meant to him. Even though he'd be running his own practice, he'd also be able to work closely with

Hazel and consult with her whenever she needed him. He wasn't sure how it was going to go, but he was willing to put his heart on the line for her, and Lizzie was thrilled with the prospect that Hazel could be joining their family.

It had been so long since he had been in love.

Since he opened his heart, but this was what he was waiting for.

He was waiting for Hazel.

Seeing her standing there in the empty rental space took his breath away. Three weeks was too long for them to be apart. He'd missed her.

Completely.

And when he'd entered the room, all he could do was stare at her for a few moments. He was remembering each inch of her. The silken feel of her skin, the way her hair felt between his fingers.

The way she tasted.

She was everything he wanted.

His thorn.

Hazel wrapped her arms around him. Her dark eyes were full of tears, but she was smiling up at him.

"We both overreacted, and then Lizzie lost the baby and…it took me a long time to process. Can you forgive me for taking so long?"

"Only if you can forgive me for being so stubborn too," she said, leaning her head against his chest.

"Deal."

She smiled at him, the dimple showing up on her cheek, and he bent over and lightly kissed her on the lips. "I love you, Hazel."

"I love you too, Caleb. So much, it's kind of terrifying because I didn't think that I would ever fall in love again, but then I realized that I hadn't actually been in love before. So I guess I didn't think that I would ever really fall in love like this."

"Will you marry me, Hazel? Lizzie and I want you to be a part of your family."

"Yes! That sounds wonderful. Of course when you marry me, the both of you will be dragged into my big, spread out family."

"Lizzie would love that."

"She might change her mind when she meets some of my nieces and nephews," Hazel muttered. "So, are you still serious about opening a practice here?"

He looked around the small rental space. "Of course, why wouldn't I?"

"You want to work so close to your wife?" she asked, cocking an eyebrow. "We didn't exactly always see eye to eye when we first met."

"And I'm sure we'll have plenty more to discuss, but yes, this is what I want. For now. There is always the possibility that we could both sell our practices and eventually move up to Alaska."

Hazel grinned. "My parents would like that, but I think that's way off. I just started the Women's Health Center here with Bria. I'm not leaving quite yet."

"Okay, in a few years maybe?"

"Maybe," Hazel agreed.

They kissed again and then walked out of the building hand in hand.

"So, I suppose I have to call your father up and ask for permission?" Caleb asked.

"Yes, and I'm going to have to go see Lizzie and ask for her permission."

Caleb chuckled. "She's already expecting you to pay her a visit."

"Oh?"

"She's at home, and she's having her fiancé, Derek, make dinner." They stopped in front of Caleb's car and he opened the door for her.

"I suppose we need to stop by the bakery and get another pie."

"Why?" Caleb asked.

"I have to butter her up somehow," Hazel joked.

"I suppose we can stop at the bakery and get a pumpkin pie."

"And a chocolate pie too," Hazel said. "I've been craving one of those chocolate pies this last week."

Caleb laughed and shut the door. He climbed into the driver's seat and glanced over at Hazel, who was smiling back at him. He was the luckiest man in the world, and he had almost been too stubborn and let her slip right through his fingers.

He was glad that he was able to finally get his head on straight.

He was glad that he was no longer numb and that he could finally breathe again.

For the first time in a long time, he was alive and he was glad to be alive. He had a lot to be thankful for.

He'd had to deal with the thorn in his side, and he'd been pricked by that thorn and fallen in love just like a kind of crazy fairy tale.

He had found his happily-ever-after with his beautiful rose.

EPILOGUE

Six months later

IT WAS COLD out and snow was falling.

The park service warned them that the path to the Benson Bridge would be too icy to traverse, and that was fine. Hazel just wanted their wedding picture to be taken in front of the falls; she didn't have to be in front of the bridge.

Bria had tried to convince her to wait until the spring or summer to get married, but Hazel hadn't wanted to wait that long. They had been together long enough. She was tired of waiting.

She honestly couldn't wait that long anyway, because in the early autumn she was due to give birth.

Hazel still couldn't believe what had happened the last time they'd had a night to themselves. She had been on the pill, but it was not infallible and right before she was about to walk down the aisle to marry the man of her dreams, she'd just peed on a stick and discovered that she was going to have a baby.

She was staring at the plus sign in disbelief.

"Well?" Bria asked.

"It's positive," Hazel said in shock.

"Well, that's wonderful!"

"It is."

It was everything that Hazel had always dreamed of, but

she and Caleb had plans and a baby wasn't part of those plans right now. What was she going to tell him?

"Do you want me to get him?" Bria asked.

"It's bad luck to see the bride before the wedding," Hazel said automatically.

"Oh, come on, it's not that bad." Bria got up and put on her parka over her simple bridesmaid dress. "You have to tell him."

Hazel nodded. "Yes, it's going to distract me for the whole service if I don't tell him."

"I'll send him in."

Bria disappeared and Hazel stared at the stick again.

Everyone would be arriving to the Multnomah Falls lodge where they were having their wedding. It was a small wedding, but a lot of her family had managed to fly in, despite the winter weather. She didn't want to delay the service any longer than she had to, but she had to see Caleb and tell him the news.

She was kicking herself that she hadn't seen the signs, herself, earlier.

She was a midwife, after all.

Caleb didn't see them either and he's an obstetrician.

Caleb walked into the bridal change room and he looked concerned, but then his gaze raked over her body in a way that made her tremble.

"You're absolutely stunning."

Hazel blushed. "Thanks."

Then his eyes fell to the stick that she was still holding in her hands and he paled. "Is that…is that a pregnancy test?"

She nodded. "I'm pregnant."

Caleb didn't say anything at first, and she began to panic.

"I know it's not part of our immediate plans, but I'm pregnant and I'm pretty happy about it. Shocked, but happy."

Caleb pulled her up into his arms and held her. "I'm

happy too. I guess I'm a little shocked as well. When did it happen?"

"That night when we both were off duty and Lizzie had moved in with Derek. The night in the living room, remember?" she teased.

He grinned. "That would make sense."

"I can't believe I didn't notice my symptoms sooner."

"Ditto." He reached down and touched her belly. "I'm really thrilled, Hazel. Another child."

"Do you think that Lizzie will be okay with this? She'll be nineteen years older than the baby."

"Are you kidding? She wants a brother or a sister. She'd gladly take one of each."

"One of each!" Hazel fake swooned and then set down the pregnancy test. She wrapped her arms around his neck.

"It would be perfect."

Hazel cocked an eyebrow. "Perfect, eh?"

"Your parents will be thrilled to have another grandchild."

"Grandchildren," Hazel corrected him. "They have already claimed Lizzie as one of theirs."

He smiled. "Yes. That means so much to me."

"You mean so much to me." She reached up and kissed him. The kiss deepened as his hands went around her, pulling her flush against his body.

"Why don't we skip the wedding?" he murmured in her ear, nibbling down her neck in a way that made her blood heat.

"No. We can't do that. Everyone flew in to see us get married. We have to go do that."

Caleb groaned. "I suppose, but I feel a bit put out. You're so gorgeous. I just want to carry you off to bed."

"You can do that later," she said with a smile. "You might as well get it while you can. Soon I'm going to be too big."

"That won't stop me," Caleb whispered.

"You're awful." Except that she was so in love with him. Everything he said or did thrilled her, and she was incredibly happy right now. She was getting the family she'd always wanted. She had Lizzie as a great daughter and now she was secretly hoping for a boy, but she didn't care either way as long the baby was healthy.

Everything was working out right.

She was never one to believe in fairy tales or happily-ever-afters and she certainly didn't believe in Prince Charmings, but somehow the one man that she sworn she had to resist was her knight in shining armor after all.

The man who drove her crazy, who'd grated on her nerves the first time she'd met him and who now drove her wild with passion. The man she loved more than anything else, and he was finally going to be her husband.

"We better go." Caleb sighed. "The ceremony is about to start."

"Yes, but I do have one more thing to show you."

He cocked an eyebrow. "Oh, and what's that?"

She lifted her dress slightly and showed him what she was wearing underneath, in particular on her feet. It wasn't glass slippers, but she knew he would like it all the same.

"Rainbow toe socks," he chuckled.

"The source of my power. Like I said."

"You did say that, and I hope that you wear them in bed tonight."

Hazel laughed and took his hand as they headed out into the lodge to join their families legally.

Their hearts were already joined.

A family forever.

* * * * *

THE MIDWIFE
FROM HIS PAST

JULIE DANVERS

MILLS & BOON

For Karlynn, who got those quintuplets out safely.

CHAPTER ONE

BRIA THOMAS HAD spotted an impostor.

She and her best friend, Hazel Rees, strolled along the bank of Willamette River, both with a coffee in hand. Portland's weekly open-air market bustled around them, the voices of hagglers mingling in the early fall air with the strains of music from street performers.

"There," Bria said, gesturing with her coffee-laden hand. "That woman with the tan coat. She's definitely a spy."

"Are you sure?" asked Hazel. "She seems pretty ordinary to me."

"That's exactly what a spy would want you to think. She may look plain on the outside, but that handbag of hers probably holds all kinds of State Department secrets."

There was nothing Bria loved more than getting coffee with Hazel and going to Portland's Saturday Market. Like Bria, Hazel was a midwife, although her friend was a nurse practitioner, too, and the two of them were cofounders of the Multnomah Falls Women's Health Center. Pulling double duty as midwives and starting up a nonprofit organization had kept them extremely busy, but now that it was up and running, spending Saturday morning together had come to be a fiercely protected tradition, no matter how much work they had to do. The two of them would spend hours concocting elaborate backstories for people in the crowd. The human statue performing on the corner was actually in the witness protection program, hiding from the Mob in plain sight. The cyclist pausing for a drink on the sidewalk was a world-class athlete, training for glory after tragically losing everything years ago.

The spy moved on to another booth, examining various pieces of jewelry crafted by local artists.

"Hmm. Perhaps you're right," Hazel agreed, taking a sip of her coffee. "Ooh! Secret billionaire to the left." She nodded toward a man in a large hat and cowboy boots.

"*Secret* billionaire? How can you tell?"

Hazel laughed. "Bria Thomas. You, of all people, should know a secret billionaire when you see one."

"I guess I've lost my touch." Bria moved to tuck her hair behind her ears, an old habit from before she'd gotten the pixie cut that now framed her large green eyes. She didn't miss the dark waves that had once fallen around her shoulders—she'd always been petite, and all that hair had only made her look shorter. But she occasionally forgot that it wasn't there anymore. She'd been through so many changes over the past few years that sometimes it was hard to keep up with them.

Once, Bria might have been as skilled at picking the well-bred and wealthy out of a crowd as she was at spotting a real Prada handbag from a mountain of designer knockoffs. Her family was one of the oldest and wealthiest in Portland. But taking her family's money had also meant accepting being under their control. She'd stepped down from her family's trust years ago, deciding that she preferred independence to living in a gilded cage. Her life was drastically different than it used to be, back when her idea of a relaxing Saturday morning involved a trip to the Maldives by private jet, or a few days at an exclusive spa. But it was her life, and while it might not be glamorous, she was proud of what she'd been able to accomplish. She loved her career as a midwife, and she had good friends like Hazel in her life. And as far as her love life was concerned…well, she supposed one couldn't have everything.

Dating had never been easy for her. It had been years since she'd had anyone serious in her life. Part of that was because of her work. Up until last year, she'd spent two years working for an international aid organization in Haiti. There hadn't been many dating opportunities while working abroad, and she'd preferred it that way. In her experience, dating led to misunderstandings, hurt feelings and heartbreak, and she'd wanted to focus on her career without the complications that accompanied romance.

But she also wanted to have a family someday. She knew, of course, that it was possible to have a child on her own, but she'd always dreamed of having a family built on the love between herself and someone else. The trouble was, her attempts to find that someone else ranged from bad to completely disastrous.

When she'd returned from Haiti last year, she'd tried to ease herself back into the dating scene. But thus far, her attempts at dating had only led to a string of awful romantic encounters. There'd been the man she'd met online who turned out to be married—fortunately she'd found out after just a few weeks. Another man claimed to be looking for a long-term relationship, but he really just wanted to use Bria as his cat sitter whenever he went out of town, which seemed to be every single weekend. Another had texted frequently but canceled at the last minute every time they'd made plans to meet in person.

Frustrated and discouraged, she'd decided to take a break from dating. But that hadn't stopped Hazel from trying to nudge her toward men whenever possible. At the moment, Hazel seemed to have set her sights on one target in particular.

"I'm telling you, Bria, he's a secret billionaire. He probably thinks he's fooling everyone by walking around in those dusty, worn-out jeans—which are quite flattering to the figure, I must say—but the quality of the boots gives him away. And I don't see a wedding ring." She raised her eyebrows meaningfully at Bria.

Bria shook her head. "Nice try. With my luck, Mr. Secret Billionaire over there would probably turn out to be Mr. Secret Serial Killer." She knew that Hazel meant well, but she also thought that Hazel tended to think about relationships through the biased lens of her own success. Hazel had found her own happiness with Dr. Caleb Norris, who until recently had been chief of obstetrics at St. Raymond's, the birthing hospital across from the Women's Health Center. Bria knew that Hazel simply wanted her to find as much happiness as she had. But Bria was starting to doubt that she'd ever have a real chance at love. Her attempts at relationships had at best led to awkwardness and discomfort... and at worst, life-shattering heartbreak. She'd been through that kind of heartbreak once in her life, and she had no desire to repeat the experience.

"How's Caleb feeling about leaving St. Raymond's now that he's finished working out his notice?" she asked Hazel, hoping to change the subject. "Have they found a replacement for him yet?" Caleb had quit his job at the hospital so he could set up his own private practice at the Women's Health Center as an obstetrician, as he'd developed a desire to do more holistic work with patients. Bria was excited to have a physician of Caleb's ability available to them, as that would only help the center's reputation grow. Normally, Hazel's eyes brightened whenever the subject of Caleb came up. But Bria was surprised to see Hazel's brow tighten with worry.

"Hazel? Is something wrong?"

"Look... I need to tell you something. And there's no easy way to say it."

Bria instantly felt guilty. Here she was obsessing over her own problems with love and dating when Hazel needed to talk about something. "What is it? The center didn't lose more money, did it?" Although the Multnomah Falls Women's Health Center was wildly popular among patients, many of their clients couldn't afford to pay for the entire cost of their care, and the center was dependent on grants and donations. Recently, a major donor had decided to shift their funding to other causes, which had left Bria and Hazel scrambling to find new sources of support.

"No—nothing new has happened in that department. And don't worry, I know that if we keep working on the problem, we'll find a solution. I wanted to talk to you about Caleb's replacement at St. Raymond's."

"Why would you need to talk to me about that?"

"Because they've found someone who can take over for him. Not permanently, but for a few weeks, so that they have time to conduct a thorough search for the new chief of obstetrics." Hazel sighed. "I've been dreading telling you this all morning, ever since I heard who it was. It's Eliot. Eliot Wright."

Bria almost dropped her coffee cup. "Eliot's coming back?" Her voice was barely a whisper.

"He's the one you used to date, isn't he?"

They'd been engaged, actually. Six years ago, she'd had a fiancé for less than a week—until her father had ruined everything.

Hazel looked mortified. "I didn't realize until this morning, or I swear I'd have told you sooner. Caleb never told me the new doctor's name. He just said it was an obstetrician from Boston, a good friend of his from when he did his residency there. And then this morning over breakfast I told him that you used to date a medical student who'd gone to Boston to finish his residency, and that's when Caleb told me a bit about the new doctor, and I realized it was *the* Eliot Wright. I was furious with Caleb for not telling me sooner, but he said—" Hazel abruptly cut herself off, as though she'd suddenly said too much.

"He said what?"

"He…said that Eliot had never mentioned you to him at all."

Bria tried not to feel hurt. She told herself that she didn't have any *right* to feel hurt. She'd broken up with him, after all.

Still. Had Eliot really not mentioned her to his friend at all?

Had he even thought of her again once he'd left for Boston?

She tried to regain her composure, for Hazel's sake. There was no need for her friend to look so worried. Six years was a long time. She and Eliot were ancient history. True, she was surprised to learn that he was coming back to Portland. But it was only surprise, not devastation, or grief, or any of the other terrible feelings she'd had when Eliot left. It wasn't as though she still had feelings for him.

When they'd broken up, she'd fallen into a deep well of heartbreak, and she'd spent most of the last six years climbing out of that well. It hadn't been easy, but she'd done it. She'd done it by focusing on the future, and by refusing to allow herself to dwell on painful memories.

It had been incredibly hard. She'd had to accept that Eliot was gone, and to let go of her dreams of the life they'd planned together. But, painful as it all had been, she'd managed to do it. And if he was back in Portland now, then she could not, would not allow his return to disrupt the hard-won stability she'd finally found here.

She'd had no reason to feel the pang that shot through her heart when Hazel said that Eliot had never mentioned her to Caleb. *I was just surprised to hear his name*, she thought.

"I'm really sorry," Hazel continued. "I should have asked

Caleb more about his friend from Boston sooner. I should have realized that it might be Eliot."

"It's not your fault. Eliot and I dated before you and I met in nursing school. And there are a lot of obstetricians in Boston. There was no reason for you to guess it might be him." She probably shouldn't be surprised that Eliot hadn't talked to Caleb about her, either. Why would he ever bring up an ex-girlfriend to a close friend?

You told Hazel about him. True, but she had none of the difficulty with vulnerability that Eliot had. As she recalled, Eliot had rarely spoken of anything personal to anyone. He was a compassionate man with a deep desire for closeness, but he'd also built heavily fortified emotional walls for himself. His protective outer shell had been the source of so many of their problems. She'd longed to reach the inner warmth that she knew was there within him, but so often, his guardedness made that impossible. She was always left guessing at what he was thinking and feeling because he couldn't lower his defenses enough to let her know.

If he could, then maybe their breakup wouldn't have ended in the worst way possible.

They'd met shortly after she'd graduated college, when he was in his final year of medical school. They hadn't met on campus, but in her home: Eliot's mother cleaned houses for many of the families in Portland and had worked for Bria's father for years. Bria had often heard Eliot's mother speak of her son, who was going to be a doctor, but they'd never actually met until Eliot had appeared on her doorstep to give his mother a ride home. As Bria got to know him, she realized there was an authenticity to him that she hadn't felt with anyone else in her father's world, where everyone seemed preoccupied with their own wealth and self-importance.

They began dating, and things quickly became serious. They might have been young, but they both knew what they wanted. When Eliot asked her to come with him to Boston for his residency—as his wife—her response had been a heartfelt *yes*.

But then her father had interfered, as she should have known he would. The only thing Calvin Thomas loved more than money was control.

In addition to being the head of Portland's wealthiest family, Bria's father was also a retired surgeon. His wealth and privilege had given him lofty ideas of the respect due to the Thomas family. Both of Bria's sisters had lived up to their father's expectations and married men who came from families with generations of inherited wealth.

But Eliot's situation was different. He was raised by a single mother with very little money. He'd funded most of his education through scholarships and student loans. Calvin was convinced that Eliot's only interest in Bria was her family's fortune. Even if Eliot hadn't been deep in debt with student loans, there was the insurmountable fact of his background: Eliot simply wasn't good enough for her.

Bria didn't believe that for a minute. And when her father realized his threats to cut her off from the family trust wouldn't work, he changed tactics and threatened Eliot instead. He'd warned her that if she didn't break off her engagement, he'd do everything he could to ruin Eliot's career.

Bria knew her father would follow through with his threat. He was a major donor to numerous medical charities and sat on the board of more than one medical philanthropic organization. As a former surgeon, he still had connections in the medical field. If he'd made a concerted effort to hold Eliot back, she knew he would have been successful.

And she could not be an obstacle in Eliot's career. She knew how hard he'd worked, and how much his mother had sacrificed, to get him through medical school. She could not live with herself if she stood in the way of his success.

She couldn't tell him what her father had done, because Eliot wasn't the kind of man who backed down in the face of threats. But Eliot didn't know Calvin Thomas like she did. He didn't know what he was up against. Devastated as she was, she knew the safest course of action for him was for her to break things off with him and hope that he would find happiness with someone else.

She'd written him a note, an awful, horrible note, telling him that she'd changed her mind. They were from two different worlds, and they couldn't possibly be happy together. She'd tried to be convincing, because otherwise he'd find out she was lying to him, and then her father's threats would come out. But perhaps she'd not been convincing enough, because he'd shown up at her home, demanding to hear from her in person that she meant all that she'd written.

The result was an argument that grew far more heated than she'd expected. He accused her of being utterly selfish. He said he couldn't believe how shallow and materialistic she was. And even though she knew that, to an extent, his reaction was understandable, his accusations still hurt. She'd spent her life trying to prove that her privilege hadn't made her selfish, or materialistic, or proud, and now here was Eliot, a man she'd loved and trusted more than anyone, accusing her of being exactly those things. She tried not to fire back at him, because he didn't know the whole story, but his words had burned. And eventually she did lash out, because he knew where she was sensitive, and just what to say to shock her.

He'd told her that she was a naive, spoiled, out-of-touch princess whose money insulated her from any real-life issues. She'd responded that she'd never realized what he really thought of her, or how cold and uncaring he could be. They'd traded insults for a while, and when they finally parted, it was with far more hurt and anger and pain on both sides than Bria would have ever thought possible.

She'd never known just how sensitive he was about her family's money and status, because he hadn't told her how he felt. Nor had she realized that he could see her exactly the way she'd always feared people would: as shallow and privileged, with no understanding of how the real world worked. Their marriage never would have worked with all that resentment locked inside him.

There was one silver lining to the breakup, despite all the misery involved. Breaking the engagement had given her a stark clarity about the amount of control her father and his money had over her life. She was determined that Calvin Thomas would never be able to control her or anyone else she cared about in that way again. And so she'd removed herself from her family's trust, despite her father's derisive assurances that she would never be able to survive on her own. She'd gotten a job and used the income from that and her personal savings to pay for a nurse-midwifery program, where she'd met Hazel. She'd managed to build a new life for herself that was very different from the one she'd had before, but she absolutely loved it. It might be a smaller life, but it was all hers, and she was proud of her independence.

She wasn't the same woman she'd been when Eliot had last seen her. She was far more self-possessed, far less naive and far more knowledgeable of the world. So there was no reason Eliot's return should disrupt her life. She'd managed to recover from all the hurt they'd caused each other, and she hoped he had, too.

In fact, maybe it was a good thing that Eliot was returning. How else would she be able to prove to herself that she'd made peace with their breakup unless they saw one another again? Now that he was back, she'd have a chance to greet him calmly, one medical professional to another, and to show him all the confidence and independence she'd gained. After six years, she should be able to manage that.

"It's going to be fine," she told Hazel with all the certainty she could muster. "Eliot and I have been over for a long time, and I've never wished him anything but a happy life of his own."

Hazel still looked skeptical.

"Really, Hazel. It'll be all right. Given the amount of work we have at the center, I'm going to be far too busy while he's here to dwell on the past."

As if to prove Bria's point, the emergency on-call phone began to buzz. "See?" Bria said, holding up the phone. "I barely have time to spend with *you*."

Hazel still looked unconvinced. "If you need a little time to process all this, Bria, I could take that call for you."

"Absolutely not," said Bria. "Duty calls, and anyway, it's your turn for a day off." She opened the phone. "Multnomah Falls Midwives," she said with a firm glance at Hazel that brooked no further negotiation. "How can I help?"

Even though it meant the end of her relaxing Saturday morning, Bria was grateful for the emergency call. Work had always been a refuge for her.

After the breakup with Eliot, she'd realized how desperate she was to escape her father's control. But she'd also realized how much she wanted to do something meaningful with her life. Calvin had been scornful of her decision to become a midwife. In his mind, midwifery wasn't as prestigious as becoming a surgeon. But Bria hadn't wanted prestige. Her mother had passed away when she was in college, and she'd found herself feeling drawn to the bond between mothers and newborns. There was something about the experience of birth that made her feel close to all mothers in general, and to her own mother in particular.

She couldn't imagine any career as rewarding as midwifery. Birth was a sacred ritual, shared by every human being. It was all the more meaningful if she could help women give birth in their homes, with their loved ones close at hand.

But babies had a way of coming in their own time, rather than when they were expected. And the Schroeder family's fifth baby was about to make its way into the world nearly a month early.

Bria raced to the Schroeder house, trying to keep her car within the speed limit. She'd asked Hazel to call for an ambulance to St. Raymond's before she left. She didn't anticipate any difficulties, as Mrs. Schroeder's pregnancy had progressed without complication—until now. Still, with a premature baby, it was best not to take any chances.

Mrs. Schroeder was inclined to agree. "It's too early," she said, her face worried as she clasped Bria's hand.

"Don't be afraid," Bria replied. "I've delivered babies earlier than this. We're going to be fine. But for now, I need you to start breathing, just as we practiced." She pulled back the sheets to begin her assessment and asked Mr. Schroeder to bring more towels.

As Bria felt for the baby's head, she felt a thick loop fall into her hand. Her blood ran cold. A prolapsed umbilical cord. She took in a long, slow breath, trying to steady herself. Thank goodness Hazel had already called the ambulance. Even now, she was relieved to hear sirens in the distance.

"What is it?" asked Mrs. Schroeder, noting Bria's worried expression. "What's wrong?"

Adrenaline rushed through Bria's veins, as it always did during a medical emergency. "The umbilical cord has dropped past the cervix and is coming out before the baby's head."

"Is that bad?" said Mr. Schroeder, who had returned.

"It's something we need to take care of right away,"

said Bria. A prolapsed cord was a serious emergency. Mrs. Schroeder needed to be transported to the hospital for a cesarean section as soon as possible.

Bria adopted her calmest demeanor. "Hear those sirens outside? Since Mrs. Schroeder went into labor so early, my colleague Hazel called an ambulance before I left. And that's a very good thing, as now we do need to get Mrs. Schroeder to the hospital right away. If you'll be so kind as to head downstairs to let them in, Mr. Schroeder, then I can help Mrs. Schroeder until the paramedics arrive." Mr. Schroeder nodded and rushed downstairs.

"Now," said Bria to her patient, "it's very important that you don't push. We need to keep the baby's head from pressing against the umbilical cord. I'm going to hold the baby away from the cord until we can get you to the hospital, where they'll do a cesarean."

Mrs. Schroeder looked at her with pleading eyes. "But you'll stay with me until then?"

Bria smiled. "All the way."

The ambulance would have Mrs. Schroeder at the hospital within minutes, but until then, her only option was to manually push the baby's head away from the umbilical cord until they arrived.

She explained this to Mrs. Schroeder, who grimaced. "I hope you've got strong arms."

"I do," Bria replied, with a wink. "But we'll both have to be strong now. Your job is to keep doing your breathing, stay relaxed and *not push*. Meanwhile, I'm just going to hold the baby in position for…for as long as it takes."

Bria kept her right arm extended, as still and straight as she could make it. She wasn't sure how long she could hold her arm like that. The answer, she supposed, was for as long as was necessary. No matter how tired her arm was, she wasn't going to let go of the baby's head.

Though how the paramedics were going to get her and Mrs. Schroeder down the stairs was a mystery.

One thing at a time, Bria told herself. *Focus on holding the baby's head for now. You can worry about the stairs later.*

She hadn't been lying when she'd told Mrs. Schroeder she had strong arms. She was a midwife; upper-arm strength came with the territory. But as a bead of sweat formed on her forehead, she couldn't help thinking that the sooner the paramedics reached them, the better.

She could feel the baby's pulse through the umbilical cord. The steady throb reassured her that the baby wasn't in distress. If she could keep holding the baby in position until the cesarean was performed, all would be well. Probably.

A clatter on the stairs informed her that help had arrived. "Prolapsed cord," Bria called as they entered the room. "I'm holding the head away from the cord."

"Great," said the first paramedic in the room. "Keep doing that." She addressed Mrs. Schroeder. "Ma'am, we need to get you down these stairs and out the door. So my colleagues and I are going to lift you onto this stretcher while your midwife keeps making sure the baby is getting enough oxygen."

"What does that mean?" asked Mrs. Schroeder.

"It means the three of you—mother, baby and midwife—are all about to go for a ride," the paramedic replied.

Climbing onto the stretcher between the knees of a pregnant woman, while holding a baby in position and keeping her right arm perfectly still, was a gymnastic feat Bria hadn't known she was capable of. The paramedics helped her find her footing as she focused on holding the baby's head in place.

"Don't be afraid, Mrs. Schroeder," Bria said as the paramedics lifted the stretcher and then tilted it to begin their descent down the stairs. "The good thing about going down these stairs is that it puts you exactly in the position we want. We need to keep your head below your feet to keep the pressure off the cord, right up until we can get baby out." That part was true enough: with a prolapsed cord, Mrs. Schroeder would need to give birth in Trendelenburg position, with her head tilted below her feet. It was just that the Trendelenburg position didn't typically involve mother and midwife both being hoisted into the air, the midwife unable to move one arm and clinging to the stretcher with the other for dear life.

Her right arm was aching now, but she didn't dare move it. By the time they arrived at the landing, both she and Mrs. Schroeder were covered in sweat.

"The hard part's over now," she said to Mrs. Schroeder. "Compared to getting down those stairs, driving to the hospital and getting baby out safely will be a breeze." Her arm was starting to go numb, but Bria barely felt it, bolstered by the adrenaline and the knowledge that they would be at St. Raymond's within minutes. She could hold this baby's head for five more minutes. She could hold it forever, if that was what it took to see it delivered safely.

Fortunately, forever wasn't necessary. The ambulance reached St. Raymond's in record time. The paramedics placed the stretcher holding Bria and Mrs. Schroeder onto a gurney, and they burst through the doors of the obstetrics department before Bria even had time to take note of her surroundings. She began shouting out the medical history to the obstetrician on duty the moment they entered the room.

"Multigravida in preterm labor, cervix dilated to—" And her voice faltered.

Because the obstetrician on duty was Eliot.

Eliot was already working at St. Raymond's.

As focused as she'd been on her patient while on the way to hospital, she hadn't had a moment to consider that she might be about to run into Eliot for the first time in six years. But now he stood in front of her. Just over six feet of tall, dark and handsome. His hair, so dark it was almost black, fell over his forehead, a few wayward strands brushing against familiar brown eyes. His body had always been lithe and graceful, but from the way his white coat outlined his shoulders, he seemed to have put on more muscle than when she'd last known him. His jaw was a firm, contoured line, but his lips were as alluring as she remembered.

Her traitorous heart was performing backflips. She'd tried so hard to convince both herself and Hazel that she was Completely Fine with Eliot working at St. Raymond's, but now it was obvious that she Completely Wasn't. Now that he was here, inches away from her, his body towering over her and smelling faintly of cinnamon, just as it always had, and his eyes were glowering at her with an intensity she couldn't recall ever seeing in them before.

"Well?" he barked. His voice brought her back into the room. "How long has she been having contractions? What's the fetal heart rate?"

Bria tried to respond, but it was as though the words couldn't get past her throat. She knew what she wanted to say—and her lips actually formed the words—but somehow, she couldn't get them out.

"Let's go," he said, a note of impatience entering his voice. She couldn't exactly blame him. She wanted to speak—she'd hadn't thought, that morning, that she would have any trouble speaking to him—but now, with all six feet two of him in the flesh beside her, she couldn't seem to find her voice.

He turned away, clearly exasperated. "We'll begin anesthesia immediately." Numerous nurses bustled about the room, preparing for surgery, drawing blood and setting up monitors for mother and baby.

Her right arm was very tired. She tried to distract herself from the numbing sensation spreading from her fingers to her elbow by thinking about other things. Clouds. Happy dogs. Coffee with Hazel. Exes that suddenly reappeared without warning.

She would not have moved her hand from the baby's head under any circumstances, but she would be damned if she failed in her duty as a midwife in front of Eliot Wright. Whatever else he thought of her, she was determined to make him see that she was competent and professional. She gritted her teeth and held her arm stiff and motionless.

She was so focused on keeping still that she didn't notice that Eliot had returned to her side.

"The baby's heart tones on the monitor look reassuring," he said. Bria let out a careful breath of relief at the news.

"Then there's no fetal distress?" She was pleased that she'd recovered her voice. As long as they kept their focus on the patient, she should be fine.

"So far, so good. You've done well. You'll only need to hold the head for a few minutes more."

Bria kept her arm straight as Eliot began the cesarean. *Just a little more*, she told herself. *You can make it through this. Just a little bit longer.*

Whether she was referring to her rapidly numbing arm, or standing near Eliot, she wasn't quite sure.

When he finally pulled the baby from Mrs. Schroeder's womb—a girl, with a healthy set of lungs—Bria felt the surge of tears that pricked at the corners of her eyes with every birth. She eased her arm back, rubbing her elbow to bring back circulation. For just a moment, she was lost in joy and relief as the other nurses patted her on the back and Eliot's familiar smile turned from the baby toward her.

But then their eyes met, and her heart sank as the smile faded from his face.

"Well," he said, gruffly. "A fine job done by all."

"Eliot," she began, without even the faintest idea of what she could say next.

"Excuse me," he cut in. "I need to see to other patients."
And without another word, he left the room, leaving Bria
with a numb feeling that had nothing to do with the stiff-
ness in her arm.

CHAPTER TWO

ELIOT HAD SPENT nearly six years trying not to think about Bria Thomas. It hadn't been easy to recover from having his heart shattered into a million pieces, but he thought he'd done an admirable job of moving on with his life after Bria broke off their engagement. Once, he'd thought he wouldn't be able to live without her, but that was before he'd learned that she wasn't the person he'd thought she was.

Their lives were very different—she'd been the child of wealth and privilege, while he'd grown up among the wealthy, but not one of them. His first impression of Bria was that she was just another one of the snobbish elite who felt themselves better than Portland's working class, but as he'd gotten to know her better, he'd formed a different impression. She'd seemed down-to-earth, caring and adventurous, and he'd thought she was the woman he wanted to spend the rest of his life with.

They'd had one blissful year together before the night he learned just how wrong he'd been about her. Not only did she not want to marry him—she'd changed her mind only days after accepting his proposal—but during their breakup, she also confirmed his worst fear: that after growing up in such a rich and powerful family, a life with him wouldn't satisfy her. *Two different worlds*, she'd said. The phrase still infuriated him. There was only one world, and he'd thought they could find a place for both of them in it.

But she'd made it clear that that wasn't what she wanted, and if she didn't want to marry him, there wasn't much he could do besides let her go.

Over the past six years, he'd finished his residency in Boston, started a private practice, participated in a few extremely successful business ventures and spent plenty of time *not* thinking about Bria. But not thinking about her was a lot easier when he wasn't working with her.

More than thirty-six hours had passed since his encounter with Bria, and he still felt shaken. He'd had no idea that she'd become a midwife, let alone that she was working at a women's health center across the street from St. Raymond's. He'd known there was a chance she might still live in Portland, but as he'd planned to spend most of his time at the hospital, he'd thought avoiding her would simply be a matter of staying away from restaurants they used to go to. He'd assumed his chances of running into her were slim.

Apparently, his assumptions couldn't have been more wrong.

Any hope he had of avoiding her evaporated as he learned more about the close relationship between St. Raymond's and the Multnomah Falls Women's Health Center. The two facilities shared patients regularly. Not only was he not going to be able to avoid Bria, he'd probably have to work with her frequently.

And he had no idea yet how he was going to handle it.

He sat over his lunch in his office at St. Raymond's, glaring at his computer screen. Monday at noon, his schedule read. Tour of Multnomah Falls Women's Health Center.

Dr. Victor Anderson, the hospital's chief of staff, had urged him to get to know the center so that he would be familiar with the experiences of their shared patients when they arrived at St. Raymond's, and so he would know the layout of the center if he was called there for an emergency. It was a completely practical suggestion, yet Eliot couldn't help feeling as though the universe was conspiring to throw him into Bria's path. He was dreading the tour.

Come on, she's just an ex, he thought. *It's hardly the most stressful thing you'll face this week.*

He wished he could believe that was true. Over the weekend he'd dealt with two sets of twins and a placental abruption, but none of it had left him reeling as much as his encounter with Bria. He felt embarrassed by the brusque way he'd treated her on Saturday. No matter what was in their past, they were both medical professionals, and he should have acted accordingly. Eliot had great respect for midwives, who could afford to spend more time with their patients and often got to know them better than physicians. But by barking questions at Bria like he had, he'd probably come off as exactly the kind of elitist obstetrician he couldn't stand.

His curtness had been a clumsy attempt to cover his shock at seeing her again. Most people would have grown flustered by his manner. But instead of jumping to respond, Bria had remained silent, patiently waiting for him to settle down and address her more professionally. He'd been impressed, and a little ashamed, of the way she'd waited for him to collect himself. Fortunately, he'd been able to focus on the patient and the emergency at hand, but he was certain she'd noticed that it had taken a moment for him to recover from seeing her.

He couldn't believe how different she'd looked—and how familiar. Her dark brown hair was now cropped into a pixie cut, with short strands that framed her face and accentuated her large green eyes. He couldn't help noticing how well it suited her, even though a small part of him might secretly miss the feeling of running his hands through the tresses that once fell to her shoulders. Despite the surface changes, there was a warmth about her that felt the same as it ever had. She radiated a calmness about her that was almost palpable, even as an emergency swirled about them.

There had been a time when he'd taken great comfort in that calmness. Trusted it enough to open up to her in a way he'd never opened himself to anyone before. He wouldn't make the same mistake again.

For years, Eliot had tried to avoid ruminating over their breakup, but now the memories came racing back. She could have given him any number of reasons for breaking off their engagement, but she'd chosen the one that would hurt worst of all. She'd told him that she'd realized they couldn't relate to one another because they were from different worlds. She'd meant that she was accustomed to the finer things in life, things that he would probably never grow to appreciate, no matter how hard he worked or how successful he became. And the fact of their different backgrounds was something that would never change, no matter what other work they put into their relationship.

At first, he couldn't believe those words were coming from her. He was certain her father had influenced her. He knew Calvin Thomas—his mother had introduced him to the man in high school, thinking that her son who wanted to be a doctor might benefit from getting to know a renowned retired surgeon. And Calvin, flattered, had paternalistically taken Eliot aside and given him advice about how to prepare for medical school. Even then, Calvin had struck Eliot as a pompous man with an inflated sense of self-importance. And years later, when he'd begun dating Bria, he found that Calvin still held rigid, outdated ideas about class differences.

But Bria had often criticized her father for holding those opinions, for caring so much about money, and so it had come as a complete surprise to suddenly hear her parroting his words. She'd insisted that they were her own words— that her father hadn't pressured her or threatened her. She'd thought it over, she'd said, and there were just too many reasons their relationship wouldn't work. He couldn't afford to give her the kind of lifestyle she was used to. True, she could buy things on her own, but would a man as proud as Eliot really be comfortable with an arrangement like that? The condescension in her voice had galled him. And her words had hurt all the more because they rang true: he didn't want Bria to pay for everything in their lives. He didn't want to be her prince consort, hovering in the background while she made all the financial decisions.

The more he'd felt as though she was talking down to him, the more heated their conversation became, until eventually they were shouting at each other. Finally, he'd pleaded with her that even though he might not be able to afford the lifestyle she was used to, at least they'd have each other.

Yes, she'd responded, *but we wouldn't have anything else.*

It had been those words, more than anything, that finally convinced him that she meant it when she said she didn't love him and had changed her mind about marrying him. He'd thought, perhaps hoped, that her father was behind her decision, but he didn't think she would try to cut him so deeply unless the way she felt about him really had changed.

And so he'd left. Moved on. Tried to accept that he was probably better off without someone who'd turned out to be so materialistic and shallow. He wouldn't make the same mistake of trusting her again. Even if he did have to work with her for the next few weeks.

At least she seemed to be a competent midwife. No matter what bitterness he might feel about their breakup, he had to admit he was impressed with how she'd responded to her patient's crisis. The way she'd held that baby perfectly in place—God only knew how long she'd been holding the head before reaching the hospital. Her arm must have been terribly sore. But she'd done what was required, without complaint. And she'd seemed genuinely concerned for her patient. He recalled the relief in her eyes when he'd reassured her there was no sign of fetal distress. She'd always had such large, expressive eyes. And now that he had a moment to think about it, other memories came to mind: memories of those eyes staring at him over a pillow, of her arms reaching for him...

He couldn't let himself indulge in old memories. His time at St. Raymond's was supposed to give him six weeks immersed in the medical world so that he could make a decision about his future. He couldn't do that if he got distracted by Bria's eyes, however alluring they might be.

When Caleb had called to ask if he'd be interested in taking over the obstetrics department at St. Raymond's for a few weeks, he'd jumped at the chance. It had been a few years since he'd done any hospital work, and he missed it. His career hadn't turned out the way he'd expected. His original plan had been to go to medical school and discover his calling, which turned out to be obstetrics. Unfortunately, he'd quickly learned that while medicine might be a path to a fulfilling career, it was no guarantee of wealth, and Eliot had needed money.

Between his medical school loans and his desire to provide for the single mother who'd raised him, he couldn't wait the ten or fifteen years it took for most doctors to begin earning a large income. And so he'd turned to business, using his knowledge of the medical field to guide his investments.

Those investments had paid off more than he could have hoped, and now managing them was almost a full-time job. He still spent a few hours a week at his private practice, assisting with difficult cases or supervising new trainees. His business partners had urged him to give up his medical license entirely, arguing that delivering babies was cost-ing him money. His tax attorney said that if he quit medi-cine and spent that time working on his portfolio instead, he'd easily make another million, maybe two million each year. But Eliot couldn't bring himself to quit obstetrics completely. He loved being a doctor.

It was nice to have the security that money brought him, especially as it was something he'd never known growing up. But being a doctor brought him a sense of fulfilment that the business world had never been able to provide. No matter how much money he made, there was nothing as powerful as helping a new life come into the world. Obstet-rics made him feel connected to a part of life that seemed truly magical, and giving it up would be like abandoning part of his identity. Working at St. Raymond's felt like a vacation compared to his days spent reading market reports and analyzing profits.

The senior partners at his firm hadn't been pleased when he'd announced he would be taking six weeks off to work at a hospital. They'd only agreed to it because he'd gotten another doctor to cover his private practice patients while he was away, and he knew they were hoping that he would leave his practice for good once he returned to Boston. One partner had even told him they were looking forward to Eliot "getting medicine out of his system once and for all."

As much as Eliot loved medicine, it *was* becoming in-creasingly difficult to balance both of his careers. He was at a crossroads, and he didn't know what to do. Caleb's call had come at the perfect time. Six weeks working full-time at a hospital would help him feel more certain about what he wanted to do with the rest of his career.

He'd intended to spend his time at St. Raymond's find-ing answers to his questions about the future. Instead, he'd been put face-to-face with his past.

And now, instead of focusing on his career and what he

wanted to do about it, he was stressing over how he was going to deal with seeing Bria again.

It's only for six weeks. You can do anything for six weeks.

As uncomfortable as it had been, Saturday's emergency had proven that he and Bria could put personal feelings aside and focus on patient care. If they'd done it once, they could continue doing it until he left Portland for good. He'd never had plans to stay, and he was eager to leave the moment his obligation to his friend was complete. If he wanted to ensure a smooth exit, then the best thing he could do would be to make it clear that he was a professional who didn't let personal issues get in the way of his work.

In fact, he decided that he was *glad* Dr. Anderson had scheduled his tour of the Women's Health Center for today. The sooner he ran into Bria again, the sooner he'd be able to demonstrate in no uncertain terms he felt no differently about working with her than he would with any other midwife.

He thought about Bria's green eyes again and swallowed. He wanted very much to prove to her that he wasn't at all affected by seeing her again. But a small part of him thought that he might need a chance to prove it to himself, too.

Bria was in a meeting with Hazel, their heads bent together over budget spreadsheets, when they were interrupted.

"There's a Dr. Wright at the reception desk." Joan, one of the students who staffed the front desk, stuck her head into the doorway. "He's been scheduled for a tour."

Bria groaned inwardly. The day was already off to a rough start, as she and Hazel had spent the morning taking a closer look at the center's financial situation, and they were becoming increasingly concerned at what they found. Eliot's arrival would have been difficult for Bria under the best of circumstances, but at the moment, it was a particularly unwelcome surprise.

"Did you know anything about this?" she asked Hazel.

"Not at all. I'd have given you some warning, I swear."

"Dr. Anderson called and asked if their new interim chief of obstetrics could take a tour of the center, so I scheduled one for today. I'm so sorry if it's not a good time."

"Not at all, Joan." Bria mentally kicked herself. She should have seen this coming. All of the hospital's obstetrics staff had toured the center at one time or another, just as she'd needed to become familiar with the layout of the hospital when she'd first started. No one wanted to have to waste time searching for the right office or operating room when they were dealing with a pregnant patient in crisis.

"Joan, let Dr. Wright know we'll be out in just a moment," said Hazel. When Joan had shut the office door behind her, she said, "Bria, if you need me to, I can give Eliot the tour."

Bria felt her spine stiffen. As much as she dreaded facing Eliot after Saturday's fiasco, letting Hazel give the tour felt far too much like hiding. She was going to have to see Eliot again at some point, and she didn't want to wait until the next crisis arose. Better to establish their working relationship on her own turf, without a pressing emergency.

"That won't be necessary," she said. "You've got more than enough work for today."

"Still, I'm right here if you need anything," Hazel said. "And you and I are meeting up for a postmortem after work tonight, is that understood? Even if one of us has to work late and it's a virtual meet-up."

"I'll be fine," Bria insisted. She poked her head outside to look down the hallway. There he was, chatting with another receptionist. Though the hallway was long, she could faintly pick up on the deep tones of his voice. She could remember exactly how it felt to be wrapped in those long arms of his, her head pressed against his body, his baritone voice resonating through his chest.

That's not helpful, she thought, willing herself to ignore the memories. Since Saturday, she'd had some time to think about how she would cope with Eliot's presence over the next few weeks. When they'd parted, he'd accused her of being materialistic and self-centered. And despite his understandable reasons for making those accusations, the words had hurt her deeply. Eliot might think that that her privilege blinded her to the realities of life, and maybe—though she hated to admit it—maybe there had been a time in her life when that was true. But that wasn't who she was anymore. She'd worked hard to build her career as a midwife, and if she wanted Eliot to respect her as a professional, then she'd need to act professional. Which meant not allowing herself to be distracted by that resonant voice of his. Or by the memories of being pulled close within those strong arms.

She forced herself to put on a warm, professional smile and headed toward the reception desk.

As she approached, she saw that he was holding a familiar blue box. Despite her nerves, her smile became more genuine.

"You brought donuts from Donut Stop Believing!" She cracked the box open, and the familiar scent of vanilla icing wafted out. "There's even—oh my god, is that a passion fruit cake donut?" The upscale bakery a few blocks away was a familiar treat from her past life; the bakery made some of the most outrageous—and expensive—donuts in the city. Now that her financial situation had changed, donuts this pricey no longer made it into her regular rotation of creature comforts.

She tried not to read too much into the fact that he'd remembered one of her favorite treats. It was probably mere coincidence, as doctors from St. Raymond's brought baked goods and lunches for the center's staff all the time. It was all part of networking.

"They're for your staff," he said, his voice cool and businesslike. "I thought they might enjoy something special."

"They certainly work hard enough to deserve it," she replied, taking the box from him and setting it behind the counter. As she did, her fingers brushed against his, their first physical contact in six years, and her heart gave an unexpected jolt. *Move it along*, she thought. The sooner she got the tour underway, the less time she'd have to spend noticing how his dark eyes stood out against his white medical coat.

As she grabbed a clipboard from the reception desk and ushered him into the hallway, she again caught a faint waft of cinnamon. She'd thought it was from the donut box, but now she knew it was him. He used to enjoy a dash of cinnamon in his coffee, and evidently, he still did. The scent teased at her nose.

Yep, definitely need to get this over and done with.

"I'll give you the five-cent tour," she said, trying to keep her voice steady.

"I've been curious to see this place," he said. "Everyone at St. Raymond's has been singing your praises. I understand that things got off to a somewhat rocky start, but now it seems that the hospital finds the center to be indispensable."

She appreciated his comment about the center, but his tone was unmistakably cool. It was one thing to be professional; it was another to keep his voice entirely devoid of emotion. Did he really expect her to believe that he wasn't having any reaction to the utterly surreal situation in which they now found themselves? If there was one person she never thought she'd be taking on a tour of her center, it was Eliot. He had to feel *something* about seeing her again.

But if he did, he clearly wasn't going to show it. That fit with what she remembered about him. Rule number one in the Eliot Wright playbook: hide your feelings at all costs.

Well. If he wanted to act as though this situation was completely normal, no different from a tour of any other health center, then that was his prerogative. She matched his cool, informational tone.

"We do share patients quite a bit. For uncomplicated pregnancies, women are able to give birth here at the center, or at home if they prefer, but it's best for more complicated cases to move to the hospital for delivery. Case in point—here's Mrs. Patterson." A heavily pregnant woman in a blue dress had just left one of the exam rooms. "Sandra Patterson, meet Dr. Eliot Wright. He's chief of obstetrics at St. Raymond's."

"Interim chief," Eliot corrected. "It's just for the next six weeks."

"Six weeks?" Sandra laughed. "Then it sounds like we'll be meeting again."

"Mrs. Patterson is expecting quintuplets," Bria explained. Despite her determination to match Eliot's coolness, excitement crept into her voice. Everyone at the center was looking forward to the delivery of the quints.

"Any day now," Sandra affirmed. She let out a long exhalation. "I've just had the loveliest massage. Nobody who talks about the miracle of life ever brings up just how much lower back pain is involved in miracles."

"I hope you're feeling better now," said Bria.

"Goodness, loads better," Sandra replied. "I don't know what I'd do if it weren't for this place."

"Should a woman expecting quintuplets really be getting services at a birthing center?" Eliot frowned as he watched Sandra go. "Surely a hospital is the best place for her."

"Mrs. Patterson is the perfect example of the kind of patients we share. You're absolutely right that she should give birth at the hospital. But until then, what's wrong with letting her take full advantage of more holistic, integrative approaches? If you were about to give birth to five children, wouldn't you feel better with some massage or aromatherapy from time to time?"

"If I were giving birth to five children, I don't think all the aromatherapy in the world would be enough to make me feel better."

She gave him a sidelong glance, and for a split second, she thought they both might be about to laugh. Or share a smile, at the very least. But the moment passed almost as soon as it had begun, as they both made a hasty retreat back into their professional shells.

"Yes. Well. You're probably not wrong," she said, trying to collect herself. Once, it had felt so easy to be in his presence. This stiff formality between them didn't feel right at all. And yet it didn't seem as though she had any alternative.

She walked him past the clinical offices, describing the care they offered to patients, and paused when they reached the larger rooms down the hall. "We try to offer everything our pregnant patients could hope for in a birthing center and beyond. Prenatally, we offer everything from acupuncture to yoga. Down *that* hallway are some of our therapy rooms. We have counselors on staff to treat postpartum depression. And, of course, we have a pool for water births."

She saw an apprehensive look cross his face, and she hastily added, "I know the medical research is mixed on water births. But lots of single case studies point out that buoyancy makes it easier for mothers to shift position during labor."

"It's not that," he said. "It's just that you offer quite a range of holistic services. I'm very impressed, but…"

"But what?"

"Who pays for all this? Unless you serve incredibly upscale clientele, then I can't imagine how an operation like this could keep running for very long. And I know that many of the hospital's patients couldn't afford a facility like this."

"Actually, we're able to offer care to every patient who walks through our doors, regardless of their ability to pay."

"Ah. Of course. I forgot who I'm talking to."

"Excuse me?"

"It's just that I'm sure it helps to provide state-of-the-art services when you have a family fortune to finance everything."

Bria felt a burst of irritation. She supposed it was natural for him to assume that she'd founded the center with her father's money, but the assumption rankled deeply. She and Hazel had spent countless hours on fund-raising, researching grant proposals and conducting community outreach programs. The center was hers, she had been there for every step of its formation and she was not going to have its success attributed to her father.

"Actually, the center subsists solely off grants and private donations, as well as what our clients pay when they can afford it. It's completely self-sufficient, and my father's money has nothing to do with it. I haven't even spoken to him in years."

She felt a pang of guilt as she realized that what she'd said about the center's self-sufficiency wasn't entirely truthful at the moment, considering her conversation with Hazel just a moment ago about their recent shortfall of funds, but she decided that was a detail she didn't need to mention immediately.

"Really?" The expression of surprise on his face was gratifying, but also irritating. He didn't need to look *so* shocked.

"Yes, really," she said, her voice coming out more sharply than she meant it to. "I may have had some things in life handed to me, but not this." She cringed inwardly over her choice of words. He'd said almost those exact words to her during their final, terrible argument: that she couldn't understand him because she'd had everything handed to her instead of working for it.

But if he noticed, he didn't mention it. He held up his hands. "I'm sorry. I'm sure it took a lot of work to make all of this possible." She suddenly felt foolish. Based on what Eliot knew about her, it was completely natural for him to assume she'd built the center with her father's help. He hadn't been trying to bring up the past, and she should steer clear of it as well.

"The center's very important to me," she said, hoping she could think of a way to explain her strong reaction that wouldn't bring up the past. "I didn't mean… You don't have to…" She hesitated, unable to find her words while Eliot maintained his cool, unemotional gaze. Dammit, if he'd just give her a clue about what he was feeling, this wouldn't be so hard. Finally, it was too much. "For God's sake, Eliot, are we really going to pretend as though this is a normal situation? Are we going to act like we don't have anything else to talk about?"

"What else should we be talking about?"

She fought the impulse to smack him with her clipboard. "How about the fact that we're here, working together, when we both thought we'd probably never see each other again?"

A look of pain flashed across his eyes, and for the first time that day, she saw his professional shell begin to crack. "That's right," he said. "Neither of us thought we'd see each other again. But now that we have, I don't see what difference it makes. We may have a past, but I think the best thing for both of us will be to let it stay there." Whatever she might have seen in his eyes a moment ago was gone. He'd reverted back to his detached, unemotional self.

"Then your plan is to just ignore it? Act like our engagement never happened?"

"My plan is to be professional," he replied. "I don't live in the shadow of my mistakes. I came here for six weeks to help out a friend, and that's still what I plan to do. There's no reason you and I shouldn't be able to work well together as colleagues for a while. So, no, I don't plan to 'pretend' this is a normal situation. I'm going to *treat* it like a normal situation, because that's what it is. You and I are no different from any other doctor and midwife working together."

His brisk, businesslike tone made her reel, but only for a moment. It hurt to think that he could so easily dismiss what had once been between them. But as much as she disliked his tone, she agreed with his words. For once, Eliot's tendency to put up emotional walls might be the right step forward for both of them. If they were going to work together, it would probably be better not to delve into the past. They needed to focus on their patients, not their personal issues.

But six weeks of seeing Eliot? Six weeks of pretending that it was completely normal to work with someone with whom she shared such an intimate history? Not to mention that he was every bit as attractive as she remembered. Seeing him had stirred up memories she hadn't attended to in quite some time, memories of heated nights together and long, luxurious mornings…

"Perfect," she said, trying to sound as though she meant it. "That's what I want, too. For the two of us to work together just as we would with any of our other colleagues." That part was true. She *did* want to work well with Eliot. She did want him to respect her as a professional.

It was just that being in such close proximity to him reminded her of times when she'd wanted other things, too. Like his smile directed at her. His arms wrapped around her. The warmth of his body close to hers.

After seeing him twice in only a few days, she'd found herself having to work harder at putting thoughts like that out of her mind than she had in years.

It was going to be a long six weeks.

CHAPTER THREE

THE NEXT DAY, Eliot was back in his office, hitting refresh on his computer screen.

He was trying very hard to keep his internet search focused on medical journal articles, but it was difficult to focus when images of Bria kept popping into his mind.

Don't look her up, he thought.

People look up their exes online all the time, his mind countered.

Not after six years.

He'd never bothered trying to see what Bria was up to before. After their breakup, he'd avoided all signs of her. He'd wanted to move on as quickly as possible, and looking her up online seemed to run counter to that plan.

But their conversation yesterday continued to nag at the back of his mind. The way her eyes blazed when he'd mistakenly assumed her father had paid for the Women's Health Center.

She hadn't spoken to her father in years, she'd said. Why not? Was it because of their breakup?

Even if it was, that didn't change the past. It couldn't erase what they'd said to each other during those final, awful moments.

Although Bria herself seemed to have changed. He'd never seen her eyes look like that before.

The memories of their relationship had flooded his mind

over the past few days. The way her head fit right under his chin when she stood close to him. The softness of her skin against his fingers. The taste of vanilla lip balm and the smell of coffee that wafted from her.

She was still one of the most attractive women he'd ever met. Even now, after all that had happened between them, he couldn't help feeling something in his chest quicken when he'd watched her approach the reception desk yesterday. But he'd learned his lesson six years ago. He hadn't been good enough for her then. He didn't know whether learning that he was now a millionaire several times over would change how she felt about him, and he didn't care to know. If his money made him more attractive to her, then she wasn't the kind of person he wanted to be to be with.

But that fire in her eyes. She'd had the look of someone who'd had to fight hard for something. The Bria he knew had never had to fight for anything, because she'd already had everything.

He wondered what else about her had changed.

The internet beckoned.

If he wanted to know about her life, he should ask her, he thought. He shouldn't be a creepy internet stalker.

But didn't people *expect* to research one another online? And now that he'd run into Bria again, it was only natural to be curious about what had happened in her life.

Five minutes later, he was scrolling through a list of search results.

There was the usual handful of articles on Bria's family from the gossip pages. Members of the Thomas family were always getting into the news for one reason or another, whether it was because they'd made some huge charitable donation, or because of more licentious behavior. But there was a surprising absence of articles that specifically mentioned Bria. Almost any mention of her seemed to be in connection with the center. What else had she been doing for the past six years?

That was when he saw the image that made his heart stop.

There was a paparazzi-style photo of Bria in a wedding dress, outside Abernethy Chapel, surrounded by her family.

She was married?

He clicked through the pictures, willing himself to stop.

Oh. His heart, which had been jackhammering in his chest, slowed with relief. Upon closer inspection, the woman in the wedding dress was one of Bria's sisters. Bria had just been a bridesmaid.

Ridiculous, he thought, as his heart rate settled. He had no reason to get so worked up over what Bria might or might not have done over the past six years. Why should he care about whether she'd been with anyone else? He hadn't exactly been celibate.

He shut his computer screen. He'd made it clear yesterday that he would treat her like any other medical colleague. And he wouldn't be poking around in the history of any other colleague online. This foolishness had to stop, immediately.

But try as he might, he couldn't stop the questions from swirling in his mind. What was Calvin Thomas's privileged daughter doing working as a midwife? She was obviously proud of building her career. But was she aware of how he'd built his?

Eliot had had to fight for most things in his life. Growing up, he'd attended one of Portland's most elite prep schools on extensive financial aid, because his mother couldn't afford the high tuition fees on her own. She cleaned houses for most of the wealthy families in the area, families who sent their children to the school Eliot attended.

His father had only been in his life intermittently and left for good when he was twelve. Before he did, he gave

Eliot one piece of advice. "Don't let them know you're a scholarship student," he'd said. "In fact, don't tell them anything about yourself unless you absolutely have to. These people already think they're better than you. Don't give them any proof." And so Eliot had kept his scholarship a secret, and he'd told no one that he lived on the edge of town in a run-down apartment complex. He quickly saw that it was a necessary survival strategy, because his father was right. The other students did bully each other based on how much money they had and whose family was the most well-known. Any personal information he revealed risked making him a target. He'd learned to blend in and to keep his real thoughts and feelings to himself.

But he could only delay the inevitable for so long. Eventually, the truth got out among his classmates: that he wasn't a boarding student, his parents didn't fail to attend school functions because they were traveling abroad and he wasn't looked after by servants while they were away. He lived in a one-bedroom apartment with his single mother, who was so poor that she could barely afford to buy him more than one school uniform.

They teased him relentlessly. Anything that made him seem the least bit different was interpreted as a sign of poverty. His hair, the bologna sandwiches his mother packed in his lunches, his plain shoes. He hadn't cared what they thought of him, but he did take it as a valuable lesson in trust. His father had been right: anything he revealed about himself, anything that people in power perceived as different, was an opportunity for them to put him down. Trusting anyone, or revealing anything about himself, was asking for disaster.

Even in college and medical school, his father's prediction turned out to be true. The bullying wasn't as overt as when he'd been a child, but even as an adult, he could see how people who were privileged protected their own.

He'd made some good friends, people who were working their way through and scraping by on student loans. Most of them, like his friend Caleb, were down-to-earth people who'd chosen medicine as a career because they cared deeply about helping others. But he'd also met a surprising number of people who seemed as though they were only interested in medicine because their families were pushing them toward a career with prestige. Those were the students who didn't seem particularly excited about medicine, yet who often seemed to get coveted training positions and well-paying jobs immediately after medical school because of their parents' connections.

Bria had been a breath of fresh air—at first. She might have come from exactly the kind of family he resented, but she was nothing like them. He'd thought she was authentic, genuine and compassionate. That was why it had hurt so much to find out that she did care about where he came from, after all.

Calvin Thomas had overheard every word of their final, vehement argument. As Eliot had stormed out of the Thomas mansion, Calvin had waylaid him in the foyer, and beckoned Eliot into the office.

"How much?" Calvin had said, bringing out his checkbook.

"How much for what?" Eliot replied, confused.

"How much to keep you from smearing the family name? I'm well aware of your financial situation, boy. If you can't get what you need from my daughter by marriage, I'm sure you'll find another way, and I don't want you running to the tabloids or the gossip sites. I want to know your price to keep all this quiet."

Eliot was aghast. At first, he couldn't respond. All he could do was gape.

"Come on, out with it," Calvin continued. "Everybody

has their price. After four years of medical school, I'm guessing yours is about two hundred and fifty thousand dollars."

It was almost the exact amount of his student loans. But he didn't want money from Calvin. He'd always planned to pay the loans back himself, no matter how long it took.

"I don't need your money," he said.

"But I need your silence, and I want to make sure that I get it. All I ask is that you sign this nondisclosure agreement—" he pulled a document from his desk drawer "—and the money's yours."

Eliot hesitated. He couldn't believe that Calvin had a nondisclosure agreement drawn up and ready to be signed. Calvin noted his hesitation. "It was only practical to have this ready," he said, nudging the form toward Eliot. "It could never have lasted between you two. I always told her that, and she's had the good sense to finally see it."

He wrote out a check and handed it to Eliot. "Don't be stupid, boy. Your loans will be coming due soon. It's not easy to make the payments on a young doctor's salary. All you have to do is keep your mouth shut, and the money's yours."

Eliot had taken great pleasure in ripping up that check and continuing on his way out the door. Calvin didn't need to worry about him badmouthing the Thomas family to the press. He never wanted to talk or think about any of them ever again.

He'd thought that was the end of the matter. But then his mother had gotten a Christmas bonus from the Thomas family. A check for two hundred and fifty thousand dollars.

His mother was overjoyed. When he saw how happy she was, he couldn't bring himself to tell her about the argument between him and Bria. He'd only told her that the engagement was off. She'd offered to stop working at the Thomas house, but Eliot couldn't let her do that; the Thomas family was one of her best customers. He couldn't let his mother deprive herself of that income when he knew how much she needed it.

She'd cleaned the Thomas mansion for fifteen years, and she'd assumed that Mr. Thomas was giving her this unexpected windfall to pay for Eliot's tuition. It even said in the memo, "For fifteen years of loyal service."

He'd never seen her so proud. "You see?" she'd said. "People notice when you work hard. I've always put in little extra touches for the families I work for, and even though they never said anything, I know they noticed." She was beaming; he could tell how much it meant to her to feel valued and appreciated.

He knew, too, how much his mother wanted to help him pay for medical school. He couldn't bear to tell her what the money really meant. Calvin's trap had been extremely effective: Eliot might not have signed the nondisclosure agreement, but he also couldn't tell the truth about the money without having to reveal to his mother that it had nothing to do with their appreciation for her hard work at all. She'd thought it was a genuine bonus, while he knew it was just hush money. After everything she'd sacrificed for him, he refused to take away one iota of her pride.

His mother had insisted on using the money to pay off his medical school loans, even though he'd protested that she should keep it for herself. She wouldn't hear a word of it, and Eliot graduated medical school debt-free, with a little extra money to spare. When his mother had refused even that small amount, Eliot had invested it instead. Those investments had been successful and formed the basis of Eliot's multimillion-dollar fortune today.

For years, he'd tried to tell himself that he owed Calvin Thomas nothing. But that wasn't the whole truth, no matter how hard he tried to convince himself otherwise. He felt guilty for judging Bria's wealthy background when, in the end, he'd benefited from her family's fortune just as much as she had.

He knew how Calvin Thomas's mind worked. He'd wanted Eliot to know that he'd never have been able to make his fortune without Calvin's help. Even if he'd paid the man back, it wouldn't change his situation now. If Calvin hadn't written that check, Eliot would still be struggling to pay off his medical school debts. He'd never have been able to make his investments at the time he did, nor would he have amassed his own wealth, without Calvin's help. He'd tried to alleviate his guilt by doing good with the money. As soon as he'd earned his first million, he'd funded his mother's immediate retirement, and he gave freely to many charities. But nothing could ever change the fact that he owed his entire fortune to Calvin Thomas, and it was a bitter pill to swallow. He suspected Calvin knew exactly how much Eliot hated that.

And something about those blazing eyes of Bria's told him that she would hate it, too.

Bria obviously took great pride in having built her business without her father's help. What would she think if she knew that he hadn't been able to do the same? Or was it possible that she already knew, and the blaze in her eyes had held some scorn for him? He didn't think so. Bria had seemed more defensive than anything. If she'd known about Calvin's "donation," she'd have mentioned it yesterday. And it shouldn't matter if she found out. It wasn't as though her judgment of him mattered in any way. It was simply a matter of personal pride. He preferred that she didn't know what he owed to Calvin. But that didn't make her stand out: he preferred that *no one* knew what he owed to Calvin. Which was in keeping with his determination to treat her like any of his other colleagues.

If Bria didn't know, then there was no reason for him to bring it up now. It was far in the past, and it wasn't as though he gave detailed reports to his other colleagues on how he'd made his fortune. He'd just tried not to think about it. The same way he tried not to think of the memories of certain intimate nights together. Or the way she still tilted her head in thought, exposing the delicate curve of her neck. Those things were private. What was one more secret in the face of things?

Bria stepped outside the delivery room at St. Raymond's and tore off her gloves, welcoming the coolness of the air against her hands. The labor she'd just assisted with had lasted for almost ten hours, and her lower back was aching. She tried to ease the knots out of her shoulders as she leaned against the wall. Sometimes, when she witnessed the miracle of life, she thought the real miracle would be if the baby could come out quickly.

She raised her head to glance into the window of the delivery room door—Mrs. Hatfield and her baby boy were gazing deeply into one another's eyes. Despite her exhaustion, Bria smiled. She would never be tired of seeing the expression on a parent's face when greeting a new life for the first time.

Familiar footsteps sounded behind her. Eliot joined her at the window, bending down to peer in. "It never gets old, does it?"

She gave a rueful smile. Lately, witnessing the first few bonding moments between parents and their children was bittersweet, as she'd begun to feel less certain of ever experiencing such a moment herself. Still, she knew she could never stop watching. The privilege of being present at those early moments was by far one of the best professional perks of being a midwife.

Not that she could voice any of this to Eliot. The two of them had worked well together over the past few days, but their focus had been entirely on patients. Eliot had stuck to his resolution to ignore their past and treat her like any other colleague. She, however, was well aware of Eliot's presence having an effect on her—she'd caught herself casting glances over the muscles that lined his chest and upper arms, which definitely hadn't been there six years ago. She tried not to notice, but she did, and couldn't help getting caught up in dwelling on how those muscular arms might feel when wrapped around her waist. She'd had every intention of treating him like any other doctor.

Though Eliot clearly wasn't *just* any other doctor—and not just because of their history. Even though he'd only been at St. Raymond's for a few days, she'd had the chance to see him in action more than once. He was supremely skilled, and his intuition alerted him to complications that might be overlooked by less sensitive physicians. He was a doctor she'd have been proud to work with under any other circumstances, and she found herself respecting him on a professional level.

And on an unprofessional level, if she did happen to notice those newly defined chest muscles…well, she'd just have to suffer in silence.

But Mrs. Hatfield's new baby should be a safe topic, falling firmly into the professional realm they'd agreed to share. She yawned and rubbed her back. "It never gets old, but midwives get tired. Poor Mrs. Hatfield started her contractions at ten this morning."

Eliot winced in sympathy. "You must be tired."

She stifled another yawn. "I was just about to head to the hospital commissary for a cup of coffee." She hesitated, wondering if she should invite him along. He'd brought her donuts on Monday. True, he'd made it clear that they were professional networking donuts, but maybe he'd receive her offer of coffee in the same vein. She wanted to extend an olive branch. She'd do anything to end this awful, stilted formality. They could be polite without being cold to each other, couldn't they?

"Would you like to join me?" She blurted the words out before she could overthink them.

He raised his eyebrows. "Are you sure that's a good idea?

"Look, you're the one who said we're no different from any other doctor and midwife working together. If you were any other doctor, I'd invite you to grab a coffee and ask how you were settling in."

He still hesitated, and at first she thought he was going to refuse. But then he said, "Fair enough. I suppose if you were any other midwife, I'd accept."

He was being so cautious, she thought with a wave of sadness. And yet, what else could she expect from him? She'd been the one to end their relationship. It made sense that he'd be hesitant to spend any time with her again.

The hospital commissary was abuzz with medical staff who were consulting on cases, sharing jokes and generally enjoying one another's company. Bria and Eliot got their drinks and sat down. She looked at his coffee cup and wrinkled her nose. "Is that…decaf?"

He laughed, and as he did, his face lit up for a moment with all the warmth and energy that had attracted her years ago. "The cost of getting a few years older. That, and I'm not used to these long hospital shifts. I've been relying on coffee a lot more since I started here at St. Raymond's, but I try to make every other cup decaf, so I don't go tachycardic."

"Wait, do you mean you don't work at a hospital out in Boston?"

"I haven't worked in a hospital since my residency."

She couldn't hide her surprise. He was so talented. When they'd dated, he'd been about to graduate medical school near the top of his class. Any hospital should have been thrilled to have him on staff.

"I went into private practice right away. It was the only way I could balance both my careers."

"You're not just an obstetrician?"

"I manage a firm that deals in medical holdings and investments. As you can imagine, it takes up quite a lot of time. I could never combine that with a medical career on a hospital's schedule."

She'd never pictured him in the business world. He'd always been so committed to medicine, so driven to succeed as a physician. But she was glad that he'd done well for himself.

"And you're…happy with that balance?"

He mulled this over. "Satisfied, I suppose? I've accepted it. Money is a necessary evil in American health care, and being invested in the business side of things gives me a different perspective on what my patients are facing. But it's getting more difficult to do both, so I'm thinking of giving up medicine."

She nearly dropped her coffee cup. Becoming a doctor had been a lifelong dream for Eliot. At least, the Eliot she'd known. First the decaf coffee, and now this. Could things really have changed so drastically over the past six years?

"How could you even think of giving up medicine? You're so talented." But at her words, his face became a familiar emotional wall, the classic expression Eliot wore whenever he would refuse to discuss a subject further. Clearly, the idea of giving up medicine was fraught with emotion for him. How could it not be? He'd never wanted anything more than to become a doctor. He obviously needed to talk about it. Which made it just as obvious that he never would.

"I'm not the only one who's changed. I never would have thought to see you working as a midwife."

She couldn't be sure, but she thought there might be a note of admiration in his voice. "Is it really that unexpected?"

"Don't get me wrong—you clearly have a knack for it. I'm very impressed by what I've seen so far." She tried to suppress the warm glow that rose within her at his praise. What Eliot thought of her shouldn't matter—or at least, it shouldn't matter *this much*. It was always nice to hear positive feedback from a doctor, but her heart rate was increasing just a little too quickly after Eliot's compliment.

But his next words felt as though he'd poured cold water over her. "I always thought that if you decided to work, you'd end up in some puff position at one of your father's companies."

"Excuse me?"

"You know—that your father would put you in some meaningless role where you could stay out of the way until you got tired of having a job. It's impressive that you chose midwifery instead. It's a career with meaning and purpose."

His condescension was a slap in the face. "Is that what you thought of me?"

"Don't get mad. I'm trying to pay you a compliment."

"It's a hell of a backhanded compliment. You honestly thought I'd be satisfied to stay in some useless position my father arranged for me until I got 'tired' of having a job? Is that where you saw my life going when we were together?"

He grew defensive. "Tell me I'm wrong. Tell me that if you'd asked your father for a job six years ago, or today, or tomorrow, that he wouldn't set you up somewhere with a decent salary doing something that wouldn't get in the way of all the people at the company who do the real work."

Her father had, in fact, done exactly that for both of her sisters when they'd toyed with the idea of working. But that had never been what she'd wanted for herself. Eliot might be right about her father, and her situation, but he wasn't right about her.

"I wouldn't know," she snapped at him. "I told you, I haven't spoken to my father in years. We're very different people."

"Are you," he said. It didn't sound like a question.

She knew his reaction was fair considering how she'd broken things off between them, but she also knew it was wrong. She felt all the animosity of their final fight rising up between them again. The expression on his face was an exact replica of the one he'd worn six years ago, when he'd accused her of being a spoiled princess and she'd said that he'd never even tried to understand her if he thought that and that he didn't know her at all. He'd agreed and stormed out moments later. He looked as though he might storm away now, and it made her heart ache, because she'd never meant to hurt him so badly.

But she also resented his perception of her as sheltered, inexperienced and spoiled. She hoped that wasn't the view he held of her today, but it was awful to think that he'd ever felt that way about her at all.

More than anything, she hated that her attempt to extend an overture of peace to Eliot had turned into a moment that brought them right back to where they'd ended things six years ago. They'd both changed. She knew that. So why had her attempt at a friendly conversation turned sour so quickly?

"It looks like we're back where we started," he said, echoing her thoughts.

"Wait." She shook her head. "You're not wrong about my father. I could have done exactly what you said. Gotten some job that meant nothing, whenever I wanted. Left it whenever I wanted. And my father would have been happy to arrange it for me, because it would have kept me firmly under his control. But that wasn't what I wanted for myself.

That's why I don't speak with him anymore. Because relying on him nearly cost me everything. My independence, my identity. Relationships that were important to me. He has a way of making everything impossible."

It was as close as she'd ever come to telling him that her father had forced her to break up with Eliot. It had been no secret that her father was against their relationship. But she'd always sworn to Eliot that she'd initiated the breakup under her own volition.

But to her utter surprise, he laughed. "In other words, you broke off contact with your father because he was too controlling."

"Yes. Why is that funny?"

"Because it's exactly why our relationship didn't work! You say that relying on your father nearly cost you your independence and your identity. Don't you realize that the exact same thing almost happened to me when we were together?"

She was absolutely aghast. "How can you say that? I would never, ever have used my money to control you, or anyone else, the way my father did."

"No, but you still went ahead and made all of the decisions in our relationship. You were the one who decided whether we stayed out or went in, whether we went to a restaurant or ordered pizza, even what kind of clothes I wore. Because it was your money."

His interpretation of their relationship felt completely unfair to her. She remembered the moments he was describing, but in a completely different way. It had been a joy for her to take Eliot places he'd never ordinarily been able to afford, and she'd bought him clothes because she'd known how much he wanted to fit in with his medical school colleagues—*he* was the one who'd said he felt uncomfortable wearing patched trousers and shirts that had withstood a thousand washings. She'd never meant for those gifts to express anything but love for him.

"As far as I was concerned, we were in an equal partnership."

"We were. But you were the one who decided how equal we'd be. You were the one who decided that I was good enough for you, not the other way around."

"I never felt that way. Not once."

"But that was how other people saw it."

"Who cares about what other people thought?"

"That's the point. You never had to care about that. But I did, because I was the one who was the cleaning lady's son. I was the one people were looking at, wondering how someone like me got to be with someone like you."

His words stung. She'd always known, during their relationship, that he was insecure about money, but she'd never realized his feelings ran so deep. Had he really felt so controlled by her? Had her privilege left her so totally blinded to his unhappiness over their inequalities? She'd been determined that his lack of money wouldn't matter to her. But it seemed to have mattered to him more than she'd ever understood at the time.

Even so. Eliot had never told her how he felt. Not like this. He might claim now that he'd tried, but she remembered things very differently. The lack of vulnerability, the guardedness. The shutting down whenever she tried to find clues that would help her discover his feelings. How could she have known how he felt unless he talked to her?

"You could have let me know that you felt this way," she said. "Even afterward."

"What was the point of talking about it? It wouldn't have changed anything. I thought the best thing for both of us was to move on."

"Moving on hasn't exactly been an easy road for me."

She barely tried to mask the raw hurt in her voice. After all, he didn't know why she'd had to break up with him, did he?

"I'm sorry."

"Don't be. I'm…used to making mistakes in relationships."

"Well. You know what they say about mistakes. Everybody makes them. You, me…everybody."

And that, she thought, might be the closest either of them would ever be able to come to acknowledging that they'd made mistakes with one another. It certainly wasn't enough to heal the hurt that had happened between them. But it might be enough to lay the groundwork for something else.

As hard as it had been to hear how Eliot had felt—and she was going to need to think about it before she accepted his interpretation of their relationship—their conversation had also helped her understand a little more of what things had been like for him. If only he had told her all this sooner, she might not have hurt him so badly when she'd ended things. As it was, she'd inadvertently struck a blow exactly where it had wounded him the most.

But he was telling her now. If he could change, maybe their relationship could, too.

"It's been six years, Eliot. I know the idea of the two of us being friends is a long shot. Probably impossible. But we're the only two people on earth who really know what we've put one another through. If we can't be friends, then how about establishing a truce?"

He considered this. "I suppose stranger things have happened."

"Like me becoming a midwife? And you becoming a venture capitalist?"

"Exactly. If all that's possible…then maybe a truce is possible for us."

Bria was just beginning to feel a sense of relief when he added, "Besides, I'm only here for a short time, and then

I'll be gone for good. What's the harm in two colleagues trying to get along with one another for just a few weeks?"

He was right. There shouldn't be any difficulty in the two of them trying to get along. In less than a month and a half, he would be gone from her life again.

And this time, when he left, he would be gone forever.

CHAPTER FOUR

"ONE MORE TIME, people! From the top!" Eliot clapped his hands, the signal for everyone to resume their places.

Bria paused for a moment to catch her breath. The maternal-fetal medicine team at St. Raymond's was running drills to prepare for the birth of Sandra Patterson's quintuplets. Multiple births were always complicated, and with quints, prematurity was a given. Some of the babies might weigh as little as two pounds. There were a host of other issues that could arise. Seconds would matter in ensuring that each of the five newborns was appropriately monitored during the first few moments after birth, especially since the quintuplets born last would be the weakest and in need of the most care. A smooth and speedy delivery could have significant long-term effects on each quint's quality of life. In the face of the unknown, Eliot wanted to be ready for anything, and as interim chief of obstetrics, he wanted the hospital staff to be ready along with him.

Bria returned to her place on the "baby assembly line" Eliot had designed, which was comprised of Eliot as the delivering physician, Caleb as the assisting surgeon and Hazel and herself as Sandra's midwives. Sandra herself was also there, as Eliot thought having her present during rehearsals might reduce her anxiety and help her to feel more relaxed once labor started. Bria approved wholeheartedly of Eliot's decision to include Sandra; many doctors didn't give much thought to the mother's emotional experience during birth, nor to the impact that fear and worry during delivery could have on later postpartum depression.

Though not everyone was quite as appreciative of Eliot's meticulous attention to detail. Hazel blew her bangs upward with an annoyed puff of air and leaned toward Bria. "If he says 'one more time' one more time, I'm going to start doubting his sincerity."

Bria smiled. "He's just being thorough."

And perhaps also a bit competitive. Eliot had told her that he'd learned of a hospital in Utah that had delivered quintuplets in five minutes. Five babies born in five minutes was an impressive feat, but Bria had a feeling Eliot was aiming for four minutes and thirty seconds, a record that would probably stand for some time if he could manage to achieve it.

At the moment, the team was clocking in at about eight minutes, although that was to be expected, as they were still discovering and working out new obstacles to plan around.

"Less chatter, more focus!" Eliot called out.

Eliot had turned the operating room into a miniature NICU. He'd requisitioned five of every item a newborn could possibly need: cooling blankets, bassinets, cardio-pulmonary monitors, central lines, all color coded and labeled with letters from *A* to *E* for each baby. Bria could tell that when the day finally came for Sandra to deliver, things would run as close to clockwork as they could get.

The team ran through the drill twice more before Eliot allowed them to break for lunch. "You seem pleased," she told him. "We got that last one down to six minutes and thirty seconds."

She recognized the competitive gleam in his eye. "We're getting there. There's still lots of room for improvement." He noticed that Sandra was listening and was quick to reassure her. "I hope all of this preparation isn't worrying you, Mrs. Patterson. We just want you to have the smoothest delivery possible."

"You don't have to convince me that faster is better," said Sandra. "I'll just be glad to be on the other side of this." She shook her head in awe at the complex operations of the staff. "And to think that when I first got pregnant, I wanted a natural birth at home. Something quiet and low-key. Of course, at the time I didn't know I'd be giving birth to five."

"You've been doing incredibly well," Eliot replied. "But while you're here, I do think it's time for us all to talk about when to expect the big day. Right now you're at twenty-nine weeks gestation, which is great for quintuplets. But I'd like to do everything we can to get you to thirty-four weeks. And with plenty of bed rest and good care, I think we can do it."

Sandra hesitated. "Lots of bed rest, you say?"

"It's essential that you stay home in bed as much as possible."

Sandra looked as though she might cry. "I hear you, Doctor, and I want to give my little ones their best chance. But I've had so much bed rest already. I only leave the house once a week as it is, for my acupuncture and massage sessions at the Women's Health Center, and I think I'd go mad if I didn't have that." A tear rolled down her cheek, which she wiped away. "I'm sorry. It's all these hormones."

Bria took her hand. "None of this is what you expected, is it? Five babies, and now a C-section, and a huge team of doctors instead of the quiet birth at home that you wanted."

"I know I'm being ridiculous. All I really want is for the babies to be healthy. And I know you're all trying to do the best for our family. But I feel as though my life is about to be nothing *but* babies for quite some time."

Bria thought for a moment. "How about this, Sandra? I can talk to our acupuncturist and massage therapist about doing some home visits, so you don't have to come to the center."

"Could you really? It would mean so much to me." Sandra gave her a relieved smile. "That center is such a treasure."

As Bria fell into line to take a sandwich from the lunch table in the hallway, Eliot came to stand beside her. "That was quick thinking with Mrs. Patterson," he murmured. "I was about to give her a lecture on the importance of bed rest, but you were far more helpful."

"She just needs something to help her feel special," Bria replied. "Emotional health is as important as physical health, and bed rest is difficult."

"It's a good thing your massage therapist and acupuncturist make house calls."

"They normally don't," Bria replied. "But they make exceptions for special cases, and Sandra is definitely a special case."

Eliot gave her an odd look, as though he was studying her. "You really care about her."

"Of course I do," she said, surprised. "She's my patient."

"It's not just that, though. You care about how she's feeling, whether she's happy or upset. It matters to you."

"Of course it does," she said again. "What kind of midwife would I be if I didn't care how my patients were feeling?"

He didn't respond immediately but continued looking at her as though in a new light. "You don't seem as fazed by the pressure of these drills as anyone else."

She felt that same mixture of frustration and pleasure and annoyance that seemed to come up whenever he paid her a compliment. She was pleased to hear him say it, frustrated with herself for feeling pleased and annoyed with him for seeming so surprised at her competence. But she decided that if they were going to have a truce, she might as well fill in some of the blanks about her life. "I spent two years with an international health organization in Haiti before moving back to Portland," she said. "After a few years of delivering babies with scant medical resources, prepping for quintuplets in a hospital is a walk in the park."

She could tell he was surprised, but all he said was "Well, your experience shows."

It was the first positive thing he'd said about her that didn't feel completely backhanded. For once, she didn't feel plagued by the frustration that so often accompanied his feedback when they worked together.

But before she could say anything in response, Eliot was calling the team to attention again, announcing that he wanted to run the drill three more times before the end of the shift.

By the end of the day, Bria was surprised by how cohesive the teamwork felt. She, Hazel and Caleb had all worked together before, but Eliot seemed to fit right in. He had a way of recognizing everyone's talents, bringing the team together to work as a unit. As the day went on, they developed an easy flow, so that their work felt automatic, seamless.

She'd always known he would be an excellent doctor, and it was rewarding to see him in action. Bria could see the team's confidence in him growing with each new decision he made, and she couldn't help feeling a small amount of pride, because she'd been there at the beginning, when Eliot was working so hard to make his dream come true.

It tore at her heart to think that her father had almost interfered with that dream. Watching him work now, she could tell that the hunch she'd had years ago had been right: he belonged in a hospital. He was perfectly in his element, master of all, mindful of everything from his patient's needs to how the hospital system could help or hinder a complicated delivery.

She'd seen many doctors during her career, some who were talented and others who held no passion for their work. She could tell that Eliot was born to be a physician. It was almost worth all the sacrifice and heartbreak that had brought them here, just so she could have a chance to see him in action. He'd become the doctor he'd set out to be, even though there had been so much in his way.

She couldn't believe he was thinking of giving up medicine. He was so obviously talented. Would he really give up a career that was such an important part of his identity— for money? If he'd been as successful in business as he'd said, did he really need any more of it?

A pang of guilt followed. She'd been the one to tell Eliot that he wasn't good enough for her, that he couldn't provide the life she wanted. She'd been lying, of course. To protect him. But no matter what her motivations had been, Eliot had heard from her, someone he loved and thought he could trust, that he didn't have enough money. And now she knew he'd heard that throughout his childhood, as well, from people so shallow that it shouldn't matter what they thought. For days, she'd been remembering their conversation in the commissary, when he'd revealed how he'd felt about the financial inequality in their relationship. She'd never known that he'd felt as though her money gave her the lead when they were dating. Was that what was driving him to consider giving up a career in which he was so obviously gifted?

Eliot's voice called her attention back to the drill. "We're doing great, but I want to have one more day of practice before the big day. We're just above five minutes. Let's see if we can shave another thirty seconds off our time. In the meantime, everyone on the quintuplet team needs to keep their pager on them at all times. Remember, the message is QUINTS911. That message means to report here, to this delivery room, no matter what you're in the middle of. And don't forget…this is supposed to be fun."

Everyone laughed, and Bria thought again of how skilled Eliot was. It wasn't just his medical knowledge. He put everyone at ease, patients and medical staff included. She'd even noticed it in herself after only a day of working with him. Before, she'd been excited for Sandra, but now it was more. Now she felt excited for herself, too. Delivering quints was a momentous occasion, and she couldn't imagine anything more exciting than the delivery of five healthy babies at once.

And as she watched Eliot, she knew he felt it, too. His passion and excitement were apparent in his voice, his tone, his energy, and all of it was infectious.

How could he even think of quitting medicine?

Eliot couldn't wait to get out of his scrubs and into his hiking gear.

One of the few things he'd missed about Portland was the greenery. When it came to finding good hiking spots, Portland was full of gems. He remembered numerous hidden trails and waterfalls from his youth. He hadn't been to the city in such a long time that each excursion to a trail remembered from his childhood held fresh excitement, as he was able to enjoy the natural beauty with fresh eyes. He got all the joy of being a tourist while holding all the secret knowledge of a local. And even though his financial situation had improved considerably from his childhood, he still found simple pleasures such as hiking to be the most restorative after a long day.

Running the quintuplet drills had left him excited and nervous. He'd only delivered quints once before, during his residency, and then he'd mostly been observing. This time, he'd be in charge, and he was feeling all the weight of his responsibility.

He'd always felt there was nothing better than a hike in the woods to clear his mind and help him feel refreshed. He changed his clothes in the hospital's staff locker room and began walking toward Forest Park.

It was encouraging to see how the quintuplet team was coming along. He thought he'd chosen the team wisely, as everyone seemed to work well together, but he couldn't help noticing that he and Bria, especially, seemed to have a special kind of flow. The moment he thought of something, she already seemed to have anticipated his needs. He'd noticed that Hazel and Caleb, and in fact all the other members of the medical team, were often talking. That was good; everyone should be communicating with one another. But between him and Bria, it felt as though they didn't need to speak.

Perhaps it meant nothing. Or perhaps he was even imagining it. It would, he admitted to himself, probably feel nice to think that he and Bria shared some special understanding, after all the misunderstandings that had passed between them. When they'd spoken a few days ago, they'd argued and aired some past hurts, but things had been far calmer between the two of them since then. As though they were able to see each other more accurately now, after six years apart. He'd even noticed himself looking forward to when he and Bria could work together, which was a nice change from when he'd dreaded those moments.

It had felt good to be honest with her after all this time. So good, in fact, that he had to admit she had a point about his lack of vulnerability. He'd spent years hiding his feelings. That had been his go-to strategy for surviving high school. And later, in medical school, it had been the same. He started to form a list in his mind of the people he'd ever felt really comfortable opening up to. There was Caleb, to a certain extent. His mother…but he couldn't even tell her everything. Bria's name had been on the list once, but now it was mentally crossed out.

When he'd first come back to Portland, he'd been afraid that telling Bria how he really felt would only cause more conflict between them. Now it seemed to have actually brought them closer together.

Bria was certainly full of surprises. He'd been shocked when she told him she'd worked in Haiti for two years. He wondered what service organization she'd gone with. If she'd been gone for that long, it explained a lot: why there was barely any recent information about her online, the way she was so steady in a crisis, as well as her overall skill as a midwife. If she'd had to practice without much modern equipment or medicine, it probably was a luxury to have the resources of St. Raymond's available.

Something had changed as he'd seen her interacting with Sandra Patterson. She'd been so compassionate, so empathetic. He knew what it was. He'd seen it before, among the medical colleagues he had who were among the very best. Bria's care for her patients was real.

He'd worked with plenty of colleagues who were good at their jobs, but he could always tell when a medical professional really, truly cared about their patients as people. Bria had that ability. She had a passion for working with patients that he'd often felt, too. She was nothing like the overprivileged medical students he'd gone to school with, or the burned-out colleagues he'd met who could no longer muster empathy for their patients. Her feelings were genuine.

Careful, he thought. *You've been down this road before.*

He was all too aware that it wasn't safe to trust that Bria stood out, that she was different. And yet…he'd felt a burst of warmth for her when he'd seen her comforting her patient earlier. Something that went far beyond feeling impressed with a colleague's skill.

The feeling was so strong it was palpable, and it took him utterly by surprise.

He'd spent six years trying to put the past behind him. He'd met other women but had never seemed to be able to find what he was looking for. His wealth made it difficult to know if women were interested in him or in his checking account. After all his insecurity about Bria's fortune, and the difficulties he'd faced growing up in poverty, he was well aware of the irony of his own wealth interfering with his ability to have a relationship.

Seeing Bria again, hearing her laugh, smelling that vanilla-coffee scent that always lingered about her…all of it had awakened something within him that he thought had been dormant, maybe even gone forever.

He was almost to Forest Park. There were only a few hours of daylight left, so he intended to make a short hike up to the spot called the Witch's Castle. It was a popular hike for both residents and visitors, and so he supposed he shouldn't have been too surprised to hear a familiar voice.

"Eliot." Bria.

"Are you headed up to the Witch's Castle?"

"I go up there after busy workdays," she said.

"I guess great minds think alike. I was just about to head up there myself. It's one of my favorite hikes."

"I know. You were the first one to ever take me up there, remember?"

Now that she mentioned it, he did remember. They'd gone into the park with a picnic basket and had explored all the park's various treasures.

"I come here nearly every day," she continued. "It's one of the best places in the city to unwind."

He was touched that she'd continued walking here. It was as though she'd taken something good from the wreckage of their relationship.

But he was also uncomfortable with that line of thinking. He'd spent years trying not to think about Bria, and so the idea of her hiking along one of the same routes they used to travel together left him feeling unsettled. Had she thought about him as she walked here? Or had she simply enjoyed the trail with no associations to him? Either scenario threw his emotions into turmoil.

"I could take another trail, if you'd prefer," he said awkwardly.

She cocked her head to one side. "I thought we agreed to a truce."

"Still, if you're uncomfortable…or if you want some peace and quiet, I can find somewhere else to hike. It's a huge park. It's not as though I can't find another trail." His words were coming out a bit too fast.

She raised her eyebrows. "If *I'm* uncomfortable? Is it possible, Eliot, that *you* might be the one who's uncomfortable? Or are you still not allowing yourself to have feelings?"

He stiffened, annoyed with himself for becoming flustered and letting it show. "I'm not uncomfortable at all."

"Then let's get hiking. I'm sure we can handle being civil to one another even if we're not at work."

She fell into step beside him. Though her presence had disoriented him for a moment, he realized he was glad to have company. Even if it was Bria's company. Bria, who reminded him of bakery smells and leisurely mornings spent lingering over coffee. And the nights that had come before those mornings, when both of them had felt a heat so intense he'd once thought it would consume them both.

He wondered if she ever thought about those nights. Of course, he could never ask her. And she'd never shown any sign that the memories of their love life came to her mind the way they'd come to his from the moment his plane touched down in Portland. So there wasn't any point in thinking about them.

And yet, the memories of her arms reaching for him, her legs wrapped around him, had a way of gripping his mind at the most inopportune moments. Such as right now, for example.

He searched his mind for a topic that would get them as far from speaking of the past as possible. "I don't think the tour you gave me of the Women's Health Center did it justice," he said. "The more I hear about it, the more invaluable it seems to the community."

She frowned, as though she didn't want to talk about it right now. He couldn't believe it. He thought he'd chosen the exact subject she couldn't seem to talk enough about.

But then she sighed. "I might as well come clean. I didn't want to admit it to you during the tour, but the fact is, the center's in a pretty serious financial crisis."

"I'm sorry. I know it's important to you."

"It's all right. We're doing what we can to make up what we need with fund-raising. In fact, we've decided to organize a charity gala in a few weeks. I actually came out for a hike to avoid thinking about gala planning. Frankly, there are too many details and not enough time to sort them all out. But I don't want to let Hazel down. I promised her I'd take the lead, since I've done this kind of thing before."

"I remember." He'd always hated attending black-tie charity galas with Bria. He took no pleasure in wearing uncomfortable clothes to events where people wrote large checks to feel good about themselves while looking down their noses at him. "I thought you liked planning these kinds of things. You used to be able to throw them together in no time."

"That was when I wasn't working full-time as a midwife and managing a women's health center." She sighed again. "I really wasn't looking to take on a third job right now, but it can't be helped."

"Isn't there any way you could take more time? Reschedule it for next spring?"

"No. We need to act fast. We had a change with one of our major donors, which would have been fine, but then two others left as well. One passed away, one shifted funding to other causes… It's just a run of bad luck, all at once, and the financial consequences are going to hit us soon."

"So you need to get your fund-raising underway as soon as possible.

"Exactly. Hence, the gala. But there isn't a lot of time to plan. I don't even have anything to wear."

"What's wrong, you already wore each of your Oscar de la Renta gowns somewhere once?" He instantly felt ashamed of himself. He hadn't meant to be harsh. Bria was opening up, telling him about her life. He had no reason to goad her. But old habits died hard, it seemed, and so, he supposed, did old resentments. Still. He and Bria had agreed to a truce, and he needed to respect that if they were going to get through the next few weeks.

She narrowed her eyes at him and looked as though she was about to say something sharp in reply, but then her face softened. "I sold most of my clothes to a consignment shop a few years ago."

He was taken aback. "Why?"

"I was about to start work in Haiti, and I didn't see myself having much use for designer eveningwear ever again."

"But why sell them? Why not just…put them in storage, or something?"

She shrugged. "Because I needed the money."

"What?"

She bit her lip and then said, "I haven't taken any of my family's money in years. My father is leaving everything to my sisters."

His jaw dropped. "Why?"

"I've told you, because my father sees money as a way to

control people. There are always strings attached, no matter what he says. And because as long as I knew I had the safety net of being dependent on him, I would never push myself to stand on my own two feet."

"And that was important to you."

"You have no idea how much. I wanted to be sure that I was making my own decisions, without being influenced by anyone else ever again."

A mix of emotions threatened to overtake him. Part of him was horrified at the idea of her walking away from such a fortune, yet he also felt a deep respect at her ability to stand up for her principles.

He didn't want to think about what her decision might mean regarding their past, but his mind raced on regardless of his desire. Was she implying that she had been influenced by her father to break up with him all those years ago?

The hope was irresistible, but along with hope came pain. Even if her father had swayed her, she was still the one who'd said they couldn't be together. Ultimately, she hadn't wanted to marry him. No matter what her motivations had been, nothing could change the past six years, and he refused to torture himself by getting mired in what-ifs.

"So you walked away from him."

"It's what had to be done. I was never going to have my own life as long as I was in the shadow of his."

"So that's why the center is so important to you. That's why you got so mad when I assumed your father was responsible for all of it."

She nodded. "The center is entirely mine and Hazel's. It's why the gala has to be a success."

"Is there anything I can do to help?"

"How could you help?"

He felt his old insecurity tugging at him, looking for the insult: How could *you* help? But all he could see was genuine curiosity on her face, and hope that he might have answers she hadn't considered.

"I run a holding company that buys and sells medical centers."

"Ugh. Please don't tell me that you buy family clinics and turn them into soulless conglomerates."

"Those soulless conglomerates are the reason family clinics can survive. My partners and I buy clinics that are struggling financially and make them part of profitable corporate chains. There are doctors who wouldn't be able to stay in business if it weren't for us."

"That may be, but it's not going to happen to the center. We're going to keep our independence and our identity."

"I can respect that, but given the issues you're facing, it would make a lot of sense to consider selling to a conglomerate. You and Hazel could make a tidy profit and stay on as employees to direct the center. You'd have better name recognition as part of a national chain of clinics, so you could expand your reach and help more people. It's not the terrible thing you think it is."

"But you're describing the best-case scenario, with investors who really get what Hazel and I have created and wouldn't turn on us the moment they've bought us out. Where would I find a firm like that? What firm would even understand our situation?"

"How about mine?"

She gawked at him. "I don't know if you're joking, but just in case you're not, I can think of about a dozen problems with that."

"Such as?"

"For one thing, our past."

"This would be strictly business. You wouldn't even have to deal with me, just managers from my firm. I'd be back in Boston. To be honest, buying the center would be a profitable move for me. And the expense would be minimal."

"We need to raise four hundred and thirty thousand dollars. That's minimal?"

"To me it is."

He watched her consider this. "For the record, I'm serious about the offer. It would make a lot of sense for you to sell."

"No. It's my center, and I'm going to save it my way."

Even though he knew how she felt about the center, he'd thought she might jump at his offer to bail her out. The fact that she hadn't left him all the more impressed with her passion.

"Let me help you," he said again. When he saw she was about to protest, he quickly added, "I don't mean with money. Let me help you plan the gala. I can see how important the center's independence is to you, and I'll do everything I can to make the gala successful. But if it isn't…just know that you have another option."

"Why do you want to help?"

"Because I can."

As he'd amassed his fortune over the years, he had to admit that he'd occasionally thought about what might happen if Bria found out that he'd become wealthy. He wasn't above fantasizing about how it might feel to finally be the one offering Bria money, to show her that she needed him for a change. He knew it was petty, but he'd always thought there would be a kind of satisfaction in turning the tables on Bria.

But now, as he said the words, they had nothing to do with satisfaction. He wasn't offering to help her because he wanted to lord his wealth over her or make her feel small. He'd offered to help because he couldn't bear to think of that light of passion going out of her eyes if the center failed.

After a moment's pause, she said, "Eliot, are you a secret billionaire?"

The question was so unexpected that he couldn't help laughing.

"That's not the term I'd typically use, and *billionaire* is a stretch, but… I've done well for myself. Let's leave it at that."

"In that case, maybe you could help by inviting some of your rich investor friends from Boston to the gala."

"Consider it done. I'll give you a few more names for the mailing list. But make sure to tell them you're only interested in donations or they'll just want to buy the place."

They'd nearly reached the Witch's Castle, a stony structure covered by moss. The place had an aura of magic that gave even greater weight to its name. The air, normally filled with the chatter of other hikers, had grown quiet around them.

"I've always loved this place," Bria said.

"Isn't the stone house supposed to have a bit of a ghost story?"

"I like to think of it as a love story. Sometime in the nineteenth century, Mortimer Stump fell in love with Anna, a local settler's oldest daughter. Only they couldn't be together, because…" She swallowed. "Because Anna's father didn't approve."

Eliot traced the graffiti someone had left on one of the stone walls. "As I recall, this story doesn't turn out too well for poor Mortimer."

"Well, it didn't turn out great for Anna's father, either. One of many reasons why people shouldn't thwart young love."

Now it was his turn to swallow. "They really shouldn't."

Bria clambered up the stone steps and sat atop the wall.

Eliot, tired, stayed on the ground below her. "Careful," he told her. "It's slippery."

"Don't worry, I'm used to climbing around on these stones." But even as she spoke, her ankle twisted at an odd angle, and she lost her balance and slipped backward down several steps.

Eliot caught her before she could completely fall over, wrapping his arms around her.

Let go, he thought, once he was sure she was steady. But he found that he didn't want to.

He turned her so that she was facing him, and then, before he even realized what he was doing, he bent forward to kiss her. His lips sought hers, and as she put her hand to the back of his head to press him forward, he crushed his mouth against hers, all the yearning of their years apart taking shape in a single kiss. He was intoxicated by her taste—the familiar vanilla lip gloss, coffee and the third, indefinable element that he could only classify as *her*. It was a taste he hadn't known he was craving for six years, and yet now that he'd had it, his desperation for more only grew.

He might have gone on kissing her indefinitely—if another hiker hadn't come running up to them, panting.

"Please," the man yelled. "I need help." He seemed to be in his late thirties, rather out of shape and completely unaware that he was interrupting anything.

"It's my wife," he gasped. "I had to leave her alone—you're the first other hikers I've seen. Something's wrong. I think she needs a doctor."

CHAPTER FIVE

THE KISS STOPPED almost as quickly as it began, the moment melting away at the sudden interruption. Bria disentangled herself from Eliot's arms, her heart racing. But there was no time to sort out her emotions, as complicated as they were. The hiker was clearly in distress and desperate for help.

"Please," he gasped again. "I ran all the way here, and I've had to leave her alone."

"We're both medical professionals," said Eliot. "Tell us what's wrong, and we'll help in any way we can."

"Oh, thank god. She was stung by a bee, but for some reason she won't use her EpiPen."

"Can you take us to her?"

"Yes, she's just down the road. She couldn't walk anymore, and we both left our phones in the car. I shouldn't have left her, but I didn't know what else to do.

"You did exactly right," Eliot said as they followed the man back down the trail at a rapid pace.

Bria willed herself to snap back into medical mode. Though she tried to focus herself mentally, her emotions after that kiss ran the gamut from terrified to confused to pure, unadulterated joy.

You can sort out your feelings later, she told herself.

If she and Eliot were about to deal with a medical emergency, she needed to remain in the here and now.

"Up ahead," the man said.

A woman was sitting on the ground next to the trail, her head folded over bent knees. Three or four people hovered near her; it appeared as though another hiking group had come upon her while her husband had gone for help.

"Has anyone called for an ambulance?" Bria asked as they approached the woman. One of the hikers nodded and raised his phone.

"Excellent. Then the best thing you can all do is give this woman some space while my colleague and I take a look at her. Clear away, please. Unless you're a medic, I want everyone at least six feet back."

Bria knelt to take the woman's pulse, which was weak and erratic. Her neck and chest were covered in large hives, and her lips were swollen. "What are your names?" she asked the man.

"I'm Tim, and she's Rachel." He shook his head, his face distraught. "We're from Nevada. This trip was supposed to be a chance to recover after a rough year, and…" His voice faded, and Bria could see how frightened he was. "She has to be all right."

"We'll do everything we can. But I need you to stay focused while I ask you a few questions. Is there anything wrong with the EpiPen?"

He handed it to Bria. "It seems fine, as far as I can tell."

It seemed to be in good working order to Bria as well. "You said she was stung by a bee—does she have any other known allergens?"

"Not that I know of. She hasn't been stung since she was a child, but it must have been pretty bad back then, because she's always had her EpiPen with her whenever we go on hikes, just in case. I've never seen her like this before." His lower lip began to tremble, and he looked as though he might cry.

"Tim, I want you to talk to Dr. Wright while I see to Rachel. Tell him everything you might know about Rachel's medical history. I'll see if I can help her." She nodded to Eliot, who took the hint and steered Tim a few yards down the trail, out of hearing distance.

Bria noticed that the woman's breaths were coming in a strained wheeze. "Rachel, you're showing classic signs of anaphylaxis. Your husband said you got stung by a bee?"

Rachel nodded, but as she saw the EpiPen in Bria's hand, her eyes widened and she pushed Bria's arm away.

"Don't worry, I'm a nurse-midwife, and my friend over there is a doctor. I won't do anything you don't want me to. But I've taken your pulse, and your blood pressure seems dangerously low. The sooner I give you the shot, the better."

Rachel shook her head violently. She tried to speak, but her lips were too swollen. Tears of frustration formed at the corners of her eyes.

Bria looked over at Eliot and saw that he was on his phone. He saw her looking and called, "Ambulance here in ten."

Good. Bria put her hand on Rachel's shoulder. "Medics will be here soon. In the meantime, we do need to use your EpiPen to give you the best recovery."

Rachel shook her head again and craned her neck to look at where Tim and Eliot were standing. They were deep in conversation. She looked back at Bria, shook her head and patted her stomach.

"Oh! You're—

Before she could say the word *pregnant*, Rachel put a finger to her lips and shook her head again.

"I understand." Bria lowered her voice. "He doesn't know?"

Rachel shook her head again, tears falling more freely. She tried again to speak, but her breath was coming too hard and fast.

Bria had a feeling that Rachel's harsh breathing wasn't just due to anaphylaxis but to the woman's distress. She hastily fished her own phone out of her hiking bag and opened the text function. "Here, just type whatever you want to say on my phone." She handed it to Rachel.

Rachel hurriedly texted.

Had miscarriage last year. Didn't want to tell him like this.

A recent miscarriage—no wonder Rachel was so distraught. By the looks of things, Rachel was probably early in her first trimester; even a midwife wouldn't have guessed she was pregnant without looking carefully for the signs. And after her loss, Rachel was probably walking on eggshells out of fear of losing another chance at a baby.

"Don't worry. It's very early still, right? So you can probably use your EpiPen safely. There's no known risk to the baby." Rachel's eyes were wide, and Bria knew she wanted what every worried mother wanted: certainty that she was making the right decision, knowledge that her baby would be all right.

Her hunch was confirmed seconds later when Rachel texted another message on her phone.

Probably???

There had been so many times since she'd become a midwife that Bria had longed to give her patients certainty. But she'd learned very early on in her career that making false promises only made things worse. Unable to give Rachel the certainty she craved, Bria tried for the next best thing: honesty.

"I can't promise there's no risk at all. But I can guarantee that your anaphylaxis poses a greater risk to your baby right now than using your EpiPen."

Rachel's breathing grew more relaxed. Bria could see that she was thinking it over, trying to make the best decision in a crisis. Then she gripped Bria's hand and nodded, pulling up the hem of her hiking shorts. Bria pushed the tip of the EpiPen firmly against the side of Rachel's thigh.

The injection took effect within moments. Bria was relieved to see the hives disappearing from her chest and neck, and the swelling in her face began to recede. They sat together as Rachel's breathing eased.

Bria took her pulse again. "You should start feeling better soon. Your pulse is still a bit slow, though, and that's something we'll want to get back to normal right away, because if you have low blood pressure, that can have an effect on the baby. Dr. Wright said the ambulance should be here any minute, and they'll take you to the hospital to make sure you're all right. They'll probably want to keep you overnight just to be sure."

"A hospital," Rachel whispered, shaking her head. "Tim is going to freak."

"If you like, we can just say that a hospital stay is standard procedure and nothing more. I would recommend that you go to the hospital even if you weren't pregnant."

Rachel paused. "It was so hard when we lost the first baby. I was trying to wait for just the right time to tell him I was pregnant again. I know if I tell him now, after this emergency, he'll just worry nonstop."

"But you need support, too. I can tell you're tremendously concerned about your baby. That's why you wouldn't let me give you that EpiPen."

Rachel gave a husky laugh, her voice still weak. "That was stupid. I panicked. I didn't know what to do."

"Not stupid at all. You were desperate to do the best thing for your baby. It's hard to make those kinds of decisions under pressure, when you don't have all the information. You didn't know if the EpiPen was safe. And anaphylaxis is sudden and frightening. Considering the circumstances, I think you did well. You waited for a medical professional to arrive, and you trusted their opinion."

Rachel gave her a watery smile. "I'm just lucky you were here."

"I'm glad I was, too. But think about the support you already have. The longer you keep this a secret, the more you're cutting yourself off from someone who could help."

"I know. Tim wouldn't want me to feel alone. It's just that we've wanted a child for so long. I can't stand to think of losing another one. And Tim would be devastated, too."

Though she'd never shared Rachel's experience, Bria could understand how she felt. It must have been devastating for Rachel to have her hopes raised and then dashed. No wonder she'd been afraid to use the EpiPen.

She gave Rachel's hand a squeeze. "Part of protecting your baby is about keeping you as healthy as possible. And that means having Tim's support as well." She retrieved a business card from her pocket and handed it to Rachel. "When you're ready, why don't you call the Multnomah Falls Women's Health Center? We have therapists who work with couples who've faced miscarriage, and they can give you some guidance on how to find a good counselor at home in Nevada."

The ambulance arrived, sirens blaring, and Bria returned to Eliot.

"Let's give Tim and Rachel some privacy," she replied, steering him away from where the couple sat by the roadside. They walked a little farther down the road and then heard Tim give a shout of joy. Bria turned to see him throwing his arms around Rachel.

"Well, it looks like she told him."

"Told him what?"

"That she's pregnant."

"Ah, so that's why you took over so quickly back there, leaving me to tend to the husband."

"I thought I might be able to find out why she was refusing the EpiPen more quickly without her husband around. Anyway, we aren't at the hospital now. You don't get to pull rank out here."

"So it seems. Perhaps I should refer to you as Dr. Thomas from now on."

"Hmm, that does have a nice ring to it."

"You did very well. You had her calmed so quickly. I might have just given her the injection right away, but your approach was better—asking her questions, explaining things, calming her down. Patients always do better when they understand the treatment."

Her heart warmed at the compliment, even though she'd been trying to tell herself since he'd arrived that his opinion didn't matter. And then she remembered.

You kissed him.

The medical emergency had absorbed her so much that she hadn't even had time to think about it.

What on earth had happened back there at the Witch's House?

He seemed pretty eager to kiss you, too.

It had been an accident, falling into his arms like that. But what had happened afterward had been more than an accident. She could have pushed away from him instead of allowing herself to melt into his arms. Instead of leaning her face closer to his.

She realized he'd been silent for a few moments and wondered if he was thinking of their kiss, too.

"That was pretty close back there," he said. Her heart nearly stopped.

"But I supposed it's for the best, if it means the secret's out," he continued.

"The secret?" Her lips were dry.

"At least now that he knows she's pregnant, she won't have to bear all that worry alone."

Of course. His mind was still with their patients. She was glad the growing darkness hid the blush on her cheeks.

"That's the thing about secrets," she said, searching desperately for something to say that wouldn't show him her mind had been occupied with entirely different thoughts. "It always feels better once they're out."

She'd been trying to steer away from the subject of the kiss, but somehow it seemed as though they were right back where they'd started.

They had, in fact, reached the beginning of the trailhead, where they'd begun the evening's adventures.

"Well, that was unexpected," she said, trying to keep her voice bright and casual. "We both came here looking to relax, but duty called instead."

"Ninety percent of being in the medical profession is about being in the right place at the right time. I'm just glad we both decided to come here tonight."

"Me, too. I'm so happy we were able to help in time."

He reached out as though to put a hand on her shoulder, but then his hand trailed all the way down her arm, finally clasping her hand. She shivered under his touch.

"I meant for other reasons as well."

Oh. Alarm bells rang within her ears. His hand still held hers. The pull toward him was magnetic, irresistible. She should tell him good night. She should remind him that they were friends and colleagues, and that trying to be anything more would only lead to both of them getting hurt all over again.

She opened her mouth to say all those things, but what came out instead was "Would you like to come over to my place?"

Bria didn't live far from Forest Park. Dusk was falling as they walked, and she found herself once again relieved that the growing darkness hid her expression. She'd never been very good at hiding her feelings. She was sure she looked as nervous as she felt.

Eliot, on the other hand, was his typical stoic self. It was hard to make out his face in the darkness, but even if she could, she wasn't sure she would have found much there to inform her as to what he was feeling.

If she hadn't been emboldened by their kiss, she probably would have listened to the part of her that had better sense, and they'd have parted back at the trailhead. But she could still feel her lips tingling. Could still feel the way his arms had wrapped around her, holding her as though he'd never let her go.

But we did let go of each other.

Once. A long time ago. No matter what happened next, she couldn't let herself forget that. Becoming involved with Eliot was almost a certain road to heartbreak.

But what if their involvement was for one night only?

There was so much that was unresolved between them. Their relationship was such a tangle that she didn't think it could ever be sorted out.

But maybe they didn't need to sort it out. Maybe they could be together, just for now, and get whatever resolution the night could afford them.

They reached her building, an older brownstone with creaking front steps. She unlocked the main door and led him up to her hallway.

"One second," she said when they reached the door. She slipped into her apartment, a modest one-bedroom, and flicked the lights on. Her housekeeping skills were relaxed at best, but work had called her away from home so often recently that she hadn't been home much, which meant that things were relatively neat. *Relatively* being the key word.

She dashed into her bedroom. Within twenty seconds, she had kicked a pair of old jeans underneath the bed, cleared a plate peppered with toast crumbs from her nightstand and turned the stuffed panda from her childhood to face the wall. Perfect. She returned to the doorway, where Eliot stood. Waiting.

"Come on in," she said, trying to calm her fluttering nerves.

He entered, and she instantly became nervous about what he might see when he looked around the apartment. Was there some clutter she'd forgotten to attend to?

But his eyes were fixed on her. They seemed to burn with a question. Eliot had always been had to read, but the intensity of his gaze left no room for wondering if he'd misread her intentions when she'd invited him here.

He stepped toward her, and she didn't back away.

He put his hands on her shoulders lightly and traced his hands all the way down her arms, just as he had in the park. This time, she didn't try to hide her shiver. He bent his head down until his lips just barely grazed hers. Unable to wait any longer, she pressed her mouth against his. His kisses were soft and slow, as though after all these years, he wanted to take his time in rediscovering her. His tongue entered her mouth, and a slow urgency began to build between them. He pulled her body closer, and she leaned into him, feeling herself melt against him.

He rubbed his hands along her back, her waist, as though he was exploring her body for the first time. And yet, when he reached one breast, he paused there, stroking her nipple between his thumb and forefinger. Clearly, there were some things he hadn't forgotten.

She arched her back, reveling in his touch, aching to feel his hands on her bare skin. Anticipating her desire, he began to unbutton her blouse, slipping it from her shoulders as though he'd unwrapped a present. With a flick of his fingers, he undid her bra, which fell to the floor in a crumple of black lace. He bent his head to give her breasts their due attention, his tongue attending to all the old places—and some new ones as well.

"Come over here," she whispered, tearing herself away before she became lost in sensation. She took his hand and led him to the bedroom. He kicked off his shoes, and she began undoing his belt buckle as he pulled off his T-shirt over his head to reveal the smooth planes of his body. She unbuttoned her own trousers, and he slipped them off along with her underwear in one smooth motion.

She stood before him, naked. For the first time in six years.

She felt self-conscious, but at least he was naked, too. He still seemed as perfect as she remembered. His thighs were long and lean, his abdomen well-defined. As he gazed at her, she saw him growing hard, and she knew she wasn't the only one whose need was becoming urgent.

He drew her close and muttered something in her ear. Caught up as she was in the thrill of feeling his bare skin against hers, it took her a moment to realize he was asking about protection. She reached into the nightstand, where she had an endless supply of condoms, not because she had need of them often, but because such were the perks of working in women's health care.

He laid her on the bed and took her mouth with his, both of them releasing themselves to the desire that overtook them. Her thoughts melted away as she became lost in the sensation of his body atop hers, her limbs intertwining with his.

His hands moved down to caress the space between her legs, and the need within her became a fire that she was unable to control. She writhed under him and gasped his name to let him know she wouldn't be able to hold on much longer.

He shifted his hips, and she could feel him, hard and hot against her. As she tilted her hips upward to meet his, he entered with a long, slow thrust that made her moan with pleasure.

He moved within her, slowly at first, and then his pace quickened as she joined him, their bodies coming together in a rhythmic dance that they knew of old, yet that still somehow felt brand-new. She arched beneath him, and he thrust until she was teetering on the edge of ecstasy.

Finally, she let herself go. She heard his groan as though from a great distance, heard him calling out her name. She felt the sensation of stars bursting inside her over and over again. Finally, her body collapsed against his, sated and replete. An empty place within her, one that she'd denied even to herself for so long, had been filled at last.

Stars, she thought, barely able to form thoughts in her mind. Her last thought, before her eyes closed, was that she hadn't been aware of wishing on one. But if she had, she would have wished for this.

The first rays of morning light made their way through Bria's window. She blinked her eyes open and saw that Eliot was still there, his eyes shut, his face in peaceful repose. She'd forgotten those gentle snores of his: quiet enough to let her sleep, but just loud enough to make her feel his comforting presence. She snuggled closer to him, allowing herself to inhale the faint cinnamon spice scent that always lingered on his skin.

She couldn't remember the last time she'd had sex that had left her feeling so satisfied, so complete. The few encounters she'd had, scattered over the last six years, hadn't held much significance for her. She'd been seeking something, and after failing to find it for so long, she hadn't merely decided it didn't exist—she'd forgotten that she'd ever hoped for it in the first place.

But last night had awakened that forgotten part of her. She'd given in to her feelings and her memories, allowing the two of them to return to the past for one fleeting, shining moment.

Of course, their future remained to be determined. Eliot shifted in the bed. One of her rumpled sheets nearly slid off him, not leaving much to the imagination. She relaxed her body against his. She refused to spoil this moment by worrying about the future when she had such a scene of actual perfection in front of her right now.

He stretched and rolled over to face her, batting his eyes open. He saw that she was awake and smiled.

"Are you cold?" she asked. "I can grab another blanket from the closet."

He put an arm around her waist and pulled her even closer to him. "I've got everything I need to keep me warm right here." She nestled against his chest, indulging in the hypnotic rhythm of his heartbeat.

"Besides—" he kissed the top of her head "—you've got the heat blasting away."

"That's radiator heat for you. I can't control it." The only buildings in which she'd been able to afford the rent for a one-bedroom apartment had been more than a hundred years old. Central air was one of the luxuries she sorely missed from her past life. Her inefficient radiator meant that she rarely slept with blankets and often wore shorts and tank tops when home alone, even in the winter. At least she was never cold.

His eyes wandered around her apartment. It wasn't fancy, but it was cozy, and it was special, because it was hers. She'd found that she enjoyed decorating on a budget. Her room might not look as stately as it had when she'd lived in her father's mansion, but each item had personal meaning to her. She noticed him taking in the wall hangings, the collage of photographs artfully displayed on her bureau.

"I like your place. It's a fantastic location, and even though it's small, it feels homey."

"That's what I was going for."

"It must be a far cry from what you're used to, though."

She nodded. "I think this whole apartment could probably fit into one of my father's guest bathrooms."

"Was it hard to adjust, coming from a place like that to a place like this?"

"No. Not for a second." She saw his eyebrows lift, so she explained further. "After spending two years in Haiti, I understood how much everything was relative. My family's estate might be opulent compared to this apartment. But my apartment has everything I need. Warmth, a refrigerator, a solid roof. All I had to do to get comfortable was add a strong Wi-Fi signal and a decent coffee maker."

"What made you decide to go to Haiti?"

"I had just finished my nurse-midwife program. That was where I met Hazel. I was so impressed by how she knew exactly who she was. But I still didn't know myself at all. I needed a change, and that change needed to be something meaningful. Something that would show me who I wanted to be, rather than the person everyone thought I should be."

"And did it work? Did you find yourself?"

She thought for a moment. "I definitely found a new appreciation for different parts of my life. Friendships became so much more valuable to me. Things I'd always took for granted, like electricity and clean drinking water, became small miracles to enjoy. I don't know if I exactly found myself, but I think I came to understand my own life far better than I used to."

"I think it would have been hard for a lot of people to give up so much."

She hesitated, and then admitted, "Full disclosure—my

coffee maker is a Breville. I may have given up my family's fortune, but I didn't become a saint."

He buried his face in her hair and laughed. "I don't know what that is, but I assume you gave up as much as you could stand."

"Everybody has their limit."

"I'm not surprised at all to hear that the coffee maker is yours. Speaking of which. What are we going to do for breakfast?"

"Well…" She held the pause for as long as she could, not wanting to let the moment go. But she couldn't put it off any longer. Last night had been exquisite, but the sun was in the sky, and a new day had begun. They couldn't avoid talking about the night before without engaging in more denial than she could tolerate.

"Breakfast is a problem that's easily solved," she said. "But first, what are we going to do about last night?"

"Do we need to do anything about it?"

She'd been sitting up with the sheets around her, but at his words, she flopped backward into the bed with her hands over her eyes. This was exactly why she hadn't wanted to have this conversation. It was why she'd wanted to linger against his body, enjoying the cinnamon scent of him for as long as possible. Last night had been exciting, an unexpected opportunity to reignite the heat that had once existed between them. That clearly *still* existed between them.

But if she expected him to reveal any feelings about their night together, she was sorely mistaken. Mistaken, but not surprised. She knew Eliot. If she was going to get any feelings out of him, she'd have to go in with a pair of pliers.

Was he regretting last night? Did he feel it would create unnecessary complications, for them to be romantically involved while they were coworkers?

"We need to at least talk about it," she said. The room,

which had seemed so warm just a moment ago, now felt tense and uncomfortable. She took a deep breath and decided to get things over with. Things between them were already complicated, and she would rather rip the bandage off all at once instead of allowing the two of them to labor under any further misunderstandings. "Do you have any regrets?"

"Absolutely not," he said, to her utter relief. "In fact, I'd be glad to repeat the experience as often as possible."

That was unexpected. She'd assumed he'd merely given in to physical attraction, just as she had. Her heart felt lighter than it had in years, and yet she cautioned herself, *be careful, go slow.* She'd need to make sure she understood his intentions perfectly before allowing her heart to soar even the slightest bit higher. "But you're leaving in a little over a month."

"Then what would you say to making the most of that month?"

Her heart no longer felt as though it was soaring. It was more like spinning, leaving her uncertain of her direction. She knew what he was about to suggest, and she saw the sense of it. Eliot's life was in Boston. Hers was in Portland.

"Are you suggesting what I think you're suggesting?"

He put an arm around her. "We obviously have an attraction to one another. Maybe we could enjoy the physical part of that attraction without the other complications that always get us into trouble. No romance. Just sex. And then at the end of it, we say our goodbyes."

She hesitated. A fling with Eliot. Part of her leaped at the idea; another part warned her that she was setting herself up for hurt. But how much could they really hurt each other in a month? And given their past, these might be the only terms on which they could realistically be together. Even after last night, her body craved closeness to his. He was right about their attraction to one another. After last night, there was no mistaking that. But she couldn't see how they could ever have anything more. She'd hurt him so badly in the past. How could he ever trust her with his heart again? She couldn't imagine it was possible.

If she was completely honest with herself, she'd been longing to touch him, to feel the heat of his skin against hers, from the moment he'd returned. Despite her best efforts, she hadn't been able to stop thinking about him, and she was beginning to doubt whether she ever would. A brief fling might be her only hope of ever getting over him, once and for all. It wasn't a rekindling of their relationship. That could never happen. But it might be the next best thing—closure.

"Just one month, then?" she said, wanting to be absolutely clear.

"Just one month. No promises. No romantic involvement. We keep things purely physical. And then at the end of it, we say our goodbyes."

After all that had passed between them, did she really have anything to lose? Breaking up with him had been like having a piece of her heart torn out. But this would be different. This time, there would be no breakup, because there would be no relationship.

"All right. I'll agree on one condition."

He cocked an eyebrow at her. "What's that?"

She looked him in the eye. "That when you leave, we have a *real* goodbye. No taking off suddenly, without warning. When the time comes, I'll drive you to the airport, we'll hug and we'll have an actual goodbye instead of a painful one." Their last goodbye had been so harsh; they'd hurt each other so much. She wanted this chance for closure, for them both to be able to move on.

Last night had been about reminiscence, about connecting to the heat between them that had always made their relationship special. But she held no false hope that one night together had anything to do with their future. She'd killed any real feelings he might have had for her by breaking up with him, and by now they'd both built separate lives apart from each other. She wasn't so naive as to think that his desire for her was about anything more than being caught up in the moment and the memories between them. Allowing herself to want anything more than that would only result in getting hurt.

But she thought it was fair for her to want a kinder farewell than they'd had six years ago. Maybe their month together could give them a chance to write over the pain of their last goodbye. It couldn't hurt to try.

"All right," he said. "I think I can offer you that."

"Great," she said, kissing him on the cheek. She extricated herself from the bedsheets. "Now, about that breakfast. Let me make you a cuppa, and then maybe you'll understand why I kept the fancy coffee machine."

She fixed their coffees the way they both liked them—his with a dash of cinnamon, hers with a scoop of cocoa. Even the smell brought a sense of nostalgia. She'd have to be cautious about getting swept up in that, though. Revisiting some memories might be fun, but she didn't want to get her heart broken all over again. All she wanted to do was enjoy the present moment, however fleeting it might be.

CHAPTER SIX

"IT SEEMS LIKE everyone on staff just loves you."

Eliot shrugged, but inwardly, he was pleased by Caleb's words. He hadn't seen much of his friend since he'd come to Portland, but Caleb had stopped by his office at St. Raymond's to see how he was enjoying being interim chair.

"*Love* is a strong word—I'm just glad to hear I'm fitting in. I appreciate the feedback, though. And the opportunity. I didn't realize just how much I've missed doing medicine full-time. Working at a hospital like this has been like stepping into another world, if only for a few weeks."

"It doesn't have to be just for a few weeks, you know. I've talked with Dr. Anderson. He'd be glad to end the search for a new hire now and keep you on permanently."

Eliot frowned, the old conflict welling within him. Caleb couldn't know just how tempted Eliot was to take him up on his offer. But the salary he'd make at St. Raymond's was barely a fraction of what he could make working at his firm in Boston. And the senior partners were counting on him to return. He couldn't simply walk away from his responsibilities.

But more importantly, there was the matter of Bria. He liked the way things had been between them since they'd established their arrangement of a purely physical, no-emotional-strings-attached affair. Their physical chemistry had always been good, and now it was exhilarating, perhaps because he'd been trying to ignore his attraction to her from the moment he arrived. But now he didn't need to hold back. They could both enjoy one another without having to worry about feelings from the past. Or any feelings at all, really. Emotional attachment made things far too complicated.

But if he stayed in Portland permanently, he risked deepening things with Bria. Even now, after only two weeks with her, he felt himself growing more involved. He'd noticed himself looking forward to spending time with her and feeling disappointed when she wasn't nearby. These were dangerous feelings. He couldn't allow himself to grow close to her again. He was enjoying their physical connection, but he had no interest in anything else. Especially not when the chances of having his heart shattered again were so high. The sooner he returned to Boston, the better.

"I'm afraid I have too many obligations in Boston," he told Caleb.

"Is that right? Because I was wondering if a certain midwife might be affecting your decision."

Eliot jerked his head up. "What do you mean?"

"I've been talking with Hazel, and she said you two have a history. I hope that hasn't created any problems. When I asked you to work here, I had no idea that you'd be in such close proximity to your ex. I'm sorry."

"Don't be. How could you have known? I never told you about her."

"Is there…anything you'd like to tell me about her now?"

"Why do you ask?"

"Because Hazel and I get the impression that whatever is between you two right now might be *more* than just history."

Eliot paused. He and Bria hadn't discussed how open they planned to be about their fling. But if she was talking to Hazel about it, then she couldn't fault him for saying anything to Caleb. "We've figured out an arrangement that works for both of us. But it won't complicate anything. We've both agreed, no talking about the past and no emotions."

"No, that definitely won't complicate anything," Caleb said dryly. "Those kinds of arrangements tend to work out really well."

"This one will," Eliot insisted. "It's not like other short-term relationships. We didn't just meet each other. We have a past. So we already know that getting emotionally involved is a mistake. We don't have to go through all that again. This is just about…moving on."

"Having sex with your ex is moving on? Eliot, you're one of the most brilliant people I know, so I'd never question your judgment. But doesn't getting involved with someone from your past feel more like moving backward than forward?"

"That's the beauty of it. We're not getting involved at all. This is more like a long goodbye."

Caleb shook his head. "Well, you're the medical and financial wizard. I'm just a lowly obstetrician. I won't presume to give you advice. But… I'm around if you want to talk, okay?"

He left Eliot to his work. But try as he might to focus on chart review, Eliot's mind kept swirling with questions.

Caleb's doubts about his arrangements with Bria could be easily dismissed. Eliot was perfectly satisfied with the ground rules of their affair. Caleb might not understand because he didn't know the full force of his attraction to Bria. And knowing that she was attracted to him, too, was like a drug he couldn't get enough of. But Eliot was certain that if he and Bria acted on their attraction, they could get one another out of their systems by the time he left. He'd be able to move on and finally find someone else, because he wouldn't be preoccupied with the way he felt about her any longer.

Caleb had also dropped something of a bombshell with his suggestion that Eliot might stay on at St. Raymond's permanently. Eliot had often thought about working full-time at a hospital, but only in an abstract sense. Caleb's suggestion had thrown his decision into stark reality. For the first time in a long time, Eliot wasn't sure what to do.

He felt more energized than he'd been in years. He'd meant it when he told Caleb that being at the hospital was like being in another world. One he hadn't realized how much he'd missed. Immersing himself in a medical environment offered a dramatic change from his career back in Boston. It was a change he had needed, badly.

His life in Boston had become rote, mechanical. But hospital work made him feel alive. Even days like today, which consisted mainly of signing off on charts and reviewing complex cases, left him feeling excited rather than worn-out. The cases piqued his interest and his curiosity. Even the background conversation of the nurses and physician's assistants felt invigorating. Everything about the hospital made him look forward to coming to work in the morning.

At home, his business partners were constantly trying to convince him to give up his medical license so that he'd have more time to spend on his work. But here, he had colleagues nearby who understood and valued the satisfaction of a career as a physician.

His office door was open, and he happened to hear Bria's voice from down the hall. She was talking over a case with one of the nurses.

Everything about the hospital felt right to him, including working with her.

He'd been so afraid of running into her when he returned to Portland. But the moment he kissed her, all those fears had fallen away. Kissing her had felt like he was coming home again. And when they'd made love, it had felt as though he'd found where he belonged.

When they'd arranged their fling, he'd initially been concerned that there might be some awkwardness between them at work. But if anything, they worked even better as colleagues now. It felt as though their physical connection had somehow given them an understanding that needed no words.

Though all seemed well between them, there was one small worry that had been nagging at the back of his mind ever since he and Bria had helped those hikers on the trail to the Witch's Castle. It had arisen after Bria's comment about secrets.

It always feels better once they're out.

He did have a secret, and it could make her feel differently about him. He'd realized he didn't want to tell her, but he knew it would only get worse the longer it remained unsaid.

He'd never told her about his mother's Christmas bonus, and the more he saw of her, the more certain he felt that she didn't know anything about it.

It wouldn't be that surprising if Calvin had never told her. The man had found it difficult enough to see his daughter as a person, let alone care about her feelings. The Thomas reputation was far more important to Calvin than any preferences of Bria's.

Would Bria feel any differently about him if she knew that his money essentially came from her father? She'd told him that it had been years since she'd lived off her family's trust. What would she think of him for having taken Calvin's money at such a critical time?

It was so important to her not to feel controlled by her father. Would she think less of him? Especially after she'd been able to step away from her family's wealth?

Even if she did, he didn't know what he could have done

differently. He could never have stopped his mother from taking that money. It had meant too much to her, and she'd sacrificed too much for him. She'd been so proud to bestow it on him, believing that her years of work had finally enabled her to provide for him the way she'd always wanted. Not only was he not going to take that happiness from her, he'd fight anyone who did. But what if Bria saw it as a lie? What if she thought he'd deliberately been keeping this a secret from her?

And was it really a secret, or simply something he'd decided not to tell her? Was there even a difference?

He had a feeling Bria might think so.

But he didn't want to bring it up with her. And morally, he thought he would be in the clear even if he never told her. He and Bria had agreed that they weren't in a relationship. They'd probably never see each other after he returned to Boston. So telling her about the money would only risk upsetting her for no reason. After six years, there was no point in rehashing old history. He didn't want to spoil their time together by bringing up the past, and he didn't think she did, either.

Bria had been excited when Eliot asked if she'd wanted to meet for dinner after her shift. She was doing her best not to analyze the connection between them. For right now, she simply wanted to enjoy what they had together.

If she thought about it too much, she'd have to recall that Eliot was leaving his position at St. Raymond's soon. Which would mean that there was nothing keeping him in Portland. But she didn't want to dwell on those thoughts, because they interfered with what their time now was supposed to be about: tying up the loose ends of their relationship and saying goodbye in a kinder way than they'd been able to six years ago.

She was loving the sex, but even more than that, she'd

been enjoying spending time with him outside work—and outside the bedroom. Though not all their excursions went as planned.

She poked at her duck confit, her stomach growling. "I didn't realize this was what you had in mind when you suggested we meet for dinner this evening."

She'd thought they might go out for something casual, but Eliot had surprised her with reservations at L'Epicure, one of Portland's most exclusive French restaurants. It had opened within the past year, to much fanfare, and reservations quickly became impossible to get. Eliot, however, had simply called a few hours before they arrived to reserve a table.

The chef at L'Epicure was well-known for his emphasis on taste and flavor. But most of the food was served in the form of small cubes—hardly enough for two hungry medical professionals coming off a busy shift.

Bria's duck confit with field greens was a small cube of—presumably—duck, about the size of half a domino, and two lettuce leaves, artfully placed so they crossed one another.

She poked again at the cube dubiously. "Is it supposed to bounce?"

"I think the bouncing is what makes it fancy," said Eliot. His own small cube of sea bass seemed even smaller in the center of the vast, otherwise empty white plate.

Their waiter approached to ask if they were ready for the next course.

"What is it?" Eliot asked.

"Lobster roe, bathed in a sea of crème fraîche."

Bria's heart sank. Why was the most expensive food always the most unappetizing? She was all too familiar with these kinds of restaurants, though it had been a long time since she'd set foot in one. The restaurant was so focused on being exclusive that it had forgotten to make sure to serve good food. In her experience, the quality of the food didn't matter in a place like this. No one ate it. People came to places like this to see who was here and to be seen themselves.

The waiter removed their plates and set the next course in front of them. Bria looked at Eliot with pleading eyes.

"What's wrong?" he said. "Don't you like your, um… your fish eggs?"

At that, they both burst out laughing.

"I'm not sure this type of place is my thing anymore," she said.

"It's kind of a bust, isn't it?" he replied. "I was hoping that coming here might be a nice change of pace for you, since I got the impression that it's been quite some time since you went anywhere really special for a meal."

She picked her fork up and then set it down decidedly. There was simply no way she could eat the dish in front of her. "I think I've been a midwife for too long for this to count as an actual dinner."

"Damn. Guess my timing was off."

She gave him a quizzical look, and he explained. "I wanted to impress you. Back when we were dating, I always wanted to take you to a fancy restaurant."

"But we went to nice places all the time."

"Yes, but you paid for our meals. You got the reservations that were impossible to get. I, on the other hand, was lucky if I could dig enough money out of my sofa cushions to pay for pizza once in a while."

"Oh, Eliot, what does it matter who paid for anything? You were my fiancé. I never resented having to pay for things. I was always happy to share with you, to make both of our lives better."

"Yes, because you could afford it."

"So what? What difference does it make? You'd have done the same if our positions were reversed. In fact, this dinner proves it. Our positions *are* reversed. Am I supposed to feel embarrassed and insecure because you're taking me out to a dinner I can't afford myself?" An even worse thought occurred to her. "Or is this supposed to be some attempt to pay me back for all the times I took you out while you were dating? As though I was keeping some weird sort of ledger system regarding who spent what?"

"No! Not at all." He seemed to be struggling to explain, and she tried to be patient. She wanted to understand. "I did want to be able to take you somewhere nice tonight. Yes, because of the past. But not in the way you're describing. I only wanted you to enjoy yourself. I was hoping to impress you."

"But you do impress me. Your medical skills impress me. Who you are as a person impresses me. I don't care about what restaurants you can get reservations at or what you can buy. That's not the kind of thing that matters to me."

"But it does matter to some people."

"I've already told you those people don't matter! Why does what other people think have to be important at all?"

His face had a familiar withdrawn expression. She wondered if he was going to shut down, just as he always had every time a conversation got emotional. Six years wasn't nearly enough time to make her forget that pattern: they'd disagree, he'd shut down and she'd feel abandoned and hurt. But this time, instead of withdrawing into himself and leaving her feeling alone and confused, he seemed to think better of it.

"Because sometimes those people will treat you differently. Look, I agree with what you're saying. The best way to deal with other people's judgment is to not care about it. But you have to understand that the cost of being yourself and not caring what other people think is different for me than it is for you."

She wanted to hear more. "Go on."

"I've been trying to live in two different worlds ever since I got into high school," he explained. Bria knew he'd attended an elite prep school in the city. "Word got around that I was a scholarship student, despite my best efforts to keep anyone from finding out. People started spreading rumors that I was poor. Which was true, but you know how cruel kids can be."

"Children can be absolutely horrible little monsters, and that's coming from a midwife who loves children."

"That may be the case, but ultimately children learn their views from their parents. Some of my friends at school had actual live-in servants in their houses. How do you think their parents treated those servants?"

"I can't imagine."

"Well, I have a pretty good guess, because my mother started cleaning some of my classmates' houses after the hotel she worked at shut down. I was so embarrassed. I begged her not to tell anyone she was my mother. And the worst part was, she understood."

"Why was that the worst part?"

"Because there was no reason for either of us to be embarrassed. Cleaning houses is honest work for honest pay. When she agreed to keep it a secret, it was as though she was agreeing that we had something to be ashamed of."

"Eliot, you were only a child. You were just trying to fit in."

"I suppose…but at the time, I felt as though I was betraying our family by not wanting to tell anyone what my mother did. I went to great lengths to keep the secret. I'd try to come up with excuses to keep from having to invite my friends over to our one-bedroom apartment after school. I'd tell them that my mother was away on business, or that we were having our pool cleaned. But I'd go over to their houses. Until, of course, the inevitable happened."

"What was that?"

"One of my friends… I think his name was Langdon… he invited a group of kids over after school to play video games. I was so excited. It was the newest game system. And Langdon lived in this huge thirteen-bedroom mansion. I remember his housekeeper greeted us with snacks, and it was the most substantial meal I'd had all day. I didn't like bringing my lunches to school, you see, because my mother always packed me bologna sandwiches on white bread, and I was embarrassed for the other kids to see how sparse my lunches were. It would have just fueled the rumors that I was poor.

"Anyway, we went into the kitchen to get some more snacks, and there was my mother, cleaning."

"That must have been hard. You were with all of your friends, after all."

"But she was my mother." He paused, and Bria could see it was hard for him to tell this story. "At first, her face lit up when she saw me. But then one of my friends asked if we knew each other. And I said no.

"And I saw her expression slip into nonrecognition. She was going to cover for me. And I couldn't stand it. I said, 'Actually, she's my mother,' and I walked around their expensive kitchen island with the granite countertop and hugged her."

"Oh, she must have been so proud of you."

"Maybe. I can't forget the look on her face when she decided to cover for me. I swore I'd never deny her, or myself, ever again. But there were consequences. The biggest was that I became a total outcast at school. There were no more invitations to play video games with anyone after school. I got picked last for all the team sports."

"I want to repeat what I said before about children being little monsters."

He sighed. "And I'll repeat what I said about their parents."

She couldn't disagree with him.

"College and medical school were better, though," he continued. "Medical school was a great equalizer, because even though there were people from wealthy families, merit and skill counted for a lot. It didn't matter quite so much where you came from, as long as you performed well and got good grades. Or, at least, while in school it didn't matter. After graduation, the people you're connected to made a big difference in the kinds of jobs everyone landed. I saw lots of people beat out better candidates for jobs because they had relationships with major donors or people on the board of directors."

"Hmm, that's a problem we know about all too well," Bria said, rolling her eyes.

"Indeed we do. So I went into business, to give myself some more freedom, and so I could take care of my mother. She's retired to a mansion in Aruba now."

As she listened to Eliot's story, she realized that independence was just as important to him as it was to her. He'd needed to make money to gain his independence, just as she'd needed to give it up to gain hers.

"I'm sorry," she said heavily. "I should have been more perceptive to how you felt about money, especially because I grew up with my father and saw how he manipulated everyone with it. I learned from birth that money was his way of exerting control. I could have anything I wanted, as long as it was something that he wanted to buy me. So I could have the best of everything, but not necessarily what I wanted."

"I'm sure that was hard." She couldn't tell if he was being serious or not, so she tried to explain.

"It was, actually." She tried to think of how to put it into words. "When I was six, an animal shelter had an adoption event downtown, and I begged my parents for a dog. I wanted the sweet brown mutt they had at the shelter. But my father refused to get anything other than a purebred Samoyed. That dog was incredibly bad-tempered and terrorized me for ten years. But my father didn't care, because it looked perfect in our family pictures. He had to control everything, and if I fought against it, it meant I was spoiled, because how could anyone fight against having their life handed to them on a silver platter? But everything I had was completely on his terms."

"So you gave it all up," he said. His voice seemed uneasy. She wondered if it was hard for him to hear her talking about stepping away from her family's fortune when he'd worked so hard for his.

"I needed to build something for myself. And I found midwifery, which allowed me to do that." She laughed. "It seems ironic now that you found your freedom in business, and I found mine in the medical field."

He hesitated and then said, "I don't know that I've found much enjoyment in the business world. But independence, yes. It's going to be hard to leave the hospital in a few weeks. The partners want me to give up my medical license for good so I can focus on the firm full-time, and the only way I could convince them to let me have these six weeks off was to promise that I would."

"You mentioned to me before you were thinking about giving it up, but seriously, why would you do that?"

"I think I have to. The partners are depending on me."

"Yes, to make them more money. But there are patients depending on you, too. It's a lot harder to find a good, compassionate doctor than someone who wants to make a million dollars. I think you could help a lot more people as a doctor than as a millionaire."

"I'd like to think so, but it's not that simple. If I'm not there to lead the firm, and it loses money, that affects the salaries and job security of many medical professionals.

I've been in it for too long now, and at this point I don't see that there's any other way out."

She could see that it was a tough choice for him, but she had a feeling that his career in business hadn't left him feeling very happy. From what she'd seen at the hospital, working with patients made his face light up. He brought an energy to working out difficult diagnoses and helping patients overcome obstacles that she hadn't seen from other doctors. But the expression on his face when he discussed his business career simply looked…dull. As though he was talking about a tiresome chore or discouraging weather.

But at least he was talking about it now. That was a big difference from what she remembered from six years ago and even when he'd first mentioned it to her a couple of weeks ago. He'd never talked about anything. When something was bothering him, he'd always hidden it. She'd always wondered why.

"How come we never talked about these things while we were dating?" she asked him.

He shrugged. "What difference would it have made?"

She couldn't believe it. "Eliot, it would have made *all* the difference." Knowing what Eliot had gone through as a child made his insecurity around money make so much more sense to her now. "Didn't you think I'd understand?"

"The trouble was that *I* didn't understand. It wasn't until long after medical school that I realized I'd tried to fit into two worlds for so long that I'd forgotten how to be myself. When I was younger, and when I was with you, I dealt with things by trying to be the person I thought people wanted to see. But then, with my family, or even in medical school, I didn't want anyone to know how much I was pretending not to be myself. So I hid that, too. The result was that I couldn't be myself anywhere. It felt as though I'd almost forgotten how. And when we broke up, I knew I couldn't try to get back together with you, because as long as we were together, I'd still be trying to fit into your world instead of figuring myself out."

She couldn't help saying, "I thought we could figure ourselves out together."

"No, we couldn't. I was always going to be Bria Thomas's plus-one, instead of my own person."

"But you never even tried to explain this to me. You just held it all in. You're doing the same thing with medicine right now. You're just assuming it can't happen. Maybe if you'd actually talk about this dilemma, you might understand more how you feel about it. I've seen you with patients—and I've seen how they respond to you. You don't belong in a boardroom. You belong in a hospital. I understand why money is important to you, but really, how much more do you need? It doesn't seem to have made you any more secure in yourself."

She instantly regretted her words, worried that she'd spoken out of heat and gone too far.

"I don't belong in a boardroom, do I? Well, thank you very much for telling me. Maybe you can do what you do best and make all of my decisions without asking me."

"I'd love to ask you, Eliot, I'd love to know how you feel, but I need to know that you'll actually tell me instead of shutting down."

"Maybe it's hard to tell someone how I feel when they've already decided what's best for me. It's easy to ask how much money I need when you've had everything you need for your entire life."

"But I gave all that up, Eliot."

"It was still your choice to do that. You could have done a lot of good with that money. For all you know, if you hadn't given up your fortune, you wouldn't need to scramble to raise money for the center now."

"That's not how it works and you know it. My father controls the family trust. Any money from him would have come with major strings attached. And I don't see how you get to judge my financial decisions. Or any of my life decisions, really."

"The way you were just judging mine, you mean?"

"I wasn't trying to judge. I was trying to understand how you feel!"

"Well, maybe you can't."

She put her head in her hands, exasperated. It was so frustrating that they always seemed to arrive back at the same place, no matter how hard they tried not to.

"I'm sorry," Eliot said suddenly. He reached across the table and took her hand.

"What?" She blinked. "Why are you apologizing? I'm the one who spoke out of line first."

"But I'm the one who said we should keep things physical. No trying to rehash the past, no relationship stuff. And yet here we are."

He was right. They'd agreed not to talk about the past, and yet somehow it had a way of coming into the present. And every time it did, they found themselves having a different version of the same old fight.

"We need a reset button," she said.

"Want to start over?" he asked.

"Only if we can start over at a place with some better food."

He poked again at the unappetizing glob on his plate. "This place has two Michelin stars. I'm not sure if there's a better place in Portland."

She smiled and rose from her chair. "I can think of one."

Half an hour later, Bria's eyes closed in pleasure as she sank her teeth into the cheeseburger from the greasy spoon around the corner from the hospital.

"Of all the places we could eat, this is what you wanted," said Eliot, cautiously inspecting his chili.

"Mmm… Now this is a meal. This is real food, not tiny little experiments on plates."

"If I'd known all those years ago that a cheeseburger could smooth things over so easily, we both might have been a lot happier."

She crumpled a napkin and threw it across the table at him playfully. "Hush. Just enjoy the moment." She took another bite. "This diner is the restaurant that should be charging exorbitant prices, not that fancy place up the street. This right here is the breakfast of champions."

"But we're not having breakfast."

"You're right. Maybe we should pick up some extra in case we need to refuel tomorrow morning."

"For breakfast? That sounds unappealing in about eight different ways."

"I know, but hear me out. Babies come at all different times, with absolutely no regard for conventional mealtimes. As a midwife, you get used to eating what you need when you can, rather than worrying about whether your food is appropriate for whatever mealtime it's supposed to be."

"Rather like traveling to different time zones and craving pizza when you arrive somewhere at nine in the morning."

"Exactly." She ate a French fry with great satisfaction. "I can't believe we didn't come here first. I'll take one of these burgers over haute cuisine any time of day."

"Hmm. Well, you *could* take away some cold diner food for breakfast. Or you could try what I think would be a far more enjoyable option."

"And what might that be?"

"Something you don't know about me is that over the past six years, I've nearly perfected the Spanish omelet."

She smiled. "Are you offering to make me breakfast in the morning?"

"Not just any breakfast. I'm offering to make you the best breakfast you've ever had."

She didn't doubt it.

CHAPTER SEVEN

BRIA STARED AT the unopened box, wondering what to do.

The past few weeks had been a blur of work, preparation for the charity gala and nights with Eliot. She'd never been so busy in her life.

She'd been worried that her purely physical fling with Eliot would complicate her life. But as she'd spent long days planning, organizing and generating publicity for the gala, she'd found it all much easier now that she no longer had to spend so much time trying not to think about him. Now that they'd given in to their physical attraction, she didn't have to worry if he noticed a sidelong glance. She didn't have to question whether a look he gave her meant that he was attracted to her. She knew the answer. He *wanted* her. And knowing that he wanted her meant that she didn't have to put so much energy into hiding how much she wanted him.

He would be gone in two weeks. Despite their agreement to keep things on a purely physical level, she knew that when he left, she would be sad. But she also knew that she needed to accept her time with Eliot for what it was: a second chance to end their relationship on peaceful terms. She couldn't allow herself to want anything more than that. And as long as she didn't, she wouldn't have to worry about getting hurt.

Experience had shown that getting emotionally involved with Eliot was a mistake for both of them. Every time they discussed the past, and every time they tried to discuss their feelings for one another, they ended up fighting. Somehow, when she was with him, she couldn't seem to find the right words to express how she felt. And she knew all too well how difficult that was for him. She felt their choice not to allow things to go beyond the physical had been the right one for them both.

But she found it hard to keep herself from getting emotionally involved when Eliot did things that were so unexpected.

Like the box, for example.

It was a pale blue box with a large silver ribbon around it. It had been delivered to her door that morning, but she hadn't had time to open it. A lifetime ago, she'd had such boxes delivered to her home by the dozens. But she hadn't seen one in years.

There was a note from Eliot underneath the ribbon.

Just in case you still need something to wear.

The truth was, she did need something. She'd been so busy that she hadn't had time to rent a ball gown until the last minute, and the one she'd nabbed wasn't exactly flattering on her petite frame. It was formalwear, and it was within her price range, so it would have to do. Hazel had offered to lend her something, but Bria was far too short, and her sewing skills weren't even close to good enough for her to hem up six inches of one of Hazel's dresses.

She didn't want to wear the rented dress, but it wasn't as though she had a range of other options. As the coordinator of the gala, she needed something formal. All eyes would be on her, and she'd be representing the center. The rented dress might not be the best thing she'd ever worn, but at least it was serviceable, and she'd resigned herself to wearing it.

But then the box had arrived. If she was surprised to see it, she was even more surprised to see that it was from Eliot.

She'd held back from opening it for a moment, uncertain of what the box might mean. They'd agreed that their relationship was purely physical. No emotions, no attachment.

So what could he possibly be thinking by sending her a couture dress?

She opened the box with tentative fingers and couldn't help emitting a small gasp when she saw the gown. It was a dark green, the same color as her eyes, made of sleek satin. It was strapless, with a sweetheart neckline and a fluted skirt with a hem that rose up in front just a bit, enough to show off a pair of high heels, and then came down behind her to brush the floor in the barest hint of a train. It had been years since she'd worn anything so beautiful.

And—wonder of wonders—it had pockets.

Gorgeous and functional. The perfect dress for the midwife who needed to slip back into princess mode, just for one night.

Since Bria had become a midwife, her life had gotten considerably less glamorous than it used to be. She spent her days dealing with squirmy newborns, placentas and all the delightful bodily fluids that were involved in the natural order of childbirth.

But that didn't mean she'd forgotten her knowledge of high fashion. This gown had easily cost several thousand dollars, and quite possibly more. It was an incredibly generous gift. He'd remembered their conversation about how she'd sold all her fashionable dresses. She was touched.

Then again, Eliot had made it sound as though a few thousand dollars was the kind of money he might find lying within his couch cushions now.

Still, he couldn't have known how much a dress like this, on a night like this, would mean to her. She'd been to plenty of galas in the past, but this was her event, for her cause, and it was also a celebration of every way she'd changed and everything she'd built over the past six years.

She hesitated, wondering if she could even wear the dress. If Eliot's gift meant far more to her than it did to him, then by wearing it, would she be crossing the boundaries they'd set for their arrangement?

They'd said no emotions. But she didn't think she could wear this dress without getting emotional.

She decided to call Hazel for advice.

"Damn," Hazel said once Bria tried the dress on in front of her. "He even knows your size. Are you *sure* you understand the terms of the arrangement you two have? Because this dress is not the kind of thing you get for the ex you're just having a short-term affair with."

Bria shook her head. "I don't know. We both agreed that we were keeping things strictly physical, but this…this is too much. I can't accept a gift like this, can I?"

Hazel was still rummaging through the box the dress had come in. "Oh, my. Did you see that it comes with gloves as well? You are going to look absolutely gorgeous."

"But I can't wear it, Hazel. We agreed that this was just sex. And now he's sending me one of the nicest dresses I've ever seen, to wear to the most important gala I've ever attended." With the most significant man from her past in attendance, she thought, but didn't say. "This dress has to mean something, doesn't it? He couldn't just have sent it to me on a whim."

Hazel pursed her lips. "What do you think it means?"

"I have no idea. All this time, I thought that getting back together was just a way for us to say goodbye. But now there's this dress. I thought we'd agreed we just wanted closure. Was I wrong? Does he want more? Is he going to think *I* want more if I wear this?"

"Let's step back about twenty paces. Maybe you're overthinking this. You said he's rich now, right? Maybe the dress isn't some grand, romantic gesture. Maybe he just knew that you were rushing to get everything done, up to the last minute, and he wanted to do something nice for you."

It was possible. Maybe he didn't think of the dress as a terribly expensive gift but simply as a kind gesture.

Though the neckline of the dress was awfully low for a kind gesture.

"What do you think I should do, Hazel?"

"Well, it's strapless, so I definitely recommend some long earrings. And with the way the hem rises in the front, you'll need a killer pair of heels to show off. I can let you borrow mine. I've got some Hermès stilettos my grandmother gave me for Christmas."

"Hazel! I mean what do I do about the fact that the dress is from Eliot?"

"Does something need to be done about it?"

"Of course it does! If I wear it, what kind of message does that send?"

Hazel eyed the dress's swooping neckline. "A strong one."

Bria pleaded with Hazel to be serious.

"I'm trying to be," Hazel replied. "Look, the two of you are just together for now, right? He's going back to Boston in a couple of weeks, and then, presumably, he'll be out of your life for good."

"That's the plan," Bria said weakly.

"So as your best friend, while I don't think this fling is the *wisest* plan you've ever come up with, I can kind of see the appeal. But if he's going to be gone in two weeks, what are you afraid of? Don't hold back. Put the rental back in the closet. Wear the hot dress. Be spectacular tonight. Give him something to remember two weeks from now."

Bria tilted her chin, bolstered by her friend's words. Hazel was right. No matter what, Eliot would be gone in two weeks. Nothing would change just because she was getting emotional over a dress. She might as well wear it and enjoy herself.

And if the thought of Eliot leaving made her heart crack just a bit, she'd just have to let herself worry about that when it happened. After he was gone, she could let herself become emotional. But if she wanted him for now, she'd have to keep her feelings to herself. They'd said no emotions, and she planned to stick to that agreement. Otherwise, she'd end up spoiling her one chance at finding closure over their relationship.

This time, when Eliot left, she didn't want to feel devastated. Instead, she wanted them both to feel as though they could move on. And she wouldn't accomplish that if she indulged in daydreams about a future that would never be. Even if part of her wanted the dress to be more than just a thoughtful gesture, she needed to accept that it wasn't. Because in two weeks, Eliot would be gone, and she wanted to be mentally prepared for that. And so, instead of wishing for anything more, she should focus on tonight and give both of them something to remember after he left.

Eliot pulled up to the entrance of the event hall in his Lamborghini and handed his keys to the valet. Dusk was just beginning to fall. He was a little early, but he didn't mind. He hoped Bria would wear the dress he'd sent her, and if she did, he didn't want to miss her entrance.

He couldn't explain what had possessed him to buy her a dress. But as he'd watched her prepare for the gala over the last few weeks and seen how important its success was to her, he'd wanted to help in any way he could. He could make a donation, of course, but he wanted to do something more personal. At the last minute, he'd remembered their conversation about clothes and decided to send her something she might like. And even though they'd agreed not to become romantically involved, he didn't think it was too far out of the bounds of their arrangement for him to get her a dress. Tonight was important to her, and she'd needed something to wear other than the rental gown he'd spotted in her closet.

He had to admit, too, that it felt good to be able to do something to help her, for once. When they'd been together, she'd always bought things for him: clothes for practicum interviews, tickets to events. He'd tried to accept those things graciously, but he couldn't help resenting that their relationship seemed so imbalanced. It was nice to finally be able to return the favor and offer her something that she needed. It helped provide the sense of closure he was looking for.

The event hall was a Tudor-style mansion, with a long stone pathway leading to heavy wood doors. Glittering partygoers walked under a tunnel of archways covered with ivy and softly glowing fairy lights. With only a few weeks to plan, Bria had made the event look like something on a par with a major awards ceremony. Given how much money the center needed to raise, she'd known she would need an event that would attract the kind of people who didn't just want to donate money but wanted to make the news while doing so. Judging by the amount of opulence around him, she might have pulled it off.

In the past, these kinds of events had always bored him to tears. But tonight's atmosphere seemed more relaxed. The gala was somehow glamorous without feeling formal. Maybe it was because he knew so many people. Most of the staff from St. Raymond's were there. Dr. Anderson, the hospital's chief of staff, gave him a wave before taking over the dance floor with an enthusiastic jitterbug. Caleb and Hazel arrived and immediately engaged Eliot in conversation. Hazel gave him a few knowing looks that confirmed his assumption that Bria had indeed told her everything.

He'd also invited a few of his friends from Boston, because he thought they might be willing to donate to Bria's cause, and he was pleasantly surprised when they showed up.

He had to admit that he was actually having fun.

There were even a few patients who'd come to support the Women's Health Center. Sandra Patterson, the soon-to-be mother of quints, was there, her husband spinning her around in her wheelchair. She'd made it to thirty-three weeks of pregnancy despite her frustration with constant bed rest. Her cervical stitch, which had been put in earlier on in her pregnancy to prevent her from miscarrying, had already been taken out in preparation for the labor, so she was good to go as soon as her babies gave her the green light. It couldn't be much longer now, so he'd given her medical clearance to attend the gala tonight under strict conditions. Mental stimulation was so important to women restricted to bed rest, and she'd been growing so despondent that he'd thought the outing would do her more good than harm. She looked happier than she'd been in weeks.

As the song ended, he crossed the dance floor to speak to Sandra.

"Not too much excitement, remember. And you're expected to leave within the hour."

Sandra rolled her eyes. "I know, Doctor. Home by 9:00 p.m., or I'll turn into a pumpkin."

"And don't you forget it."

Someone came up behind him and took his hand. "You're off duty tonight, Doctor. Let's allow Sandra to enjoy her evening out."

He turned around to see Bria. She was wearing the dress he'd sent her. The low, strapless neckline clung to her perfectly. She'd worn the silk gloves as well; her hand, which still held his, felt light and smooth as water. She was gorgeous. The dress was made even more beautiful by the fact that she was wearing it.

He tried to greet her, but his voice caught in his throat. She looked positively delectable. Seeing her like this was having more of an effect on him than he'd anticipated.

For the first time, he found himself thinking about his departure in two weeks with a pang of regret. It would be hard to say goodbye to her again. But also necessary, for both their sakes. He needed to move on. And he was sure he would, eventually. But not right now. Not tonight. Tonight, he wanted to enjoy the vision of Bria in the fairy-tale gown he'd bought her. And to fantasize about taking the gown off her later, if the opportunity arose.

The band struck up again, and he found his voice at last. He lifted her hand to his lips. "I wonder if we could dance?"

She smiled. "That's what we're here for. That, and to raise a whole lot of money."

He took her hand and put an arm around her waist. He'd planned to make a large donation himself, and he was about to tell Bria about it, but then he stopped himself. Bria had worked hard on the gala. He didn't want to flaunt his wealth by bragging about how much he could donate. Better to do it quietly, he decided, and keep the donation anonymous.

When he and Bria were together, there had been so many times when he'd felt as though they were on uneven footing. But over the past few years, he'd built his career and grown more secure in himself. And now that the tables were turned and he was the one able to help Bria, he had a perspective on their relationship that was different than the one he'd held for the past few years. Her family's wealth might have made him uncomfortable, but it was never Bria herself who'd tried to make him feel that way. He'd been uncomfortable because of the situation, not because of her. He'd had a chip on his shoulder about money for years, yet Bria hadn't put it there. It was there because of the bullies he'd gone to private school with and the medical students from wealthy families who'd looked down on him. Students who hadn't really wanted to be doctors but were there because it was the only career their families thought was respectable enough.

Calvin Thomas had probably been one of those medical students once, he realized. Coming from such a wealthy family, he couldn't just have any career. No, he'd have to be a surgeon, an eminent one, because nothing else would satisfy the family's pride. He doubted Calvin had chosen his career out of a desire to help people. Everything the man did was about how things would look to someone else.

Bria laid her head against his shoulder as they swayed about the floor. She was so unlike the rest of her family. And with that thought, his certainty grew: something—or should he say, some*one*—had influenced her to break up with him that night six years ago. She'd always insisted it was her own choice, but he had his suspicions that Calvin had played a part in it. At the time, he'd given in to his own fears instead of thinking it through logically. He hadn't believed she was really so materialistic, but his own fear that he wasn't good enough had erased his doubt and led him to accept her words at face value.

But now Bria's life looked nothing like what he would have expected of someone who was selfish, materialistic and spoiled. Because she *wasn't* those things. Since he'd earned his millions, he'd met plenty of women who were only interested in money. None of them were anything like Bria. None of them had passion for their careers, or worked with service organizations, or with patients whom they genuinely cared for. Bria was different. She wasn't the kind of person who cared about background or financial status.

He should have known that about her back then as well. But he'd been too afraid to believe it. Too insecure, too defensive. There was still too much of the young boy in him who'd been bullied so harshly about who he was and where he came from. But he wasn't that boy anymore. He was secure in himself now, and he had a right to know the truth.

He and Bria might have agreed not to discuss the past, but he needed answers. If they were going to find the closure they were looking for, he wanted to know the real reason she'd broken up with him. He didn't buy that it had been her choice. Not for a moment. And he wondered how on earth he'd ever been convinced that it had.

He held her body closer against his, marveling at how perfectly they fit together as they danced. He was so glad she didn't wear perfume. For as long as he'd known her, she'd smelled like coffee, and vanilla, and herself, and he couldn't imagine any combination of scents that he preferred more.

He'd lost count of how many events like this they'd attended when they were together. He'd always felt obligated to go, and he'd never enjoyed himself. This time, he was almost disappointed when the band ended their song and began something faster. Bria's eyes lit up, and he could tell she wanted to keep dancing, but suddenly her smile faded.

"What's wrong?"

Her expression hardened. "Don't turn around, but my father's here."

Eliot's jaw tightened. "Perfect. I'd like to go talk to him."

"Wait! Please don't. I mean, don't bother. He isn't worth getting upset over."

Eliot disagreed, but he saw the panic in Bria's eyes and decided not to pursue the point. He had plenty to say to Calvin Thomas, but he didn't want Bria's event to be spoiled by a confrontation.

"I didn't know you'd decided to invite him."

"I didn't. But I should have known he'd show up anyway. This is a major charity event. *Of course* all his friends would expect him to be here. And everyone would talk if he didn't attend a gala hosted by his own daughter. He couldn't stay away."

Eliot could see the rage burning in her eyes. A minute ago, he'd been worried about causing a scene and spoiling Bria's gala; now he had a feeling she might be on her way to accomplishing that herself. "Do you want me to see about having security remove him from the building? They might be able to do it quietly." And judging by the look in her eyes, they might prevent her from tearing off Calvin's head.

"No need," she said, her lips forming a firm line. "Stay here for just a minute. I'm going to go deal with him myself." She stalked off the dance floor, her face so furious that Eliot could almost pity Calvin. Almost.

Bria elbowed her way through the crowd of gala attendees, trying to fix a smile on her face as she nodded to each patron who waved at her. Inside, she was seething. Her father had absolutely no right to be here. Six years ago, he'd ruined the most important thing in her life when he'd threatened Eliot. She refused to allow him to cast a shadow over her career as well.

In a way, she was glad he was here. The past few weeks with Eliot had shown her exactly what she'd given up—their physical connection, the way they worked together so seamlessly, the way he seemed to anticipate her needs. She'd walked away from it all once, because her father had been in control. But he couldn't control her any longer. She knew it, and it was time for him to know it, too. Elliot had enough of his own money and prestige now and couldn't be threatened by him anymore, and she had earned her own independence. For the first time in her life, she was ready to tell her father that he couldn't bully her ever again.

She reached the edge of the crowd, where her father stood. His face was grim, his brow furrowed, but she could match him glower for glower, and she wasn't afraid to let him know it.

"Hello, Dad. What brings you here?"

He scowled at her. "Don't be ridiculous. A few weeks ago I learned that you were putting on a major event at extremely short notice, despite knowing that doing so would throw you into the public eye and subject you to all the scrutiny that is typical for a member of the Thomas family."

"Well, I managed to pull it all together, and disaster didn't strike. Despite what you may believe about me, I was actually able to accomplish something on my own. The world hasn't ended, and as you can see, the gala is going very smoothly."

"I disagree. For one thing, my invitation seems to have been lost in the mail."

"It wasn't lost. You weren't invited."

"You call that good event planning? How do you think it will look when it's reported in the press that you didn't invite your own father to your fund-raising gala? What kind of publicity would that create for your little charity? I saved you by coming here tonight."

She bristled. "The center is doing just fine on its own. It doesn't need saving, especially by you."

"No? Then I suppose you just got everyone out here in their finest getup for fun, then."

The anger, already strong within her, threatened to overflow. There was nothing she hated more than when her father was right, and he was right on both counts: she *had* been worried about how it would look to other potential donors if she didn't invite her father, and the center *was* in a financial crisis. But she hadn't worked this hard over the past few weeks to allow her father to swoop in and act as though he'd rescued her from the brink of disaster.

He pulled out his checkbook. "I may as well do my part,

since it seems you're so committed to your little scheme. How much do you need?"

She scowled. "No, Dad. Your money isn't welcome here."

"Oh, really? I wonder how your friend Hazel might feel if she heard you say that."

"Your money always comes with strings attached."

"That's how the world works. It's best you learn now that everyone owes somebody something."

"Even where family is concerned? Even where love is involved?"

"The sooner you give up all of your idealistic fantasies, the better off you'll be."

"If those are fantasies, I'm going to do my best to make them a reality," she retorted.

"There you go again, showing your typically bad judgment. Making all your typical bad decisions," he jeered.

"Every decision I've made since I stepped back from the family has brought me to exactly where I wanted to be."

"Really? Living in that tiny apartment? Working as a *nurse*?"

"I'm a nurse-midwife, actually. And I don't have to care about your opinions anymore. Neither does Eliot. You can't threaten his career again. He's been very successful on his own, no thanks to you. You can't control either one of us."

"Ha! He's been successful on his own, has he? No thanks to me? Is that what he's let you think? That he's one of those idealistic types? Don't be so naive. There are some things about him that I know better than you, my girl."

"You don't know him at all."

"Oh, but I do. You think he made all those millions of his on his own? Nonsense. Everybody in this room owes me something, including him. You don't believe me? Ask him. He'll tell you. He thinks he's honorable, after all."

Bria had no idea what he was talking about, but she was so angry that she didn't want to hear another word.

"Dad, if you want to stay, you're welcome to do so. If you want to donate money, fine. But know that I can do this without you. In fact, that's what I need most from you tonight. Not your money, but your confidence that I can do something on my own. And I can do it all far better without you involved."

She stormed out of the ballroom, leaving him sputtering over his drink at the edge of the crowd.

She scanned the hallway for a private corner where she could compose herself and opted for the stairwell, next to the elevators. She leaned against the wall and took a few deep breaths.

She should have known her father would show up uninvited. He claimed to care so much about appearances, but it was just like him not to care about anyone else's feelings. He wasn't the kind of person who worried about whether he was welcome or not. He simply showed up, caused his havoc and then left everyone else to deal with the consequences. It was a pattern that had repeated itself constantly throughout her childhood.

It was therefore no small pleasure to be able to tell him exactly what she thought, and to leave him choking on his drink. She smiled. No matter what else happened this evening, telling her father off had been deeply satisfying.

Now that she was feeling more composed, she realized she should get back to the ballroom to see what Eliot was up to.

But just as she turned to leave the stairwell, she encountered Sandra Patterson, her husband pushing her wheelchair.

"Heading home for the night?" Bria pushed the button for the elevator for them.

"I'm afraid so," said Sandra. "Those are the doctor's orders. It was wonderful to be out for an evening, even if it was only for an hour."

"I'll see you down to the first floor."

"We don't want to trouble you," said Sandra.

"It's no trouble at all." Bria stepped on the elevator after the Pattersons.

The elevator seemed to be taking a strangely long time to travel only one floor. Bria and the Pattersons waited and then exchanged confused glances. A moment later, the elevator began moving, and they all relaxed.

"There it goes," Dan Patterson said, relieved.

But then the elevator came to an abrupt stop, and the doors didn't open.

"What's the matter?" said Sandra, her voice worried.

"I'll check." Bria hit the button to open the doors. Nothing. Then the elevator moved a bit lower before coming to a sudden stop. The doors opened...to reveal an inch of space between the bottom of the doors and the next floor.

"Oh, dear," Bria said. "It looks like we're stuck." She pressed the emergency service button, which blinked on and off but gave no other indication of what might happen next. "Not to worry. I've got my phone with me. We can call for help, and hopefully we'll get out of here before too long."

Sandra winced. "I hope so. These babies seem to think they're trying out for a world gymnastics team. I've been getting so many little pokes and kicks today."

Bria examined Sandra's face more closely. "Have the babies been more active than usual?"

"All day long. I think they're all doing somersaults in there. But a few minutes ago, they really started kicking."

"Why didn't you say anything?" Dan asked.

"I didn't think it was any different than usual. Between the five of them, someone's always giving me a good kick. But it usually stops much sooner than this. And—ouch! They usually don't kick quite so hard."

Bria put her hand on Sandra's stomach and felt her own body grow cold with dread. "Sandra, those aren't kicks. You're having contractions."

CHAPTER EIGHT

BRIA TRIED TO calm the panic rising within her. This couldn't be happening. Not here.

Dan Patterson seemed to be thinking along the same lines. "What do you mean, she's having contractions?"

"Exactly what I said."

"But the elevator's stuck! She can't have the babies now. It's the worst possible moment."

"I agree with you, Dan, but it's happening now, stuck elevator or not. But don't worry. Getting scared isn't going to help anything, and also, it's unnecessary, because we're going to do everything we can to get these babies delivered safely. We'll call an emergency services team that will get us out of here before you know it, and in the meantime, I'll be with you, Sandra and the babies every step of the way." She took her pager from her pocket and shot off the message—QUINTS911. She was about to put the pager away but then thought better of it and sent a second message: IN ELEVATOR.

Dan and Sandra looked terrified. "Dan," Bria said, trying to keep her voice even, "Sandra needs your help now. Can you take her hand and practice breathing, just like we've done in the practice sessions?"

Dan nodded and put his arm around Sandra's shoulders. Bria's cell phone rang—it was Eliot.

"Just got your page. Please tell me it doesn't mean what I think it means."

"Yep. The quints are on their way. Dan, Sandra and I are in the elevator near the south stairwell, stuck between the first and second floors."

"Any chance Sandra can make it to the hospital?"

Bria glanced at Sandra. "Maybe. Her water's broken, so it depends on how quickly you can get us out of here."

"Understood. We've already started making phone calls. Most of the quint team is here at the gala, so once we get you out of there, you'll have lots of support available. In the meantime, what do you need right now?"

Aside from nitroglycerin, for the heart attack she was about to have? Bria tried to keep her composure for the benefit of the Pattersons. "I need Hazel. Ask her to scrounge up any tools she can find for emergency premature birth. Tell her there's an opening of about one inch between the elevator doors where someone could pass through small items."

"I'm on my way, along with the entire team. You're not alone. We'll all be right outside. And, Bria? You've got this."

She hung up, trying to take heart from his confident tone.

She turned to Sandra, who looked close to tears.

"I'm not going to have the babies in an elevator, am I?" asked Sandra. "Not after all those drills we practiced."

Bria made her voice as soothing as possible. "I know this isn't what you expected. But help is on the way, and they may have us out of here soon. And if not, I want you to know that I've delivered babies in stranger places than this." It was true. At least an elevator gave them four walls, a roof and overhead lighting. When she'd done her service work in Haiti, there'd been times she hadn't even had that.

She'd never had to deal with five babies at once, but she decided not to dwell on that detail right now.

She tried to prepare Sandra as best she could. "I want

to get you out of that wheelchair. Just as a precaution. It'll be easiest to move you to the floor now rather than later." Bria and Dan helped Sandra move to the floor, and Bria showed them how Sandra could be more comfortable if she positioned herself so she was leaning back against Dan.

"We need to do everything we can to slow your labor, so I want the two of you to continue to practice rhythmic breathing while I take a look at your cervix," she said.

Bria knelt to check on Sandra's progress, the skirt of her evening gown crumpling beneath her knees. So much for couture fashion. The ballroom floor seemed a million miles away. She'd have given anything to have Eliot here with her now.

Sandra was already five centimeters dilated. Unless something changed quickly, these babies were going to have quite a birthday story to tell. Assuming everything went smoothly. She tried not to think about the numerous things that could go wrong. As she'd told Dan earlier, fear wasn't going to help anything.

She heard a commotion outside the elevator doors, along with a great deal of banging. Did that mean rescuers were on their way? She didn't have time to give the question more than a fleeting thought, as she was giving all her attention to taking Sandra's pulse and helping her with her breathing. She was so absorbed in assessing Sandra's progress that Dan had to get her attention.

"Nurse Thomas? They're calling to you from outside."

"Oh!" She looked over to the gap in the doors, where Eliot and a firefighter had been trying to get her attention.

"The whole team's outside," said Eliot. "An ambulance has already arrived to whisk you off to the hospital the second the fire department can get you out. You and I can ride with Sandra, and the quint team will follow in their cars."

"That's a great plan, Eliot, but I'm not sure it does much to change our situation right now."

"This might. It's everything Hazel could get together." Eliot shoved a packet through the small opening.

Bria almost cried with relief. Hazel had included five gallon-size plastic bags—she must have found them in the event hall's kitchen—along with a shoelace, a single tea towel and a pair of scissors.

"We've got more tea towels if you need them. The hope is that we can get you out before it comes to that."

"The sooner, the better." Bria turned her attention back to Sandra, who was crying out as a strong contraction overtook her.

Bria took another look at Sandra's progress. "Sandra, the first baby's coming very fast. I want you to keep breathing, just as you are now, but when the next contraction comes, I want you to push."

Sandra's eyes were wide with alarm. "But I thought you said we were going to try to slow down the labor!"

"I don't think we have any choice in the matter at this point. But look at me." She clasped Sandra's hand and held her gaze. "I'm going to do everything I can to give your babies the best start in life. You and Dan have protected them so well, and now we're all going to work together to make sure they arrive safely. That was always the plan. The way we follow that plan is just going to look a little different than we thought."

Sandra nodded, and when the next contraction came, she pushed and cried out.

"That's it, Sandra." Bria was relieved to see that the birth was proceeding fairly smoothly. If she hadn't known to expect multiple newborns, she would have felt that the birth was completely routine.

Routine was good. She had enough unexpected surprises to deal with at the moment; she didn't think she could handle any more.

Sandra's first child, a boy, made his way into the world

and immediately demonstrated a healthy set of lungs. Bria laid him on the tea towel and used the shoelace from Hazel to clamp the cord. After a few minutes, during which she took the baby's vital signs as best she could, Bria cut the cord and then wrapped the baby in the tea towel and handed him to Sandra.

Sandra's face was aglow. "He's perfect."

Bria cut a hole for the baby's head in one of the large Ziploc bags. "You can hold him for a minute, but then I'll need to put one of these around him."

"A Ziploc bag?"

"I know it seems odd, but it's similar to what we'd use in the NICU to keep preemies warm. Here, I'll show you." Sandra handed her the baby. Keeping him wrapped in the tea towel, Bria deftly slipped his head through the hole so that the bag draped around his shoulders, like a poncho. She then sealed the edge of the bag and gave him back to Sandra.

"It's like a little rain suit," said Sandra.

At that moment, the elevator lurched and then proceeded smoothly to settle at the first floor. The doors opened, and Sandra was promptly surrounded by medical staff. They had her loaded into an ambulance in short order. Bria marveled at what seemed now like a surplus of medical equipment.

Within moments, Sandra had been loaded into an ambulance. Eliot and Bria climbed in with her.

"City employees have temporarily closed some of the roads between here and the hospital," Eliot said. "We'll be there in no time at all."

By the time Sandra's second baby was born, they were already in the delivery room that had been set up during Eliot's drills. The last three babies were born by cesarean, which was far safer for the quintuplets, and easier on Sandra. The baby assembly line worked just as Eliot had planned, and since the hospital had set up five of every necessary piece of equipment ahead of time, everything was ready and waiting for the quints. Despite the chaotic way things had started, the rest of Sandra's labor couldn't have gone more smoothly.

As soon as the team ensured that all members of the now greatly extended Patterson family were resting comfortably, they left the delivery room to congratulate one another.

"Three babies in three minutes," Bria said to Eliot. "You would have broken that record if only things had gone according to plan."

He sighed. "The important thing is that all the babies are doing well. Maybe I'll have another chance to deliver quintuplets someday."

"Not if you quit medicine."

"Who knows? Hospitals aren't the only place mothers give birth. There are all kinds of places that people need medical professionals. Elevators, for example." His eyes twinkled as he teased her. Then he grew more serious. "You did very well under incredible pressure."

Bria shook her head. "I tried not to show it, but I was so scared. I can't believe Sandra and the quints are all right."

"I can. They were in very good hands the entire time. You probably saved their lives."

"What saved their lives was having a well-trained team set up and ready to receive them at a moment's notice, which was your plan all along."

"Let's agree to call it a team effort, then."

She gave a weary smile as she stripped off the disposable surgical gown she'd put on over her eveningwear. No one had had time to put on regular gowns. Eliot checked the time. "What now?" he said. "There's still time to attend the last half hour of the gala. Do you want to head back and see how it's going?"

She was bone tired. "Let me check in with Hazel first.

I'd rather not go back, to be honest. I'm exhausted, and I don't know if I can go back there without thinking about how I almost delivered five babies in an elevator."

Just as she fished her phone from her pocket, she got a text from Hazel. "Oh my god! It looks like I don't have to go back after all!"

"Is something wrong?"

"Far from it. Hazel says we got an anonymous donation of two hundred and fifty thousand dollars right before the quints were born and that it pushed us well over our target amount." She flipped her phone case shut, her eyes sparkling.

"This has been quite a night for you," said Eliot. He had also taken off his disposable gown. He was still in his tuxedo, though he'd removed his black tie and loosened the top button of his collar. His jacket outlined his lean frame and the sharp angles of his shoulders.

She smiled back at him, flushed with success. But only for a moment. Her time with Eliot was growing so short.

But it was all she had, and so she might as well make the most of it.

"They can't need me at the gala now that we've exceeded our goal," she said. "I suppose I have the rest of the evening free."

"In that case, I know a great diner next door where you could show that dress off. Are you hungry? Neither of us got to eat at the gala."

"Starving."

"Care to accompany me to the finest of greasy spoons?"

"Only if we order it to go."

As hungry as they were, they didn't quite make it to dinner.

They'd brought cheeseburgers from the diner back to Bria's apartment. But when they entered, he dropped the bag on the kitchen counter and simply looked at her.

And the way he was looking made it seem as though he was starving, but not for food. He looked as though he wanted to devour *her*. He kept staring, eating her up with his eyes, and she kept letting him stare.

Tonight, she wasn't going to waste her last chance by thinking about how their fling couldn't last forever. Nothing lasted forever. That was life. For now, she just wanted to focus on what was in front of her.

Which, at the moment, was Eliot. Dressed in a tuxedo that outlined every firm line of his body.

He moved toward her, putting his hands around her waist. He bent to her ear and murmured, "I've been wanting to take this dress off you all night."

"And here I thought you wanted me to wear it."

"I'm glad you did. It definitely serves a purpose." He gave her a wicked smile.

"And what purpose is that, exactly?"

He placed his hands on her shoulders, and it was all she could do not to melt under his touch. His hands were cool, but her skin felt hot. She didn't know how he couldn't feel the way she was burning.

"It lets me do this." He tilted her chin up, so that her throat was exposed, and planted a kiss on her neck. He nibbled his way down her bare shoulders, one of his hands grazing the top of her breast. The barely there stubble on his face gently scratched against her skin. Eliot's beard had always grown in fast—if he didn't shave twice a day, he had a full shadow by early evening. The sensation of his stubble pricking against her skin set her body aflame.

That flame began to grow even deeper, radiating from her core, as his hand slid away from her breasts and found the clasps at the back of her dress.

They hit a roadblock, then, as they both tugged at the clasps, which refused to budge. "How the hell…how did you even get this on?"

"I don't know," she gasped, half laughing, half desperate to feel him against her. "But I'm not the only one who's overdressed for the occasion." She slipped off the jacket of his tuxedo and attended to the belt of his trousers while he unbuttoned his white shirt. Finally, he was naked in front of her, while her own dress was no closer to coming off than it had been before.

"I think…" She hesitated. It was such a beautiful dress.

But that was an ever more beautiful man standing in front of her. "I think you're going to have to rip it," she said, silently dying inside just a tiny bit. But the dress didn't matter. She'd had lots of gorgeous gowns in her life. There was only one Eliot. And she needed to be close to him right now.

"Are you sure?"

Her body was sending more urgent signals now. Seeing him in front of her, a vision of sheer male perfection, was turning the rising want within her into a desperate need. She couldn't wait much longer.

"Yes, please. Get me out of here." Her tone was playful, but she was only half joking. The urge to feel his body against hers was growing with an intensity that would not be denied.

His hands grasped the seam at the side of her dress, and he pulled it apart in one long tear. She cried in relief as the dress crumpled to the floor and he gathered her body to his. She arched her back, her breasts feeling full and heavy as they melted against him.

There was nothing between them now but a few wisps of black lace. He slipped his hand down to her waist, easing one finger in between her panties and her skin, finding the sensitive nub between her legs. She felt her knees turn to water; if she hadn't had her arms wrapped around his neck, she might not have been able to stay standing.

He lifted her in his arms, carrying her like a bride over a threshold into her bedroom, and laid her down on the bed. He was hard and ready for her and quickly took a condom from her nightstand to sheath himself. Her body ached for his.

He eased himself onto the bed, keeping himself raised just above her so that his skin barely brushed hers. She could feel him against her thigh, and it was all she could do not to wrap her legs around him and pull him to her.

"Ready?" he said.

"Yes," she breathed, her voice coming out in a whisper of need.

He entered her slowly, and she felt a delicious tingle throughout her spine as her body adjusted, her hips rising to meet his of their own volition. He bent his lips to hers, covering her mouth, and she pressed her hands against the back of his head to keep him there. It was overwhelming to be so consumed by him, to feel the fire they'd created grow beyond their own control.

He moved slowly at first, letting the intensity build, and then their hips began to sway, finding their own rhythm. Their bodies rocked together faster and faster, performing a dance far more intimate and timeless than the one they'd shared earlier that evening.

They pushed one another back and forth over the brink of ecstasy, her body feeling as though it was melting into his. And still the need within her burned and burned, until, finally, he gave one last powerful thrust and shuddered against her, and she felt herself shatter around him.

For a moment, she was unable to move. Her body felt completely satisfied; she couldn't conceive of moving or of ever wanting to leave this exact spot. He recovered faster, disentangling himself from her and lying on his side next to her. He put an arm around her waist and pulled her to him, cupping his body around hers.

Two weeks left.

She'd tried so hard to focus on the present rather than

the ending of their arrangement. She had to keep reminding herself that no matter how delicious, how *right* things with Eliot felt, she couldn't allow herself to want any more than he was offering. Their time together was about writing a new ending to their story, one that didn't involve so much pain. In two weeks, they wouldn't break up. Instead, they would say goodbye to each other. They'd allow each other to move on.

You can't lose something you don't have, she reminded herself.

So why did it feel as though she was about to lose him all over again?

The next morning, Bria woke first. She allowed herself to indulge in a few seconds of gazing at Eliot. As always, his face was so unguarded in sleep, his breathing deep and untroubled, his muscular frame relaxed. It would be a shame to wake him, but they both needed to be up for work soon.

She started their coffee, fixing his just the way he liked it.

Last night had felt surreal. The dress, the ballroom, dancing with Eliot—all of it had felt like something from a fantasy. As terrifying as delivering one of the quints in an elevator had been, when all five babies were born, she and Eliot had shared a moment of triumph. She cast her gaze over the clothes strewn about the floor. The ruined dress.

Worth it, she thought. Sometimes a girl had to sacrifice a great dress for even greater sex. She had no regrets.

Telling off her father had been incredibly satisfying as well. She paused while stirring her coffee, suddenly remembering what her father had said. He'd claimed he knew something about Eliot that she didn't. That everyone owed him something, including Eliot.

She tried to ignore the nagging feeling. Her father was pompous and controlling. Perhaps he simply wanted to *be-*

lieve that Eliot owed him something. Or perhaps whatever he'd said was utter nonsense.

The emergency births of the quints had pushed the question out of her mind, but now she found herself mulling over it again. She and Eliot had agreed not to talk about the past. But what if there was something in his past that she needed to know?

Isn't that a little hypocritical? her conscience goaded her.

After six years, there were probably plenty of things she didn't know about Eliot. But there was also something she hadn't told him. She'd never come clean about the real reason she'd broken up with him.

Last night, she'd told her father that there was nothing he could do to hurt Eliot now. But she suddenly realized that was true for her as well. Eliot was no longer a vulnerable young doctor at the start of his career. He had built his fortune independently, and he was successful enough that there was little her father could do to affect his career. Which meant that there was no reason for her not to explain that she had broken up with him under pressure from her father. She'd lied to him, and she'd hurt him deeply to cover up that lie.

She had to tell him the truth, she knew. The past few weeks of sleeping with Eliot had been magical, but whatever she'd tried to tell herself, she knew they hadn't provided the sense of closure that she'd hoped for. After standing up to her father last night, she thought she might know why. After all these years, she finally had a chance to undo the hurt she'd caused Eliot years ago.

They'd agreed not to talk about the past, but she needed to explain this. She needed him to know that she'd only done it to protect him. She hoped it wasn't too much of a reach to think that he might understand and forgive her. Maybe then, when he left to go back to his successful business in Boston, she'd finally have the closure she was looking for.

He shifted in the bed, then stretched and batted his eyes open. She sat beside him and handed him his coffee, which he set on the nightstand so he could pull her close and nuzzle her hair with his nose.

"What's for breakfast?" he murmured.

"Oh, were you going to make us breakfast?" she teased. "I've got cereal and some eggs in the fridge. Feel free to fix anything you like."

He took little nibbles of her shoulder. "I've already got what I want right here."

For a few moments, there was silence as the subject of breakfast was forgotten. But then he groaned as she disentangled herself from him. "We have to go to work," she said, standing up and heading for the kitchen.

"Just a few more minutes."

"Nope. We can't be late. And there's, um, something I want to talk about with you first." She had to tell him today, she decided. Now that she'd decided to tell Eliot the truth, she wanted the secret to be out as soon as possible.

"What's on your mind?" He was pulling clothes from the small tote bag he'd begun keeping at her apartment. She watched as he slipped into a pair of jeans and then began buttoning a white collared shirt over his chest.

She took a deep breath. "It's about what happened six years ago."

He cocked an eyebrow at her. "Are you sure you want to go there? Every time we talk about the past, we end up fighting."

"I don't think we will this time. Because there's something you don't know. Something I've never been able to tell you, until now."

"Well, now I'm intrigued. What is it?"

She squeezed her eyes shut, then forced them open. She

owed it to him to look him in the eye as she told him this. "My father forced me to break up with you. I was never ashamed of you. I never once felt that you weren't good enough for me. I was just afraid of what my father would do to you if we stayed together."

His jaw had formed a firm, hard line that she couldn't read. "What were you afraid he'd do?"

"He threatened to ruin your career. I knew he'd do it, too. Nothing stands in my father's way when he's determined. And I knew that if *you* knew he'd threatened you, that you wouldn't run from him. You'd want to face him. You'd want to prove to him that he couldn't control you. But you didn't know him like I did. I knew that if he wanted to, he'd destroy your career before it even started, and I couldn't let him do that to you."

"So instead you let me believe that you didn't care about me? That you thought I wasn't good enough for you?"

"To protect you," she said weakly.

"To protect me." His voice was cold. Somehow, he didn't seem to be taking this with the relief she'd anticipated.

"I couldn't see any other solution," she tried to explain. "I knew you'd want to fight my father, and I knew he'd win. I'm sorry, but at that time, given who he was and where you were in your life, I knew he'd win. He always did. And he'd have ruined you."

He finished buttoning his shirt and began to put on his shoes.

"Where are you going? Don't you want to wait for breakfast?"

"I don't think so. I think I've had enough for today."

"Why are you so upset?"

"Do you really not understand?"

"No," she whispered. She couldn't imagine how her attempt at honesty had gone wrong so quickly.

"Then maybe I can help you with that. You say you broke

up with me to protect me. But you did it by telling me that I wasn't good enough. That I could never make you happy. That we were from two different worlds, and that no matter who I became, my background would never change. You said we'd always be two different people who would want different things. Do you have any idea how that made me feel? After years of being teased and bullied, can you imagine how it felt to hear the woman I loved, that I wanted to marry, say that I wasn't good enough for her? You've got a really strange idea of protection."

"I know it hurt you to hear those things. I didn't understand how badly until recently. But I only knew that I needed to say something that would throw you off track so you wouldn't think my father was behind it all. Something you'd believe."

His eyes burned into her very soul. "And you knew I'd believe that, because I did grow up poor. You knew that I'd heard I wasn't good enough from people just like you, and you used it against me."

"I had to, Eliot. It was for your sake."

"Is that right? If it was for me, then why did you make the decision yourself, without ever telling me about it? You knew I'd want to stand up to your father, to stand up to him together, and so you decided all by yourself to take that choice away from me."

"Was I wrong, though? Look at all that's happened since. You're a respected doctor *and* a multimillionaire. Could you have done that if my father had been bent on trying to destroy you so early in your career?"

"I'd have found a way to make my life successful. And it would have been my choice. And—" he almost choked on the words "—we could have been together. If you'd trusted me, if you'd had any faith in our relationship, we could have had six years together. But instead of the two of us being a team, you kept this secret and made the decision on your own. Just like you always did with everything else."

Now she was upset, frustrated that he couldn't seem to understand that she was just as upset about the loss of the last six years as he was. It had been a sacrifice that had felt like she'd torn her own heart out, but she'd made that sacrifice for him. Yet he seemed determined to blame her for it.

"You should be the one to talk about secrets," she retorted. "I talked to my father last night, and I know you've got one of your own."

His face blanched, and she realized she'd been hoping that he would deny it. That he'd say her father was just trying to stir up trouble. But she could tell from the look in his eyes that she'd hit on something he didn't want to talk about.

Whether he wanted to talk about it or not, she deserved to hear it. The time for secrets was long past. "What is it, Eliot? Why does my father seem to think you owe him something?"

"Because I do." The expression on his face looked utterly defeated. It was how she felt, too.

"What do you mean?"

"After we broke up, your father offered me a large sum of money to keep quiet about our breakup, and to sign a nondisclosure agreement promising that I wouldn't say anything about your family in the press."

"And you took it?" she asked numbly.

"No! I tore the check up in his face. But then…"

She nodded mechanically. She knew her father well enough. Whatever the details might be, he'd have found a way to force Eliot to take the money.

"He made it impossible for me to refuse."

"How much did he give you?"

"Quite a bit. Enough to pay off my medical school loans and start investing. Two hundred and fifty thousand dollars."

The amount jogged something in her memory. "Then the

anonymous donation that came into the Women's Health Center last night?"

"Yes. It was from me."

"Wow. Just wow. So your donation didn't really have anything to do with wanting to support me or the center. It was just some sick, twisted way of paying my father back."

The hurt cut deeper than she'd ever thought it could. The idea that Eliot would use her, and a cause she cared about, to settle some old score with her father was appalling. For the past six years, she'd done everything she could to earn her independence. But now, the night after she'd organized a gala to save her own health center, she learned that her success wasn't about her at all. It was about something her father had done years ago. And it hurt her more than she could say to think that Eliot had been a part of it.

"You don't have to look at it that way," he protested. "The truth is that I can never pay that money back. If I hadn't gotten it at that exact time, I'd have spent the past six years watching my student loans grow larger and larger with interest, instead of paying them off and investing. The fact is that I do owe my entire fortune to your father, and I hate that. You can't imagine how much I hate it."

"How do you think I feel, with you donating the same amount he gave you to the center?"

"It wasn't about him. I wanted to help you. Or is that only all right when you're the one doing all the helping, making all the decisions?"

"Not fair, Eliot. You don't get to hold on to your resentment about the disparity in our incomes when your wealth came from my father all along!"

"You don't understand."

"I understand that you kept a secret from me. One that makes you a total hypocrite. You objected to me keeping something from you when you did the same. And you knew

I stepped away from my family's money to get away from my father's control, while you'd taken it all along."

"But that's not how it was. There were extenuating circumstances."

"I'm sure there were. My father's great at finding those. But the point is, you didn't tell me about it. Whatever the circumstances were, you held back from telling me, just like you always do, and left me out in the cold. And I can't do that. I can't keep wondering what's going on with you, what you're thinking and feeling. What you're keeping from me."

"Well, you won't have to wonder too much longer," he said bitterly. "I'll be leaving in two weeks. And not a moment too soon, I'm sure."

She felt as though he'd slapped her. She'd thought there were no longer ways they could hurt each other, but apparently she'd been wrong. "You should go now," she said icily. "We've gotten our closure. We've shared our secrets. If there's anything more to say, I don't need to know. I just need you to leave."

"Gladly," he said. He grabbed his tote bag and stormed out the door.

Funny, she thought as he left. She thought she'd cried all the tears she had over their relationship. But somehow, she'd just managed to find a few more.

CHAPTER NINE

"I HAVE SOME good news."

Caleb seemed to be in a cheerful mood. Eliot raised his head from his hands. After his disastrous morning with Bria, he'd gone home, showered and gone straight to his office. His attempts to start the morning anew had not been successful. He kept hearing the pain in Bria's voice.

Caleb's visit was a welcome distraction from his thoughts. "We've found a doctor to take over as chief of obstetrics," he said. "His name's Dr. Phillips. He's older and very experienced."

"That is good news." Eliot tried to muster some enthusiasm. The hospital had performed an aggressive search for a new chair of obstetrics during his time there, hoping to find someone permanent before he left. St. Raymond's small budget had made the search difficult, as the most talented doctors often went elsewhere for higher pay. They'd been very lucky to have someone as dedicated as Caleb working there for so long, and though he wouldn't say so himself, they'd been just as lucky to have Eliot to replace him.

"Hey, try to look a little excited," Caleb said. "This means that you can return to Boston earlier than expected. You can enjoy some time off, or get back to work and your own life sooner, if you'd like. I thought you'd be glad to hear it." He gave Eliot a sidelong look. "Don't tell me you've changed your mind and decided you want to stay, now that we've finally found someone else to take the job."

"Oh, no. In fact, I think going back early might be a good idea."

"Really? Because the way you and Bria were dancing last night, I thought…that maybe there'd be something to keep you here a little longer. Or someone."

"No," Eliot said brusquely. "Not at all. Bria and I are just friends." His tongue almost tripped over the word *friends*. If there was a less accurate word to describe their relationship, he couldn't think of it.

"I see," said Caleb, giving Eliot a long look. "Then maybe I just misread things."

"Yeah. Well. Easy mistake to make." He knew that Caleb would be willing to listen if he wanted to talk, but he didn't think he could bring himself to discuss Bria. It had been difficult enough getting over her the first time. And now, even though they'd meant to keep things on a physical level, he somehow found himself feeling an overwhelming sense of loss once again. He didn't understand how things had gotten so out of hand, and he didn't think he had it in him to tell anyone else. Even his most trusted friend. He tried to turn the conversation back to business. "I think the sooner I go back to Boston, the better. I've got a lot of work waiting for me there. I'll take a couple of days to help with the transition of the new doctor, and then I'll head home."

"I understand. It's been good to have you for as long as we did."

Two days left in Portland, then. He wondered how he should tell Bria. When she'd agreed to a solely physical relationship, she'd done so on the condition that they'd have a proper goodbye. But that had been before their argument. She'd practically kicked him out of her apartment that morning. Did she even want to see him again?

He'd leave her a note, he decided. That way, he couldn't

be accused of breaking his promise. But he'd also be able to avoid seeing the hurt in her eyes again and hearing the accusation in her voice. Accusations that he still didn't think were completely fair considering her own actions six years ago.

He'd be back in Boston before he knew it, and he wouldn't have to worry about her judgment then. And then he could finally go about the business of moving on.

Bria stood up from her desk and stretched. For once, her workday was ending at a reasonable hour. It was just after 5:00 p.m., and she and Hazel had accomplished a long day of administrative chores. As tedious as all those tasks had been, it was also heartening to see that the center's financial situation had improved hugely. At least one thing in her life was going well.

Eliot had been gone for a week. The note that he'd left her lay crumpled at the bottom of her wastepaper basket. It had been brief, and even without looking at it, she recalled perfectly well what it said.

Bria,
I know you wanted us to have a proper goodbye this time, but I'm not sure either of us wants to go through that. Maybe this note can be something in between. I don't have any regrets about our time together, back then or now. But you're right, I did keep a secret from you when I shouldn't have, and I'm sorry for that. I'm sorry we both hurt each other as much as we did. At least we know now that it just wasn't meant to be.
Eliot

Upon reading it, she'd immediately crumpled up the paper and thrown it away. What was wrong with him? How could he leave without any warning, almost two full weeks before his time in Portland was supposed to be over? She knew the hospital had found a new doctor, so there was no reason for him to stay at St. Raymond's. And in fairness, he had no reason to stay for her, either. Not after that terrible morning together. But she hadn't expected to say goodbye so soon. And she hadn't expected that their goodbye would be via a note.

So much for closure, she thought.

Their sex-only, no-emotions-involved fling was supposed to help her get Eliot out of her system so she could move on. Instead, she now found her mind swirling with more questions than ever.

Why on earth had Eliot had to ruin everything with his stupid pride? Why on earth had he had to donate two hundred and fifty thousand dollars? Why couldn't it have been two hundred thousand, or three hundred thousand, if that amount of money was so easy for him to give away?

When she'd first learned of Eliot's large fortune, she hadn't ever thought that he could be like her father. She'd trusted that for Eliot, money wasn't about control. But by donating the exact amount of his medical school tuition, Eliot had done the exact thing she'd never wanted anyone to do. He'd taken something she'd built and made it about her father, and about money, too. She'd spent the past six years connecting with the things that felt truly important to her in life, and money hadn't been one of them. But Eliot didn't seem to have learned any lessons from the past. His action proved that he was just as insecure about money as he'd ever been.

The fund-raising gala had been a huge success. But it was a bittersweet victory for Bria. She was glad the center had what it needed—for now—but she knew they wouldn't have reached their goal without Eliot's huge donation.

As upset as she was about his choice, she couldn't help

wondering if she'd done the same thing to him. Eliot's furious reaction to her revelation about their breakup and the accusations he'd thrown at her had been so unexpected. And yet, on reflection, she had to admit that he had a point. She'd made a decision for both of them, without even having a conversation about it with him. She'd just assumed that her father would crush Eliot, because she'd seen him crush people before. She hadn't imagined for even one second that Eliot might have triumphed over Calvin Thomas. Where had her faith in her fiancé been?

She hadn't known, back then, that he'd felt as though she made all the decisions in their relationship. But he was right. Back then, that was exactly what she'd done, right up until the breakup. That had been her decision, too. She'd chosen to protect him when she should have confided in him instead. Not only had she told him he wasn't good enough, which had devastated him, but she'd also reinforced that lie by choosing not to trust him with the real story of why she'd felt she had to end things.

And now he was gone, along with any chance of the two of them ever being together.

As much as she'd tried not to let herself want anything more than the physical fling they'd agreed on, she'd been fooling herself all along. She loved Eliot. She'd known the moment she'd seen him again a few weeks ago that her feelings were as strong as they'd ever been. Stronger, in fact, because she'd grown.

Growing up, Bria's life would have looked perfectly charmed to any outside observer. Everyone told her that she was treated like a princess. But she'd never felt like a princess, or special in any way. Until she'd found Eliot. He'd been the only person in her life who'd ever made her feel that sense of warmth, of rightness, of *family*. Since her mother died, she hadn't had that sense of comfort, and of being at home, until she met him.

That was why it had hurt so much to have it torn away from her. After their first breakup, she'd felt herself drowning, and she'd floundered for a long time before she'd figured out how to save herself.

She'd tried to make a few other relationships work in her dysfunctional love life, but the way she felt after losing Eliot was on a completely different level. There was no one else like him, she knew. Certainly there wouldn't be for her. After losing him twice, she knew that for sure. She still loved him, despite how complicated things had grown between them. She'd probably always love him. But they'd ruined their second chance, and she couldn't see how they would ever have a third.

Thinking of him was as painful as it ever had been. She was looking forward to going for an after-work hike to find some solace in nature. But just as she was about to leave, she thought better of it. One of the quints had been showing signs of labored breathing, and she thought she should run over to St. Raymond's to check on him.

"Are you heading out, too?" asked Hazel, who was also leaving her office.

"I was going to. But I just thought that I should do a quick check on Sandra and the quints."

"Is that necessary? They're in good hands with the staff there."

Bria hesitated. She hated to speak ill of another medical professional, but she had her doubts about Dr. Phillips, the new obstetrician working at St. Raymond's. He was an older man whose résumé contained a long list of previous hospitals he'd worked at. But the more Bria saw of him, the more concerned she became that Dr. Phillips's résumé was so long because he couldn't get along with the staff at those other hospitals. At St. Raymond's, he was short-tempered, dismissive of staff suggestions and had a paternalistic, all-knowing attitude.

Dr. Phillips was a physician with twenty years of experience, and she was only a midwife. Intellectually, she knew she should trust that Dr. Phillips would look after his patients with whatever care was necessary. But her gut instinct told her that something was amiss, though she wasn't sure what it was.

Hazel noted her hesitation. "Dr. Phillips doesn't exactly inspire confidence, does he?"

Bria grimaced. "I know it's not really my place to challenge how he cares for his patients. But I don't think it would hurt anything to do a few extra check-ins with the quintuplets."

"Tell you what. You look like you're eager for a nice hike. Why don't you go off and enjoy yourself, and I'll run over to St. Raymond's to check on them?"

"Oh, Hazel, you don't have to do that. Especially when there's probably nothing wrong with them—it's just me being paranoid."

"I don't mind. I've had an easy day today—it's no trouble to do one thing more. And between you and me… I have my doubts about Dr. Phillips, too."

"He's only been here a short time."

"That's true. Maybe he'll settle in after a while and everyone will get used to him. But I don't think any of us are thrilled with the first impression he's made."

Bria hated to create more work for her friend, but she was relieved by Hazel's offer. She longed to be in the open air and to have the quiet solace of nature around her.

When she arrived at Forest Park, she opted not to take her usual hike up past the Witch's Castle. Her nerves were far too sensitive to visit a place that held recent memories of Eliot. She swallowed the lump in her throat and headed down another, less frequently used trail. It was a trail that didn't attract nearly as many hikers, which was fine with her. Solitude was what she craved.

She trudged through the woods, the hike somehow not providing the comfort that she'd so often felt in the past. The trees around her were lush and green, their branches bending over the trail to create inviting archways to pass through. The air was completely still except for the occasional rustle of leaves as some small chipmunk or insect hopped about its business. The earthy smell of foliage hung thick around her, and she inhaled deeply, trying to lose herself in the peacefulness of the setting.

She was so lost in thought that she hiked much farther than she meant to. By the time she realized she should be getting home, she was very far down the trail. The sun was setting later these days, but she knew she'd have to move fast if she was going to make it out of the park before sundown.

But as she was trudging back, she came to a fork in the road. She realized she'd been ruminating so much on thoughts of Eliot that she hadn't noticed which direction she'd taken on her hike out. She picked the way she thought she'd come, hurrying even more now, but the road only seemed to take her deeper into the forest.

Frustrated, she decided to turn back again. But now darkness was falling, and it was getting difficult to see.

She passed a large rock that she was absolutely certain she didn't remember and sat down on it, confused.

Where the hell was she?

"Hey, try not to look like you're going to a funeral." One of the firm's senior partners clapped Eliot on the shoulder. "This is great news. You've just graduated from millionaire to billionaire. And let me tell you, you're going to enjoy the difference."

He was back in Boston, sitting in his company's boardroom. They'd called him in to share what they thought would be some good news: they were promoting him to senior partner.

His time away at St. Raymond's had led them all to realize just how badly they needed him, they'd said. They wanted to make sure he realized the vast amount of earning potential he had, not just for the firm, but for himself. That led into yet another discussion of his medical license. The partners were putting even more pressure on him to give it up, once and for all. It wasn't just that his time away had cost the firm money. He was costing himself millions, as well. If he put the time he spent on medicine into the business, he'd eventually retire at an early age with a stock portfolio potentially worth billions.

The partners seemed certain that Eliot wouldn't walk away from such an offer. And honestly, he didn't see how he could. It was so much money. Wasn't that everything he'd wanted? After a childhood of being bullied and teased about his poverty, he'd never feel disrespected again in his life.

He didn't see any reasonable way he could walk away from what they were offering. He'd nodded and listened as they'd spoken, only pausing to ask if it wouldn't be possible to keep his medical license current for the sake of nostalgia. Absolutely not, they'd replied. They didn't want to risk him taking off for any more "medical vacations," as he had at St. Raymond's. Everyone seemed to think that Eliot should be thrilled with this turn of events.

He was trying, very hard, to see it as good news. If he couldn't have a life with Bria, then at least he could have this.

He'd lost her forever, he knew. He'd thought that amassing a fortune of his own would finally give him the security he was looking for. And yes, all his millions had made his life easier in certain ways. But his money still hadn't brought him the happiness he'd been looking for. Even before he'd reconnected with Bria, his love life had been an absolute mess. The women he met all seemed far more interested in his money than in his personality.

But Bria had repeatedly proven to him that she was different. He'd just been too blinded by his own insecurity to see it. It was true that she'd hurt him badly by ending their engagement the way she had. He wished she'd talked to him first. But ultimately he could see now that she'd done it out of love for him. She'd hadn't wanted to break up with him, but she'd sacrificed their relationship so that he could have the career he'd said he wanted.

He might blame her for making that decision without him, but wasn't he just as much to blame? If he'd been more open about what he was feeling back then, would she have been able to put more trust in their relationship, in *him*, and talk to him about what her father was threatening to do? Maybe he could have convinced her that he wouldn't have cared about having to work longer and harder to build a career outside of her father's influence, as long as they had each other. He was no stranger to hard work.

Instead, she'd tried to protect him from her father and from himself. And she hadn't felt she could discuss that decision with him. Even then, she'd known how insecure he was. He'd accused her of using that knowledge against him, but he knew now that he was his own worst enemy. All she'd tried to do was make a sacrifice for his career. A career that he was about to give up, throw away—all for money.

Rich or poor, Bria had shown him what was important to her. Loving someone, and being loved in return, mattered far more to her than what someone had, or how much. He'd been the one who couldn't see that. Who'd let his resentment of their financial disparity come between them.

He didn't deserve her, and he couldn't imagine that she would ever take him back. He knew he loved her. But when you loved someone and failed them, weren't you supposed to let them move on?

He tried very hard to take some pleasure in the opportunity the senior partners were offering him. But his smile didn't come naturally. Supposedly, the partners were handing him everything he'd ever dreamed of, and yet he felt as though someone else were in control, telling him when to smile, when to nod and when to sign on the dotted line.

He went back to his office and rested his head in his hands. He couldn't turn down the offer. He needed to take it. If not for himself, then on behalf of every kid like him who'd ever struggled to fit in as a scholarship student, everyone who'd been told that they'd never make it because they didn't live in the right kind of house or didn't have the background or connections they needed.

But the truth was, he missed St. Raymond's. He missed the pride he'd felt after helping every single newborn into the world. He missed the exhilaration he felt with special cases, especially the quints. They'd been named Joseph, Murphy, Rosemary, Oliver and Sophie. All of them had been doing well when he'd left, although he'd been a little concerned about Oliver's breathing. The new chief of obstetrics had told him not to worry about it, as all premature babies needed extra time for lung development. Still, he hoped someone was keeping a careful eye on Oliver. He was sure Bria would watch over him with extra care. She was such an attentive midwife. If there was anything to worry about, she wouldn't miss it.

But thinking about Bria again only led to wanting her—again. He wished there was some way to shut off his thoughts, but they came rushing into his mind regardless of his wishes. The way his head fit perfectly into the crook of her neck as they lay in bed, the scent of her hair as he buried his nose in it. The heat of her skin as he kissed her neck, the feeling of her moving next to him.

It's over, he thought. *Accept it. Try to think about something else.*

At least at St. Raymond's he'd been able to immerse himself in work that interested him. Here, he had nothing better than stock reports to focus on, and those barely held his attention.

Suddenly, he sat straight up in his chair. The quintuplets. Baby Oliver's wheezing. He knew what was wrong.

His hand hovered over his phone, ready to call St. Raymond's. He hesitated. Surely the new doctor would catch anything amiss. But at that thought, his unease grew. He hadn't been impressed with Dr. Phillips and had only grudgingly relinquished his patients to the man's care because he hadn't seen that there was any other option. He wasn't sure that Dr. Phillips would make the right diagnosis. And he might take umbrage at Eliot's interference, since Eliot was no longer the attending physician.

But this was no time for professional niceties. Eliot dialed St. Raymond's and asked to be connected to the NICU.

"I need to speak with Dr. Phillips immediately," he said. "It's a matter of some urgency about one of the quintuplets."

Hazel had answered the phone. "I'm sorry, Eliot, but that won't be possible."

"It's an emergency, Hazel."

"I understand, but Dr. Phillips is no longer here. He was fired and left immediately. He really wasn't able to get along with any of the staff, and then he and Dr. Anderson had quite the falling-out."

Fired? So St. Raymond's was without a chief of obstetrics again? He pushed the thought from his mind; that wasn't important now. "Look, it doesn't matter. Baby Oliver needs to be tested immediately for respiratory syncytial virus."

"Oh my god. You suspect RSV?"

"I didn't at first. I attributed his trouble breathing to

underdeveloped lungs, just as Dr. Phillips did. But the more I thought about it…"

"No, you're right. The wheezing, the fast breathing, the way his nose and chest look…it all fits. I'll get him tested immediately. Thank you, Eliot. I'm so glad you called."

So was he. Even if he'd lost Bria forever, the phone call had given him clarity about one thing: he was a doctor.

The knowledge hit him in the gut, the same way he'd made baby Oliver's diagnosis. No matter how much money someone offered him to do something else, he would always be a doctor. And there was no denying it. He'd tried for years, and he'd ended up right back here—on the phone, saving a patient and knowing he would never quit.

The partners would be perfectly fine running the company without him. He didn't need more money. But there was a hospital in Portland that needed him now. Even if Bria didn't want him, that hospital was where he belonged. He might not be able to be with her, but at least he finally knew who he was. If he couldn't have her, then that would have to be enough.

He opened his mouth to ask Hazel if he could talk to the chief of staff, but before he could speak, Hazel said, "Eliot, I think you should know something."

"What is it?" Her tone made him apprehensive.

"It's Bria. She's…she's in bad shape."

His heart suddenly felt very full. Was she struggling just as much as he was? Was Bria there? Could he talk to her? There was so much he wanted to say. "I know," he said gently. "But I'd really like to speak with her, if she's willing."

"You can't," said Hazel. His heart plummeted. *What else were you expecting?* he admonished himself. *It's over, she doesn't want you.*

He'd thought Hazel would hang up, but she continued, her voice tearful. "She's been injured. She's here, in the ICU. She's been here for a few days. I don't know if she would want me to tell you or not. I couldn't ask her, because she's…" Hazel paused and seemed to fight for composure. "She's in and out of consciousness. But I thought you should know." Hazel hung up. Eliot stared at the phone, frozen.

Bria was in the ICU?

His mind swam with questions. From the sound of things, her condition was very serious. *Don't panic—it won't help.* He could almost hear Bria's voice saying the words. He knew that if she were here, the first thing she'd do would be to try to get him to calm down.

But she wasn't here. She was in a hospital bed, thousands of miles away, and he had no idea what had happened or how to help.

Half a second ago, he'd thought he'd finally gotten his life figured out when he realized he needed to go back to Portland to be a doctor. But now it seemed that everything was wrong. Bria being injured was wrong. Him being in Boston was wrong.

Everything was wrong, and he wasn't sure how to fix any of it.

But he had an idea about where to start.

CHAPTER TEN

Bria faded in and out of consciousness. She was dimly aware of having been brought to the ICU, but it seemed as though her memory was playing tricks on her. She wasn't entirely certain of what was real. She thought she remembered the concerned face of a park ranger, an ambulance ride and then doctors speaking over her in urgent, quiet tones. But at other times she felt as though she was still in the forest, waiting for someone to find her.

She'd gotten lost in the woods. It had been getting dark, and she was starting to grow concerned about just how deep she'd traveled into the park without paying much attention to her surroundings. Her phone wasn't getting any reception at all, and her maps application simply showed her as deep in the woods somewhere, with no clear instructions as to how to get out. The compass kept reorienting itself in different directions.

She'd finally found a rock that she could sit on comfortably, but when she did, she'd been so frustrated and so tired that she'd made a rookie hiking mistake: she'd put her hand on the ground behind her to steady herself without looking to see what was there first.

She'd heard an unearthly rattle, and before she could move, there was instant pain. Whatever had bitten her disappeared in an instant, but the two small, bloody dots on her hand only began to look more serious as time went on. Within five minutes, her hand felt as though it was burning.

She'd never heard a rattlesnake's rattle, except perhaps in films, but there had been no mistaking that sound. She'd earned her first-ever snakebite, and at the worst possible time. She was lost in the woods, and it was growing dark.

Snake venom, she knew, traveled not through the blood but through the lymphatic system. As long as she didn't move, the venom wouldn't travel through her tissue fluid. In theory, she could lie here indefinitely. Assuming she didn't die of exposure first. Or another snakebite. Or starvation.

Stop that. It's a popular hiking trail in a public park. Someone will come along eventually.

Yes, eventually, but how long would that take? And it was a huge public park, with long, winding hiking trails. She'd chosen one of the less popular trails specifically because she'd wanted to be alone. And night was coming on fast.

The pain in her hand made it hard to keep still. She wanted nothing more than to cradle it to her chest and curl up in pain. Instead, it took everything she had to remain flat on her back, willing herself not to move.

Her strategy wasn't going to work, she realized as the minutes ticked away. For one thing, she couldn't keep her hand completely still. The pain was so bad that her hand jerked every few minutes, and it was impossible to keep her face an expressionless mask—fear and pain led her to gasp and cry out. She couldn't stay completely motionless for the amount of time it would take for someone to find her. She needed to try something else.

She stood up. She'd give herself three minutes, she decided, to walk briskly in the direction of a trailhead. Any trailhead. It didn't matter whether it was back the way she'd come. She just needed to get to a place where other hikers were more likely to walk by. Or where she could get a phone signal. A phone signal would be even better.

She headed down one of the trails, keeping an eye on her phone in case the reception bars sprang up. When three minutes had passed, she'd come close to a fork in the road. Hopefully close enough that someone would see her when they passed by. Her entire arm was on fire now; she didn't dare walk any more. She lay flat on her back again. As she did, she noticed that her phone had one tiny reception bar that flickered in and out.

Her strength was rapidly ebbing as she dialed the emergency number with her good hand. After that, her memories became less reliable.

Sometimes it seemed as though she could hear Hazel's voice calling to her. At other times, it felt as though she was still lying on her back in the woods, listening to the rustle of the leaves and wondering whether the noises she heard were caused by people or wild animals. Sometimes it seemed as though she could hear Eliot's voice, but that made the least sense of all, because Eliot was gone. She'd lost him forever, because she hadn't seen that she could trust him after all.

She could make out voices every time her mind roused itself, but it was difficult to stay focused on them. She heard little snatches of conversations. Everyone sounded so worried, and she tried to let them know that they didn't need to be. But every time she spoke, someone told her to rest.

People kept telling her that she was brave, that she was showing so much courage. She didn't have the strength to tell them they were wrong. All she was doing was lying in a bed, while other people drew blood and gave injections, doing their best to save her life. All she could do was trust them.

Thinking about trust brought her back to Eliot again. She'd always told him he needed to be less guarded, more open, but had she proven herself to be the kind of person he could open up to? She didn't think so.

And now, even if she survived this ordeal, she'd be just as alone as ever. She knew she was drifting in and out of consciousness, but part of her didn't even want to fight to stay awake. Eliot still wouldn't be there, and it was hard to think about waking up without him.

She'd been so naive to think that she could ever agree to a meaningless fling with him with zero consequences. Eliot was the love of her life. That would always be true, even if she never saw him again.

She heard Hazel speaking with two doctors. One of them did sound like Eliot, but she was dimly aware that she was probably delirious and that her mind was likely to fabricate things.

"Her arm's swelled to twice its normal size," she heard one of them say. "There's a serious risk of compartment syndrome."

"Isn't there anything you can do?" That was the doctor who sounded like Eliot.

"She's already had more than twenty vials of antivenin. If we'd gotten to her any later, she would have died. She'll be very lucky if we can save her arm."

"Whose arm are you talking about?" she wanted to say, but when she heard her voice come out, it only sounded like a dull moan. They couldn't be talking about her arm. She was a midwife; her hands and arms were her tools. How many babies had she cradled with her own arms? Maybe one hundred? She needed her arms to work.

"We should have this conversation somewhere else."

"I don't want to leave her," said the Eliot-sounding doctor. Now she knew it definitely couldn't be him. She'd ruined her second chance with him, and there wouldn't be any more. Eliot wouldn't say he didn't want to leave her, because he was already gone.

"I understand, but she might be able to hear us, and I don't want her disturbed. The best thing we can all do right now is let her rest."

Three days later, Bria blinked her eyes open. She could see now that she was, indeed, in an ICU. She'd had some sense of it while she was delirious, but she hadn't been sure. There was a heart rate monitor next to her, and her right arm was splinted and completely wrapped in bandages.

But the most surprising sight of all was Eliot, sitting in a chair across from her bed.

There were dark circles under his eyes, but she could still see the light buried within their brown depths as they gazed at her with warm concern. He looked as though he hadn't slept in days. His face was worn and haggard, his hair askew, and his stubble almost grown into a beard. He'd never looked better to her.

But why was he here?

"Hey," she croaked, her voice dry from disuse. "Aren't you supposed to be in Boston?"

"Don't worry about that right now. Here, have some water." She sipped from the straw he held for her, grateful to feel the coolness on her parched throat. But her curiosity about what he was doing by her bedside was too great to ignore.

"You're the one who looks worried," she said, her voice coming out more clearly now that she'd had something to drink. "What are you doing here? Why did you come back?"

He hung his head, almost as though he was afraid to meet her eyes. But then he did look up at her, and his eyes were warm and full of contrition. "Because from almost the minute my plane landed back in Boston, I realized I'd done something incredibly stupid. I wasn't where I needed to be. I'd left people who were depending on me. And…"

He reached across Bria and took hold of her good hand. "I made a mistake that almost cost me the most important person in my life."

The warmth of his hand felt so good against hers. She noticed tears in his eyes, and she felt tears forming at the corners of hers, as well. And then a tear did fall down his cheek. She moved to wipe it away, but he said, "Don't. The doctors want you to move as little as possible."

"But I don't want you to be sad," she said.

"I know," he said. "I should have known that a long time ago. You've only ever wanted me to be happy."

She leaned back into the hospital bed. Despite her low energy, she was fighting a strong desire to leap up and throw her arms around him. She longed to tell him everything she'd realized over the past few days, about how unfair she'd been and how much she regretted that she'd wasted their second chance. But she'd also just been delirious, and she had no idea for how long. She was still trying to convince herself that he really was here, in the flesh.

"You're really here?" she asked him.

"I'm really here. And I'm not going anywhere."

But what about his job in Boston? Clearly, there were a few gaps in her understanding of recent events. "Um, Eliot? Could you catch me up a little on what's happened?"

"Well, first of all, it's been a week since you came in."

"A *week*?" Bria sat up in alarm.

"No sudden movements, or you'll get me kicked out of your room and Hazel will bite my head off."

She relaxed. Now that Eliot was here, she didn't want anything to send him away. Even a well-meaning best friend. "A whole week?" she said, shaking her head. How could she have lost that much time without realizing it?

Suddenly, she remembered something important. Something about the way one of the quintuplets had been breathing had raised a red flag in the back of her mind; she'd meant to keep an eye on it. "Eliot—how have the quintu-plets been doing? I wanted to keep Oliver closely moni-tored."

"Oliver is fine."

"But—"

"Bria." His hand over hers was firm. "Will you please let me take care of you first before we start talking about patients?"

"Sorry," said Bria, mollified. "Please continue."

"You were brought in and treated for a real beauty of a rattlesnake bite. You were out for about seven days, during which time your arm just kept getting bigger and bigger. Everyone was scared that you might have compartment syn-drome. There was some pretty serious talk of amputation."

So she hadn't imagined that part. Bria shivered.

"I'm not trying to scare you, I'm just trying to explain why *we* were all very scared over the past few days, and why I want you to take it easy. But the good news is that as long as you are very careful and follow the doctor's orders to the exact letter, you should be able to keep your arm." He raised an eyebrow in warning. "And I'll be watching to make sure that you take very good care of yourself."

"Because you're not going anywhere."

"That is indeed what I said. I'm glad you're keeping up."

"Okay. I want to know exactly *why* you aren't going any-where. But first, Oliver. Has Dr. Phillips looked at him? Is he going to be all right?"

"Oliver is fine. He was tested for RSV. We were able to start treatment extremely early, and his prognosis is look-ing good. As for Dr. Phillips, he is no longer at St. Ray-mond's, due to being incompetent and unable to get along with anyone. But that's all right, because the hospital has a new chief of obstetrics."

"Who?"

"Me."

"Then you chose medicine!" she said, relieved. She'd known he was born to be a doctor, and she knew it brought him joy he couldn't get in another profession, no matter how much money he made.

"I did." Eliot smiled. "I got the partners in Boston to buy me out. I'm a doctor full-time now. All I have is my meager salary, a fulfilling profession…and a fortune in the bank. I think I'll be all right."

"And you really are staying in Portland!"

He shook his head. "As we've now established for the third time, I'm not going anywhere. But I hope you don't think that's because of a job."

"It's not?"

"No. Not at all. I can get a job anywhere. That's not why I'm staying in Portland."

She'd thought that might be the case, but she couldn't quite let herself believe it. A torturous, agonizing hope was rising in her chest.

She'd ruined everything. She'd spoiled their time together, and she hadn't trusted in him or in their relationship. She'd been just as closed off as she was always accusing him of being.

And yet he was here. He'd said she was the most important person in his life. And apparently, he wasn't going anywhere.

"But *why* aren't you going anywhere?"

"I'm working up to that part," he said softly.

"Does it need working up to?"

"It does. Because, you see, I thought you might die." The tears were coming back into his eyes again.

"Hey," she said. "How come I'm the one who suffered a snakebite but you're the one who looks like they've been run over by a truck?"

"Because I thought I'd lost you."

She smiled, trying to reassure him. "Well, guess what? I'm not going anywhere, either."

"I'm glad to hear it. Because when someone you love almost dies, it helps you to realize a few things."

The agonizing hope that had been rising within her began to soothe itself. It was turning into a warm glow. It was no longer the kind of hope that tortured. Instead, it was the kind of hope that breathed life into her. All because of that little four-letter word he'd uttered. It was going to be hard to concentrate on anything else he had to say, because that word kept looming larger in her mind. He loved her.

"Bria, I have to tell you something."

She smiled. "I think you might have already told me the most important part."

"Which is?"

"That you love me."

"But I have to tell you all the other things first. I have to apologize for being a fool, and for not understanding that you were trying to help me when I needed it. For doubting you when you had the best of intentions. For not seeing you for who you really are. I let my own past get the better of me, and it cost us...*us.* And even though I know it's unlikely, I came here hoping against all hope that you might consider giving me another chance. Because I love you, Bria Thomas. You make me feel alive, and I promise you that if you let me love you again, this time I'll never let you go."

She squeezed his hand. "What about my apologies? I made so many mistakes, too. I lied to you about wanting to break up, and I didn't trust you when you needed me to. I didn't trust you when you could have helped both of us. I could have confided in you, but instead I just made a huge decision on my own. One that cost us six years of happiness."

"You can make those apologies if you need to. But I

don't need to hear them. Because I know how I feel about you, and frankly, I'm much more interested in hearing how you feel about me. And about the idea of the two of us, together."

"I think it's the best idea I've heard in six years," she said. "Because I love you, too. I never stopped. You're the one I want to spend the rest of my life with, and you always have been."

He kissed her then, a soft, sensuous kiss that was full of promise. She smiled a bit as she inhaled the faint scent of cinnamon on him. There were so many ways in which they'd both changed, and yet the best parts of him had always been there, waiting to be seen.

As they broke apart, she said, "I promise that from now on, I'll make sure I'm not making unilateral decisions, but that I'm including you and that we're working as a team."

"And I'll tell you what's going on with me rather than hiding my feelings and keeping you shut out in the cold."

"Wow," she said. "Call me crazy, but I think we might actually have the makings of a mature, adult relationship."

"Maybe even more than that," he said. "I was thinking that we just made something that sounded like vows to one another."

Her heart soared. "I was thinking that, too."

"In that case…" He took her uninjured hand in both of his and got down on one knee. "Bria Thomas—"

"Yes," she laughed before he could finish.

"Really?" he said. "For richer or poorer?"

"I think that has to be a given with the two of us."

He leaned in and kissed her. She could tell he meant to be gentle, but she wasn't. She put every last ounce of love she had for him into it, every bit of energy she could spare to let him know exactly how loved he was. She'd spent the past few days fretting over all the chances in life and in love that she hadn't taken. From now on, she planned to make the most of every moment, starting with this kiss.

EPILOGUE

One year later

THE EARLY FALL leaves made a satisfying crunch under Bria's feet. The air was crisp but still warm enough for a Saturday morning picnic near the open-air market. The tradition that Bria and Hazel shared had evolved over the past few months. Now she and Eliot spent their mornings at the market with Hazel, Caleb and Caleb's nineteen-year-old daughter, Lizzie, and sometimes they were joined by Lizzie's fiancé, Derek. Each weekend, they would all split up to find something to eat from a different booth—perhaps some local honey, a new kind of cheese or a loaf of artisan bread. When they returned, they made a picnic out of their findings. It was quickly becoming one of Bria's favorite Saturday rituals.

This morning, she and Eliot were the first to return to the agreed-upon spot by the river. Bria had brought an old wool blanket once owned by her mother to spread upon the ground, and she snuggled into Eliot's arms as they sat on the riverbank, watching people make their way into the market.

"It's nice to have a moment to ourselves," he said, his arm around her, his nose nuzzling into her hair. "I thought being married meant we'd have *more* time to spend together, but I feel like I haven't seen you in days."

"That's your fault for being such an important doctor," she replied, leaning back to kiss him. Over the past year, word of the quintuplets' birth had spread within the medical community, and St. Raymond's was becoming even more well-known as a hospital that specialized in complicated pregnancies. Eliot now spent his days immersed in hospital work, and Bria could tell that he loved every minute of it.

"I've been working too much, haven't I?" he said, his face drawn with concern. "We could have had a more elaborate wedding if I'd taken more time off."

"Nonsense," she said, putting a hand on his arm. "Our wedding was perfect." After Bria's recovery, they'd both wanted to get married as quickly as possible, and so the ceremony had been a tiny affair, nothing more than a small gathering of their closest friends at city hall. Eliot's mother had flown in from Aruba; she'd welcomed Bria with open arms and made her feel like family.

"Perfectly efficient. I can't imagine it was the wedding of your dreams."

She nudged him playfully. "Now you're just trying to get me to say it."

"To say what?" he said, his eyes wide and innocent.

"To say that any wedding to you would be the wedding of my dreams." She leaned back to kiss him again.

"You're right," he said. "I have to admit that I do enjoy hearing you say that."

"Ahem!" Lizzie had arrived with a loaf of bread. "Are we here to have a picnic or engage in PDA?"

"Sorry, Lizzie," Bria said, motioning for the girl to sit down beside them. "We'll try to keep the public displays of affection to a minimum."

"But no promises," Eliot said wryly, wrapping his arms tightly around Bria's waist.

Lizzie rolled her eyes as she sat next to Bria and dropped

her loaf of bread onto the blanket. "I can't believe you haven't gone on your honeymoon yet. When Derek and I get married, we want to take a grand tour of Europe, starting with Paris, and then hit all the romantic spots in Italy. Well, that's what we'd do if we had loads of cash, anyway. How can the two of you stay here when you've got millions in the bank?"

"Lizzie!" Caleb had just arrived over the knoll. "Don't be rude."

"It's all right." Bria smiled. "Everyone has a different idea of what makes them happy. For us, happiness means being here with our friends."

"It's kind of you to say that, but I know you've delayed your trip for Hazel," Caleb said. That had indeed been a strong practical reason to delay the honeymoon, as Bria refused to leave the country before Hazel gave birth. She was overdue now and very ready to meet her baby.

"There couldn't be a better reason for us to stay," she told Caleb. And she meant it. There couldn't have been a better reason to delay the honeymoon...except, perhaps, for the additional information she and Eliot had received last night. But she'd need to wait for Hazel to arrive before she revealed that particular piece of news.

"Where is Hazel, anyway?" asked Lizzie, echoing Bria's thoughts. "I'd have thought she'd be back by now."

"Me, too," said Caleb. His expression was worried, as it always was these days whenever Hazel left his side for more than five minutes. Bria knew that Caleb's first wife had died due to a pulmonary embolism after an emergency cesarean section, and she understood Caleb's anxious hovering. She could even relate to it, to a degree. Even though Bria had assured Caleb throughout the pregnancy that Hazel was doing wonderfully, she'd been absolutely determined to be Hazel's midwife. She knew that Hazel would be in excellent hands no matter who assisted with the delivery, but she still felt more comfortable with the idea of overseeing things herself. It must be hard for Caleb, she thought, to focus on being a husband rather than an obstetrician.

Just as she was wondering if she should text Hazel to check on her, everyone's cell phone began to whirr at once. As Bria opened her phone, she saw a group text from Hazel: BABY911.

A moment later, a second whirring followed up the first: CHEESE STALL.

After a stunned moment, Bria felt her brain snap back into action. "Caleb," she said. He was staring at the phone in shock. "Caleb?"

"I can't believe I left her alone," he gasped. "She wanted us each to go to different stalls, like always. I should have said no. She's all alone and it's my fault."

"Caleb!" Bria almost shouted, using her most authoritative voice. "She's not alone, she's got us. That's why she texted. Where are your car keys?"

"My keys?"

"Give them to Lizzie, right now." Bria turned to Lizzie. "You're going to be our driver. Run and get your dad's car and park at the bottom of the hill. We'll meet you there as soon as we can."

Unless things progress a lot faster than expected.

A glance at Eliot's face told her he was thinking the same thing.

But if it came to that, she was ready. One baby in a cheese stall couldn't be that difficult compared to some of the other situations she'd encountered. At least she wasn't facing quintuplets in an elevator.

"Don't worry," she said to Caleb, infusing as much confidence as she could into her voice as they hurried down the hill toward the market. "We'll have her at the Women's

Health Center in no time. You'll be celebrating the birth of your second child before you know it."

Caleb nodded at her, but the look of dread on his face didn't change.

They did, in fact, make it to the Women's Health Center in time, thanks to some bold driving on Lizzie's part. Hazel was glad to see Caleb become noticeably less distressed once they finally had Hazel set up in one of the birthing rooms, though the worry never completely left his eyes.

"You're both doing wonderfully," Bria said. Caleb held Hazel's hand as she breathed steadily.

"How much longer?" gasped Hazel.

"Not long at all now," Bria reassured her. "You're fully dilated."

Both Hazel and Caleb grew tense. "Then why—" they both began at once.

Bria cut them off. "The labor's progressing, but more slowly than it should. That's not surprising, given that the baby's in breech position."

Hazel lay back and groaned.

"She needs a cesarean," Caleb said. "We should get her to St. Raymond's immediately."

"Hold on," said Bria gently. How true it was that doctors made the worst patients. Caleb was ready to jump into action at the exact moment she needed both him and Hazel to calm down and take things slowly.

But that, she supposed, was why they had a midwife on hand. Bria was determined not to let her best friend down.

"No one's going anywhere until you start breathing again, just like we've practiced," she said to Hazel in her firmest tones. To her relief, Hazel began her deep breaths again. Caleb, however, still looked recalcitrant.

"She needs to be in a hospital. In case something goes wrong, in case we need to act quickly…"

Bria knew that the loss of his first wife had to be weighing heavily on Caleb's mind. But that was nearly twenty years ago now. He was wrapped up in his fear from the past, and she needed him to be with her today, right now, with her and Hazel.

"Caleb," she said gently, "look at Hazel. Look at how well she's breathing. I want you to squeeze her hand." He did as Hazel smiled up at him.

"We're going to get through this together, but we need to go *slowly*. Can you do that?"

Caleb looked at Hazel. "It's your call," he said.

"I want our baby to be born here," she replied. She nodded at Bria. "I'm ready."

Bria smiled. "Good, because so is baby." As Hazel had resumed breathing, the baby's hindquarters had slowly been making their way into the world. Bria gently eased the baby along with each of Hazel's contractions until the baby's legs were out.

She'd known the baby's sex for months, but Hazel and Caleb had wanted to be surprised. She gave them both a wink. "Just a few moments more and the big secret's out. Ready, Hazel?"

Hazel gasped and nodded, and Bria rotated the baby until she could feel the cheekbones with her fingers. "One more big push," she said to Hazel, and with the next contraction, a slippery bundle shot into her arms.

Caleb was still shaking with relief, so Bria opted to hand the tiny bundle to Hazel. "Would you like a few moments to yourselves?" she asked as Hazel and Caleb gazed down into the brand-new pair of eyes before them.

"No," said Hazel. Tears streamed down her face as she tore her gaze from the baby and looked up at Bria. "I want everyone here. Lizzie should be part of this, and you and Eliot, too."

"Agreed," said Caleb. "Joy is better when it's shared, and we…" His voice choked. "We have a lot to share."

"I'll go get them." Bria stepped into the hall, where Eliot and Lizzie had been waiting. "Well?" Lizzie cried as she rushed in. "Do I finally get to know whether I have a baby sister or brother?"

"It's a boy," said Caleb, barely able to contain his pride.

Hazel beamed up at him. "We've got our little Darcy."

Bria felt Eliot's arm around her waist. As happy as she was for Hazel, she didn't resist as he pulled her back into the hallway. After the intensity of the birth, it was a relief to feel his arms around her, sturdy and reassuring.

He pulled her close and murmured into her ear. "Think we'll be that happy when our turn comes around?"

"Shh! They'll hear you. I don't want to intrude on the moment with our big announcement."

Eliot glanced into the birthing room, where all eyes were fixated on baby Darcy. "I have a feeling you don't need to worry about them overhearing us for now." He put a hand on Bria's stomach. "Still, you should probably give Hazel a little warning that you'll be needing her services as a mid-wife in a few months."

Bria twined her arms around Eliot's neck and leaned up on tiptoe to kiss him. "I'll be sure to let her know well before the time comes. We'll let them celebrate today and share our own joy tomorrow."

Eliot's arms grew tighter around her waist. "I never knew," he said, gazing into her eyes. He seemed about to say more, but his lips bent to kiss her first.

As much as Bria was interested to know what he had to say, she found she was quite unable to pull herself away from his kiss, and so quite some time passed before she was able to say, "You never knew what?"

"Hmm?"

"You said, 'I never knew,' and then we got a bit distracted."

"Ah. Yes. I was going to say that I never knew how much there could be to celebrate in life. So much, in fact, that for the first time in my life, I feel…rich."

Her heart burst with love for him. She knew exactly what he meant. After all the years they'd lost waiting for each other, after all the times they'd nearly missed finding each other again, it was hard to believe that there could be so much joy in their lives. The new life growing within her was a miracle in more ways than one. They were indeed rich, with so much to be thankful for.

"We both are," she said, tears brimming her eyes. "In all the ways that count."

He gave a sigh of deep contentment. "Shall we head back in there?"

"In just a moment," she said, pulling his head toward hers again. Just like Eliot, she'd never known, never even dreamed, that she would have so much joy in her life. And now that she did, she wasn't going to let it go.

* * * * *

COMING SOON!

We really hope you enjoyed reading this book.
If you're looking for more romance, be sure to
head to the shops when new books are
available on

Thursday 23rd June

MILLS & BOON®

Coming next month

THE NIGHT THEY NEVER FORGOT
Scarlet Wilson

She met his gaze. There was so much there. Twelve lost years between them. She lifted a muffin from the plate and walked around her desk, gesturing to the seat at the other side as she moved to flick some switches on her coffee machine.

He could sense she was trying to decide how to play this. He'd turned up unexpectedly. They'd had literally no contact since that last awkward morning after graduation. He'd replayed that day over and over in his head so many times. It had seemed clear that Caitlin had thought they'd made a mistake; she'd made a quick comment— 'at least we got that out of our system'—and that they could get back to being rivals again. He hadn't said a word. Hadn't told her how much that cheapened what had happened between them and how, after one taste of Caitlin, she would never be out of his system. He'd let the hurt feelings go; he'd wanted to respect her wishes. The embarrassing retreat and hasty exit he'd had to make had been imprinted in his soul. He'd lost the person he'd been closest to for six years. It shouldn't have been worth it. Not for one night.

But, strangely, that night had meant everything. And he was still glad they had gone there. Even if the next morning had been a disaster.

He couldn't help it. His eyes went to her left hand. No ring. The sense of relief was unexpectedly overwhelming.

Ridiculous. And he knew that. He also knew he couldn't take a lack of ring to mean anything at all. Caitlin might well be married and just not want to wear a ring—she was a surgeon after all. She could also be in a long-term relationship. But he couldn't help but hope not…no matter how shallow that might make him.

He swept his arm around the room. 'Corner office? They must like you.'

'Of course they do. I'm their shining star.'

It was the way she said those words. The confidence in herself that had brought him here.

He glanced out at the dark view of the beautiful city of Barcelona, with all the familiar structures easy to pick out.

'You've done really well for yourself.' He said the words with a hint of pride. When any other physician mentioned Caitlin he always said that they'd trained together, and that she was a fine surgeon.

'I like to think so.' Her gaze narrowed slightly. She was getting suspicious of the small talk.

'We should catch up?'

Her eyebrows raised.

'I mean, twelve years is a long time. You could be married, divorced, a mother of ten.'

Her eyes widened.

Continue reading
THE NIGHT THEY NEVER FORGOT
Scarlet Wilson

Available next month
www.millsandboon.co.uk

MILLS & BOON

THE HEART OF ROMANCE

A ROMANCE FOR EVERY READER

MODERN

Prepare to be swept off your feet by sophisticated, sexy and seductive heroes, in some of the world's most glamourous and romantic locations, where power and passion collide.

HISTORICAL

Escape with historical heroes from time gone by. Whether your passion is for wicked Regency Rakes, muscled Vikings or rugged Highlanders, awaken the romance of the past.

MEDICAL

Set your pulse racing with dedicated, delectable doctors in the high-pressure world of medicine, where emotions run high and passion, comfort and love are the best medicine.

True Love

Celebrate true love with tender stories of heartfelt romance, from the rush of falling in love to the joy a new baby can bring, and a focus on the emotional heart of a relationship.

Desire

Indulge in secrets and scandal, intense drama and plenty of sizzling hot action with powerful and passionate heroes who have it all: wealth, status, good looks…everything but the right woman.

HEROES

Experience all the excitement of a gripping thriller, with an intense romance at its heart. Resourceful, true-to-life women and strong, fearless men face danger and desire - a killer combination!

To see which titles are coming soon, please visit

millsandboon.co.uk/nextmonth

JOIN US ON SOCIAL MEDIA!

Stay up to date with our latest releases, author news and gossip, special offers and discounts, and all the behind-the-scenes action from Mills & Boon...

 millsandboon

 millsandboonuk

 millsandboon

It might just be true love...